Love o .... on

"Funny, fast paced, charming, and totally relatable. Friedland gives us a brilliant love story and reminds us it's nice to pick up a smart book instead of a smartphone for a change."

—Jennifer Belle, bestselling author of
High Maintenance and *The Seven Year Bitch*

"A delicious and timely novel. Friedland takes a look at how our addiction to social media brings us together while keeping us apart." —Molly Jong-Fast, author of *The Social Climber's Handbook*

"Wholly irresistible—smart and poignant and laugh-out-loud funny." —Sara Houghteling, author of *Pictures at an Exhibition*

"An extremely fun reminder that we can all survive without emoticons. #greatread!"

—Erin Duffy, author of *On the Rocks* and *Bond Girl*

"A witty, wonderful, and thoroughly modern love story. Friedland's writing is sharp and funny, tender and true. I couldn't put it down." —Cristina Alger, author of *The Darlings*

love
and miss
c♥mmunication

love
and miss
c♥mmunication

Elyssa Friedland

WILLIAM MORROW

An Imprint of HarperCollins*Publishers*

P.S.™ is a trademark of HarperCollins Publishers.

HarperCollins books may be purchased for educational, business, or sales promotional use. For information please e-mail the Special Markets Department at SPsales@harpercollins.com.

FIRST EDITION

Designed by Diahann Sturge

Library of Congress Cataloging-in-Publication Data has been applied for.

ISBN 978-0-06-237984-9

15 16 17 18 19   OV/RRD   10 9 8 7 6 5 4 3 2

For Mom, my biggest cheerleader

Technology is nothing. What's important is that you have a faith in people, that they're basically good and smart, and if you give them tools, they'll do wonderful things with them.

—STEVE JOBS

love
and miss
c♥mmunication

Prologue

Evie scooped up the glossy black-and-silver invitation perched on her vanity. In tiny cursive, she read the words "festive chic attire." What the hell did that mean? Whatever it was intended to convey, it felt like a tall order after a ten-hour workday on a Saturday. She pulled open the bifold doors of her overstuffed closet, filled mostly with conservative work suits that blocked the view of her formal-wear options. From the back, she pried out the navy blue crepe dress that she had last worn to her great-aunt's memorial service. By substituting sensible pumps with strappy sandals and adding dangly earrings, the dress could likely make the transition from funereal to celebratory. After struggling with stubborn jewelry clasps and nearly throwing out her back trying to force a side zipper, it appeared that "festive chic" might be achieved after all. She couldn't help smiling to herself as she took a glance in her full-length mirror before heading out the door. True a blowout and an eyebrow wax would have gone a long way, but the reflection staring back wasn't that bad, considering her rush. Fortunately the humidity had given her amber hair a nice wave. Clear olive skin made foundation and blush almost unnecessary, which was a good thing because she had no time for either.

Her BlackBerry screeched like a rattlesnake from its perch on her bookshelf as she hastened to throw on lipstick and apply eyeliner. She forced herself to ignore its mating call. Instead she snapped up the phone and tried to fit it into her matching evening bag, a tiny sequined rectangle that she hadn't used in months. No such luck.

Shit. She didn't know what to do. No feat of physics or geometry would get her BlackBerry into the purse. Carrying her phone all night was out of the question. Her friends would be merciless about her "Crackberry" addiction. Leaving it home was also a nonstarter. A corporate attorney without a BlackBerry at arm's length might as well not bother showing up for work on Monday. Quickly, and trying as best she could not to consider the implications for the rest of her evening, she hiked her dress over her waist and slipped the bulky PDA into her cotton panties. The plastic hit her flesh like a cool breeze. She could feel the tiny buttons digging crannies into her skin. Evie checked her BlackBerry so often that it was actually fitting it should take on the role of a bodily appendage. Someday, a more evolved version of her would emerge from the womb with a smartphone already implanted. Evie 2.0. She reached back down to lock the keys so she wouldn't accidentally call anyone from down there. When her phone was safely secured between the grooves of her body and the fabric of her underwear, she actually felt satisfied with her solution and took a deep breath, sucked the air to the pit of her belly, and released. Everything would be okay. Just some minor discomfort. No big deal, really. She was late, as usual, and there was no time for reconsideration.

Chapter 1

Another wedding for Evie Rosen. Not her own though. Tying the knot were Paul Kindling and Marco Mendez, Evie's college and law school friends, respectively. They officially were married in a private ceremony at unromantic City Hall a few days earlier. Friends and the more tolerant members of their families waited to fete them in grander style at a lavish party downtown. Sixteen years, she thought, smoothing the fabric of her dress over her midriff one last time. That's how long she'd known Paul. He was her first friend in college. And she was late to his wedding. Tardy, is what he would say.

Worse than her tardiness, though, was what she was think-ing. Across the country, millions of people were trying to prevent unions like Paul and Marco's, and yet they had still beaten her to the altar. Evie tried her best to be happy for them—to silence her envy and vanquish any useless questions like "Why not me?" Because Paul was a true friend, a co-navigator in that terrible thing called freshman year and now a formidable partner in the madness of New York City life, and while he could be flighty at times, he'd never let her down in any significant way in a decade-and-a-half-long relationship.

With an aura of sophistication that far exceeded his years, Paul had stood out from the other newbies at Yale, a dichotomy of prep school kids from the coasts and public school valedictorians from small towns in between. Dressed in a dark shirt and slim trousers, he resembled a salesperson at an expensive boutique, while Evie looked like someone pretending to shop there so she could use the bathroom. On move-in day they chatted in the center of the freshman quad, where they exchanged the prepack-aged bios every freshman brings, along with a computer and a forbidden halogen floor lamp. It turned out they were assigned to the same dorm, which Paul helped her locate while her clueless parents ambled behind. It was hard to believe she'd known Paul for so long already—that after a chance conversation on the first day of school, she was rushing to get to his wedding.

As Evie was about to step into the hallway of her building, at last presentable enough for what was sure to be a chic affair, she felt an unfamiliar sensation ripple through her body. When it stopped and started again, she realized it was her BlackBerry, rhythmically buzzing inside her panties. She dislodged the phone and saw the call was from her grandmother, Bette. She debated letting it go to voicemail. But Bette was too sharp. All the way from her white-plastic lounge chair on the balcony of her Century

Village condo in Boca, she would know her granddaughter was dodging her call. Besides, her grandma was probably just calling to warn her about an outbreak of Listeria she heard about on the five o'clock news. Why deprive her of the opportunity to show Evie how much she cared?

Bette, Evie's paternal grandmother, was an octogenarian force of nature—a survivor of the Holocaust who had long since parted with her oral filter. She referred to Evie's singledom as "ze situation," as in "vhat are ve going to do about ze situation?" Evie's grandmother even had a signature move. When Bette would see Evie after any meaningful length of time, she would extend her hand—palm facing down—and point to her engagement ring, a tiny sapphire stone surrounded by diamonds on a yellow gold band. Bette wore the ring every day, even though Evie's grandfather, Max, had been dead for a quarter of a century. Then she'd ask "Nu?" (shtetl slang for "so?") and widen her eyes in expectation. Over the phone, Bette would resort to summoning a feeble cough and saying, "Don't forget, your grandmother's getting older. I'd love to see you settled." And then the clincher, "I know your father vould feel ze same vay, may he rest in peace," invoking Evie's late father, Henry, who died when Evie was finishing her freshman year of college. Bette was a professional meddler and probably the person who thought the most about Evie on any given day. No, she would not ignore the call.

"Hey, Grandma," she said breathily, hand still on the door-knob.

"Evie-le, vhat's new?" Bette asked, her thick Eastern European refugee accent already making Evie feel guilty for needing to rush her off the phone. That accent was made for guilt-mongering. One *w* pronounced like a *v* and Evie crumbled.

"Not much. I'm on my way to a wedding," Evie said. "I'm actually late so I can't really talk."

"Oh, very nice. Vish zem mazel tov," Bette said. It still hadn't occurred to her grandmother that not everyone Evie knew was Jewish. Imagine if she knew the couple getting married was short one X chromosome. "Anyvay, I just called to say hello. Oh, but zat reminds me, I just heard Lauren Moscovitz is engaged."

Ahh. The real reason for the call.

"Good for her," Evie said blandly. She used the extra moment on the phone to touch up her speedily applied makeup, lamenting that the call would surely get dropped if she got into the elevator. A disconnected call could easily send Bette into a nervous spiral about a possible terrorist attack in New York.

"He's an orthopedic surgeon. Rose, Lauren's bubbe on her mother's side, called to tell me. You know Rose. She has zat horse face. Her husband vas a terrible gambler. Anyvay, she just couldn't vait to tell me. It does seem like zis boy is a real catch."

Evie sighed deeply, not sure what there was to say.

"You remember Lauren, no? She vas a little zaftig. I think you babysat for her a few times."

Evie couldn't say for sure if her grandmother was truly trying to help her recall Lauren, or was purposefully showing her that someone whose diapers she changed was getting married ahead of her. Evie did remember Lauren. She had been an especially ugly child, with frizzy tendrils and a nose that always seemed to have a precariously dangling booger.

"Anyvay, the vedding is at the Ritz-Carlton in Boston, vhere ze boy is from. Apparently he's extremely vealthy."

Despite the fact that Bette moved to Florida shortly after Evie's father died, she managed to keep apprised of their old Baltimore neighborhood, and seemed particularly keen to share news of marriages and births with Evie. Surely some of their former neighbors were getting divorced, but those stories never extended from Bette's grapevine to hers.

"That's great for her," Evie repeated, trying to keep her annoyance in check. "You know, Grandma, the wedding I'm going to might as well be in Boston because that's how long it's going to take me to get there with the downtown traffic. Let me call you from outside so I can at least look for a cab."

"Okay, be safe," Bette said, as though Evie lived in the trenches and not the yuppie-lined streets of the Upper West Side.

In the warm air of the June evening, Evie spied her competitors jostling for cabs at each corner—old ladies wielding canes, moms with strollers, and throngs of teenagers in their evening hooch-wear. Evie started downtown on foot, hoping to outsmart the masses by picking up a cab in front of Lincoln Center. She jabbed her grandmother's phone number as she walked.

"Hi, Grandma. I'm back."

"Good. I vas just about to ask, Evie, if you're seeing anyone now? Someone special?"

"Not at the moment. Jack and I only broke up six months ago," Evie responded, suppressing a groan. "But I do have some potentially good news. The partnership committee started meeting. I should hear by the end of the summer. Isn't that exciting?" Evie asked, wincing as she realized just how much she thrived on praise.

"Oy. Vhat do you need to vork zose long hours for? How vill you meet someone if you're alvays vorking? Your mother tells me you are practically living zere. You are sure you vant this?"

"Of course I want it, Grandma. Why else would I have been working so hard?"

Truthfully, it wasn't crazy of her grandmother to question her desire to make partner. Evie had only gone to law school because her father had been a lawyer and every other political science major was signing up for the LSAT.

"Okay, who am I? If you vant it, zen I hope you get it," Bette said, as though this would appease Evie.

"Yes, I want it. Anyway, let's talk later. I need to focus on getting a taxi. I love—"

"Vait, I have something else to tell you. It's important."

"Yes?" Evie said, a smile creeping across her face. She knew what was coming. The warning about Listeria. Or some lifesaving tip Bette learned on *The Dr. Oz Show:* Eat jujuberries daily. Parabens are lethal. Yada yada yada.

"Listen carefully. I heard ze most vild thing at Canasta today. Louise Hammerman's grandson just got engaged to someone from ze computer. She said zere are zese places vhere you can find people who are looking to get married. And zey're all Jewish. Louise told me. Her grandson lives in Manhattan too. Vith eight million people zere, I don't know vy anyone should need a machine to get married, but vhat do I know? It vorks. Anyvay, Evie, I can put you in touch with her grandson if you need instructions."

Evie's heart sank. So much for "I just called to say I love you." This was a tactical phone call, and a useless one at that. In her grandmother's mind, once Evie signed up for this "place" on the Internet, an eligible man would pop out of her computer screen like a stripper jumping out of a birthday cake. Evie didn't want to let her down by telling her she'd already been on thirty-plus JDates in the last decade, her only welcome hiatus was when she was together with Jack. The men she met online were almost always disasters, boasting halitosis, neurosis, scoliosis, and, quite recently, osteoporosis.

"Um, thanks, Grandma, but I actually already know about JDate," Evie said, keeping her eyes peeled for an available cab. Instead, already occupied, the fleet of yellow cars mucked up her shoes as they zoomed past her strappy-toed feet.

"Oh," Bette responded. Evie could hear the disappointment in her monosyllabic response. "Vell, I'd tell Susan about zis, but you know, vy vaste my breath?"

Susan was Evie's aunt who lived in New Mexico. She was a meditation consultant who loved all things hemp. It was hard for Evie to pinpoint even one strain of DNA her late father and her aunt shared. Only by Googling her estranged relative had Evie discovered that Susan lived in some bizarre commune called New Horizons. The most Bette ever said about her daughter was "vy me?" Aunt Susan served primarily to bring into stark contrast how much Bette was counting on Evie to lead a traditional life, i.e., get married and have babies, quickly.

"I know, Grandma."

"Anyvay, Evie, did you see ze latest issue yet? I svear nobody has taste anymore," Bette said, shifting topics like a seasoned politician.

Evie's grandmother was referring to *Architectural Digest,* a.k.a. "the Bible," which she and Bette both loved to analyze each month, hankering after outrageously expensive silk carpets or haranguing total strangers for choosing outdated damask curtains. Many of the apartments featured in the monthly magazine were located in New York City, but rarely was an actual address printed. Evie would sometimes gaze up at the windowed skyline and wonder: Are you the penthouse with the fabulous double-height living room? Are you the one with the Central Park view from the master bathroom?

"Not yet. Haven't even had time to check the mail all week. Listen, I'm going to miss the entire reception. I'll call you this week. I love you."

Evie hung up, her mood deflated. She hated being a letdown to her grandmother. Despite their strong bond, when Bette started up with the whole marriage bit, her nudging had a way of eclipsing the finer points of their relationship.

Evie looked at her watch again. Shit. In front of Avery Fisher Hall, two well-heeled ladies exited a black town car and Evie threw herself in the backseat before the driver could tell her he was not for hire. Black cars charged nearly double the rates of yellow taxis, but this was no time for frugality.

"Metropolitan Pavilion, please," she said breathlessly. "Eighteenth Street."

"Thirty dollars, miss," the driver responded, and Evie nodded her acquiescence to the exorbitant price. She pressed her body into the soft leather of the seat and closed her eyes for a moment, letting herself take a one-minute breather before checking her work e-mail. It seemed hard to imagine Evie and her team would be ready for Tuesday's closing, when Calico, the country's largest manufacturer of plumbing supplies, would take over Anson-Wells, a related chemicals company in a stock-purchase agreement. But there was a certain thrill in racing to meet the deadline. As a senior associate, it was Evie's job to marshal the juniors toward the finish line. Florencio Alvez, Calico's COO, had sent her nine new messages in the last hour. She had a particular fondness for Florencio, who she knew had personally requested that she be put on the project. They had worked together previously when Calico sold off its residential parts division last fall. It was those moments—being in charge of a team, the satisfaction of a job well done, having her efforts rewarded by being personally solicited by a client—that made the tedious work and the grueling late nights almost manageable. She responded to Florencio and rested her head against the cushions once again, but couldn't find peace. She was still stressed about being so late to the wedding, and even more so, unnerved by her conversation with Bette.

Looking out the window, she noticed there was still another ten blocks of Lincoln Tunnel traffic before they would pick up any speed. She decided to call her mother, Fran, for a pick-me-up. Fran was what most daughters would consider a maternal dream come true: wholly uncritical, perpetually optimistic, and unfailingly supportive. If Fran ever expressed worry about her daughter being overworked or lonely, she was sure to mask it exclusively as concern for Evie's happiness. This was unlike Bette, who didn't bother with pretense. Bette was legally blind when it came to finding a bright side in bad situations, which was a personality trait Evie regrettably shared. Fran, on the other hand, was the master of manufacturing silver linings.

"Hi, Mom," she said.

"Hi, Evie—where are you?"

"On the way to Paul's wedding, though I'm like friendship-ending late at this point. There is so much Lincoln Tunnel traffic. Honestly, who knew so many people wanted to go to New Jersey?"

"You'll get there, sweetie. Please congratulate Paul for me. How are you doing?"

"I'm fine, but I just had the most aggravating conversation with Grandma." Evie relayed the details.

"Evie, you know how she is. She's a woman of a different generation. She wants you to get married, have kids. She never had the chance to pursue a real profession. It's foreign to her."

"What about you? Is that what you want too?" Evie asked. "I assume you're excited that your daughter might be a partner at Baker Smith in a matter of months. There are only like twenty female partners total." Twenty-two to be precise, but Evie didn't want to show that she'd counted.

Before having Evie, Fran was an advertising executive at Ogilvy in their D.C. office. After becoming a mom, Fran parlayed her experience into consulting work for local businesses, still finding time to devote considerable attention to her real passion—third-tier regional theater.

"You know I'm proud," Fran said. Evie noticed her mother didn't answer the first part of her question.

"Good. Because it's a really big deal. I wish someone would acknowledge how prestigious this is. Or at least pretend."

"I do realize. Remember the 'Yale Mom' hat I wanted to wear on Parents' Weekend but you wouldn't let me? I'm very proud. But these are your accomplishments, not mine. You don't need my validation. Or Bette's."

Don't I? Evie wondered. It certainly seemed at times that she did.

"I know that."

"Listen, honey, you have a great time at the wedding. We're meeting a colleague of Winston's in town for dinner, so I have to jet."

Winston was Evie's ultra-WASPy stepfather, who Fran married two years after Evie's dad passed away unexpectedly. Winston was tall and built like a boxcar. His face was perpetually tan. Not in an artificial orange way—more like a worn-in leather couch. Pink polos and Nantucket red pants with embroidered whales made up a good chunk of his wardrobe.

"Oh, and don't forget that April and May are also coming for brunch tomorrow," Fran added, referring to Evie's stepsisters. "It's at eleven because they have so much school shopping to do. It'd be great if you could get here early to help out. I have an early morning rehearsal that I can't miss. I swear this is the trickiest production of *Godspell* I've ever done. If you get here early enough I can drive you over to see the sets."

"Yes, I'll be there. Love you," Evie said, but just as she was about to hang up the phone, Fran cut in with, "Did you hear Lauren Moskovitz is engaged? She was an odd little girl, wasn't she? I guess there's someone for everyone." Then click, the phone went dead, and Evie was still entrenched in horrendous Midtown traffic and not one bit calmer.

She turned her attention back to the ticker tape of e-mails on her phone, several of which were from Bill Black, the supervising partner on the Calico deal. Bill's awareness of the division between weekdays and weekends was negligible at best. Evie dashed off some quick responses that she hoped would pacify him for at least an hour and checked her Gmail. She subtly returned her phone to its ridiculous spot, wondering when her next point of access would be. It occurred to her then that she could have brought a blazer to stash her phone in, but it was too late to turn back, especially now that she was a few blocks away from the tunnel entrance and her car was finally about to move.

Out of the window, from Ninth Avenue, she spotted the office tower that housed Cravath, Swaine & Moore, arguably the city's most prestigious firm and the only one of the seven she applied to from which she didn't receive an offer after law school. She had burned at the time—receiving the thin envelope in the mail with its form-letter text: *We appreciate your interest in a position at our firm. Unfortunately, we are unable to offer you employment at this time. Have a nice life.* Well, it was their loss.

From Columbia Law School, she joined another white-shoe firm that represented more than half of the major investment banks and a sizable percentage of the Fortune 500. Baker Smith had even stolen away several of Cravath's biggest clients since she'd joined (having nothing to do with her work—but it was still satisfying). For the past eight years, she had pored over contracts, revised purchase agreements, blacklined merger documents, and sat in on conference calls ad nauseam. She gave her life to the firm, canceling dates and weekend brunches with friends and at times abandoning what most would consider basic hygienic practices. Around the time of a deal closing, her bikini line was the stuff of horror films. When things got really crazy, the only way she could see friends was if they were willing to meet for a twenty-minute lunch in the office cafeteria—and even that could be cut short if her BlackBerry buzzed with something urgent. The work could be very stimulating, but with each new project that landed on her desk, she still felt like an anxious freshman unsure if she was up to the task. Luckily, with fourteen-hour workdays a regular occurrence, she had little time left for contemplation.

Finally it seemed her dedication was going to pay off. Her department, Mergers and Acquisitions, had no female partners, and all the existing partners were around the same age—sixty— and would be retiring soon enough, to finally start enjoying their lives and their nest eggs. She'd never received anything less than a stellar review. Her assignments were usually among the most high profile and complicated in the firm's portfolio. Woefully, she accepted the fact that the partnership committee likely considered having no family responsibilities a plus. She was never running off to do anything foolish like taking her kids to Disney World or the pediatrician. If things with Jack had worked out, she might be in an entirely different place now. But they didn't "work out," and unlike the reorganizations and liquidations she witnessed in the firm's bankruptcy unit, there was no orderly division of assets or mitigation of emotional damage after she and Jack split. Just two jagged halves of a former whole left to fend for themselves.

So this is where she was.

Single, but on the brink of partnership, and actually pretty damn proud of her efforts. She was looking forward to having a bigger office, and the impressive title would certainly be nice, but mostly it was the fatter paycheck that excited her. The salary jump from eighth-year associate to junior partner was enormous. She'd be more than doubling her earnings next year, meaning she could finally afford to buy her own apartment instead of renting. A charming, prewar one-bedroom near Lincoln Center that was only ten blocks from her current apartment on West

Seventy-Sixth Street had been bookmarked on her computer for the last three months. She stared at the pictures of the listing so long she had practically memorized every detail, from the working fireplace with the intricately carved gray-veined white marble mantel to the six-over-six oversize windows that framed the southern wall of the living room and looked out onto a lovely tree-lined side street. She knew where she would put her beloved tufted couch and could precisely imagine the tall lacquered bookcases she would buy to flank it.

As her town car glided to the entrance of her destination, Evie promised herself she'd e-mail the listing broker the same day she made partner to arrange an appointment to see it. Living next door to Avery Fisher Hall and the Metropolitan Opera, maybe she'd actually take advantage of everything New York had to offer. She could finally see her first opera. It was embarrassing that she'd never seen the one about the butterfly.

# # #

The reception was in full swing by the time she arrived. Through the gaggle of attractive gay boys doing an ironic nod to the Electric Slide, Evie spotted her friends seated together in a booth at the back of the room. She reached them just as they were toasting. The brilliance of their ring fingers, each boasting a sparkling engagement ring, beamed at her like flashlights. The weight of what rested on their hands, perhaps a combined total of eight carats (most of which came from just *one* of those stones), told the world that her best friends were spoken for—loved—part of a team. Evie wondered if her own naked hand, adorned only with nail polish chipped from rampant typing, signaled the opposite.

"Evie, finally!" Stasia shouted over the music. "You are so late. I told Paul your taxi hit one of those food delivery guys on bikes. So just go with that. Anyway, let's get you a drink." She motioned to her husband, Rick, to go to the bar.

"Evie, you look great," Rick said, giving her a warm hug. "What can I get for you?"

"I'd love a white wine."

"Actually, I'll help get refills for everyone," Stasia said and popped up from the banquette to follow her husband, moving through the crowd with the elasticity of a Slinky. Evie admired the back of the conservative white shift that her friend wore so effortlessly it managed to look sexy. Evie had almost chosen a white dress but decided against it, thinking it was inappropriate for a wedding. Now she felt like a fool, realizing that rule only applied if a bride was present. Her friends returned a few minutes later with beverages for all.

This was hardly the first time Evie had compared herself to the manor-born Stasia. She hailed from San Francisco, where she was raised in a double-wide town house by her father, a successful venture capitalist turned congressman, and her mother, a pencil-thin blonde who could trace her roots to the *Mayflower* and acted, with Locust Valley lockjaw intonation and a general haughtiness, like that was the only respectable means of arriving in the United States. Evie's family was more Ellis Island. Stasia reached New Haven as a freshman sans her mother's attitude, but with pedigree to spare. (She was fluent in boating vernacular; Evie knew one word—seasick.) Stasia would be so easy to hate if she didn't possess a remarkable amount of patience for Evie's occasional bouts of neurotic behavior.

"How are you feeling?" Evie asked, turning to face Tracy, who was digging her hands into a bowl filled with monogrammed M&Ms.

"Fat," Tracy responded, the word spewing from her mouth.

"I'm just pregnant enough to look chubby and not far enough along to make it clear there's a baby inside. And don't try to bullshit me and tell me I'm glowing."

"You look beautiful, honey," Tracy's husband, Jake, interjected, resting his hand on his wife's belly. Today, Jake's tenderness didn't make Evie swell with envy like Rick's often did. Burdened by the Calico closing and still smarting from the call with Bette, it was making her skin crawl.

"You look great, Trace. And you're having a baby. It's worth it," Evie said in what she hoped was a reassuring tone, though she always felt like a fraud when she tried to talk to her friends about marriage and babies. After all, she was basing her comments on nothing but guesswork.

"You're going to have to tell me what it's like—motherhood, that is. I think we're getting ready to try," Stasia said, leaning in closely so that Rick and the other men couldn't hear. It wasn't surprising to Evie, really, that Rick and Stasia were planning to start a family. But for some reason, it stung, even though it shouldn't have.

"That's great news! I'll be happy to pass down any and all information," Tracy said excitedly. "Oh, and guess what? Jake put the crib together today. I know it's early, but he finally got a break from work, so we figured why not?"

Evie resisted asking where said crib was going. In Jake and Tracy Loo's Hell's Kitchen studio apartment, the only plausible space to accommodate their new baby was the entry closet. Jake's latest professional venture—producing children's music about the environment—was not exactly lucrative. Evie worried it was only a matter of time before they were suburbia-bound. Tracy had an edge to her that Evie's other friends didn't have and was especially prone to eye rolling whenever Stasia discussed her father's political office or Caroline, the fourth in their quartet, mentioned an extravagant purchase. If she left the city, maybe to go back to Pittsburgh where Jake was raised, Evie would miss her dearly. Tracy swore she'd never go to Pitt. "You know Asian mothers— she'd welcome Jake back in the womb if he'd fit."

"Trace, you'll lose all the weight within three months after having the baby," Caroline said. "You just need to see my trainer. She's a miracle worker." She flexed her muscles, drawing out surprisingly ample biceps from inside spaghetti-thin arms.

"You'll have to give me her number then," Tracy said, and then muttered under her breath to Evie, "I think the tummy tucks in the recovery room were the real miracle."

"Shh." Evie nudged Tracy. "We don't know that."

It was true Tracy had put on some baby weight, but the hormones had managed to add some color to her ivory complexion and sheen to her reddish locks. Caroline was now a better version of her college self—Pilates-toned, airbrush-tanned, and designer-clad. And Stasia was just riding a continuous trajectory of genetic supremacy since birth: oval face, turquoise eyes, wheat-blond hair, and a sweet cleft in her chin. They were all well preserved from college, if not improved upon. Certainly their fashion choices were more sound.

Looking at her friends tonight, Evie was struck again by how cohesive their group had remained. True, it helped that they'd all chosen to settle in New York City (Stasia after medical school out west; Tracy after a two-year stint with Teach for America in New Orleans), but geography couldn't be the only reason they'd all stayed close. In a bustling city where work could often threaten to swallow her up whole, Evie cherished that she had her girls to count on.

But why they had all managed to find their *b'sherts,* as Bette would say, and she remained the seventh wheel, baffled Evie. Lifting the cool wine to her lips, she thought maybe just for the night she could find a suitable answer to that puzzle at the bottom of her Chardonnay glass.

"So, Evie, you've been with us for an entire five minutes without checking your BlackBerry," Tracy said with mock admiration. "Did your office burn down?"

"Unfortunately not. The Baker Smith fortress remains," Evie said. What would her friends say if they knew her phone was wedged in her underwear at this very moment?

"You know, I'm not the only one with an Internet habit." Evie gestured to the table where her friends had set out their respective iPhones like dinner utensils.

"I'm just taking pictures," Stasia said. "We're supposed to tag our photos from tonight with the hashtag 'hotgrooms.'"

"Classy," Evie said.

"Besides, the rest of us let three-minute intervals pass before checking our phones," Tracy quipped.

"Speak for yourself," Caroline objected, scooping up her iPhone. "I'm waiting for my nanny to let me know if Grace ate her vegetables. And my eBay auction is ending in six minutes and I'm in a death match with someone named Big Apple Luxury over a vintage Birkin." She flashed the phone in Evie's face for her to admire a cobalt blue handbag just as a text message flashed on the screen.

"Good news, Care. Imelda wrote that Grace ate four green beans and—what the hell is a treetop? Apparently she ate three of them."

"The top of a spear of broccoli," Caroline explained, as though that should have been self-evident. "Grace won't eat the trunks."

"Got it."

Caroline was the definition of a high-strung parent, applying the same intensity she brought to her former finance job to raising her girls. Grace was already one of those oddly sensitive kids, the kind that won't take a bath without goggles or wear anything with a tag in it. Pippa, Grace's younger sister, seemed a bit more resilient, but the jury was still out. Caroline's laser-sharp focus on their every move couldn't be helpful. But it wasn't for Evie to judge, of course.

"So where is the happy couple?" Evie asked. "I haven't even said hello yet."

Tracy pointed to Paul and Marco, who stood near the buffet with their arms around each other's waists. Evie knew she should be beaming, seeing as she was the one who introduced them during her 1L year. While she didn't think Paul, a celebrity publicist, would be as charmed as she was by Marco's plans to work at New Yorkers for Children, she knew Marco's hard-earned six-pack and cappuccino skin would at least garnish a first date. She was right. Fortunately for Paul, Marco Mendez had a weakness for Hollywood culture and hazel-eyed men.

She was happy for them, and proud of herself for successfully setting up a couple, though she wondered if Rabbi Berman of Temple Beth-El in Baltimore would agree that putting together this match would count toward the Jewish belief that setting up three marriages guarantees a place in heaven. Maybe someone Evie knew was only one match away from the holy trifecta and would be duly motivated to find her a spouse. Not that she should be worried. It'll happen when it happens.

Evie was thirty-four, which at times felt to her like a young and promising age and at others made her feel like she was on a collision course with an exploding biological clock. Nothing was going to get solved tonight, that much Evie knew. She vowed to have a good time and wait until tomorrow to resume her obsessive worry about the future. She let the familiar harmony of her friends' chitchat distract her until the wine kicked in.

# # #

Soon enough the hokey line dancing at Paul and Marco's wedding gave way to some turbulent bumping and grinding, and Evie made good on her promise to let the alcohol ease her troubled mind. She already regretted being so amenable to the early family brunch in Greenwich the next morning. Seeing April and May, Winston's twin daughters, was hardly the way she wanted to spend a few precious Sunday hours away from the office. They were born in November, so exactly how much Mount Gay rum Winston and his ex-wife were drinking when they named these two was up for debate. At least they weren't identical. That would just be too much to stomach.

The TWASPs, as Evie and her friends called them, were seventeen years old and in their final year at Andover. April was off to Dartmouth in the fall and May was going to Yale. There really wasn't anything particularly abhorrent about them. They just seemed so young to Evie, and so painfully unburdened by anything of real consequence. To be fair, they were still teenagers— and though they were her only siblings, relating to them was almost impossible. She'd felt like a grandmother at their recent high school graduation, more aligned with the crotchety old folks complaining their seats were too far back than the carefree teenagers in cap and gown on the dais.

If she was honest with herself, the thing she really resented about the TWASPs was that they were first starting on the path that she herself had been on many moons ago. The one that was supposed to lead to success in all things professional and romantic, the one that had somehow worked out for her friends but not for her. What if the TWASPs got married before she did? What if she had to don some horrible periwinkle bridesmaid dress and stand amid their twenty-something friends with everyone in the church whispering, "Well at least she has a great career." Evie was especially agitated by May, who never so much as asked Evie about her time at Yale. It was as if Evie had gone there so long ago her experience would be irrelevant. It was true Evie hadn't used a laptop in class, but she wasn't dunking a quill into an inkwell either.

As she was considering excuses for skipping the family brunch, Evie met the gaze of a handsome guy staring at her from the nearby bar. Her mind floated above the conversation at her table, which had turned to a heated debate over the finale of *Celebrity Truth or Dare*. He was dressed in a well-tailored dark suit and a bright yellow tie, expertly knotted. Perhaps this night was going to be more interesting than she had anticipated. She knew most of Paul and Marco's male friends and they were, almost exclusively, more interested in each other than in her. But this guy leaning against the bar was definitely looking her way.

Evie debated whether to approach or wait for him to seek her out, feeling regrettably clueless about facilitating what should be a simple meet-cute. Her relationship with Jack had obfuscated whatever little bit she thought she knew about courtship and dating. She felt bile creep up the rungs of her esophagus at the thought of her ex. They dated for two years but broke up six months ago, when she finally realized that when he had told her on their first date that he didn't believe in marriage, he wasn't kidding around. Their countless wine-filled dinners, Sunday mornings waking up together with Nespresso Arpeggio lattes and the *New York Times,* and the sight of adorable children swinging in Central Park did not change his mind. And certainly not the ultimatum she gave him last December.

It was time to focus on the here and now. She settled on sending a quick, close-lipped smile with a nod of acknowledgment in the direction of the bar. Her smile was returned on impact and with that split-second exchange, Evie felt the hope rise in her belly that maybe on this night, when it was totally unforeseen, she would meet The One. Isn't that what people always said happened? She headed toward the bar cautiously and was relieved when she saw him motion her toward the empty seat next to him.

"Hi there," he said. "I'm Luke Glasscock. Paul's cousin. Second cousin, actually. And you are?"

"Evie Rosen, Paul's friend. And Marco's too. I went to college with Paul and law school with Marco. I actually introduced them."

"Smart and pretty. I like that," he said. "Well done on the setup."

"Well thank you. So is your whole family here?"

"Just some cousins. My parents are in Cincinnati, but I moved to New York a few years ago for work."

"Oh yeah? What do you do?"

"Investment banking. At Deutsche Bank. Don't hold it against me."

"Cool. I'm a lawyer at Baker Smith. We represent DB actually."

"I know that. So can I get you a drink? I figure we better get shit-faced if we're going to hit the dance floor later?"

Shit-faced? What was this, a DKE formal? She thought again of Jack. He never would have used such a doltish frat-house phrase. He would say "Care to dance?" and lead her by the hand to the dance floor where he would put to use the ballroom dancing lessons from his London schoolboy days. But he was pompous and self-obsessed and didn't believe in marriage, so it didn't matter. She returned Jack to the sealed compartment of her brain, the lockbox that also held the painful memories of losing her father, and refocused her eyes on Luke. "Chin chin," she responded, and they clinked glasses.

"Sure. I'll have what you're having," she said, gesturing toward his watered-down amber drink. Since when did she drink Scotch?

"I noticed you when you came in—I was hoping we could get a chance to talk."

"Oh yeah? Well, here I am. Always happy to talk."

The piercing sound of a fork clinking on a glass signaled it was time for toasts. Evie watched Paul and Marco make their way to the platform where the DJ was set up.

"Thank you all for coming," Marco began. "As my six hundred and twelve Twitter followers already know, Paul and I exchanged our vows yesterday at City Hall in front of a mail-order bride and a pair of ex-cons." The crowd emitted knowing chuckles.

Marco launched into a cheesy but moving speech about the progress of their relationship, and Evie, already familiar with the details of their courtship, tuned him out while she studied Luke. It wasn't until she heard her own name that she snapped back to the present.

Paul had apparently grabbed the microphone away from Marco while she was daydreaming. Evie could tell Paul was tipsy from the way he was shuffling like a child on the verge of an accident.

"—Evie Rosen for setting us up. We're so glad she took time away from her BlackBerry to join us this evening. Evie, stand up and take a bow. She's the foxy brunette in the corner over there." From the DJ booth, a spotlight made its way over to her.

"That's you," Luke whispered, touching her gently on the elbow.

Evie smiled graciously and prayed for the moment to end. The harsh light stayed with her, and she squinted her eyes reflexively.

"Stand up, Evie."

She panicked. Her phone had shifted to a precarious position in her underwear, and she feared it would drop out if she rose. Wouldn't that make Paul's BlackBerry dig poignant?

She clenched her muscles as tightly as she could, attempting what her former Pilates teacher called a "Kegel," and stood up cautiously.

"She's single, by the way." Paul winked at her from the stage. For some reason, the announcement that she was single elicited cheers from the crowd. Idiots, Evie thought. She didn't dare look at Luke.

"Come up here, Evie," Marco said. "Let's get a picture with our matchmaker."

Evie clutched her wineglass for dear life and awkwardly attempted to walk across the dance floor without separating her legs too much. The spotlight maintained its steadfast position on her. It was no use. She felt the BlackBerry slide down her leg and somehow heard the crash in her head before the phone hit the floor. Around her, wedding guests gasped and laughed quietly until someone let out a roar, giving license to everyone else to let it rip. Her phone lay faceup, its red message light flashing, in the center of a white marble diamond. As she bent down to reach for it with a shaky hand, the damn thing started to ring.

Chapter 2

She felt Tracy grab her hand and pull her into the ladies' room. They stood at the sinks, Evie's flaming cheeks burning under the fluorescent lights.

"Are you kidding me, Evie?"

"I had no place to put my phone, okay!" she hissed. "You don't understand. I have a closing on Tuesday and half the people on the deal are in the Hong Kong office. It's morning there—I can't just take off because I'm at a wedding."

"So you're a slacker if you don't put your phone in your underwear? By the way, that's what pockets are for."

"It didn't fit in my purse. Stupid Judith Leiber. Caroline bought me this gajilion-dollar bag and it barely holds a lipstick."

"That's no excuse. Why the hell are you so obsessed with that thing anyway?" Tracy glared at the BlackBerry curled in Evie's hand.

"I like my phone. It helps me feel connected," she answered, adding what she believed to be an "I'm not hurting anyone" shrug.

"To what?"

"People, work, plans, news, the cultural zeitgeist . . . I don't know." Evie leaned toward the vanity to reapply her lip gloss. "Did Paul really need to announce that I'm single to the entire wedding?"

"Maybe it's not so bad he said it. Get the word out, you know?" Tracy said, eyeing Evie's reflection cautiously in the mirror.

"I think my Facebook, JDate, and Match profiles have taken care of that already."

Tracy tapped on the door to one of the stalls. "The baby makes me have to go every two seconds lately." She patted her stomach affectionately. Any discomfort the baby was causing was clearly a minor inconvenience to her. She practically jumped for joy when she felt a flutter in her belly, demanding that all her friends lay their hands on it like it was a Ouija board until they swore they felt movement too.

"So I was chatting with Paul's cousin before the toast. We were kind of hitting it off. Though let's see if he's still interested after I gave birth to a phone on the dance floor." With that, Evie ducked into the stall next to Tracy's.

"Oh yeah? What's his name?"

"Luke." She kept the Glasscock part to herself, otherwise Tracy would rename him Fragile-Dick in two seconds flat.

"Well let's go back and find him!" Tracy's voice went up about four hopeful octaves.

"I will." Evie ran a hand over prickly calves. "Is there a razor in the toiletries basket?"

"Nope." Evie could hear Tracy rustling around the basket. "I have tweezers in my purse."

"Forget it," Evie grumbled, emerging from the stall. "I haven't quite had the time for proper grooming. Been at the office every night literally until two A.M."

"They're killing you over there." Tracy gave her a disapproving look. After completing her tenure teaching in a mobile trailer in hurricane-ransacked New Orleans, Tracy took a cushier job at the Brighton-Montgomery Preparatory School, an Upper East Side institution known for its rich academics and even richer student body. She worked hard, relentlessly grateful to have a proper classroom that didn't double as a supply closet, art room, and teachers' lounge, but when she didn't have department meetings or professional workshops, she was home rubbing her pregnant belly in front of the TV by 4:30 P.M.

"It'll be better once I make partner," Evie said, not actually sure if that was true. Would she really be any less anxious about her job just because she wasn't trying to climb the ladder? There would always be some new box to check off. Getting more clients. An appointment to one of the firm's management committees. The admiration of her fellow partners. "You go back inside. I need to read my e-mail."

"Hasn't that thing caused you enough problems tonight?" Tracy asked, peering once again at Evie's phone with disdain. "Don't spend all night in here."

After Tracy exited the ladies' room, Evie scrolled through her work e-mails, where—no surprise—she found an e-mail from Bill

Black asking her why she hadn't answered his call from moments earlier and requesting that she review the latest set of closing documents before Monday.

Her mother wrote to remind her that the train to Greenwich was running on a limited Sunday schedule so she should check online before leaving for brunch.

There was also a message from her closest friend at work, Annie Thayer, her first office mate at Baker Smith and another single-girl-about-town with whom Evie exchanged dating war stories. Annie was writing to say she should expect a call from her brother's friend Mike Jones. How the hell would she Google a guy with that name? He had recently split from a longtime girlfriend and was looking to reenter the dating world, heaven help him. Annie swore he was worth meeting but didn't provide much in the way of background or pictures.

Before rejoining the party, Evie briefly glanced at her Facebook and Instagram accounts, where already the #hotgrooms feed was exploding. Satisfied with her catch-up, she went back to the dance floor, where she found her girlfriends gathered to watch the happy couple glide to Etta James's "At Last," an unfair choice of song in Evie's estimation, since Paul and Marco, thanks to her, hadn't had to wait long at all to find each other. Luke was still stationed at the bar, looking down at his phone, and Evie fretfully chewed her lip as she walked over.

"She's back," he said.

"Yes I am. Just so you know, I don't always carry my BlackBerry around in there. I'm also working on a big deal at the moment and my phone didn't fit in my purse." Evie lifted her phone in one hand and her purse in the other to illustrate her mea culpa.

"Nah, it was funny," he said with a forgiving smile. "I certainly won't forget meeting you."

"Well that's good. Always happy to leave a lasting impression." *Phew.*

"You certainly did," Luke said. "Listen, my mother will kill me if I don't say hi to her sister's kids, and it looks like they are getting ready to leave. Can I trust I'll find you here when I'm back?"

"I won't budge."

Alone at the bar, she scanned the crowd for her friends. She spotted Caroline and Jerome shimmying to a popular dance number, the top of Jerome's bald head reaching to just under Caroline's cheekbones. Caroline wasn't naturally stunning, but she reeked of sex appeal in a way that Evie never would, no matter what lacy getup she put on or how high she pushed her décolletage. Dallas born-and-bred, in college Caroline had all the trappings of wealth, which back in the day meant a Kate Spade shoulder bag, several Nicole Miller party dresses, and a credit card whose bill her parents paid. But she always seemed to have an uncomfortable relationship with money until her billionaire hedge-fund husband came along. Caroline professed her love for Jerome from the day she met him ten years before at an investor conference, the same day eight dozen lavender roses arrived at her doorstep along with a note delivered by an honest-to-goodness butler. Later that night at Per Se, Caroline and Jerome feasted on truffles and drank wine retrieved from a safe-deposit box. Eight months later they were engaged. A decade later, they were still going strong, laughing giddily on the dance floor.

Next she spied Rick chatting with Marco's mother and father. Rick caught her glance and put up his index finger to indicate he'd join her in a moment. Evie looked away swiftly. The sight of Marco's parents, standing hand in hand and smiling as they took in the crowd, caused the familiar ache in Evie's chest to flare. Her own father would never see her married. He wouldn't be there to halfheartedly complain about the expensive orchids Evie chose for the centerpieces or do the traditional father-daughter dance. Instead, her wedding photos would be shots of her and her mother, surrounded by Winston and the TWASPs, the pseudofamily that she could never quite grasp was her current reality. She'd already decided she would ask Grandma Bette to walk her down the aisle should the need arise. Bette would be so anxious for Evie to seal the deal it would probably be more of a sprint.

Tracy slowly ambled over to Evie with Jake by her side. "I think we're going to head home. I'm exhausted."

"Okay. I'm going to hang. Luke and I are still talking," Evie said, pecking her pregnant friend on the cheek. "I'll keep you posted."

"You better."

Luke reappeared shortly after Tracy and Jake retreated.

"Sorry about that. I didn't know my relatives were so talkative," he said. "Can I get you another drink?"

"Absolutely," she said.

She lost track of how many cocktails they downed, but it was safe to say enough for it to seem like a great idea for them to grab the mike from the DJ and serenade the crowd with Justin Timberlake's "SexyBack."

"You're really fun, Evie," Luke said when the two of them found themselves in the empty coat check. He was running his hands up and down her bare arms.

Then his lips were on hers, their tongues at battle. It felt amazing. The mixed-up sweat, the feel of his stubble, the panting. Oh, how she'd missed this. She pulled away from him for a moment to admire his face and smiled. It seemed there was life beyond Jack after all.

Their makeout lasted until a tuxedoed wedding attendant ahem-ed them.

"Night's over, kids," he said.

"Let me put you in a cab," Luke said. "Evie Rosen at Baker Smith. I'm going to look you up first thing tomorrow. Let's get together for a drink."

"I would love that," she said, taking the hand he offered her.

He flagged down a taxi and helped her inside. Through the open window he said, "Get home safe. Oh, and Evie, hang on to your phone a little better next time." He winked one brown eye at her and sent her off.

Seat belted into the backseat, she looked out at the city, all sparkly from the glow of the headlights and traffic lights. The rows of flowers in planters, illuminated from tiny spots, formed pink pillows in her mind. It had been a great night.

# # #

Back home, Evie quickly swapped her dress for cozy pajamas and flung her dizzy self into bed. Now she remembered why she never drank Scotch. Eyeing the blur that was her laptop on the night table, she almost sent Luke a Facebook message—just a quick "what a fun night" opener to get a dialogue going, but she resisted on account of inebriation.

She did not want to end up like Jeffrey Belzer.

Jeffrey was a summer associate with Evie. After returning from a three-bottles-of-wine lunch at the Harvard Club (normal in the course of the seduction of the Big Law summer programs), he dashed off a quick e-mail to his fellow associate Allen Jacobs.

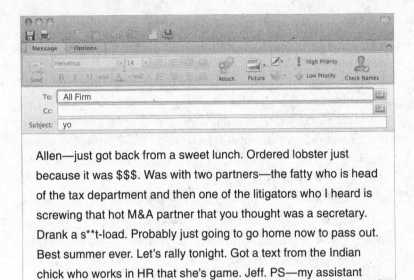

Allen—just got back from a sweet lunch. Ordered lobster just because it was $$$. Was with two partners—the fatty who is head of the tax department and then one of the litigators who I heard is screwing that hot M&A partner that you thought was a secretary. Drank a s**t-load. Probably just going to go home now to pass out. Best summer ever. Let's rally tonight. Got a text from the Indian chick who works in HR that she's game. Jeff. PS—my assistant just brought in my paycheck. Sweet!

Why, oh why, did Allen's parents have to spell his name with two *l*'s? Jeffrey Belzer must still be pondering that very question. When he selected the recipient of this soon-to-be-legendary e-mail, he didn't click on Allen Jacobs, but rather All Firm. The stream of the Sancerre at lunch couldn't have helped. It was done. There was no taking it back. Well, yes, an attempt was made to take it back. Not sixty seconds after sending the e-mail, someone must have alerted Jeffrey, because what followed in everyone's inbox was the following message: "Jeffrey Belzer would like to recall the message that was just sent." Now everyone who had ignored the message (it had had the bland subject line "yo") decided it had to be juicy. Within an hour, it had gone viral. The infamous blog *BigLawSux* had picked it up and then it appeared, verbatim, in the next day's *Wall Street Journal*.

Baker Smith was quick to issue a press release stating that Jeffrey Belzer's employment had been terminated as a result of his lapse in judgment. The statement further clarified, to clients who were already calling up to contest their bills, that the cost of the summer associate program was fully absorbed by the firm and not passed down to clients. Finally, and most comically to Evie, the firm said in the release that it encouraged every employee to recognize other individuals for their inner qualities and not their outer characteristics. Evie guessed that was the diplomatic way of saying that it did not condone referring to people as the "fatty" or "Indian chick." Fortunately for Baker Smith, its white shoes were quickly repolished and it retained its status as one of the city's premier law firms. Jeffrey, on the other hand, apparently fled to Thailand for a while and was last spotted taking drink orders at an Italian restaurant in the West Village.

The episode gave rise to Evie's hard-and-fast rule: no e-mail or texting while drunk.

Far less tragically, she had once signed an e-mail to a senior partner, Mitchell Rhodes, with "xoxo, Evie." Mitchell had responded to the otherwise professional e-mail with, "Thanks. I can't even get my kids to tell me they love me!" Evie and Mitchell had worked together many times since that e-mail exchange, and considering he was on the partnership committee, she felt fortunate they had shared that moment of intimacy, even if it arose from her carelessness. Still, there was no need for anyone else to receive an unintended electronic hug and kiss or a smiley face emoticon.

At the time of the Jeffrey Belzer episode, Evie reacted much like the other young associates—with a mixture of uproarious laughter and collegial pity. Things would be different if she made partner. She would be a partial owner of the firm (okay, her share of the profits would be like 1/250), but nonetheless a media crisis like this would have a totally different effect on her. She felt so grown up thinking about that. In the professional arena, she was exactly where she was meant to be at this age. Romantically, she felt like an insecure high-schooler. Besides the two years she dated Jack, her love life had been a series of three-date-max relationships.

What would Luke find when he looked her up? She did a quick self-Google. Her Baker Smith profile was the first return. The picture was a total disaster, taken after she'd pulled a double all-nighter. There were a few better images of her on NewYork SocialDiary.com from society events that Caroline had dragged her to. Her name appeared in a list of participants in a 5K Juvenile Diabetes fun-run, even though she'd actually bailed last minute due to a head cold. Her father's obituary in the *Baltimore Sun* was there. There was no trace of her and Jack. He didn't love pictures.

She curled up with her laptop tucked under her arm like a blankie and hoped for a new message ding from Luke, but the only thing she heard until she fell asleep were the soothing sounds of ambulances and car horns—the New York lullaby, she liked to call it.

#

Radio silence. That's what she got from Luke Glasscock after Paul's wedding. It was aggravating. He had seemed to forgive the whole birthing-a-phone-on-the-dance-floor mishap. She thought they had made a connection. They shared a hot and heavy make-out at the end of the evening. He had gallantly put her in a taxi, coolly handing the driver a twenty. He promised to be in touch. Could he have forgotten her last name? Where she worked? Even so, he could have asked Paul.

Now at work she found herself thinking about him too much, moving her head from one giant monitor to the other, like she was watching a tennis match at her desk, but not actually focusing on anything. The Calico closing had gone off without a hitch, but instead of being able to celebrate, a new matter was put on her desk moments after the final signature page had been faxed. She felt like Lucy in the chocolate factory.

Rumor had it the partnership committee was having a deliberation session that day, at least according to her BFF Renaldo on the maintenance crew. He had just delivered four sandwich platters and eight yellow legal pads to the forty-second-floor conference room.

Amid the stream of e-mails advertising summer sales, Evie noticed a message from Joshua Birnbaum, a tech entrepreneur she'd met on JDate three months earlier. They went out twice— two no-sparks-but-could've-been-worse evenings that left both of them fairly apathetic. But here was Joshua again, suggesting they meet for a drink as though ninety days hadn't passed since they'd last been in contact. She was actually considering accepting when her phone rang.

"Hi, lady," Caroline chirped. "We didn't recap the wedding yet. How've you been?"

"Eh. Swamped at work, as usual, and annoyed Paul's cousin has vanished into thin air."

"He's probably just busy at work. If his job is anything like yours, he doesn't have a ton of spare time to make dates."

Evie didn't have the strength to fight Caroline on that point—to state the plain fact that drafting a simple "It was great to meet you" e-mail could be accomplished in less than thirty seconds. No one knew that better than Evie. She managed to send dozens of personal e-mails out during the day. The letters on the keyboard of her computer were practically tattooed on her finger pads. She could dash off a one-liner blindfolded and with one hand tied behind her back.

"I think you should just put him out of your head," Caroline went on. "You know how that whole watched pot business works anyway. Can you hang on a sec? I'm in a cab." She heard Caroline ask the driver to take her to the Plaza Hotel on Central Park South. Then, in a far more hushed tone, she heard Caroline tell him to pick her up in two hours. Last time Evie checked, taxis didn't do round-trips. Clearly Caroline was talking to Jorge, her chauffeur, but at least she was embarrassed about it.

"Sorry, I'm back. I'm walking into a luncheon. Text me if you hear from him. You know how boring these charity things are—I'll just be staring at my phone. Like you." She giggled.

"Touché," Evie conceded.

Glancing at the BlackBerry on her desk, Evie thought about how her smartphone helped drown out the loneliness, almost like the background noise of a rerun she'd committed to memory. Acknowledging that a three-ounce electronic device was substituting for a genuine mate hit a sour note, but Evie was too cognizant of its usefulness to consider quitting the habit.

"Well have a good time. Don't forget to save some endangered pocketbooks for me."

Evie couldn't resist. In February, Caroline had purchased a table at "New Yorkers for Wildlife" and convinced Evie to duck out of work for lunch in the Waldorf ballroom. The trouble was that it was minus six degrees outside and most of the ladies were bundled in fur.

Unsatisfied with Caroline's dismissal of her angst over Luke, Evie phoned the ever-honest Tracy, hoping to catch her during a free period. After she went straight to voicemail, Evie started to dial Stasia's number but replaced the receiver midway. It was easier to speak to Caroline and Tracy about this type of thing. Both of them were married, but Caroline's husband was geriatric and Tracy's an ambiguously employed loafer. She believed they were both content, but still Evie took some comfort in feeling that compromises had been made. Relating agonizing dating stories to them was certainly tolerable, usually cathartic.

Stasia was different. She and Rick were a golden couple—attractive, well educated, from "good" families. They looked like they stepped out of a Slim Aarons photograph. Without—gasp—the help of a wireless connection, they found each other at Stanford Medical School (albeit over a cadaver dissection). After his training, Rick, an East-Coaster from birth, convinced Stasia to relocate with him. He became an ENT with a successful private practice on Park Avenue while she was slowly rising up the ranks in the research department of a top pharmaceutical company based in New Jersey.

After her announcement at Paul's wedding, Evie knew they were planning to start a family. It was natural to picture Rick as a father. He didn't seem to mind when Evie crashed their date nights and was quick to offer up the guy's perspective when she needed relationship advice. Plus Rick helped people for a living, even if it was only from the discomfort of deviated septums. That was more than she could say for Caroline's husband, whose daily task at work appeared to be printing money. It wasn't really her place to get high and mighty about professions, since working at Baker Smith hardly likened her to Mother Teresa. *But still.*

Her office phone rang. Tracy.

"Hey, I just saw a missed call from you. What's up? I'm on lunch."

"Nothing. Just annoyed. Stupid Luke from Paul's wedding. He hasn't e-mailed me yet."

"Evie, you are killing me. I saw him. He's cute, but you can do better. Didn't you say he was kind of a jerky banker type?"

"I don't remember that." (She did.) "And I hate to ask the obvious, but if I can do better, then shouldn't he be banging down my door? And by the way, when you did see him at the wedding, you said he was adorable."

"Uch, never mind what I said. Hormones talking. Stop checking your e-mail and think about where you want us to take you out to dinner for your long-overdue birthday dinner. We thought maybe the Beatrice Inn. Caroline can get us in." Evie had canceled on two previously scheduled celebrations because of work obligations. Things had a shot of getting quieter over the summer, but Evie wasn't much in the mood for merriment.

She chose to completely ignore Tracy's attempt to change the subject.

"In my entire adult life, I've only met one person that I've truly loved and who loved me. You know I never should have given him that stupid ultimatum. I could be happily—"

"Happily what?" Tracy cut her off. "Happily dating? You can't happily date for the rest of your life. You said you wanted a real commitment. Marriage. A wedding. Kids. You deserve that, and breaking up with Jack was the right thing to do."

"I guess you're right." Evie decided it was easier to agree than to draw out this debate again, which she had had with each of her girlfriends at least a dozen times.

"I am right. But I gotta go. The bell just rang."

Evie rested the phone in its cradle and opened up her lower file cabinet. She shifted a few heavy-duty hanging folders to the front, and pulled out the silver picture frame, now badly tarnished, that used to sit to the right of her computer. It housed a picture of her and Jack from a Halloween culinary event. Jack was one of the featured chefs. For a costume, the farthest he would venture was letting Evie attach feathers and silly pins to his toque. She, on the other hand, went all out and dressed as a sexy version of Remy, the chef from the Disney movie *Ratatouille*.

She'd met Jack just a month before the Halloween party at

the Soho Grand bar while out with the girls celebrating Stasia's move back from the West Coast. In the swanky lobby, she had flopped down happily in between Stasia and Caroline on a velour banquette and quickly downed a glass of Cabernet. She relaxed and imbibed, taken in by a sensual red diptych hanging next to the bar. That's when she noticed Jack. He was getting up from a nearby table and shaking hands with a pretty young woman holding a tape recorder and a heavily inked cameraman. Evie was instantly curious.

After about an hour of sneaking glances at each other, he approached Evie when she stepped away from her table to listen to a voicemail, and offered to buy her a drink. The first thing she heard was his accent. It was definitely British and definitely hot.

Evie assessed that he was handsome but not out of her league. He stood about three inches taller than her in her heels and had fair skin, steely blue-gray eyes, and brown hair worn a touch on the long side. She guessed he was about midthirties. The small gap between his two front teeth immediately made Evie curious about his background. Where she was from, everyone got braces the day after their bar or bat mitzvahs. He had a raw sexiness about him, emphasized by a five-o'clock shadow and the motorcycle jacket he managed to pull off without any irony. In a word—he had swagger.

"I'm Jack," he said, grabbing a few handfuls of smoked nuts at the bar. "And I'm absolutely starved after a rubbish sushi dinner in Midtown."

"Midtown? Why were you eating there? My office is in Midtown and the restaurants are terrible. I'm Evie, by the way."

"And what is it that you do? In Midtown?"

Courtesy of the alcohol ratcheting up her self-esteem a few notches, Evie responded proudly that she was a corporate attorney at Baker Smith, instead of muttering "lawyer" under her breath.

They ended up discussing for ten minutes which neighbor-hoods in Manhattan had the best restaurants—teasing, joking, and spritedly fighting their way through a mock dispute. For the first time in ages, she actually ignored the persistent buzz of her BlackBerry, even though she knew a team of attorneys in the firm's Menlo Park office was waiting on her feedback. Jack was just so passionate as he spoke—though really anything he said with that accent would have magnetized her.

"So, Jack, what do *you* do that you have so much time to go out to eat?" She hoped to get at some explanation of why he was being filmed earlier.

"Well, I suppose now is a good time to tell you, I'm a chef. Jack Kipling is my full name. Perhaps I should have told you that before we got into it." He chuckled, obviously enjoying her jaw-dropped reaction.

Jack Kipling was arguably the city's hottest young chef. She was surprised that she hadn't recognized him. He was not only a chef but also a successful restaurateur, owning several well-regarded restaurants in the city, most notably JAK, a French-style bistro on the Upper West Side near her apartment. He was a close pal and rival of Marcus Samuelsson.

"But don't worry, no offense taken about your comment that uptown restaurants are almost as bad as Midtown," he said.

"Wait—no—I actually love JAK! I eat there all the time. Honestly. Check your receipts. You'll see lots of Evie Rosen AmEx charges."

"I believe you. Though I won't quiz you on what your favorite dish is, just in case you're lying to make me feel better. Listen these nuts are not really doing it for me—I'm still rather peckish. Do you want to—wait, sorry, I forgot I saw you over there with your friends."

"No, no, it's fine. We were getting ready to leave anyway," she lied. "I'll just go say good-bye to them and we can get something to eat."

And that was the start of Evie's relationship with Jack.

Three shrill rings of her office phone brought Evie back to the present. Her secretary, Marianne, whom she shared with another associate, was away from her post, as per usual, so Evie scooped up the phone herself. Marianne was all big hair and big lips and something always seemed to need reapplying in the bathroom.

"This is Evie."

"Evie, it's Mitchell Rhodes. Could you come up to the conference room on the forty-second floor please?"

Evie immediately felt nauseated. It couldn't be that she was already going to be named partner, could it? It was too early for that, unless the firm was changing its protocol. Maybe they wanted to grill her on her recent matters, to see if she was really up to snuff. Or could there be some secret society–like initiation process where she'd be blindfolded and forced to drink a drop of blood from the pinkies of each of the partners on the executive committee? She didn't like the sound of Mitchell's voice on the phone. Why did everyone at her firm have to sound so formal? She wished they would just say, "Hey, get up here, we want to give you a huge office and loads of money."

"Sure, I'll be right up," she muttered, and grabbed her ID card so she could access the executive-level conference floor.

Two minutes later, she found herself seated across from the five members of the partnership committee. Mitchell was scanning his BlackBerry and did not look up when she entered, which seemed peculiar. The conference room had one wall of solid glass and the afternoon sun streamed through, forcing Evie to squint while she faced the grim-looking partners. She steeled her body against the powers that be. The long mahogany table around which the partners were seated was covered in boxes filled with papers—the kind used for due-diligence projects. There had to be at least ten of them, each overflowing. *Good grief, please let this not be the mound of paperwork she'd be expected to review in her newest assignment.*

"Evie," Patricia Douglas, the freshest member of the partnership committee and a highly regarded litigator, said. "You know how outstanding we think your work has been since you've joined the firm. Your reviews have been consistently glowing."

"Thank you. I really try my best." When nobody cracked a smile, Evie wondered if maybe she shouldn't have responded.

"As you know, the choice of who makes partner at Baker Smith is not one that we take lightly."

No shit. Out of her entering associate class of 120, only 5 or 6 had a shot at partnership. Evie barely knew her competition. The other associates whose names were being whispered in the hallways worked in different departments and rarely, if ever, surfaced at firm social events. The rest of the associates from her entering class had been gradually weeded out over an eight-year period. Blood, sweat, and tears were expected by-products of the journey. And still there were no guarantees for those still standing. It could be one careless error in a closing document. Or a faux pas at a client meeting. She was immensely proud of herself for not having made any missteps, at least none big enough to come to the attention of upper management.

"However," Patricia continued, "there is something concerning that has recently come to our attention. About your performance."

Suddenly, the temperature climbed to Bikram Yoga proportions. What could this be about? She couldn't remember ever feeling so clueless and so unsure of what was coming next.

A million thoughts raced through her mind at once, but none of them made much sense. She'd once feigned a terrible cold to get out of a mentoring program so she could attend a special event at Jack's restaurant. Who could have known she was lying? She'd purposely ducked out of pictures that were Instagram-bound. More recently, she had forgotten to mute her phone while on a call with the Calico accountants and had made an appointment for a haircut on her cell phone simultaneously. But those were hardly capital offenses.

"Evie, do you see all these papers on the table?"

Of course she did. She nodded yes.

"Do you have any idea how many papers are here?"

Evie shook her head no. What was this? A guess-how-many-jelly-beans-are-in-the-jar contest?

"Ten thousand," Patricia said. "Actually, more than that. And do you know what's in those papers?"

Evie looked down at the floor, unable to blink, and watched as the checked pattern of the carpet took on a distorted and frightening pattern.

"Doc review?" Evie whispered. "For my next project. The tech merger." Her voice lilted upward, like a little girl's.

"No, they are not, Evie." Mitchell Rhodes spoke for the first time in the meeting. All of the other partners present had remained silent, most of them expressionless. One of them—whose name Evie couldn't recall—seemed to be stifling a smile. "Evie, these papers are the more than one hundred and fifty thousand personal e-mails you have sent while at work over the last eight years. As you no doubt recall, we were having server issues recently. Many associates complained about the Internet speed and said LexisNexis was almost unusable. So we hired a consulting firm to look into the matter. It turns out a number of our associates have been abusing their time at work by sending extensive personal e-mails. But you, Evie, were by far the worst offender. We calculated you sent, on average, seventy-five personal e-mails every day. At first we assumed you were running a private business from the office, which is strictly prohibited, but from a review of the data that appears not to be the case."

Evie felt her rib cage collapse like an accordion. She worried her skeleton wouldn't be strong enough to lift her from her chair to get to the bathroom, where she desperately wanted to throw up. Could it really be possible she was the worst offender at the firm? Wasn't everyone addicted to e-mail? All the younger associates were probably just texting instead. But could she prove that?

"Evie," Mitchell continued, "we're very disappointed. Frankly, you were almost a shoo-in for a partnership. But we can't in good faith promote somebody who in one day sent over ninety e-mails back and forth to someone named Caroline Michaels with the subject line 'Is Jack getting sick of me?'"

Evie remembered that day. She couldn't focus at work because Jack had declined her offer to accompany him to the Aspen Food & Wine Festival for no discernible reason. All he'd said was "I'm fine to go alone." Evie felt like she was nagging him every time she offered to come along. She tasted a salty drop on her lip at the memory, which released a full batch of fresh tears at the thought of what was happening to her now. She was losing her job. The most stable thing in her life. Her livelihood. A good part of her existence. And she was crying at work. Something she had vowed never to do.

Patricia spoke up again, undeterred by Evie's tears. "In case you are wondering, our review of your e-mails is perfectly legal. When you signed your employment contract, you gave us express consent to review anything on our servers." Jesus, it was like she was reading from a script in a wrongful termination defense manual. "Evie, I'm sorry about how this turned out. But we can't imagine you have been devoting your full energies to work when you are spending so much time on personal matters at the office.

We wish you luck, but your employment at Baker Smith is now officially terminated."

Without a word, Evie stood up from the conference table and headed to the door. Summoning all the strength left in her body, she whispered, "Then I guess this is good-bye."

"Evie—wait," Patricia said. Evie turned back with her hand still on the doorknob. She thought for a brief moment that maybe they had changed their minds, reaching a silent decision after seeing her anguished face that, yes, they could overlook her e-mail infractions and give her another chance.

"Yes?" Evie said, a hopeful note in her voice painfully obvious even to her.

"We're going to need your BlackBerry back."

All she could think about as she palmed the featherweight piece of black plastic that had been her lifeline to the outside world for the last eight years was—if she wasn't evie.rosen@ bakersmith.com who was she?

Chapter 3

Naturally Marianne was at her station for the first time in recent history when Evie got back to her desk. She hung up the phone and appeared at Evie's side in an instant, fake-comforting her. Marianne and Evie never liked each other. Marianne resented working for a girl half her age, and clearly thought Evie was an idiot every time she asked for help with the copy machine. Evie was confident being a good lawyer didn't require a Ph.D. in toner replacement. She also wanted to tell Marianne to stop talking to her neighbors on Staten Island for three hours a day about whether her husband, Mickey Jr., was cheating on her and prepare Evie's expense reports instead. It was a strained relationship, to say the least. Which made Marianne's faux concern that much worse.

"Poor thing. Did they fire you? I heard about that from Jamila in payroll. Let me get you a tissue to wipe your eye makeup. No sense in you leaving here with everyone remembering you looking like hell."

That was the act of kindness that Marianne had decided to leave as Evie's lasting impression of her. At least Evie wouldn't have to see her anymore. It was a paper-thin silver lining.

Marianne was right to bring the tissues quickly, though. Baker Smith gave Evie four hours to vacate the building and turn in her ID pass. An e-mail waited for her with "departure instructions." Those motherfuckers in HR had simply been waiting to hit Send. Ten minutes later a burly man with MOM tattooed on his bicep dropped off twenty cardboard boxes. He was followed by a crusty woman from the Records Center who looked dangerously deficient in Vitamin D, thanks to her omnipresence in Baker Smith's basement. She explained the methodical way that Evie was expected to label and package her old files. It was so typical of this place that she was expected to work until her last minute in the building. She was tempted to submit a recording of her remaining hours in the standard six-minute increments used for billing purposes: 2:02–2:08—cried while reading departure instructions; 2:08–2:14—glared at Marianne while she gossiped with the other secretaries about her boss getting canned; 2:14–2:20—cradled BlackBerry in her palm wondering how it was possible she had sent that many e-mails over the last eight years; 2:20–2:26—extended trip to bathroom to compose herself and plot impractical revenge on Baker Smith.

Evie's cabinets were overflowing with nearly a decade's worth of mergers, spin-offs, stock purchases, and leveraged buyouts.

She briefly debated intentionally mixing up all of her papers and mislabeling the boxes but realized it would just create more work for her and nobody would even notice. When she was done, she made her way over to say good-bye to the few good friends she'd made over her tenure. She hugged Annie in front of the frozen yogurt machine in the cafeteria, their favorite spot to meet up during the workday. Annie made Evie swear to call her after the blind date with Mike Jones that she had orchestrated a while back. Since Evie had basically written off Luke Glasscock, she knew she had no legitimate reason to put off meeting Mike. She was glad that Annie didn't probe her on the firing. Evie hoped the story would never come out—the partnership committee wouldn't want the whole episode to be public because it would look bad to clients, and she certainly didn't plan to divulge it when she'd soon be pounding the pavement looking for a job.

After finishing her last vanilla-chocolate swirl compliments of Baker Smith, Evie visited Julia, her workplace next-door neighbor for the past two years, a friendly associate in the white-collar crime division who was fond of bringing in homemade cookies. She couldn't help notice that Hotmail was open on her friend's screen. Why was she not getting axed too?

Last she found Pierce, a sassy administrative assistant with whom Evie had built up a lively rapport based on making snide comments about other lawyers. They dished one last time about Harry, the grabby tax associate with the lazy eye, and promised to stay in touch. There were others. Lawyers who'd listen to her grumble about her breakup with Jack at "Fat Al's," the dive bar across the street that regularly played host to Midtown's overworked and horny professionals. Ladies in the printing room who listened to her complain while they expertly formatted her documents. The dorky crew in IT who had saved her butt countless times. She had genuine fondness for these people but was realistic about keeping in touch with them. She'd been on the other side for too long—taking down people's personal e-mails before they left the firm with empty promises to meet for coffee. Only Annie would be different. They were friends since the summer internship program at Baker Smith, had the same know-it-all partners belittle them, ate lunch together at least once a week, even shared Marianne as an assistant for a while.

Evie's last stop on her departure journey was Mitchell Rhodes's office. She knew of all the partners he would be the most sympathetic, and the most likely to offer her a letter of recommendation. His door was slightly ajar when Evie approached and she could see through the crack that he was on the phone.

"Stop yelling at me. I'm at work. Stop yelling. I said stop yelling." She could hear Mitchell barking quietly like a muzzled dog. "Loreen—I work sixteen hours a day. How the hell was I supposed to notice she developed a drug problem? You're the one who's home all day doing God knows what. How about knocking on her door once in a while instead of another trip to Bloomingdale's?"

Mitchell's tone was frosty. He was the kindest partner she knew at the firm, but now she was scared to even knock. He went on, enraged.

"No, I don't know what Twitter is. She tweeted that she was high? Loreen, you're not speaking English." He broke off momentarily. "No, I can't come home to talk to her. I have a client conference call in an hour, then a closing dinner, and then I have to come back to the office to speak to some partners in the Tokyo office. Someone has to pay for all of her drugs, right?"

Evie, still in turmoil, couldn't control the laugh that escaped her. She didn't know the always genteel Mitchell Rhodes, king of the corner office and rainmaker extraordinaire, had it in him.

"Sorry, no, that wasn't meant to be a joke," Mitchell pleaded.

"I'll try my best to get home before eleven. And I promise we'll deal with this in the morning."

He hung up the phone. No love you, no miss you. Just a promise to deal with family drama, and then a click. No wonder Mitchell had been so pleased to receive her *x*'s and *o*'s e-mail. From the sounds of his phone conversation, he wasn't getting too many hugs and kisses at home.

"Evie, you all right?" Mitchell asked, after spotting her lurking in his doorway. "Why don't you come in?"

She sank into the same armchair she sat in just last week, taking orders from Mitchell on how to revise an offering memorandum. Only this time she was slumped over instead of upright and perky with pen and paper in hand. She looked around for family photos, hoping for a glimpse of his wayward daughter. None could be found.

"Evie, I know you were surprised by how things went at the meeting. We all feel terrible. You are an excellent associate. Frankly, we're all surprised how you managed to perform at all given how much time you spent on personal matters. It's actually rather impressive."

"So give me another chance. At my last review, I was led to believe I was on partnership track. My clients are going to be upset that I'm gone. Can't I just have a warning? I assure you I will not make the same mistake again."

Even as she said it, she wondered if it was true that she could control her urges for distraction during the day.

"Besides, I remember when the server was slow. That was at least six months ago. How long have you known about this? Why wait to get rid of me?" Evie remembered precisely when the Internet was moving at a glacial pace. It was just at the time of her breakup with Jack, and they were exchanging those last awkward e-mails—coordinating picking things up from each other's apartments and debating whether it was practical to remain friends (it wasn't).

"Well, Evie, it took some time for us to investigate the server problems, and then you got so entrenched running the Calico-Anson merger. It wasn't the right time. You're such a good associate—we just didn't want to part with you any earlier than necessary."

This was like Tracy telling her that she was too good for Luke. If everyone loved her so damn much, why the hell were they putting her out to pasture?

"I do have some good news for you though. The compensation committee has agreed to a six-month severance package for you. Three months is standard but we are extending it in light of your service to the firm."

That *was* a relief. In her state of shock, she hadn't yet given thought to how she'd manage without her monthly paycheck.

"Thank you," Evie responded awkwardly.

"The truth is, I was holding out hope you would announce you were leaving and this wouldn't have had to happen." He paused and looked at her squarely. "A lot of female associates around your age tend to leave at this point. Even younger."

So you were counting on losing me to attrition by marriage and kids, Evie thought bitterly. Sorry to disappoint.

"Obviously, that didn't happen," Mitchell went on. "And in this case, well we don't really have a choice about giving you a second chance. You know, with the website." His voice trailed off.

"In this case what? What happened?"

Mitchell rotated his computer screen toward Evie. "Oh—I guess you haven't seen this yet. They posted the article a few minutes before we met with you."

Evie rose from her seat and looked at the familiar homepage of *BigLawSux,* the wildly popular legal blog where disgruntled attorneys came to gripe and gossip about their jobs. It was started by two former attorneys and had a massive following. The headline read: BAKER SMITH DUMPS E-MAIL–ADDICTED ASSOCIATE— EIGHTH-YEAR EVIE ROSEN SAID TO HAVE CAUSED SERVER BREAKDOWN. To the right of the text was the picture of her from the firm's directory—that damn photo she couldn't escape, with the greasy hair and the day-old makeup.

Evie knew then, for certain, what it would feel like to have a boxer land an uppercut to her cheek. She struggled to keep her knees from buckling.

"Evie," Mitchell said, biting his lower lip and looking toward the corner of the room before refocusing his gaze on her. "I'm afraid with this kind of publicity there's nothing we can do. I know it all seems rather Draconian, and for that I'm sorry. I just wish for your sake the comments hadn't gotten so nasty."

Evie leaned in closer to see the smaller font beneath the headline, which was only one paragraph long. The article stated pretty much what she'd been told at the partners meeting and cited the source as an unnamed associate "close" to someone on the management committee. What the hell did "close" mean? Sleeping together? That associate should get fired, not her! The comments below, three times as long as the article, sent her gasping for air.

The first comment, the one that set off the maelstrom, read: "I'm not surprised Evie Rosen didn't make partner. Every time I walked into her office she was playing online Scrabble or shopping on OneKingsLane. I heard she padded her billable hours too." It was signed by the rather unheroic "Anonymous."

"That's not true," Evie exclaimed, searching Mitchell's face for signs that he believed her.

"Evie, maybe you've read enough," he said and gently patted her arm, almost like he was guiding her away from the screen.

"No, I need to see this."

Next came: "Evie Rosen thought she was better than everyone. She pawned off the tough work on the junior associates but took all the credit." That vitriol came from a girl who identified herself as Legal Biznatch.

At least several associates came to her defense. LoonyLawyer wrote, "Evie was always nice to me. She was a pleasure to work with and I'm sad to see her go." Other commentators added that she was smart and capable and that Baker Smith dumping eighth-year associates was total BS. Then the conversation rerouted, thanks to Legal Eagle NYC's remark: "Whatever, at least she was a nice piece of ass at the office. Now all we're left with are the dogs."

Then came the clincher. The one that hit her like a sucker punch.

"Evie Rosen's not even that hot. Polly Yang in Bankruptcy is way hotter." Signed, Juris Dokta.

She was incensed. The Scrabble comment had to come from that third-year associate who was always making disgusting smacking noises with his yogurt. She never should have asked him not to eat in her office. And who the hell was Polly Yang?

Evie cringed thinking about Jack seeing this. It wasn't that he frequented legal blogs—she knew that—but if he ever looked her up from time to time (and she liked to think he did) this might be the first thing to come up. Negative press always had a way of floating to the top, like oil in a dressing.

She sank back into the chair across from Mitchell's desk, speechless. He looked at her with what appeared to be genuine empathy before speaking.

"I'm sorry, Evie. We really just had no choice. Our clients actually read these blogs. Our services are expensive, and they want to make sure they are getting their money's worth. Now more than ever we have to be careful about our image. I'm not even sure how this blog got ahold of our internal partnership memos. Evie—you are a wonderful lawyer. I don't know if this is really your passion, but you are damn good at it. If the economy wasn't in the gutter, maybe we could have overcome this little setback," he said, gesturing once again at the screen. "But with the market conditions as they are, we're basically looking for any reason to keep new partners to a minimum. I'm not sure if that helps you feel better, but in some ways this decision had more to do with us than you."

Evie actually laughed. Baker Smith was breaking up with her and giving her the oldest line in the book—it's not you, it's me. Pathetic.

"Thank you, Mitchell. For the record, I have never once padded my hours. That was actually me, working all the time, for this place." She stood up abruptly, offered her hand to him, and turned to leave before he could reply. Her watch read 4:11. Less than an hour until she'd be booted out of the building. In a daze, she made her way back down to her office. Seated in the chair whose vinyl seat had taken the permanent imprint of her butt, she instinctively tried to log into her computer but was denied access. The words INVALID USER burned holes in her retinas. She swiveled around to take one last look at the view from the thirty-ninth floor—the one that used to make her feel triumphant, but now was making her queasy. It was a long way down from here.

Per firm protocol, a uniformed security guard came upstairs to escort her out of the building at five o'clock.

"Ready, miss?" he asked, hulking in the doorway to her office.

"As I'll ever be," Evie said, and rose from her chair. She gathered the few personal effects she had on her desk (an immortal orchid; a framed picture of her, Fran, and Bette taken at Thanksgiving a few years ago; a picture of her clad in a bridesmaid dress with her girlfriends at Tracy's wedding; and an Ansel

Adams black-and-white print hanging on the wall). She debated leaving the picture of her and Jack in the file cabinet, where it would languish eternally in Records. That was probably where it belonged, but she snatched it up at the last minute and threw it in her tote bag.

The office she left looked more bare than usual, but then again she had never taken the time to properly decorate it since, like all associates, she was bounced among the firm's smaller offices every time the new hires started. She had been expecting to move into a partner suite, where she would have had the benefit of the firm's generous decorating stipend. She had so many ideas for the larger space. A buttery-leather couch in a rich shade of camel would go along one wall, opposite two wooden armchairs fabricated in a deep pink silk. Three oatmeal-colored cashmere pillows with cable braids would sit equally spaced and perfectly upright on the sofa, and she'd place a matching cashmere throw over the back of her desk chair. Her desk would be curvy and modern, unlike the heavy mahogany models that the male partners favored. And she would hang draperies. Nobody ever remembered that detail. But she would have. Gauzy taupe curtains trimmed in suede, with gray satin tiebacks. What a waste of good ideas.

She flipped the light switch. It was symbolic really. Someone from maintenance would be by shortly to sterilize the place, scrubbing her keyboard with disinfectant so that not even a trace of her essence remained.

She was about to leave the BlackBerry on her mouse pad, per the departure instructions, but instead she wrapped the outdated relic in a few paper towels and dropped it in the trash can. Striding beside the guard down the hallway, she felt like she was doing a perp walk. Her ears popped as the elevator shuttled between the twenty-second and twenty-first floors, but when she stepped onto the busy sidewalk at 5:00 P.M. she couldn't hear a thing.

# # #

Stasia called Evie two times on the day of Evie's date with Mike Jones to make sure she didn't bail. It was an exceptionally humid and rainy day in July, the kind that no amount of hair-styling product or waterproof makeup could combat.

"Maybe this is what you need to distract you from what happened at work," Stasia said. "Mike sounds like he could be promising."

In the background Evie heard Rick say, "If she doesn't want to go, then she shouldn't go."

"I'll go, because I trust Annie," Evie said. After a more aggressive search online, including using LexisNexis with her not-yet-terminated Baker Smith passcode, she had finally turned up some information on her date. A black-and-white photo revealed he was a handsome graduate of the University of Pennsylvania undergraduate and dental school. None of that would she admit to Stasia.

"I'm proud of you for putting yourself out there," Stasia said. "It's so important."

Evie wondered what life experience Stasia was drawing from. In college, she dated the hunky quarterback of the football team for two straight years and then broke his heart when she traded him in for the equally hot lacrosse team captain, who also happened to be the son of a famous actress and the grandson of the Post-it note inventor. Her love life was a seamless flow of enviable relationships. She didn't understand how difficult it was to be "out there." Nevertheless, Evie knew Stasia was just trying to be helpful, so she didn't challenge her with a snarky comment.

Later that night, Evie met Mike at Café Lalo, a coffee bar near her apartment famous for its appearance in the movie *You've Got Mail,* a rainy day favorite of hers. The place was half-full and

Evie surmised by the nervous postures and din of throaty laughs that many of the patrons were on first dates.

"Evie?" the man lurking next to the hostess asked.

"You must be Mike," she said. He looked younger in person than in the picture she found online, with faded freckles across his nose. His hair was the unlikely, but pleasing, combination of white and red. What did that make him—salt and paprika? Dressed in a stylish checked button-down and slim trousers, he was a far cry from Dr. Hamburger, the aptly named orthodontist who forced a dreaded palate expander on her when she was eight and slapped on braces a few years later.

"It's so nice to meet you in person," Mike said, and gave her a light peck on the cheek. He smelled like musky aftershave and powdered latex gloves. "You look great." She thought she saw relief in his eyes. He probably saw it in hers too. The first inter-action was over. No hairy moles. No extra fingers. No need for either of them to feign a heart attack.

"Thanks. I'm glad we could meet too," Evie said, and actually meant it. Stasia had been right to make her go.

The hostess seated them at a corner table, but it only had one bench and they were forced to sit side by side. It reminded Evie of the way her parents would sit when they went for dinner at Hunan Garden every Sunday night, but it seemed so much more awkward to sit shoulder to shoulder with a stranger.

"So I had a crazy day today," Mike started, and Evie was grateful that he wasn't the quiet sort. "My practice is on the Upper East Side and my patients, well actually their parents, are a little high-strung. I had to beg a mother today to let me put braces on her son, but she refused because she thinks *Avenue* magazine is going to do a spread on her family."

"You're kidding?" she asked, with a casual hair flip. *Avenue* was one of those magazines given out for free in higher-end co-ops and condos—like the building that housed the one-bedroom apartment she'd wanted to scope after making partner. So much for that.

"Not at all," Mike said, taking a sip of his Irish coffee. "But that wasn't even the worst of it. I did oral surgery on a sixteen-year-old girl today and when I gave her a prescription for Percocet she just laughed and said she had plenty at home."

Evie relaxed as she swigged her drink. Mike was growing more entertaining by the minute as the alcohol slipped into her bloodstream. His face blurred when she looked at it through the bottom of her glass. She started to fill in his thinning hair in her mind and plucked a few strays between his eyebrows. She thought he had the sort of face that could be on a label for expensive toothpaste: "Dr. Jones's All-Natural Gingivitis-Fighting Whitening Toothpaste."

"What about you, Evie? Do you like your job at Baker Smith?" Mike asked at just the right moment, when he was teetering on the edge of talking too much about himself. Not that she was eager to have the spotlight shifted to her.

"Well," Evie said, with a deliberate head scratch, "I recently left. So I guess I'm not a lawyer anymore. Or at least not an employed one. But I am starting to think I didn't really like it that much anyway. It was just something I did. Does that make any sense?" It did to her, but it was probably the first time she'd ever articulated her feelings about her job so clearly out loud, or even to herself.

"It makes a ton of sense," Mike said, and she remembered that she was speaking to an orthodontist. Chances are he wasn't that passionate about molding retainers either. She knew from Google that both of his parents were dentists, so he probably fell into his career rather than sought it out.

Over drinks and a shared slice of key lime pie (which Evie

awkwardly split and jiggled onto separate plates), they chatted for almost two hours until the waitress started to hover.

"Well, I hope we can do this again," Mike said as he was paying the check. "I'll be away next weekend for an alumni council meeting at my college, but maybe the weekend after?" He looked up at Evie hopefully.

"Sounds great," she said, genuinely pleased. "That's so nice you're still involved with school. I guess you liked Penn?"

"I didn't go to Penn. Why did you think that?" he asked, seeming confused, maybe even put out.

Evie racked her brain. Why did she think he had gone there? Hadn't he mentioned it over the course of the evening? Obviously not. It dawned on her that she gathered that tidbit from the Internet. She flailed trying to cover.

"Um, I don't know, I think maybe Annie told me that," she hedged.

"I doubt it," he said. "I went to Arizona State with Annie's brother, Jordan."

Evie flushed even more.

"There's another orthodontist in Manhattan named Michael Jones. He went to Penn," Mike said. "We always get calls at my office from patients looking for him. Evie, did you Google me?" He didn't sign the credit card statement that was placed in front of him. Evie wondered if he was backing out of paying for the date.

Her only viable option was denial.

"No, no. I must just be getting confused. You know what? My friend was talking about Penn today. I'm just all mixed up from the rum in this drink. So we'll get together in two weeks?" Evie asked without making eye contact.

"I'll be in touch," Mike said in a tone that could best be described as noncommittal. He signed the bill and stood up abruptly.

"Nice to meet you," he said and did the unthinkable—put out his hand. When they first met, he kissed her on the cheek. Now all he wanted was a handshake. Evie had never been on a date that capsized so quickly.

Back home in her apartment, sprawled out in bed with a *Seinfeld* rerun in the background, Evie replayed the night. She was embarrassed about what happened, even though in her heart she believed Googling a date was routine and necessary due diligence for dating in the digital age. It wasn't lost on her that generations of people prior had met and lived happily ever after without giving each other web colonoscopies before the first date. But things were different now. So much information was available online that it was irresponsible *not* to use it. Still, being outed as a Googler was another story. And that was how Evie knew she would not be hearing from Mike Jones again.

At least it was no great loss.

Evie stacked up everyone she met against Jack, creating Venn diagrams in her mind to assess areas of overlap. It wasn't that she never met men that matched, even surpassed, Jack in attractiveness, humor, and intelligence. But that je ne sais quoi factor, that "something extra," that part of the diagram was tougher for other men to fill.

During their time together Jack opened two more restaurants—Paris Spice, a formal French-Asian fusion restaurant on the Upper East Side, and a high-end dessert lounge in Tribeca called Eye Candy. Before Jack, she knew little to nothing about restaurants beyond where *Time Out New York* said she should eat and what new cuisines the *New York Times* announced had merged in the fusion craze. But soon she was talking "front-of-house" and "table turns" with restaurateurs and critics at culinary events and openings.

When she was on dates with guys who worked in finance, ubiquitous in Manhattan, she wasn't impressed by talk of currency hedging and derivative patents. Evie worked on those same deals, and they didn't interest her on a date any more than they did at work. Her mother once intimated that Evie liked Jack because he was a known entity—a desirable plus-one at dinner parties. But he wasn't even really famous. He was only a household name among the rarefied circle in New York with enough disposable income to justify a twenty-three-dollar slice of cheesecake (the menu did claim the crust had actual gold flecks in it). For Evie, of course Jack was much more than a name to drop, though she never tired of the way diners looked at him in awe when he would emerge from the kitchen in his uniform. Besides being handsome and successful, Jack was self-made, ambitious, and passionate about his profession. He was the whole package. What Evie couldn't readily say to her friends, and what she was even too embarrassed to say to Fran, was that she was also the complete package. They matched.

Begrudgingly, she reached for her computer to send Annie an e-mail thanking her for the setup. She assumed Mike would tell Annie about the Google snafu, but there was nothing she could do about that. She simply said that she really appreciated the introduction to Mike but didn't think they had much of a "spark." Her grandmother always admonished her to be grateful for setups lest people get the wrong idea that she wasn't interested in meeting someone. Bette would be proud that she was remembering the bigger picture in her despair.

"Finally, my Evie is getting her priorities in order," she would say, while sipping lukewarm herbal tea with the gang of widows she played mah-jongg with in Florida.

Chapter 4

July in New York City was like purgatory. Every year when it arrived, Evie wondered if some noxious bus fume would sweep her into the fiery hell of the August heat or whether one of the infrequent breezes from the trees lining Broadway would mercifully carry her directly into fall. This year especially, it seemed wiser just to stay home. The city was abandoned anyway. Most New Yorkers fled the concrete jungle in summer, seeking refuge in the country. Even virtually, life seemed to have slowed to a halt. Nobody new was popping up on JDate. The Facebook news feed had slowed to a crawl.

Evie's building had strong air-conditioning, the kind that could make you forget the season. She could order in food delivery at any time of day, though that was an expensive habit she'd need to drop. Without a BlackBerry, her home laptop was her bridge to life outside. Her personal cell phone—practically an antique by today's standards (it literally had a flip top)—didn't have Internet access, and her iPad screen was cracked beyond recognition after she dropped it three days earlier while attempting to check Instagram and brush her teeth simultaneously. She should really go out and buy an iPhone but just couldn't bear the judgmental glances of the Upper West Side mothers juggling strollers and lattes, wondering as they gaped at her: where's your baby and overpriced caffeine? Nor could she stomach the working crowd— hurriedly trekking to the subway or competing for cabs in their suits and sensible pumps. She imagined them recognizing her from the *BigLawSux* article and thinking one thing: *pathetic*.

Four weeks had passed since her dismissal from Baker Smith, but the sting of what occurred felt like yesterday's wound. She would never again see the green-on-green checked carpeting that covered every inch of her firm's office, nor would she hear Marianne's chatter about her "scumbag" of a husband. She wouldn't lean into her ergonomic desk chair for a lower back stretch while a junior associate sat opposite her, nervously asking if she was satisfied with their assignment. She wouldn't play a part in deals that made *Wall Street Journal* headlines. She wouldn't watch CNBC in the mornings and think to herself, I helped make that happen.

The worst part of reflecting on all these never-agains was her ambivalence. She missed the camaraderie of the all-nighters— fighting about who knocked over the pyramid of Chinese takeout containers on the conference table, munching on Julia's triple-threat chocolate cookies in the coffee room, and playing twenty questions with colleagues at midnight while the printer churned out three-hundred-page prospectuses. She longed for the symphony of machinery: the hum of the copier, the rumble of her computer starting up, and the click-clack of the mail cart had become the de facto soundtrack of her life.

What she didn't miss were the mind-numbing continuing legal education classes offered at Baker Smith, or the endless hours spent overseeing junior associates sentenced to document review in a windowless cellar crowded with file boxes. A pat on the back for a job well done—that just wasn't enough to sustain her in the long term.

Leaving her apartment post–Baker Smith, seeing the masses with newspapers tucked in the crook of their arms rushing to the subway, would make deciding her next steps unavoidable.

Evie's campout in her apartment prompted concerned e-mails and calls from her friends, including Annie, who had indeed proven to be more than a casual office acquaintance.

"Sorry the date didn't work out," she started off, playing dumb to the whole Google episode.

"It's all right. What's going on at the office?"

"This thing that happened to you is a cruel joke," Annie said. "I mean, I'm on Facebook the entire day and so are most of the associates. I think the trick is to keep it open all day instead of closing and reopening. At least that's what I read on *BigLawSux*. No doubt, you got a raw deal. They just targeted you since you were about to make partner. I hear they are planning to let a whole bunch of juniors go for the same reason."

"Whatever. With the goddamn blog post and those nasty comments, I'm doomed."

"Not true. The article hasn't been on their most e-mailed list for a while already. It's old news. You'll be able to get another job in no time."

"If I even want one. Sleeping past seven A.M. does have its charms."

"I wouldn't know," Annie said. "Maybe I'll join you in early retirement."

Evie eyeballed her ratty sweat suit in the mirror.

"Trust me, it's not as glamorous as it seems. Keep your day job."

Evie's mother had taken to calling her more frequently, often from the regional playhouse where she practically lived. While she tried to spin Evie's dismissal from the firm into the best thing that ever happened to her, Evie could hear a soprano rehearsing "I Feel Pretty" in the background. Of course Fran had no idea why Evie was actually terminated, which meant she also had to listen to her mother rant on about the crash-and-burn economy and the bleak futures of American college graduates. She was relieved that she didn't have to delve into the particulars with her father. Henry Rosen had worked at the same Maryland firm since graduating from law school until the day he died.

"Who needs that miserable place?" Fran said. "Want me to call some Ogilvy contacts for you?"

Evie declined.

"All right. I'm sure you'll find a job you love."

"That's an oxymoron," Evie said.

The prospect of a blank slate excited and terrified her at the same time. Her career at Baker Smith had been motivated primarily by the goal of making partner. The idea of starting over at another firm, assuming that was even a possibility, was daunting. More Mitchell Rhodeses to impress. More Mariannes to avoid.

"At least now we can see each other more often," Fran said.

At that comment, Evie felt a pang of guilt, followed by a flight of panic. She had definitely used the excuse of work on more than one occasion to get out of family get-togethers—just recently to get out of brunch with the TWASPs. It pained her to think that her mother never saw through her excuses. But at the same time that she was experiencing this guilt, she realized that she no longer had a ready excuse to duck out of anything she didn't feel like doing.

Why did she put off visits to see her mother? The TWASPs were rarely around—they had been off at boarding school and worked ridiculous jobs over the summer (barista-ing in Aspen last year, giving tours of Martha's Vineyard the summer before). It wasn't the ever-amiable Winston, who never meddled in her life. He always gave her a hearty hello and an avuncular hug, and knew enough to retreat to his man cave in the basement to play with his bank-breaking golf simulator while Fran and Evie caught up over fruit from the Greenwich farmer's market.

After Evie's father first passed, she worried about bearing sole responsibility for her mother. What would Fran do for companionship? Evie was an only child. She started picturing Fran arriving at Yale on the weekends, shacking up on the couch in Evie's common room, waiting up for her with a cup of hot chocolate in hand. It made her feel callous the way she dreaded that scenario. But maybe that was just the way it was between parents and children. Parents live selflessly for their children, and kids are just selfish.

But Fran's solemnity lasted until the unveiling, which took place a year after Henry's death. After the gravestone was laid, while Evie was still entrenched in doing "cemetery math"— calculating life spans by computing the years carved into the neighboring headstones—Fran's psyche flipped like a light switch. She enrolled in a pottery class at the local Y, signed up for Krav Maga at her gym and returned to her beloved community theater. In fact it was in full Eliza Doolittle costume that Fran first met Winston, in line at Starbucks. He was in Baltimore on business when half of his latte landed on her lace-and-silk ball gown. He insisted on paying for dry cleaning. She handed him complimentary tickets to the show. A year later, Evie found herself with a new stepfather and two stepsisters. She hated to think she resented her mother for moving on, for leaving her daughter to wallow solo in the grief. But Evie did, even knowing that it was unjustified. And it was probably what made Bette and Evie even closer—the two of them were still flailing while Fran had managed to propel her life forward.

Evie's mother shifted happily into her new life in Connecticut, embracing the unexpected role she took on as a stepmom in her forties, her only lament being that the Pikesville Players were far superior to the Greenwich Town Thespians. It was Evie who felt alone. But how much could she discuss dating, loneliness, and sex in the twenty-first century with Fran anyway? Heaven forbid her mother knew Evie was accepting dates requested via text message in the form of "U free 2nite? Want 2 hang?" The mention of Tinder would have her picturing fireplaces.

Evie wondered if she wouldn't be able to truly come to peace with losing her father until she had a nuclear family of her own. She didn't have any more urge to put herself out there on the romantic front than she did on the job front. An unemployed lawyer who idled away her time searching for gray hairs to snip and watching *Golden Girls* could very well be the definition of unsexy. It was one thing to step away from a busy day at the office for an hour to meet someone for coffee or a drink. It was quite another to spend an entire day at home preparing, letting her hopes creep up, and then coming home from the date disappointed without even work to distract her. This would just have to be a season of hibernation for Evie. Luckily with her computer and her TV to keep her occupied, she had enough "acorns" stored up to last her a while.

# # #

"I saw on Facebook that you've still listed Baker Smith as your employer," Tracy said when she and Evie reached the lobby of Evie's building.

They were back from a power walk. Evie knew things were bad when a pregnant lady was the one coaxing her to exercise. Tracy phoned her early Saturday morning, saying she was itching to get out of the house and away from Jake, who had been strumming on his guitar without any consideration for his pregnant wife, or their downstairs neighbor, who had taken to his broom.

Evie was already up when Tracy called, busy in bed Googling "numbness in arms and legs" because she could swear her limbs were falling asleep more than usual. According to WebMD, her best-case scenario was nerve damage. Her worst-case scenarios were a brain tumor or stroke. With thoughts of fatal diseases permeating her consciousness so readily, Evie was happy to receive Tracy's invitation for an old-fashioned constitutional.

While they lapped the Central Park Reservoir, Tracy agreed to go with Evie to the International Fine Arts & Antiques Show at the Armory, which would be taking place soon. Evie normally went with her grandmother during her annual pilgrimage to New York in early fall, but Bette still hadn't bought her ticket and was vague when Evie last brought it up. She and Bette hadn't spoken all that much since Evie left her job. Bette was sympathetic when Evie told her about getting fired but reacted more like Evie had lost a favorite bangle than like her entire career had capsized. She lied and said she was busy interviewing, worried that if Bette knew she was home all day she'd call Evie to watch *The Price Is Right* and discuss "ze situation" during commercials.

The Antiques Show, forty thousand square feet of highly curated furniture and decorative items, mostly from France, was just so much better to see with someone. Maybe it was finally getting too hard for Bette to make the trip and uproot herself from her familiar surroundings—a possibility that Evie did not want to face.

"You're right about Facebook," Evie said. "I guess I've sort of put off removing it. Like at least online I could pretend to be employed. But I really should take it off. The firm probably would be upset if anyone realized."

"It's better to shed the past," Tracy said. "People use Facebook these days to find jobs—maybe some other firms will reach out to you if you take down Baker Smith from your profile."

"That's not really how it works," Evie said, it occurring to her how little even her best friends knew about her profession.

"You never know. Anyway, I gotta run to a birthing class. Shoot me. Aren't you glad you got out of the house?" she asked, and then headed in the other direction without waiting for an answer.

Settled back in her apartment, Evie went about deleting Baker Smith from her online profiles. There were a number of pictures from Paul's wedding she'd been meaning to upload anyway—one of which she thought would make a good profile image for a new website Annie had joined called DateSmarter.com, which was supposed to cater to professionals with a no-fail algorithm for matchmaking.

Without any plans for the rest of the day, waiting around for "hearts," "likes," and flattering comments on Facebook and Instagram seemed as good a way as any to spend the afternoon. She logged on to Facebook and began reviewing her personal information page. It listed her favorite movies (*Father of the Bride, Old School, Casablanca, Citizen Kane*), music (The Beatles, Rolling Stones, Sarah McLachlan), and books (*The Grapes of Wrath, The Namesake, The Picture of Dorian Gray*). It included carefully selected pictures of her with all of her girlfriends, listed her hometown, her current residence, her age, relationship status, and the results of random Facebook polls and quizzes she had taken over the years. It was an amalgamation of truths and half-truths, things she truly loved and things she wanted people to think she loved.

Her profile picture was similarly ambiguous. It was a flattering side shot of her face, showing off her shiny locks and one sparkly green eye, but it didn't reveal enough of her appearance to make her recognizable if she was encountered head-on. The whole profile made her feel like a chameleon when she studied it.

She got sidetracked for a while looking up old boyfriends and guys she'd had casual dates with—trying to glean from their pictures what they were up to. She also looked up various girls she knew from New York and old friends from summer camp and school whom she hadn't spoken to in years. Nothing of any significance seemed to have changed since she last checked. And Jack wasn't on Facebook—she knew he considered social media far beneath him. He had his own website. He didn't need to post photos of himself on vacation in South Beach for the world to see he was flourishing.

After returning to her own page with the task of deleting Baker Smith, she decided to click on her firm's link one last time. Someone at her office had organized an unofficial Baker Smith group, and all the lawyers who were on Facebook were able to join at their discretion. It was mostly young associates who joined, and Evie started combing through their profile pages. Once she removed herself from the list, she would no longer be able to see these people's profiles unless she was independently friends with them. She quickly got sucked into looking at their photos of swanky travel, dreamy weddings, and Raphaelian babies. One woman, whom she recognized from passing in the firm's hallways as a fairly new litigation associate, had posted pictures of a recent trip to Turkey, where she and Jack had mused about visiting when they could both get away from work.

She studied the pictures, Photoshopping herself into the scenery. The girl had visited all the major sites, including Ephesus, Cappadocia, and Istanbul. After a dozen sightseeing photos, Evie came to a group of wedding shots. The affair appeared lavish, and Evie became engrossed looking at the fashionable dresses and colorful jewelry. Some of the guests were adorned with intricate henna tattoos snaking all the way up their toned arms. There were several shots of just the food. Platters of vibrantly colored Turkish delights made Evie's mouth water.

She started clicking through the photos faster to get to the bride and groom. She found a striking photo of them from the back. The bride's scalloped-edge veil rivaled Princess Di's in length and intricacy. The groom stood about a foot taller than the bride and had wavy brown hair circling a tiny bald spot. Evie grew curious for a front view. The next few pictures showed the couple from a distance standing under the wedding canopy. Finally, the last photo in the album showed the bride and groom, knot tied, walking happily hand in hand back down the aisle. The bride was radiant. She was exotic—impossibly thin, with Mediterranean skin and black straight hair tied in a chic knot resting on one shoulder. Her white teeth appeared like tiny index cards in a neat row. Her dress managed to be fashion-forward but still elegant. Evie was so caught up in studying the bride that she barely glanced at the groom.

When she finally did focus on him, she saw that it was Jack. The groom was Jack Kipling.

Evie vomited everything she had eaten that day right there in her bed, directly onto her laptop.

# # #

It was a full five minutes before Evie could get off the bed. She sat shivering, stunned into paralysis even as her throat was burning. When she finally unfroze, she wiped her computer screen with some crumpled tissues and brought it closer to her face to confirm that her eyes weren't playing cruel tricks on her. The groom was her Jack. The man who told her on date number one that his parents' messy divorce had turned him off from marriage for good. The man who clung to those beliefs after two years in a loving and supportive relationship. Their breakup rivaled the pain of losing her father. She had coped primarily by telling herself that at least Jack would die alone.

Who was this girl?

Evie needed to know every single detail about her. There was no question that Jack's new wife was beautiful. God help her if she had an amazing career to boot. Maybe she was pregnant. A baby could explain everything. Evie stared at the screen, tilting it backward and sideways to see if a sliver of a swollen belly was visible under the bride's silk gown. The only thing she could make out under the dress's bodice was a protruding rib cage. If the bride wasn't with child, she was probably a Turkish princess. Evie couldn't compete with royalty. But she didn't even know if Turkey was a monarchy. Jack would know. Apparently he'd made it to Turkey after all.

Evie slid off her bed and went to the kitchen for some paper towels to wipe off her keyboard. The empty roll stared at her from the top of the garbage. She ducked into the bathroom instead and reached for a wad of toilet paper. She plopped back down on the bed and set about cleaning out the nooks and crannies of her computer. Once the mess was cleared, she double-clicked the Google icon. It took a full minute to load—much longer than normal, but at least it appeared to be working. Without looking up, she typed "Jack Kipling" and "Turkish princess" and hit Search. Again she thought, who was this girl? What magic had she worked on Jack? What qualities did she have that made her "forever" material and Evie a mere stopover?

She glanced up at the results and didn't see Jack's name anywhere. She wondered if she accidentally typed in the wrong search terms in her distressed state. She checked the search box and saw a series of random numbers and letters in no apparent order. The recent numbness in her legs probably was symptomatic of a brain tumor. Now the delusions were starting.

She closed Google and double-clicked to reopen it. Nothing happened. She triple-clicked. Quadruple-clicked. Nada. She tried Microsoft Excel. That opened with no problem. She felt temporarily relieved that her computer wasn't totally fried. So she couldn't look up anything of any consequence. She could make charts!

Without much hesitation, she threw on shorts and a tank, hoping the weather was still as warm as when she was on her morning stroll with Tracy. Normally, she'd be one click away from a humidity analysis and a minute-by-minute precipitation graph. Without a BlackBerry, or a working iPad and computer, she just stuck her head out the window and decided her outfit would do.

As she rang for the elevator, it dawned on Evie that she had no idea where to get her computer fixed. That was just the sort of thing she would have looked up. If she hadn't been in such a foul mood, she would have chuckled at the irony. Instead she stood in her apartment building's long hallway and considered which of her neighbor's bells she could ring. Most people were at work, where Evie would also have been if her life hadn't recently overturned. There were a few elderly people on her hall, but she didn't think any would be too welcoming. Mrs. Teitelbaum had it in for Evie ever since she wouldn't sign the old lady's petition to ban music after 9:00 P.M. Mr. Warren, who smelled like cigars and Depends, was also a no. Evie had been dodging him for six months after he suggested fixing her up with his grandson, a coroner in Sioux Falls. She rushed to the lobby, thinking she could ask one of the doormen for help.

"Nico!" Evie gushed, gripping at the sleeve of the doorman's uniform with her free hand. "Where can I get my computer fixed?"

"I think there might be a place on Seventy-Second Street," he said, gently trying to free his elbow. "Oh wait, never mind, that closed. Oh—I know. There's a repair shop near my place in Queens that'll charge you half what you'll get fleeced for around here. Want me to get their info? It's called Al's Technology World. Or is it Abe's? You know what, I'm not sure. You better just look it up. Rockaway Boulevard."

"I can't look it up! That's the problem," Evie explained. "Thanks, Nico, but I gotta go."

She flung herself through the revolving doors and headed north on Broadway until at last she came upon a Best Buy. The service department was tucked two levels down in the subbasement. She hoped it wasn't too unrealistic to expect her computer to be fixed within an hour. Luckily there was only one person ahead of her in line. It was midafternoon on a workday, and she no longer had to cram her errands in on the weekend with the rest of the employed masses.

While waiting for her turn, her cell phone rang.

"Hello?" she asked cautiously, praying it wasn't her mother or, God forbid, Bette, on the other end. Eventually she would tell them about Jack, but today was not the day.

"It's Stasia. Where are you? You didn't e-mail me back. I got nervous."

"Phew, it's you. I'm at the electronics store—my computer's broken."

"Yikes. I knew something was wrong when you didn't respond in two minutes. I'm just calling because Rick thought you might want to come to see a movie with us tonight. I told him you were staging a be-in."

Evie sighed, with a deep inhalation through the nose that she held on to until she felt nauseated. To think it was Rick's idea to invite her out with them to make sure she was doing all right. Maybe Stasia and Rick would have infertility and Evie could get a break from secretly envying them. God, what an awful thought that was. Evie winced at her jealousy.

"Yeah—maybe. I'll call you later. Listen, I have some big news. Jack's married."

"WHAT? TO WHO? HOW? ARE YOU SURE?" At least she hadn't known.

"Yes—I'm sure. I stumbled onto his wedding pictures online. It's a long story." Even as she said it, she knew Stasia wouldn't believe her. She'd think she was snooping on Jack. Not that it was above her to do that, but in this case she had happened upon the pictures by sheer coincidence.

"He married some Turkish princess who looks anorexic but might be pregnant."

"She's anorexic and she's pregnant? Evie—what are you saying?"

The bell dinged and it was Evie's turn at the service window.

"Stas—I gotta go. It's my turn. I'll call you later about the movie."

Evie approached and placed her laptop on the desk. The service technician wrinkled his nose in disgust. Obviously the smell of vomit hadn't fully worn off.

"Ma'am, what happened here?"

"My three-year-old niece threw up on my laptop and it doesn't seem to be working now. Can you fix it?" At least she was a quick thinker. That and clovering her tongue were her special talents.

"I'm sorry but I don't think we'll be able to fix this. Once a computer gets this—um—soiled, it's usually toast. I suggest you go upstairs and look for a new one." He handed her back the laptop, along with a rebate coupon for an iMac.

Evie dashed back upstairs, taking the steps of the escalator two at a time. A salesperson with trifocals and a muffin's worth of crumbs in his beard offered help. Geek Squad, indeed.

"Is there a computer that's working that I could use—you know, to try it out?"

"Of course, ma'am. This one right here is connected to the Internet." He babbled on about the hard drive and megapixels, but Evie's fingers were already busy at work. She repeated the search on Jack that she had attempted earlier. A slew of articles came up about his restaurants, but she couldn't find anything on his wedding. Her eyes darted all over the screen, looking for the words "bride" and "ceremony" or anything else nuptial-related.

"Jack Kipling, huh?" the salesperson said. "Just took the wife to one of his restaurants for our anniversary. That was a good meal."

This guy's married? Every pot has its cover, Bette would say.

"Oh yeah? Well he onced bribed a health department official not to report mouse droppings in the kitchen." How many times had she pledged never to repeat that? At least one for each time Jack swore he'd never get married. So much for promises.

"Listen, I'm afraid I'm not ready to commit to another computer right now," she added, grabbing her things and heading out in search of an Internet café where she might continue with more privacy.

Miraculously she found one a few blocks away from the electronics store, in a second-floor shop above a Korean restaurant. The café smelled like a mixture of disinfectant and kimchi, and was almost entirely abandoned save for a sleeping hobo wearing shoes fashioned out of hand towels. Evie cringed as she sat down at the computer farthest away from the homeless guy and slid her credit card into the machine. An error message appeared.

"Excuse me," she said to the attendant, a Goth teen with blackened lips and indecipherable words tattooed on her forearm.

Evie desperately didn't want to know what they said. "This computer isn't working."

"Sorry, lady. You'll have to use that one," she said, pointing to the computer adjacent to the homeless man. "Next to Sleeping Beauty."

Evie held her breath and booted up the machine. Her knee shook vigorously as she waited for the monitor to load. Just as she was about to open Google, she froze.

What was she doing?

She was sitting next to a reeking hobo in a dirty Internet café so she could look up Jack's wife. It wouldn't do her any good to find out more information. He was married. Finding out what school his wife went to, or whether she was a successful entrepreneur or even carrying his child, wasn't going to make him any less married.

It was unhealthy, to the point of pathological, her obsession with knowing everything about everyone. What good had stalking people online done her? She'd rejected perfectly good dates because of meaningless things she'd discovered on the Internet—a job title she didn't think was impressive enough or an unflattering photo. Her last decent date ditched her because she cyber-snooped on him—and she had the wrong guy anyway.

She lost her job because of her Internet addiction. That should have been enough of a wake-up call, but no. Instead, she was spending her unemployment surfing the web for upward of seven hours a day. She spent way too much time agonizing over her profile pictures on Facebook, JDate, and Match.com. Her vision was all but shot from the hours wasted staring at her inbox waiting for e-mails from guys she'd gone out with once. If someone really liked her they could pick up the freaking phone and call.

She was going to quit the Internet! But what did that mean? All good things, as far as she could tell at that moment:

No more stalking people on Google.

No more Facebooking exes.

No more reading twits on Twitter.

No more posting pictures and waiting for "likes."

No more refreshing Gmail every thirty seconds.

No more hashtagging meaningless combinations of words.

No more Instagramming every instant.

No more Foursquaring her whereabouts.

No more bidding on eBay for the thrill of competition.

No more pretend job hunting on Monster.

No more blogs. (She was slandered on one, for God's sake!)

No more watching two-year-olds boogie to Beyoncé on
     YouTube.

No more playing Scrabble against house-bound Aspergians.

No more Candy Crush, that time-sucking psychedelic mess of
     sugar balls.

And, best of all, no more OkCupid, JDate, eHarmony, and
     Match.

Evie felt empowered. She flexed her wrists, which now would be saved from carpal tunnel syndrome—another bonus! Maybe her reproductive organs would gain a few more useful years without her laptop battery burning holes in them. She lifted her hands symbolically from the keyboard and rested them in her lap. Sure she couldn't order the heavenly throw pillows from Anthropologie she found online the night before. But she could just as easily go to the store and buy them, couldn't she? It was a measly twenty-minute walk from her apartment, and some brick-and-mortar shopping would probably be refreshing.

Contentment spread through her body like a vapor rub until she looked down at her legs and remembered about the mole on her right thigh. She had meant to look up signs of melanoma, because she could swear the mark above her knee had changed shape and color. She couldn't remember if the cancerous ones were round or asymmetrical. Maybe she'd just check that one last thing on WebMD—and then she could use Facebook to find some pictures of herself in shorts and see just how much the mole had enlarged in the past few months. As she was about to reopen the browser, she stopped herself. WebMD had led her to the very improbable conclusion that she had a stroke just weeks before. And tuberculosis last spring after she ran a 3:00 A.M. Internet search on bad coughs.

Now she just needed to notify her closest friends that she was planning to go off-line. She opened Gmail, taking in the primary colors of the Google logo one last time, and began a message to Tracy, Caroline, Stasia, and Paul. She would tell her mother when they next spoke. Fran, with her prehistoric AOL account, wasn't such a wiz with e-mail anyway. This was the woman who recently asked Evie how a deposed Nigerian prince in need of $10,000 got her e-mail address.

She typed slowly and deliberately.

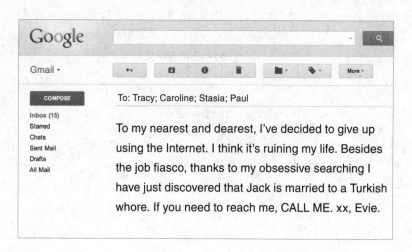

Google

Gmail ▾

COMPOSE

Inbox (15)
Starred
Chats
Sent Mail
Drafts
All Mail

To: Tracy; Caroline; Stasia; Paul

To my nearest and dearest, I've decided to give up using the Internet. I think it's ruining my life. Besides the job fiasco, thanks to my obsessive searching I have just discovered that Jack is married to a Turkish whore. If you need to reach me, CALL ME. xx, Evie.

Not thirty seconds passed since she pressed the Send button and she got three new messages. The first was from Paul.

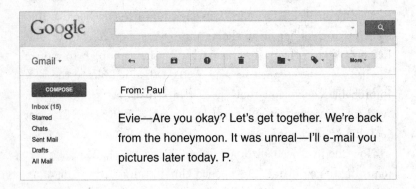

From: Paul

Evie—Are you okay? Let's get together. We're back from the honeymoon. It was unreal—I'll e-mail you pictures later today. P.

Next came Stasia.

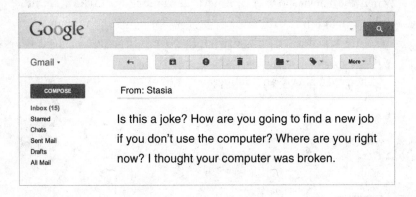

From: Stasia

Is this a joke? How are you going to find a new job if you don't use the computer? Where are you right now? I thought your computer was broken.

She followed up with a text message.

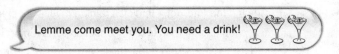

Lemme come meet you. You need a drink!

A far more startling text message from Verizon followed seconds later:

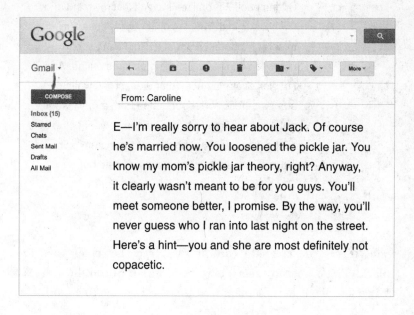

> YOU HAVE REACHED THE MAXIMUM NUMBER OF TEXT MESSAGES IN YOUR SERVICE PLAN. EACH TEXT MESSAGE SENT AND RECEIVED FROM THIS POINT ON WILL BE CHARGED AT THE RATE OF $1.99. TO ORDER A NEW DATA PLAN, VISIT WWW.VERIZONWIRELESS.COM.

Verizon better not be charging her for the message they just sent her. She abruptly decided to quit texting while she was at it. It was just another form of insincere, truncated communication, where a misplaced comma could inadvertently set off World War III.

Caroline's e-mail followed.

Google

Gmail ▾

COMPOSE

Inbox (15)
Starred
Chats
Sent Mail
Drafts
All Mail

From: Caroline

E—I'm really sorry to hear about Jack. Of course he's married now. You loosened the pickle jar. You know my mom's pickle jar theory, right? Anyway, it clearly wasn't meant to be for you guys. You'll meet someone better, I promise. By the way, you'll never guess who I ran into last night on the street. Here's a hint—you and she are most definitely not copacetic.

Naturally, Evie was curious. It could be the girl Evie accused of peeing in the communal shower in their freshman dorm. Or the slutty reservationist at Paris Spice who was always trying to get in Jack's pants. Or maybe it was Marianne. She proudly resisted e-mailing back "WHO?"

Only Tracy had the brains to call instead of e-mailing. Evie let it go to voicemail, feeling too busy quitting the Internet to chat. She sent out a follow-up e-mail to the group.

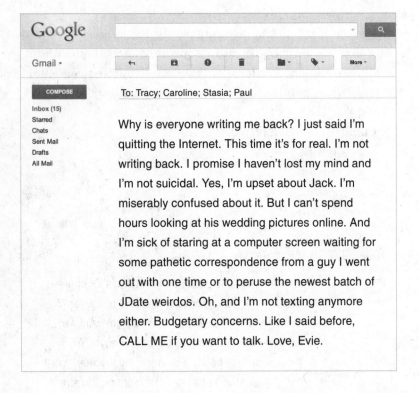

To: Tracy; Caroline; Stasia; Paul

Why is everyone writing me back? I just said I'm quitting the Internet. This time it's for real. I'm not writing back. I promise I haven't lost my mind and I'm not suicidal. Yes, I'm upset about Jack. I'm miserably confused about it. But I can't spend hours looking at his wedding pictures online. And I'm sick of staring at a computer screen waiting for some pathetic correspondence from a guy I went out with one time or to peruse the newest batch of JDate weirdos. Oh, and I'm not texting anymore either. Budgetary concerns. Like I said before, CALL ME if you want to talk. Love, Evie.

Evie ejected her credit card and watched the screen turn to black. There was no exact plan in her mind. Stasia did raise a fair point about her job search. Without being able to e-mail her

résumé and access her online Rolodex, it wasn't entirely clear
how she'd get a job. But in the time that she'd been out of work
so far, her attempts to find employment could best be described
as nonexistent.

Somehow quitting the Internet felt right. Like it was taking
the bite out of the knockouts she'd been dealt recently. At least
this would make her different from everyone else, more unique
than another faceless lawyer at a big firm or single girl in Manhattan looking for love. At least she'd have something to talk
about on a date, if she ever went on one again. But that was just
it. She was relying on the Internet for dates—now she'd go out
and meet people in the flesh.

She gathered her belongings and headed outside, where the
perpetual sound of sirens and pushy pedestrians couldn't prevent
her from feeling lighter and less burdened. Even her stomach
felt better. It was like a snowplow was working its way through
her body from head to toe, clearing away impurities. Since her
go-to activity of web surfing in pajamas all day was now out of
the question, she decided she would take a long walk through the
park. There was no particular rush to get home—no e-mail to
check, no blogs to read or dating accounts to monitor. Maybe just
a movie night with Stasia and Rick. She wound her way through
the maze of trees and playgrounds and jogging trails and ended
up back at the Central Park Reservoir, where she had been with
Tracy earlier that day. She paused to admire the stillness of the
water.

Then she threw her decimated laptop in and watched as the
once calm blackness rippled from the unexpected entry of an
Apple MacBook Pro.

Chapter 5

Over the weeks that followed, long walks through the park became part of Evie's daily ritual. She observed Labor Day by doing zero labor. A slower pace of life was fighting to set in, though her entire being was conditioned to resist it. She had always been more of a power walker than a rose smeller; more a scroll-to-the-bottom type than a read every word.

At first, the withdrawal from the Internet was unbearable. She felt anxious all the time, her hands actually twitching. Every time she saw someone using a smartphone, she wanted to pry it from them for one last fix. She'd heard that reading e-mails triggered a release of dopamine—how true she knew that to be now. It was unsettling to be so out of touch with the world—with her friends, with the news, with everything.

But there was an undeniable calmness in not being beholden to a tiny device that demanded she be on call 24/7. She found peace alone in not having to multitask—trying to text while crossing the street or e-mail while juggling shopping bags had caused her enough headaches and bruises. The day she discovered Jack was married, Stasia had been shocked when Evie hadn't written back to her e-mail immediately. Something just wasn't right about the world when people expected a response to a movie invitation in under five minutes. The pace of New York City was rapid enough without the added rush of insta-communication.

Still, her body was accustomed to constant connection, and when a runner would brush past her on the Big Loop, the motion would remind her of the vibration of her BlackBerry and she'd involuntarily look inside her bag to check it. Every twig snapping in the Ramble reminded her of a new message ding. Then she'd remember there was no e-mail to check or text to respond to and she'd continue on her walk, forcing herself to admire a sprawling tree or take notice of a chirping bird overhead. What was she missing, really? A message from Tracy with a sonogram picture of her unborn child that looked like a white, fuzzy alien? An e-mail from Paul notifying her that he saw a celebrity pick a wedgie at Tao?

It was definitely harder to be off-line at home. There she took on professional puttering, choosing a new drawer or closet to organize every time her mind revisited the image of Jack at his wedding. But it didn't take long to color-code her sweaters and arrange her shoes by heel height. She really would have loved to use her free time to redecorate her apartment. Swanky Barcelona chairs in white leather would be much chicer than her dated wingback armchairs. And her lonely mattress would be so much more fulfilled if it was butted up against a custom-made headboard in lavender shagreen, but it was impossible with her dwindling savings account.

It was time for Evie to return to work. To see people. To use her brain. To rejoin actual society, since she'd thoroughly dropped the virtual one. She just didn't feel ready. Jack—her Jack—was married. The world as she knew it was forever changed, and she was nowhere near acclimated to the new reality.

# # #

"Evie, let me in." Caroline's voice drifted to Evie's bedroom. "I have a surprise for you."

Evie was startled by the 8:00 A.M. knock on her door. Outside, the heavens had opened up and the pedestrians were struggling under cheap umbrellas intent on inverting. She couldn't imagine what was bringing Caroline across town in the tempest.

Through her peephole, Evie made out Grace, Caroline's older daughter, by the sliver of plaid pinafore showing through the space between her mother's calves. Evie normally loved children, but in her maudlin state a playdate with a preschooler did not qualify as a pleasant surprise. She unlocked the door.

"Hi, Evie," Caroline said as she forced Grace into Evie's apartment with a tug on her chubby wrist. "I booked us a full day at the Plaza Hotel spa. You don't even have to get dressed. Jorge is downstairs and ready to take us." Caroline lowered her voice. "And don't look so nervous. I'm dropping Grace off at school on the way."

"But I love Grace," Evie protested, but Caroline put up her hand to shush her.

A day of beauty was a splurge Evie would barely consider even with her plush salary, let alone in unemployment. She drank up

Caroline's generosity, happily stepping into the chauffeured SUV that sailed them to Midtown past the agitated commuters with their arms stretched out of sockets trying to hail taxis.

Thirty minutes later, they were nestled in a cocoon of tranquillity only twenty blocks from Evie's apartment, but it may as well have been a different universe. Evie was surprised when her manicurist starting pouring hot oil on her feet and rubbing it in with heavenly circular motions all the way up to her knees.

"Is this what a pedicure is supposed to be?" Evie mumbled to Caroline, who was seated in the cushiony white leather chair next to hers. The room looked more like an Italian furniture showroom than a spa. Enya played in the background, the only noise other than the rhythmic dripping of a waterfall on one of the walls. "My usual lady just gossips about my blisters in Korean. But I get a free lip wax on Mondays."

"Shhh," Caroline said, with a sideways glance that made Evie feel like she deserved to be gossiped about in a foreign language. "Just enjoy yourself."

"You're right. Thank you again for this," Evie said, and then because she was desperate not to be a total downer added, "Did you watch *Preggers* last night? I'm psyched Jolie is getting back together with Todd."

"No way. Jolie can do better. Plus Todd is never going to marry her." Caroline looked down to examine the vampy shade of plum she had painted on her toes, or maybe to avoid looking at Evie. "Sorry, I shouldn't have said that."

"It's fine. At least I'm not fifteen with twins on the way," Evie quipped.

"That's the spirit," Caroline said as she was whisked away by a tiny woman wrapped in a kimono taking her for a salt scrub. Moments later a different woman in a matching robe led Evie into a room with a bubbling stone bath and massage table.

Still it was difficult for Evie to free her mind, even as the expert therapist worked magic on her tense muscles. When she felt the masseuse's strong hands press into her temples, the only effect was to sharpen her mind's focus on her dismal state of affairs. Job-less. Man-less. BlackBerry-less. Soon-to-be penniless. There was a sign in the spa that said NO PDAS ALLOWED, but if she still had her BlackBerry, she'd no doubt have snuck it into the treatment room and checked her e-mail while her face was pressed down into the doughnut-shaped pillow at the head of the massage table. At least the constant buzzing of new e-mails would divert her from the far more perilous distraction of her own thoughts.

After several more indulgent treatments, including an African head massage and a dubiously effective tummy-toning rub, she and Caroline reunited in the luxurious waiting room to sip cucumber- and acai-infused water.

"Want to head to the Oak Bar for a real drink?" Evie asked, lifting her glass to show the inadequacy of its contents. After the spa services, many of which were sticky and goopy, a stylist had come in to do a ten-minute touch-up on Evie's hair and makeup. The results more than compensated for Evie's less than desirable outfit and were too good to waste sitting at home.

Caroline glanced at her watch.

"I would just love to, but I've got to be gettin' home to fix some dinner for Jerome." Her Texas-speak always emerged when she was fibbing. Evie was too appreciative of the spa day to ask Caroline what her chef would be doing while she prepared dinner. "But let me give you a ride home."

"Thanks. Drinks another time." Evie went to her locker, where her sweats and raincoat were stashed. The combination was the same one she always used—04-04-46—her father's birthday. For some reason, those six digits had always been her family's passcode for everything—the safe, the alarm, you name it. Even though she felt a pang each time she used those numbers, she couldn't bring herself not to. Today, it was hitting her harder than usual. Having stepped out of her isolation, it suddenly seemed unbearable to go home again. In her modest apartment, she felt like a mannequin sentenced to watch real life through a window. She piled into the backseat of Caroline's SUV, noticing that one of her freshly painted nails was already chipped.

She took stock of the day. Although it was shorter than she would have liked, it had been the best she'd had in a while. As the car glided across Central Park South toward the West Side, Evie wondered if a quiet life at home, peppered with meaningful time with her friends, could sustain her until she figured out her next steps. She could probably swing at least six months without a job if she was prudent about her expenditures. Baker Smith had given her that much severance. The trouble was the ridiculously high monthly rent she paid for her five-hundred-square-foot apartment, but she had seen too many episodes of *Law & Order: SVU* to consider living in a nondoorman building. Leaving the Upper West Side, her beloved neck of the woods, was also out of the question. She'd have to make cutbacks elsewhere.

Suddenly Caroline's driver slammed on the brakes. Tires screeched and Evie rolled down her window to see what had transpired. A taxi had cut in front of Caroline's car, a run-of-the-mill traffic incident in Manhattan, but the scare had been enough to draw her attention to the street, where her eyes landed on a sign in an empty store window at the base of the Ritz-Carlton hotel. In a petite and exquisite font it read DEGUSTATION: A NEW RESTAURANT BY JACK KIPLING—OPENING THIS FALL. FOR INFORMATION, VISIT WWW.JACKKIPLINGCUISINE.COM.

"Give me your phone," Evie said, reaching for Caroline's tote.

"No," Caroline reproached her. "I'm not giving you my iPhone so you can look up his restaurant. What's that going to do for you? So you'll see a few glossy photos of him. Maybe read about his sanctimonious views on farm-to-table cooking. Who cares? He's married now. And you deserve someone who is totally crazy about you."

It was strange how Caroline had put it. "You deserve someone who is totally crazy about you." Was that what her friends thought? That Jack didn't propose because he wasn't truly in love? That hurt, even though she didn't believe it to be true. Something else must have changed for Jack to one-eighty on marriage. Some pheromonal clutch this Turkish girl had on him. A baby. An impending bankruptcy. *Something.*

Her friends certainly seemed excited for her when she and Jack were dating. They never complained about complimentary dinners at his restaurants or VIP access to the annual NYC Food & Wine Festival. A few times Stasia had made disparaging comments about these "don't-believe-in-marriage types," but Evie dismissed them forgivingly because her friends didn't know the gory details of his parents' divorce. When Evie first met Jack she chalked up his gap-toothed smile to the stereotype about the English and their teeth. It turned out his teeth were just one of many things neglected during his preteen years while his parents went through their four-year bitter divorce and custody battle. She grew to love the vulnerability that Jack's parents' turbulent marriage fomented in him. It made him more accessible to her and needy of her validation when he was otherwise closed off emotionally. She took it as her duty to show him that a loving, stable partnership was possible. The kind her parents had had.

Stasia's straight-to-the-altar route was lucky, but most couples Evie knew endured more tortuous twists along the way. Not to mention that reaching the chuppah was no guarantee of living happily ever after. Evie had a handful of friends and acquaintances with broken engagements and divorces on their CVs.

Caroline never said much about Jack's unwillingness to tie the knot. If Jack was wary of the idea of marriage, Jerome celebrated the institution. Caroline was his third wife. She was a stepmom to a litter of kids, some of whom were almost her age, so she basically kept mum on the subject.

Paul had been so enamored of Jack's celebrity and his food that his enthusiasm for their relationship was actually overbearing. When they broke up, Paul moaned about having to rely on "reservations." After the split, all of her friends and closer confidantes at work offered the usual platitudes, like "you'll find someone better" and "it wasn't meant to be," but they spoke with palpable restraint, thinking they might reunite and Evie would harbor the nasty things they said about him. Despite their hesitation to speak freely, Evie did recall the words "narcissistic" and "self-aggrandizing" thrown around on more than one occasion.

"You're right," she agreed, rather than squabble. "Thank you so much for this fabulous day." She hugged Caroline and popped out of the backseat. "Thanks, Jorge," she called behind her.

Stretched on her sofa upstairs, Evie felt physically rejuvenated but emotionally drained. She wished the aesthetician could have dug just a little deeper, extracting her memories of Jack along with her blackheads. She couldn't shake the sight of his new restaurant sign.

During their two years together, they had attended four engagement parties and six weddings. While Jack was perfectly content to be a well-wisher, a rice-thrower, a gift-giver, what have you, Evie couldn't wait to be the guest of honor.

Having kids was something he said he'd love to do, but "down the road" when his career was more settled and he didn't have to travel as much. That was confusing to Evie, because all of his restaurants were accessible via the subway, but she assumed he had bigger ambitions and was just getting ahead of himself. Still at times he'd comment how fortunate they were not to be tethered by children. It wasn't like Evie was against sleeping late or pro diaper-changing. She knew being a mother was a lot of fucking work, unless you were Caroline who espoused the "it takes a village" (from the Philippines) theory to raise a child. Being childless was a chance at a self-indulgent life. But *she* was Evie Rosen, a nice Jewish girl from Baltimore who wasn't game to jump red-eyes to Paris and party until sunrise. She wanted to have a family like the one she grew up in—it was their Rosen triangle against the world. She didn't know if being a stay-at-home mom would be for her, but she felt more excited about motherhood than corporate mergers.

On the marriage front, Jack was far more definitive. When Evie would manifest signs of disappointment, he—the broken record—would say, "Evie, I love you. But I just don't want to get married. I hope that's enough for you." Evie torpedoed everything a few days before last Christmas. Jack had announced he'd be flying to see his ailing mother and Evie was welcome to join if she "felt like it." There was, apparently, no expectation on Jack's part that they would behave like Siamese twins whenever family obligations were involved. They were not a de facto married couple, no more wedded together than a pair of teenagers who could break up over a text message. She pressed the point, emboldened by the low-cut dress she was wearing and the two glasses of wine she'd consumed at the bar of JAK, waiting for him to finish up for the evening. In fact, she didn't let up even when they returned to his apartment and started to make love. She pulled apart from him, sat up with the covers gathered around her frame like a shield, and presented Jack with an ultimatum: get engaged in the new year, or they were done.

Somehow he'd managed to extricate himself from the conversation, assuring her that 2:00 A.M. was not the time for such a heavy discussion. But by morning, both of them knew something monumental had occurred—they had reached the point of no return. By the time Jack boarded his Virgin Atlantic flight, they were broken up. She never forgave herself for choosing that time as the do-or-die moment of their relationship. After all, he had just found out his mother had suffered a mild heart attack. His new restaurant was having trouble acquiring a liquor license because of its proximity to a school. Besides, Jack didn't want to be coerced into a binding commitment, nor did she want to get him there with threats.

Caroline was right to hide her phone from Evie. Reading about Jack's burgeoning success, so shortly after her own employment catastrophe no less, was like trying on bathing suits in fluorescent lighting: nothing good to see here.

# # #

With a *Wall Street Journal* spread on her lap, Evie scrunched her forehead and pondered what she had just read. The London-based firm of McQualin, Craft & Breslow was hoping to double its presence in New York, specifically its M&A department. She'd poached the newspaper from a neighbor she was *pretty sure* was out of town after the front-page headline caught her eye.

According to the article, the firm was looking to hire at least five partners and twenty associates with this type of corporate experience. Several New York-based firms had approached them about merging, but they resisted, hoping to grow internally. This could be the perfect opportunity for her to rejoin the workforce. So why wasn't she on the phone with the HR department trying to arrange an interview? What was holding her back?

It looked like a perfect September day outside. If she really were to return to law firm life, her opportunities to explore the city would come to an end. Besides her park walks and a few matinees at The Paris, she hadn't done much to culturally engage with the city she loved so much. So before she called over to McQualin, Evie decided to do something as completely uncharacteristic as throwing her computer into the muddy waters of Central Park—go to a museum just for the hell of it. Not to tell an artsy guy that she saw the de Kooning exhibit. Not to prove to herself she was multifaceted. No, she would visit the Metropolitan Museum of Art because she had lived in New York for twelve years and had never stepped foot inside. And that, in her mind, suddenly seemed despicable. Without the shackles of Baker Smith and the lure of her laptop tethering her to the couch, she had no more excuses.

Dressed in dark leggings and a long-sleeved shirt with a paisley scarf tied on for whimsy, she set out for the Met, pleased to discover the ideal autumn weather she had anticipated was even crisper than she imagined. Over the course of her thirty-minute walk, she passed five different Starbucks. The aroma of the macchiatos and Americanos was the perfect complement to the smell of chestnuts roasting in the vendor carts. Though she was still full from breakfast, she hungrily took in the scent of New York. This was where she was meant to be—outside, absorbing sunlight and breathing fresh air instead of recirculated air-conditioning. The trail of the season's first fallen foliage, each leaf more vibrant than the next, made a far better footpath than the dizzying geometric pattern of the Baker Smith carpet. Everything was sharper when her face wasn't pressed up against a plastic screen.

Her mother called while she was walking but Evie just let it ring. She still hadn't told her mother about Jack being married. Nor had she been very clear about just how little effort she'd put into finding new employment. A voicemail beeped as she reached the museum's famed granite steps. Evie's heart muscle tensed when she listened to the message.

"Evie, it's Mom. Please call me."

From the tone, Evie knew right away the message was ominous. Her mother wasn't calling to share the Greenwich Town Thespians spring musical announcement or to invite Evie to the mother-daughter Columbus Day brunch at the club. No, her mother had news. Bad news.

Evie called back, her fingers shaking as she dialed the number. It took her three tries until she was able to type it correctly.

"It's me. What's going on?" Evie didn't even try to disguise the worry in her voice.

"Honey, Grandma Bette is sick. She has cancer."

Evie felt queasiness overtake her. Her knees buckled and she had to take a seat.

"What kind of cancer? Is she all right?" Evie demanded of her mother.

"It's breast cancer."

Evie felt some of her tension ease up.

"Well, that's treatable, isn't it? She's going to be fine, right?" Evie asked, trying to convey how much she needed the answer to that question to be yes.

"Well . . ." Fran said, her voice trailing off, and immediately Evie knew there was more to the story.

Evie wasn't a stranger to hearing bad news—not by a long shot, and she knew better than most that a single phone call could turn the world upside down. She was in her freshman year of college when her dad passed away, after suffering a heart attack at work. Evie remembered her dorm phone ringing while she was hanging out with her girlfriends, widening their waistlines with pizza and beer to celebrate the end of midterms. She had almost ignored the call but for some reason she was guided by an inexplicable impulse to answer it. Maybe she had some extrasensory perception for tragedy.

There were no warning signs with her father, no prior health conditions, no bouts of extreme stress. His work-life balance was one of the reasons Evie felt optimistic about law school, though she quickly learned that large-firm life in Manhattan bore no resemblance to her father's career. Henry ate dinner with his family almost every evening, sleeves rolled up to reveal the cheap digital watch of which he was so fond, and cleaned his plate no matter what was served. He would ask Evie about her classes and lament that he should have been a history professor. Nightly, he'd retire to the couch to watch ESPN. Sometimes she would watch with him, despite her lack of interest in sports, just because his presence was a comfort. His surprising death would forever leave in Evie the belief that bad news prefers to lurk in unexpected places. Not that it ever stopped her from searching for it.

What Evie remembered most about that phone call in college was her utter feeling of helplessness. There was no ambulance to call, no doctors to interrogate, no miracles even to pray for. He was gone. It was the first time in Evie's life where there wasn't even a remote chance of turning things around. Death was, in fact, the only truly permanent thing she'd ever experienced. Everything else that had happened to her up until that point was child's play.

This time had to be different. She would not, she could not, lose Grandma Bette.

"Well what?" Evie pressed. "Is Grandma going to be okay?"

"Well we just don't know yet how serious this is." Her mother's voice, like a warm hand on the shoulder, filled the line after a long pause. "But, Evie, we'll get through this. I'll fill you in on everything when we see you. Bette's up in Greenwich with us now. She's being treated at Sloan Kettering and will be moving into an apartment in the city soon, near the hospital."

The phone slipped out of Evie's sweaty palms and she scrambled to rescue it before it slid any closer to a pile of dog poop on the bottom step. A rambunctious school group alighted the stairs at the same time.

"You've been with Grandma in New York?" Evie shouted over the din of the children. Why hadn't her mother told her she was in the city? Didn't Fran need her help or at least want her to visit Bette? Her mother no doubt was overwhelmed with Bette's care falling on her. And everyone knew Evie was just sitting home these days counting her beauty marks.

"Honey, Bette didn't want to upset you. I think she was hoping this would turn out to be overblown. That the doctors up here would say it wasn't a tumor, just calcification."

"You should have called me right away!"

"What difference does it make? Bette was clear that she didn't want you to worry until we had more information. We all know you've got a lot going on," Fran said cautiously.

What did that mean? She had nothing going on. Literally nothing. It was as if the absence of having anything in her life made her this fragile person whose sanity everyone was afraid to dismantle. Was her nothingness so great that it was becoming a "something"?

"Anyway, why don't you hop a train and come up to see us today if you can? Grandma would love to see you."

"Of course, I'll leave for Grand Central now," she said. She jumped into a taxi, inappropriately thinking how circumstances were conspiring to keep her from ever visiting a museum.

# # #

The train wasn't crowded, thankfully, so Evie was able to have an entire row to herself. She was in no mood to put up with sweaty commuters dripping meatball sub juice or slurping Big Gulps. Without the distraction of a neighbor, she was able to process what she'd just found out. The image of Bette's ring finger waving in her face flashed through her mind. How she never expected that one day she'd look back on that with nostalgia? She would love to burst through the doors of Fran and Winston's house and say, "Surprise, Grandma, I'm engaged! You may have cancer but look at my rock!" Bette vould probably say, "Evie-le, if I had known my getting cancer vould get you get married, I vould have gotten sick a long time ago." And she would have meant it.

Bette and Evie were always a tight pair, so much so that Fran would accuse her daughter of being all Rosen and no Applebaum. But Lola Applebaum of Great Neck, Fran's mother, never took the time to get to know Evie. She was too busy keeping up with the Joneses (in her case, the Kleins and the Cantors) to pay much mind to anything other than when she'd be able to lease a new Mercedes to park in her circular drive. Bette was totally different. She would often take her to school when Fran was working, and she sat front row at every one of Evie's dance and piano recitals (despite her obvious lack of talent). In grade school Bette showered Evie with lollipops (usually given on the walk to school before 8:00 A.M.) and Barbies, then twenty-dollar bills in high school, and then pearls of wisdom like "no one buys ze cow if zey get ze milk for free" in college. When Evie was dumped by her high school boyfriend the day before the homecoming dance, Bette stroked her back and watched *Family Ties* reruns with her until she fell asleep. When her first SAT score came back about 100 points light, Bette coaxed her into the car and drove all the way to New York to distract her with a favorite activity, pretending to shop for a very important customer at the Decoration & Design Building on Third Avenue.

They hatched a story during the four-hour drive that they were the two principals of the formidable design team Rosen & Rosen, based in Baltimore, and were tasked with finding imported damask silk woven with real gemstones for an "A-list" celebrity client. After delivering their spiel a few times with straight faces, they collapsed in laughter at Scalamandré, a purveyor of wall coverings so luxurious they made Evie's knees weak, and suddenly her poor showing on the math section of the SAT seemed to matter quite a bit less.

But after Henry died, their bond really climaxed. They—the generational bookends—seized on to each other like life preservers, and the thought of losing her grandmother now made Evie feel like she was drowning. She shivered on the over-air-conditioned train, wrapping her scarf more tightly around her.

At the New Rochelle stop, two ladies shuffled up the train steps. Out of an empty car, they selected the row right behind Evie. The women appeared to be about Bette's age. They announced their arrival on the train with the heavy scent of Chanel No. 5 and the clanging of gold bracelets.

"I'm worried about her, Gladys," one of the women said. "She's no spring chicken."

"Edith, relax. What is she again? Thirty-two?"

Evie felt her shoulders tense. She knew she should get up right now and switch seats, but some masochistic tendency forced her to stay put.

"She's almost thirty-three. And not a single boyfriend in the last year. Imagine my Gayle, as pretty as she is, an old maid. Look at this picture."

Evie heard Edith fishing around in her oversize purse. She was curious to see the photo, curious if Gayle was more or less attractive than she was.

"She's a beauty, all right. Lovely skin," Gladys said, after

Edith must have produced the picture. "And she's not going to end up an old maid. No one would dream of calling her that until she's at least forty."

"You're crazy. People probably already call her that. Or they will soon enough," Edith said. "Her standards are too high. Of course, you think she listens to me? Of course not. I'm just an old-fashioned bubbe with too much to say."

Evie was tempted to turn around and invite these women for lunch in Greenwich. They could have a nice chat with Bette over rugelach and iced tea.

"None of them do. They're too busy on those Blueberry things to listen to anyone," Gladys said.

"It's called a BlackBerry. Don't those nine grandchildren of yours teach you anything?" Edith asked. Evie couldn't help but smile.

When she descended the train in Greenwich, Evie popped into the station bathroom to look herself over. She pinched her cheeks to flush them with color and fished around for lipstick in her tote. She had no other makeup with her, so she slicked some gloss on her eyelids. It was a trick she had read about in a fashion magazine. What stupidity. The stickiness made it impossible to blink naturally. She yanked out her ponytail holder and assembled her hair in the best style she could without a brush. At least Bette wouldn't fret that her single granddaughter was running around Manhattan looking like Raggedy Ann.

Winston and Fran lived just a short walk from the train station. When she tapped on the front door, she was surprised to see May on the other side of it. She hadn't counted on one of the fucking TWASPs being there.

"Hey," Evie said casually, trying to hide her annoyance. "I thought you guys would be up at school already. Orientation must be over by now."

May twirled her long blond ponytail, which was tied up with a yellow grosgrain ribbon, about one inch wide. Ribbons in hair, post–elementary school, were a thing. Evie learned that in college, when she saw the blond field hockey players lined up with ponytails tied up with different colored bows.

"April's at school, but I came home for the weekend to do some shopping," May said. "Oh, and to visit Bette," she added, as what could only be described as whatever comes after an afterthought. "Sorry that she's sick."

"Thanks. Where is she?"

"Huh?" May was distracted by her phone. More nimble fingers were hard to imagine.

Evie shifted her weight. They were still standing in the doorway of the house.

"I asked where my grandma is."

"Oh, sorry," May said, without raising her gaze. "My friend Lonny just Snapchatted that she's getting a pedicure next to Scarlett Johansson. She says her feet are nasty and covered in blisters. Uch, I'm so jealous. I mean, on the Vineyard, April saw Justin Timberlake picking his nose, but she couldn't get close enough to get a picture of it. She probably could've gotten a lot of money if she e-mailed it to *US Weekly* or something. Do you think my friend should take a picture of Scarlett's feet?"

"May," Evie repeated, "where is my grandma?"

"Sorry, she's in the guest room."

Evie climbed the stairs two at a time but paused at the top. It was always weird for her when she reached the second-floor landing. Technically she had a bedroom there, a perfectly comfortable room at the end of the hall, across from the master suite. Over the years she had subtly replaced the needlepoint throw pillows and floral lamp shades she despised. But noticeably absent, to her, were the academic awards and the framed photos of her friends that had embellished the walls and lined the desk of her childhood bedroom. The TWASPs' rooms, labeled with their names in decorative paint, were totally different. Instead of looking like fungible guest rooms in a bed-and-breakfast, they were crowded with mementos and imprinted with their individual style.

The door to the small guest room was open, and Bette was sitting in a chair, gazing out the window. She looked well dressed in a red cardigan over a cream blouse with a navy skirt. Grandma Bette never wore pants. Several chains rounded her neck, including a necklace with the figure of a little girl that Evie knew was meant to symbolize her. The only thing off about her appearance was her hair, which was styled in its usual beehive fashion but had an inch of gray roots separating her forehead and the bluish-black tint to which Evie was accustomed.

"Grandma," Evie said, and flung her arms around her.

"Evie, bubbela, I'm okay."

In a more hushed tone her grandmother said, "I'm sorry she's here. After fourteen years, I still can't remember vhich one's vhich."

"Grandma, April and May are not even identical," Evie chastised gently, but Bette waved her arms as if to say, "Zey are interchangeable to me."

"Hi, sweetheart," Fran said, standing in the doorway to the guest room. She walked over to give Evie a kiss on the cheek, and up close Evie saw dark circles rimming her mother's eyes. "Is everything okay? Why have you been so out of touch? I was thinking about checking up on you in the city this week."

It wasn't the right time to delve into her resolution to quit the Internet. It was so inconsequential compared to Bette's illness. She was seven days into her digital cleanse so far, which was six days and four hours longer than she lasted on the BluePrint juice fast she signed up for with Tracy last year.

"Oh, that. My computer is broken. It may be a while before it's fixed." Evie looked contritely at her grandmother. She knew Bette would disapprove of her move off-line, now that she was educated in JDate. Thanks a lot, Louise Hammerman's grandson.

"So, Evie, any news?" her grandmother asked, holding up her ring finger.

"Grandma! How can you even be thinking about me right now?"

Bette snorted. "Oh please. If Hitler couldn't kill me, breast cancer can't either."

But my being single might be the death of you?

"So when did you get the diagnosis?" Evie asked, refusing to go off-topic. "What kind of treatment will you need?"

"Don't vorry about me. I'll be fine," Bette said. But her face showed signs of drowsiness, and Evie found it hard not to grow even more concerned by her grandmother's uncharacteristic lack of energy. She couldn't remember the last time Bette didn't hop out of her chair to hug Evie when she came to visit.

"Stop it, Grandma. I want to help you."

"Vell, one thing you could do is come vith me ven I meet with the breast surgeon. Your mother has done too much for me and you are already in Manhattan," Bette said.

"Of course, Grandma," Evie said. "Is this your first time meeting the doctor?"

"No, I met with two different surgeons vhen I came up to New York, I knew right away vhich one I vanted."

"Why? What was wrong with the other one?" Evie asked.

"Nothing. She vas lovely," Bette said hazily, leaving Evie bewildered.

"Evie, let's let Grandma relax a bit. She's been shuttled back and forth quite a lot the past week for appointments and tests. We'll talk in the kitchen," Fran said.

"Is that okay, Grandma? Do you want us to stay?" Evie asked, but Bette's eyes had given in to the weight of her lids. She wanted to embrace Bette again—to wrap her youthful arms around Bette's wrinkled body and inhale the motley scent of her hairspray, perfume, and peppermint-tea breath—but she didn't want to disturb her rest.

She and Fran were almost at the stairs when Bette's voice sounded behind them.

"Evie-le, come back."

"Yes, Grandma? Do you want something from the kitchen?"

"No, no, I'm fine. I'm not eating any more fatty muffins your mother is alvays making."

"What is it then?"

"You didn't answer me before. Are you seeing anyone?"

Evie's heart sank as the image of Jack getting married in a lush Turkish garden pixilated in her brain again.

"No, not right now."

"Vell, I'm not going to be around forever," Bette said. "But if I needed to *hora* at your vedding, I'm sure I'd have ze strength to fight off zis cancer."

Evie bit her tongue. Bette "Guilt" Rosen strikes again.

Chapter 6

When Fran and Evie returned from a quick run into town to buy groceries and pick up Bette's medication, Winston was at the kitchen counter, clad in his signature pink button-down and khakis, handing a wad of twenty-dollar bills to May.

"Welcome, Evie," he said, giving her a hearty hug. He was warm, as always, but the "welcome" only served to remind her that she was just a guest in Greenwich. She plopped down at the table, next to May, and watched her swig a Red Bull while texting. She wondered how she appeared to her much younger stepsister: Old? Probably. Successful? Possibly. Single? Obviously.

"So, May, how's school going? Do you like your roommate?" Evie forced the overture even though May still had not asked her a single question about Yale. It had gone from surprising to hurtful to slap-in-the-face offensive. "I remember being so nervous before school started. I even drove up to Yale a few weeks before so I could find my way around on the first day. Not that it helped."

May looked at Evie blankly and said, "I'm not nervous. I already know a ton of people."

"From orientation?" Evie asked, and then corrected herself. "Oh, you mean from boarding school. There must be a lot of kids going with you."

"Yeah, a bunch. But I know like the entire freshman class at Yale. Like eleven hundred of them. Out of thirteen hundred."

"How is that possible?" Evie asked, confused.

"We're all friends on Facebook. Some computer dork started a group called New Bulldogs and got like almost the entire incoming class to join. I feel like I already know who my friends are going to be. A group of us arranged to meet up at Toad's Place for drinks," May said, and then looked at Evie apologetically. "Oh, wait, Toad's Place is like the best place to party on campus now. Not sure if it was there when you were there."

Evie wanted to strangle the little TWASPy twit, but her dad was right there. She summoned her most patronizing voice and said, "Yes, I'm familiar with Toad's. It's been around since the 1970s. The Rolling Stones played there."

"Oh, well, I didn't know that. Now it's just like a cool place to drink and dance. I guess it changed."

"No, it was like that when I was in school too . . . whatever. Never mind."

"Someone from Dartmouth did the same thing. April said this really funny girl from Hotchkiss has been Instagramming all the things she's been getting for her dorm room. It's kind of cool."

Evie thought about asking why anyone would care that someone they've never met bought an IKEA floor lamp. If Facebook had been around when she had started college, she probably would have steered clear of the very girls who became her closest friends.

Tracy's Facebook page made her seem like a demented bookworm, with her Emily Dickinson profile picture, unsolicited critiques of anything on the *New York Times* bestseller list, and membership in the group "I'd Go Gay for Jane Austen."

Stasia's page was no better. She had posted almost a dozen pictures of herself shaking the president's hand in her father's Capitol Hill office as well as the results from quizzes like "Which Element On The Periodic Table Most Resembles You?"

Caroline's profile was a virtual love letter to Texas. She was the millionth fan of the group "Everything Is Better Deep-Fried."

Evie's own Facebook presence left much to be desired. It had nice pictures and links to interesting articles, but in an ongoing attempt not to turn off potential suitors or make waves at the office, it was kept relatively neutral. Put less euphemistically, it was lame, down to her reserved, safe profile picture—that side shot that literally was a "profile." She didn't join the group "People Who Don't Pick Up After Their Dogs Should Be Tasered," though she strongly supported the cause. She didn't "like" *The Jerry Springer Show,* even though she never flipped away from it. She didn't post about being starstruck when she saw Miley Cyrus in line for the bathroom at Dunkin' Donuts. It wasn't the real her; though how much could a virtual profile accurately portray any person?

She was tempted to tell all of this to May, to warn her about choosing friends based on 140-character drivel and check-the-box, prepackaged personal descriptions on Facebook. But Evie knew better than to tell a "back in my day" story, especially to the TWASPs. She just thanked her lucky stars smartphones weren't ubiquitous when she was in college. It was bad enough having to face the people who saw her boobs flying about when her tube top slipped off at a freshman crush party. If that had been memorialized on the Internet, dropping out would have been her only viable option. She may have been jealous of the TWASPs' youth, but she wouldn't actually want to trade places.

"May, honey," Fran said. "Thanks so much for visiting Bette. You really didn't have to do that."

Yes she did, thought Evie. Winston literally paid her to show up.

Fran gave her a kiss and a big, gracious hug, and Evie found herself feeling envious. Her mother married Winston when the TWASPs were only four years old, and while they lived primarily with their mother in Westchester, Fran was a big part of their lives. Evie felt like an outsider. She had hoped her mother would complain about them when they were out running errands and Winston wasn't around, but she didn't.

"May, let me help you load up your car," Winston said, grabbing the keys off the kitchen counter.

Evie's stepsister didn't have to be told twice she was free to go. Once she left, Evie melted more comfortably into the yellow and green vinyl chair at the kitchen table. Winston's house looked like it had been frozen in time. Fran couldn't much be bothered with interior design, which is why she was perfectly fine leaving the 1970s furnishings. The Rosen home in Baltimore was a two-story Colonial Revival with a wraparound porch, a charming house whose blue front door Evie still missed walking through. She longed for the smell of potpourri spilling out of the powder room into the foyer. Winston's house smelled like cigars.

Fran settled down in the chair opposite Evie and broke off a few grapes from a bunch in a ceramic bowl on the table. Evie eyed the muffins sitting on the countertop but refrained. It didn't seem right that her grandmother was calorie counting and she wasn't.

"It's been a long week," Fran said, after a deep exhale.

"A whole week already?" Evie gasped. "How could you not tell me sooner?"

"You have a lot going on, Evie."

There was that line again. She didn't like it one bit.

"Honestly," Fran continued, "I think if Bette weren't getting treated in New York, she would have tried to keep you from even knowing she was sick. She was worried about you. After losing Dad, you know. She knows how sensitive you are."

Did loving someone—hoping to hold on to them for a long time—mean she was especially sensitive? That couldn't be. *Anyone* would be shattered by the prospect of losing a beloved family member. She always thought Bette would be one of those grannies with her face on the Smuckers jar having her hundredth birthday announced on the *Today* show. Willard Scott, or whoever would be his equally jolly replacement, would say, "Happy Birthday to Bette Rosen of South Florida. Said she attributes her longevity to a good diet, laying on guilt trips, and telling it like it is."

"Didn't Grandma want me to visit?"

"Truthfully, she said the only reason a young lady like yourself should be visiting a hospital is to bring her doctor husband his lunch." Fran and Evie burst out laughing.

"Grandma is ridiculous. But seriously, what's the prognosis? And please don't sugarcoat it."

"Breast cancer has a very high survival rate if there is early detection, which unfortunately Bette didn't have. That doesn't mean she won't be okay. I just wish we'd caught this sooner. She hadn't had a mammogram in over three years." Evie noticed her mother's eyes swell as she shifted her gaze to the table.

"Mom! This is not your fault! You are her daughter-in-law. Ex-daughter-in-law, if you really think about it. You're not responsible for her." Evie felt herself getting emotional. "Stupid Aunt Susan knitting her freaking quilts in the desert should be taking care of her."

"You're right," Fran said. "But she's not."

A chilling thought occurred to Evie. She could have reminded Bette to get mammograms the same way her grandmother could be counted on to call every October first to insist Evie get a flu shot. Bette was Evie's personal meteorologist in the wintertime. She would call from sunny Boca to say, "Evie, I heard on the news about a cold front in New York. Don't forget your scarf and gloves."

Fran read her mind.

"Don't you start feeling guilty, Evie. This isn't on you," Fran said. "Bette has her ways, but she was always a good mother-in-law to me. Henry would appreciate me looking after her. He was as dutiful a son as he was a father and husband. And we both know Susan can't be counted on, so there's no point in even discussing that."

Just then, Winston entered and joined them at the table. Fran turned to him.

"Evie's feeling like she might be to blame for Bette not taking better care of herself."

"That's crazy. If anyone's to blame, it's Sam. At least according to Bette," Winston said.

Fran shot Winston an unmistakable shut-the-hell-up look.

"Who is Sam?" Evie asked, genuinely confused. "And why is he responsible?"

Fran kept her icy gaze on Winston, who bore the look of a man who would be sleeping on the couch that night.

"Who is Sam?" she repeated.

"Sam, is, um, Sam is Bette's companion," Fran said, rolling a grapevine between her thumb and pointer finger.

Evie was in shock.

"Grandma has a boyfriend?" Everyone knew "companion" was code for boyfriend or girlfriend in the seventy-plus set, the same generation that referred to couples as an "item."

"It's not serious, Evie. That's why Bette didn't want us to tell you about him."

"Really? It's not serious? I thought Grandma and her boyfriend might want to start a family."

Winston chuckled. "That really would be something."

"It's just, I don't know, Bette just said not to mention it to you. It doesn't matter anyway, since now it's out in the open, thanks to . . . oh, never mind." Fran, looking at Winston, shook her head in frustration.

"I know why Grandma didn't want me to know about this Sam guy," Evie said, crumpling the napkin in her hand forcefully. "She doesn't want me to feel bad that my grandmother has a boyfriend and I don't. Well she's wrong. I'm thrilled for her!"

Neither Winston nor Fran said a word. They looked at each other, as though hoping to telecommunicate how to handle the conversation.

"And pardon my morbid curiosity, but why is Grandma being sick Sam's fault anyway?" Evie asked.

"Well, according to Bette, when the lump was detected, it was already the size of a small grape," Fran said. Each of their eyes noticeably wandered over to the cluster of red grapes resting in the ceramic bowl on the table. "Just under two centimeters."

"So?" Evie asked, not sure where she was going with this.

"I guess Bette doesn't understand how Sam, never, um, felt it. You know, when they were being intimate." Fran blushed, unable to look Evie in the eye. Winston dug his hand into his collared golf shirt and scratched the back of his neck uncomfortably, but Evie noticed a hint of a smile. Sam, that old dawg, he was thinking.

"Jesus Christ. Grandma's having her boobs felt up by some geezer? I think we need to move her up north permanently. Where is he now anyway?"

Fran's jaw tightened. "Actually, Bette's a little upset that he hasn't been in touch. She thinks he may be dumping her because she has cancer. Supposedly there are a lot of women after him."

Evie shook her head in disbelief. "Let me guess. He has his own teeth. Wait, wait, better yet, he can drive at night."

Winston chuckled, but Fran persisted with a grim face.

"Well, Bette's neighbor saw him playing shuffleboard with one of the less reputable women in the condo yesterday."

Evie reached for the muffins after all. She took a big bite and chewed slowly, finding it hard to swallow.

"Okay, I think I've heard enough about Sam for now. For a while, actually. Just tell me more about the treatment she's going to need."

"Well, she will definitely need surgery to remove the tumor. Following the surgery, there will be radiation and possibly chemotherapy, depending on whether the cancer has spread into the lymph nodes. You'll hear more specifics when you meet the surgeon."

"Does that mean she'll lose her hair?" Evie asked. That would kill Bette, who treasured her weekly trips to the beauty parlor to have her 'do set in giant Velcro rollers.

"I'm really not sure," Fran said. "The chemo is much better

these days. Apparently they've been able to reduce some of the worst side effects—the nausea isn't as severe, and the hair loss is not as certain. Thank God—right? Bette would, well, you know. She's vain like me. Not like you, Evie."

"What are you insinuating?"

Now Winston shot Fran a look that said, "Choose your words wisely." Fran didn't seem to notice.

"Sweetie, you know I think you're absolutely gorgeous," Fran beamed, as if taking credit for her daughter's beauty. "But you're in pajamas right now. It's the middle of the day. I could never do that, that's all I was saying. And you know how Bette is. I would have thought you'd change before coming here."

Evie knew that try as she might, there was no way she could convince Fran that Lululemon leggings and a Juicy top were not pajamas, and that her outfit was pretty decent, considering she had no notice for the visit. Why couldn't Bette wear pastel track-suits like every other grandmother? How did she manage to look pristine a week after a cancer diagnosis?

She made her face into an innocent pout and said, "Oh, I'm sorry, I completely forgot to get my hair blown out before visiting my sick grandmother. I should have booked GLAMSQUAD."

Winston intervened, forcing a détente.

"Let's move on. Evie, I want to hear what's new with you. Have you been searching for a job? I still cannot believe your firm let you go. Fran said it's the market—everyone is suffering."

"Nothing's really new with me. I read about an opportunity at McQualin, which I may pursue, but I'm not sure. I don't think I took one fully calm breath my entire time at Baker Smith. There was always some client drama or deadline hanging over my head. And all the jockeying for position was just exhausting. I need to convalesce."

"Makes sense," Winston said. "What about in-house counsel? The folks in my shop seem to have decent hours." Winston worked as a financial planner at a midsize commercial bank. Evie had seen many of her colleagues transition to similar positions, offering better hours and less pay than Baker Smith. These exits were usually billed as "lifestyle" moves, something she'd once balked at but now was coming to comprehend.

"Maybe. I don't want to jump into anything, though. But actually, I do have something interesting to report. It has to do with why I'm not at Baker Smith anymore."

Fran and Winston leaned in more closely.

"I've given up using the Internet." She waited for a dramatic reaction to her announcement.

Fran and Winston just looked confused. "How does one quit the Internet?" her mother asked.

"And why?" Winston added.

"The Internet was dominating my life. Not in a good way. I was wasting endless hours looking up people who meant nothing to me, checking out wedding and baby photos. Trying to find out where people lived and where they went to school and who they knew. It was a stupid waste of time. And depressing. So I stopped going online. I don't check my e-mail or even text anymore. No Facebook or JDate either."

"Why was it depressing?" Fran asked, sounding alarmed. "Evie, you're amazing, and I'll be damned if you can't see that."

"But, Mom, just think about it. What do people put online? All their best stuff. Their glamour shots, fabulous vacations, pictures of them with celebrities or at cool events. Videos of their kids riding their bikes in Izod shirts on sunny days. Nobody chooses a fat photo for Facebook. None of my friends would dare post their marital spats on YouTube. No, they post clips from cheery surprise parties. There have to be ten Tweets about job promotions for every one about getting fired. It's not reality. And while intellectually I know it's not reality, it still bummed me out every time I went online."

Winston and Fran continued to look puzzled. They were clearly from the wrong generation to understand the gravity of her announcement.

"I think I get it," Winston said finally. "I wish the girls would get off their stupid phones once in a while. Bunny wants to throw them out the window." He smiled. "The iPhones, that is. Not the girls."

Bunny was Winston's ex-wife. Evie had met her only a handful of times. Barbara, as Fran called her because she refused to use her pretentious nickname, worked as a real estate broker in Manhattan. Fran told her Bunny cheated on Winston with her now-husband, Albert, whom she met at an open house. Between the time of contract-signing and closing, Bunny left Winston and shacked up with Albert in the apartment she sold him. A few years later they moved out to Rye so the TWASPs would have more space. The girls were skittish about the divorce when they were small, but by the time they became teenagers they overlooked the fact that Albert broke up their family because he was a top executive at Ralph Lauren who got them steep discounts and tickets to fashion shows.

"Winston gets it!" Evie said excitedly. "Not to mention that I was constantly updating my seventy-five different online dating profiles with new pictures. I would change my list of interests or favorite movies regularly, like some guy would suddenly notice that I like Woody Allen movies and contact me for a date. Well, you can see where that got me."

Fran reached across the table and laid her hand on Evie's arm. "Evie, like I said, you're going to meet someone very soon. Men are just intimidated by you because they think you're out of their league."

"Thanks, Mom. I'll be sure to list you as a reference. But that's not the point. There's more to the story. There was a catalyst for my Internet strike. But I don't feel like getting into it right now." The day had been strenuous enough without having to bring Jack into it.

"But what's this got to do with your job?" Fran asked.

Evie sighed deeply. "Suffice it to say the partnership committee was displeased with the number of personal e-mails I was sending. And frankly, they were right. But I really don't want to talk about that either. I'm embarrassed enough."

Luckily Winston and Fran didn't push her. They just stared at her, surprised, befuddled, and concerned.

"Enough about me. Winston, are you still attempting your renovation of the basement?" Evie said, resuscitating the conversation.

Winston happily obliged the shift.

"Yes, though I had a minor home improvement injury from my new electric sander," he said, showing Evie a bandage hidden beneath his sleeve. "I think your mom is going to lose it if she has to clean another one of my self-inflicted wounds."

Winston's voice faded as Evie zeroed in on a piece of paper lying on the table. It was a letter from Yale, addressed to May, explaining how the class "shopping period" worked and directing her to the website where she could read descriptions of all the courses offered. Evie thought back to the days when her course catalog arrived. Back then it was a thick blue book, stuffed with possibilities. She remembered dog-earing it to death. By the time school started, her catalog was a mess of yellow sticky notes and highlighter streaks. The result was a class schedule with no early-morning classes and Fridays off. Despite having many more years of experience in her armor, the present Evie still wasn't far from that hopeful girl starting freshman year. She chose Columbia over Harvard for law school because she thought New York was a better place to meet men, something she'd never admitted to anyone. When she did work out, it was at the Reebok Sports Club, an extra ten blocks from her apartment, but it ran a number of amateur sports leagues that drew lots of young, professional types.

It made her feel like a traitor to feminism, all this strategizing. She enjoyed how good it felt to do the very opposite for once. Even if only in the virtual world, she was proud to take herself out of the path of men for a change.

Chapter 7

The nameplate on the door read EDWARD GOLD, M.D., PH.D., AMA, ASA, CDC, MPH. He certainly seemed qualified alphabetically. Evie tapped gently on the door to announce her arrival.

The tall, sandy-haired doctor rose to greet her. His tan skin was dusted with light freckles, the kind that looked gifted from a recent vacation. Blue eyes framed by a noticeably thick spread of dark lashes punctuated his face. She estimated he was about forty. She had been expecting to see a much older man, and definitely not someone so good-looking. He wore a white coat with his name stitched on the pocket in red. It was buttoned up so that all she could see of his outfit was the knot of his orange tie and the bottoms of his brown trousers. She despised her own outfit, a pilled knee-length cashmere cardigan draped over a mismatched tank and cropped yoga pants. If the appointment hadn't been set for 8:00 A.M., she might have had a prayer.

When they shook hands, Evie felt comforted by his grasp. His handshake was firm and steady, like a surgeon's should be, but his hands were larger than she expected. She would have thought a surgeon would have thin and delicate fingers.

"Where's my grandmother?" Evie asked, surprised not to find her in one of the two chairs opposite his paper-strewn desk, which Evie immediately wanted to organize. Besides the voluminous stacks of files, his office was sparsely decorated save for basic office furniture, numerous diplomas and certificates, and a single baseball encased on a shelf. She found two picture frames—one in his bookcase housing a picture of a cherubic little girl, probably about four years old, in a white dress with alligators on the smocking and an oversize headband. She was in a swing, laughing. Evie assumed it was his daughter. The other picture, framed on the desk, was turned toward the doctor so that Evie couldn't see it. Probably his wife.

"Bette said her stomach is out of sorts so she and I spoke over the phone early this morning to discuss the surgery in more detail. How she should prepare and what she can expect in terms of recovery," Dr. Gold said.

"Oh, so should I go?" Evie asked, taking a few steps back toward the door, where she noticed one of the framed certificates said Dr. Gold was a lecturer at Mount Sinai Hospital, the same hospital where Stasia's husband, Rick, did his residency.

"No, no. Please stay," Dr. Gold said. "Let me fill you in."

"Okay, thank you," Evie said, taking a seat. She self-consciously tucked her hair behind her ears.

"Your grandmother is a very admirable woman. She's certainly not led an easy life. I heard about your father. That's not the way things are supposed to happen, though in medicine we see it more than most. And she seems to be taking this latest challenge in stride."

"She's incredible," Evie agreed.

"She told me about you. You two are obviously extremely close."

Dr. Gold gave her a half-smile, revealing laugh lines shaped like commas and a dimple in his left cheek big enough to store an acorn. His expression made Evie wonder just what Bette had shared with him about her. If anyone else was going to sum her up in a nutshell, they'd probably say she was attractive, smart, neurotic, maybe even funny. But if Grandma Bette had thirty seconds to describe her, well that was a whole other story. Evie feared the conversation went something like: "Dr. Gold, I know I have cancer, but if you really vant to help me, can you please find someone for my granddaughter? You must know some single doctors looking to settle down. Ideally, no children or previous marriages, but I'm flexible."

"Well, hopefully she didn't say anything too embarrassing."

"All good things, I promise," Dr. Gold said, this time offering a fuller grin. Evie must not have looked convinced, because he went on. "She told me how smart, witty, and sweet you are. You know—typical Jewish grandmother stuff. My grandma told everyone I was the valedictorian at Princeton, which was not remotely true."

"I guess they're all the same," Evie said with a laugh. "What can you tell me about the surgery and the treatment plan? Will she get through this?" She noticed her knee shaking and tried to steady it.

"Like I said, Bette has been incredibly brave. Frankly, she's more concerned with burdening all of you."

"Sounds about right," Evie said ruefully.

"I reviewed the ultrasound-guided core biopsy that Bette had done in Florida, and your grandmother has something called infiltrating duct carcinoma. It's the most common type of breast cancer, but you probably already know that from doing research on your own."

Evie was ashamed to have done no research, though it wasn't for lack of concern. The breast cancer websites would have her reeling from information overload and all she would have seen were the potential complications and mortality statistics.

"She definitely needs to have the tumor removed surgically. I offered Bette the choice of having a lumpectomy, where I would remove the tumor and surrounding tissue, or a mastectomy, where the entire breast would be removed," Dr. Gold explained. "The adjuvant treatments postsurgery are different, and many patients opt for the mastectomy so they can be assured that all affected cells are gone."

"Bette chose the lumpectomy," Evie said. "I'm right, aren't I?"

Gold laughed, and when he did, the skin around his eyes crinkled in an endearing way. Evie liked that he laughed with his whole face.

"You are. I was surprised. Most women her age opt for the mastectomy, which historically has been considered a more effective treatment for preventing recurrence. Fortunately, there is new research showing that a lumpectomy plus radiation can be just as effective, with possibly even greater survival rates, than a mastectomy. I'm actually heading up a follow-up study that we hope will confirm these findings. Anyway, Bette was pretty adamant regardless."

"Well, she does have a boyfriend. I just found out."

"Sam?"

Jeez, she really was the last to know.

"Sam the Man. So, then what, after the lump is taken out?" Evie asked.

"Let me explain to you a bit about breast anatomy," Gold said. He got up from his desk and took a few steps toward her. She didn't know if she was supposed to unbutton her cardigan.

"The breast is surrounded by lymph nodes that drain fluid to the underarms," he said, pointing at an anatomical poster on the wall behind Evie's chair and motioning for her to look at it with him. She felt like such an idiot for even thinking he was going to use her body as his teaching tool.

As she rose from her seat, Dr. Gold's phone rang.

"Sorry, let me just take this. I've been expecting an important call."

"Of course," Evie said, distancing herself slightly from the D-cup breast imagery on his wall.

"This is Edward Gold," he said, phone nestled between his face and shoulder, his hands rustling through the tower of papers on his desk. He paused to put on the glasses that were resting next to his computer.

"Nice to hear from you so quickly," he said. "Of course, of course . . . Yes, yes. I can get down to Washington next month," he responded, with a huge smile on his face. "Well, that's great news. I agree, I think spectral karyotyping is key." Dr. Gold dug his free hand into his thick dirty-blond hair and mussed it into a crazy professor style. "The first trial was very successful . . . I appreciate that . . . Yes, the Tamoxifen study could be taken further. My team is going to be very excited . . . At NIH offices, absolutely. Thank you for calling."

Dr. Gold put down the phone and rejoined Evie.

"Sorry about that. Anyway, like I was saying before, when

I remove the lump, I'm also going to remove the first draining lymph nodes and test them for cancerous cells. I hope very much that after the surgery we'll conclude that the cancer hasn't spread into the lymph nodes."

He took the seat next to Evie instead of returning to his desk. She felt important in his presence, especially after that mysterious phone call, for which he offered no explanation.

"Evie, I'm going to help Bette fight this. She has a top-notch team at Sloan. I want you to relax and just be there to support her. And I'm always here for you. Don't hesitate to call me anytime with questions," he said.

He filled her in on more of the nitty-gritty details of the surgery and what Bette could expect recovery-wise. She hoped he appreciated that she just listened to what he had to say and didn't try to outsmart him with her degree in Internet Medicine. She knew it drove Rick and Stasia crazy when people acted like insta-doctors after visiting mayoclinic.org.

"I really appreciate everything you're doing."

"It's my job. Do you have any questions?"

"If you don't mind my asking, why did you decide to go into this kind of medicine?" Evie asked, surprising herself with the completely out-of-left-field interrogatory. The guy had just mentioned the National Institutes of Health on a phone call. Why was she not more intimidated? Not to mention respectful of his time.

"My girlfriend in medical school died of breast cancer. I thought I was going to be a heart surgeon or maybe a neurologist. But when she died at the age of twenty-eight, I just felt compelled to change course. I'd also lost an aunt to breast cancer the year before. It affects women of all ages, from all backgrounds. Even men."

"Wow, I'm so sorry. That must have been devastating."

"It was awful," he said. "You know, I deal with a lot of patients and their families, but so few of them ever ask me why I do what I do."

"Oh," Evie said, uncertain how he felt about her prying. "I hope you don't mind that I did, Dr. Gold."

"Not at all, I'm enjoying talking to you," he said. "Please call me Edward by the way."

"Okay, I will," Evie said, not sure she actually would.

"Anyway, I really think the experience of losing a loved one helps me connect with patients a lot better than I would have otherwise," he said.

"I totally get that. I just basically got fired and now I connect with unemployed people more than I used to," Evie said. "It's all about the human experience."

What the fuck was she saying?

Edward nodded in agreement, possibly just to save her from embarrassment.

"So is that your daughter?" Evie asked, gesturing to the picture on his shelf.

"Yep. Olivia is four," Gold said, visibly melting. "She's adorable. And doing really great now."

What's with the "now"? Was she sick too?

"Well, she's gorgeous. I see she's got your dimple," Evie said. "I love children," she added, somewhat gratuitously. She really did love little kids though, babies too—especially chubby ones with ample thighs and wrists that spilled over onto their hands. Caroline's younger daughter had cheeks like marshmallows, alabaster and soft and impossible to resist pecking.

"Best thing in life," the doctor said, and Evie reveled in the simplicity of his views.

"Oh, I noticed from your wall of honor that you also lecture at Mount Sinai." Evie pointed to the countless framed certificates in Latin behind her. Edward visibly blushed. "My friend's husband trained there. Do you know Rick Howell?"

"Yes. That was my first teaching job. I met Rick in my surgery seminar. He's your friend's husband? I didn't realize he was married."

"Oh, yeah, he's been married to my best friend from college for like three years now. They're the most perfect couple. It's actually pretty annoying." Evie didn't think she'd ever said that out loud before, though the thought had taken up permanent residence in her frontal lobe. What a ridiculous time and place for her to come clean.

"I doubt they're perfect."

"No, they are, trust me," Evie said, surprised by the detour their conversation had taken.

"You look like your grandmother, I think," Dr. Gold said, changing course again.

"Really?" Evie asked, surprisingly flattered, considering she was being compared to an octogenarian.

"Yes, the green eyes," Gold said, though he wasn't even looking at her anymore. He seemed occupied sorting through patients' charts that he had pulled from a file cabinet.

"Same genes," Evie said, and then felt foolish for explaining to a medical professional that they shared DNA.

"Speaking of that, though," Evie said, "I have been wondering if I should get myself checked out. You know, for lumps?"

Now Dr. Gold focused his eyes squarely on her face, almost like he was scared he would look at her chest after she mentioned her breasts.

"If you are feeling concerned, then yes. Though I think you can probably wait until you are forty. It could be useful to have a baseline mammogram done at thirty-five."

"I've actually been pretty worried since Bette got sick. I tried to give myself a breast exam but I had no idea what I was doing. Is that something you could do?" Evie asked. "I mean, I'd make an appointment of course." She didn't want Gold to think she was hoping for a freebie.

"Um, I don't think that's a good idea," he said. "But I can refer you to someone excellent."

"Oh, okay. I understand." Maybe asking him to give her a breast exam was like stopping Annie Leibovitz on the street to snap her picture. "I know you have much more important things to do."

"No, it's not that," he said. "Let me give you the card of the doctor I typically refer to. But really, I wouldn't worry. Given Bette's age, I doubt there's a genetic component to her illness."

Evie relaxed, taking the card he produced from his desk and putting it in her bag, which was a giant tote from Columbia Law School that she used to lug her textbooks in. She hoped Gold noticed it because she felt like she'd said some pretty foolish things during their meeting.

"As I'm sure Bette told you, the surgery is scheduled for three weeks from today—October sixth. It's my first opening."

"So far away?" Evie asked, surprised. "There's no one available to do it sooner?" Dr. Gold seemed quite competent, and he certainly was a pleasure to look at, but didn't it make sense to get the tumor out as soon as possible?

"Bette interviewed a few surgeons, but chose to go with me. Unfortunately, I have surgeries scheduled back to back and I'm taking a week's vacation in between. Don't worry—Bette is perfectly safe to wait three weeks to have the tumor removed," he said. "Patients often choose to wait if they want a certain doctor or even because of their own work schedules."

His last point made Evie think about Patricia Douglas, the litigation partner from Baker Smith who made partner after only seven years as an associate and was the youngest member of the firm's management, partnership, and recruiting committees. Her rise in the firm's ranks was nearly apocryphal. Would Patricia, were she handed a diagnosis of breast cancer, wait for a case to settle before scheduling her surgery? Almost definitely. That thought alone made Evie glad to be done with the place.

"Okay then, Dr. Gold, I guess I'll see you in October," Evie said, though she remained anchored in her seat. She wasn't ready for their conversation to end but couldn't think of any reason to prolong her visit.

She supposed she just yearned for the company of men. She missed the guys from her office—the ones she mock flirted with for sport and who often flirted back. She even missed dating, not that she was particularly great at it. Conversation with friends was a breeze for her, and the give-and-take of sharing opinions and stories was second nature. But on dates, especially first ones, she often found herself unsure of how much to say and ask. Sometimes she set out on a fact-finding expedition, and her dates looked like suspects cooking under the hot lights in an interrogation room. Other times, she'd ramble, orally presenting her memoirs to a glazed dinner companion. Neither proved a winning formula.

By now, it had been a few months since she'd summarized her life story to a perfect stranger. She hadn't sat side by side with a guy at a noisy bar or across from one at some happening restaurant waiting to feel the spark that never seemed to ignite. Normally she'd return home from a date feeling exhausted, climb into bed and review her mistakes. From the anticipation to the preparation to the conversation to the instant replay at home, the whole process could be excruciating.

How was it that in spite of the hellaciousness of the dating world, she found she longed to be a part of it again?

The doctor stood up.

"I've got rounds to do now," he said. "But here's my card. Contact me any time with any questions."

"Thank you so much. I'd actually like to request that you keep me in the loop on everything—any updates and any decisions that need to be made. I don't think my grandmother will object."

"You got it. It was really great meeting you. Sorry it's under these circumstances, but I'm looking forward to talking again."

"I appreciate your time, Dr. Gold," Evie said.

"Edward, please," the doctor said, his sizable dimple making another grand appearance.

# # #

Back in her apartment, Evie found herself thinking about Dr. Gold. She was surprisingly intrigued by him, so much so that she'd actually forgotten to ask him a number of questions she had about Bette. She didn't know how long her grandmother's treatment would be, or if that was even known at this point. They'd never gotten around to discussing the survival rates. Maybe she'd subconsciously avoided asking him.

She decided to call Stasia at the lab. Stasia was doing Alzheimer's research but certainly would know more about breast cancer than Evie. Evie dialed her at work, but her research assistant said she had called in sick that morning. Evie tried her at home and was surprised when Rick answered.

"Evie, hi. Nice to hear from you. How are ya?"

"Been better. Is Stasia there?"

Rick paused before answering and Evie heard the tapping of shoes around the apartment.

"No, she's visiting her sister in Boston."

"Oh, okay. The lab said she was sick. Whatever. Wait—what

are you doing home in the middle of the day? Nobody's sinuses need draining anymore?"

Rick didn't skip a beat. "Just home because I forgot some patients' charts that I was reviewing last night. Heading back to the office in a few. You don't sound good, Evie. Can I help?"

She hesitated. Talking to Rick without Stasia present was new for her, though hardly inappropriate.

"It's my grandmother, Bette. She has breast cancer. I'm pretty freaked-out. I know she's already older, but still I can't imagine losing her." Evie felt tears well up in her eyes, but she forced herself to stay composed. "You know I lost my dad in college. I feel like I've had to deal with enough loss already. It's not fair."

"First of all, I'm sure your grandmother is going to be fine. This isn't my field, but honestly, I think it's generally treatable if detected early. I'm here for you if you need anything."

Hearing those words—"Evie, I'm here for you"—made her ache for the type of comfort she really sought in the larger picture. Strong hands to rub her back. An ear that was always at the ready. Her lip-biting and lump-swallowing were starting to fail her. She forced a deep inhalation.

"It wasn't detected early," Evie said, at last yielding to the tears. "She didn't get a mammogram for three years because she was worrying about me."

"I'm sure that's not true. Listen, Evie, you shouldn't be alone. You're on the West Side, aren't you? Off Columbus Avenue? I can come over in a little while. Or Stasia can, when she gets back in town."

At least she was more to him than his wife's college friend who sometimes tagged along on date night. Still, she resisted.

"Thanks, that's really sweet. But I'm fine. Honestly." He protested and she almost decided to have him come over, but then his beeper sounded, and while he placed her on hold she decided she was better off alone.

"Okay, I'm here," Rick said. "Though I do have to get back to the office. Is there anything else I can do?"

"Actually, there is something. What do you know about Dr. Edward Gold? I just came from his office and he said you know each other."

"Gold? Yep, the surgeon. He led a small group of us in a laparoscopy rotation. Really smart guy. He gets crazy grant money. I am pretty sure he was even short-listed for the President's Council of Advisors on Science. Bette is lucky he was able to fit her into his schedule."

It felt strangely intimate to hear Rick say her grandmother's name. It must be that whole bedside manner thing that doctors pride themselves on. Stasia told her there was actually a class on this in medical school. It made her feel less special about the way Dr. Gold had treated her. That was just pro forma, she supposed, making patients and their families feel comfortable. At least she understood what the phone call Dr. Gold took was all about. He must have received another grant.

"Gold is terrific," Rick went on. "I actually remember that his wife and baby sat in on his lectures a few times. It was very cute."

"Well that's great to hear," Evie said, even though for some reason she got an icky feeling inside when Rick mentioned Gold's spouse.

"Listen, I'm going to head to the office, but Evie, take down my cell number."

She grabbed a pen and a scrap of paper and jotted it down, unsure that she'd ever use it. "Thanks, Rick."

"Of course. Oh, and I'll tell Stasia to call you back."

Rick couldn't have been kinder, but she felt worse than ever when she rested her kitchen phone back in its cradle. All she could think about was how getting through her grandmother's illness, and her professional troubles, would be so much easier if she had somebody constant to support her. Stasia had Rick's shoulder available whenever anything went wrong, be it a missed promotion at the lab or even something really trivial like losing a new earring on the subway. Evie had her friends, but she couldn't rely on them indefinitely, could she? What if their busy lives juggling jobs, kids, and spouses eventually started to eclipse the strength of their college bond? Then what would happen to her, she just didn't know.

Chapter 8

Days passed, and Stasia did not return Evie's call. That, coupled with her absence from the lab and her revelation at Paul's wedding, got Evie thinking. Stasia must be pregnant. Evie had been expecting it for a while. Actually, preparing for it was more like it.

Now it all seemed obvious. Rick was home in the middle of the day to care for his wife. Stasia hated her passive-aggressive sister in Boston. There was no way she'd visit her midweek for no reason. Rick didn't bring home charts to study at home. They were home midday because Stasia was brandishing a fetus and she and Rick needed to visit the doctor and read baby name books on the couch and have mock fights over nursery wallpaper choices.

How foolish she felt for even considering having Rick visit. He was busy with Stasia—holding back her straight, but not too flat, blond hair while she puked into the toilet. Rick was probably rolling his eyes during the call in a gesture to show Stasia he couldn't get Evie off the phone.

Once Stasia came clean about her pregnancy—she would likely keep it private until the first trimester passed—that would make it official. Not only would Evie be the only single one and the only jobless one, she'd also be the only childless one. Caroline already had two little girls and a baseball team of stepchildren. Tracy was due in November. She calculated that Stasia would have her baby in the spring. What a way to celebrate turning thirty-five in May. Her birthday would probably fall on Stasia's baby's christening or on one of Caroline's girls' birthday parties. While everyone else was enjoying cake and smiling for pictures, Evie would be in the corner using a plastic knife to cut vertical lines into her wrists (although Caroline and Jerome usually rented the Plaza Palm Court for birthday parties, Eloise-style, so she'd probably have access to a real knife).

Evie took a deep, solemn breath. It wasn't that she necessarily ached for a child at this moment. But she knew it was something she did want in the not-too-distant future. If she'd married Jack, she'd happily have started a family by now. It was better to do it young anyway when the risks were lower. Evie thought back to something she'd seen online several years ago, before she met Jack. She was at work, perusing Match.com, when a pop-up ad exploded on her monitor. "FREEZE YOUR EGGS!" it said. Her instinct was to click it shut, but something compelled her to read the smaller print:

At the time, Evie was outraged. How dare this company, obviously in cahoots with Match, scout her profile and target her for some sketchy egg-freezing scam? What were they going to do when she needed her "good" eggs—nuke them in the microwave? But now that it was three years later, and she was no closer to starting a family than she had been that day, she wished she'd found out more about this service. With her luck, by the time she got married and pregnant, her eggs would have salmonella.

Now she yearned for her computer, and not just to look up the particulars of egg freezing. She had plenty of other research:

1. Read more about McQualin's M&A practice.
2. Determine if Luke Glasscock had left the country.
3. Find out where Jack and his new wife were residing (could it be his studio walk-up in the West Village that he insisted on calling his "flat"?) and pass by there by chance.
4. Check how much money was left in her savings account.

She did have a vague sense of how much she had socked away; it should be enough to last for a while as long as she was prudent. This was easier said than done. The opportunities to part with money were endless now that she didn't have the commute that took her up and down the same exact streets and into Manhattan's underworld via the C train for the last eight years. Low on discretionary cash, she'd have to be merely a window-shopper of the city's fineries.

Besides the pressing inquiries, there were many other little itches that only the web could scratch. When she tossed her computer into the Reservoir, she abandoned a Words with Friends game in which she had a substantial lead over Stasia. She lost out on covetous sale items saved in her shopping cart on Net-a-Porter. And she couldn't remember who the senators from New York were but was too ashamed to ask anyone. How the hell could she ever figure that out without the Internet? Maybe at the library. But she didn't know where the library was without her computer, except for the daunting main branch on Forty-Second Street with the massive lion sculptures guarding the entrance.

Agitated by the idea of Stasia being pregnant and exasperated that she couldn't refresh herself on the egg-freezing procedure, Evie flung herself on her bed, resolved to identify a bright side in her life.

Sushi.

That was it. Pregnant women couldn't eat raw fish. But she could. She reached for the phone to call her favorite Japanese restaurant, Haru. Jack never wanted to order in from there—he was always poo-pooing its lack of inventiveness and deriding any eatery that was part of a "chain."

She dialed Haru's number, which fortunately she'd committed to memory.

"Hi, I'd like to place an order for delivery."

"For how many?"

"One. I'd like a salmon-avocado roll, one eel roll, one spicy tuna roll, and three pieces of tuna sushi, plus a house salad." She was suddenly ravenous and ecstatic about devouring sushi without having Jack critique the presentation of the avocado slices on her salad.

"You say one person?"

Evie sighed. "Yes, one person. How much will that be?"

"Forty-eight dollars and sixteen cents."

That was a bit steep for a solo lunch in her apartment. She decided to cut back.

"Which is the kind of fish that has a lot of mercury—the eel, the salmon, or the tuna?"

"You say you want add Mercury Roll. Now fifty-five dollars. Be there in fifteen minutes."

"No, no. I don't want a Mercury Roll. I was asking which of your fish has high mercury levels. It's the eel, right?"

"Okay, you want one more eel roll. Sixty-one dollars. Thank you." The woman hung up, leaving Evie alone in her apartment to await a mercury-laden meal she couldn't afford. Now she could add the inconvenience of not being able to look up mercury levels in fish to her list of living-without-Google annoyances.

It was undoubtedly getting harder for Evie to ignore the mounting inconveniences of being computer-less. But still she was confident about maintaining her abstinence. Albeit slowly, quitting the web was purifying her mind the way drinking kale shakes would detox her body. Without Facebook's news feed streaming into her mind like an IV drip, she felt freer than she had in years. Free from reading things like "Alice Saltz (a sycophantic Baker Smith associate with her lips stitched to the partner Bill Black's ass) got promoted" and "Harry Shamos (Evie's high school ex, the guy who dropped her before the big dance) posted new pictures to the album 'The Shamos Twins—6 months.'" She was free from feeling like she needed to measure up with posts of her own. Free from discovering things about people she was better off not knowing. Free from scouring dating websites for fresh meat. And that was worth not knowing who the senators from New York were for at least a little while longer.

# # #

Even though Tracy was the openly pregnant one, her bulbous stomach inviting attention and unwanted petting everywhere she went, Evie couldn't stop fixating on whether Stasia too was with child. A pit in her belly formed whenever she questioned if all her friends knew about the baby but were keeping it from her for fear she'd have a breakdown. She tried to put up a strong front to them most of the time, but who was she kidding? She had succumbed to a gloomier disposition the minute she and Jack split, and her half-hearted attempts at covering it up weren't particularly convincing.

After one week of torturous curiosity, she decided to call Caroline to sniff around.

A familiar accented woman picked up the phone at Caroline's house.

"Michaels residence, can I help you?"

In the background, Evie heard the girls laughing and Jerome yelling, "You better run. I'm going to get you!" It was strange to think of him like that, the Wall Street titan horsing around with the toddlers.

"May I speak to Caroline? This is Evie Rosen." It was frustrating that she had to identify herself, but she knew the next question would be "Who may I tell her is calling?" if she didn't.

She heard the housekeeper say, "Mrs. Michaels, are you available to take a call from Miss Rosen?" Even the freaking maid knew she was a "Miss" and not a "Mrs." Caroline and Jerome probably talked about their unfortunate single friend Evie while turning the pages of their four-volume wedding album. And the whole "Mrs. Michaels" thing was so pretentious. If this had been just five years ago, the conversation would be more like, "Mrs. Michaels, are you available for Miss Rosen to scrape you off the floor of the men's room at Automatic Slim's? Security is on the way." Caroline Michaels (née Murphy) thought being Irish and Texan meant she had a wooden leg. It did not.

Caroline came to the phone quickly and said breathlessly, "Evie, I'm so happy it's you. I have great news. First, though, how is your grandmother doing? Jerome said he knows a few of the trustees at Sloan Kettering if you need any strings pulled."

"Thanks, but things seem to be under control. My grandmother seems eerily calm, which I can't quite figure out. So what's this great news?"

"Just that I have the best guy to set you up with."

Evie gripped the phone more tightly. Caroline didn't offer to set her up frequently. If it were Tracy, she'd suspect it was some hipster friend of her husband's and be totally uninterested. Stasia's scattered attempts over the years led Evie to believe her only criteria were male and single. Paul and Marco claimed to know very few straight men and were frequently apologizing that they couldn't find anyone for her to date. Which was okay with Evie, because she wasn't just looking for "anyone."

"He's very good-looking," Caroline went on. "Black hair. Really wavy and thick. Dark eyes. And he's tall."

"Keep talking."

"He's intelligent, successful," Caroline continued. "He works for—I mean with—Jerome at JCM Capital. Started six months ago. I just met him at the corporate retreat. He's got good schools and all that crap I know you care about."

Did she care that much about pedigree? Or was it the optics? She supposed it was both. Caroline was telling her that this guy was smart, so she didn't need any independent verification, did she? She was upset she was as transparent as celery skin to her friends. She spoke often about wanting to meet a great guy and claimed that she didn't care about the résumé details—"so long as he's nice and smart" was her tagline—but here Caroline was calling her out without a second thought. And she called it crap.

"I don't care about where he went to school," Evie self-consciously fibbed. "Tell me more."

"Well, his name is Harry Persophenis. His parents are Greek."

The image of John Stamos was now complete.

"Anyway, he already has your number and is going to call you. He asked for your e-mail address but I told him your computer was hacked. I didn't want him to think you were a freak."

Evie was grateful. It was hard enough for her friends to grasp why she had disconnected—she didn't want to get into it on dates. She hung up the phone after thanking Caroline, deciding for now to avoid asking her about Stasia. Evie spent the rest of the day feeling optimistic about her new setup. She let her mind travel to ridiculous places—like two years from now when they'd get married on a Greek Island in a ceremony far more picturesque than Jack's Turkish nuptials, then Harry would leave Jerome's office to open his own office where she'd head up a crackerjack team of attorneys as lead in-house counsel.

Energized, she treated herself to a new sweater at a cute boutique on her block and then called Bette to see how she was feeling. She casually let it drop that she had a date coming up. It was a bold move, sharing this information with Bette, who was likely to ask, "Have you met his parents yet? Vhat do zey do for a living?" It was tricky for Evie to cross the two generations that separated them and explain that even if she were dating someone, meeting the family would be out of the question for at least six months.

It was safer in Evie's case anyway.

When Bette first met Jack, she asked him to repeat his last name about three times. "Did you say Kiplitz?" "No, Grandma, he said Kipling." Then Bette proceeded to drop rampant Yiddish phrases into their conversation, hoping to see if they flummoxed Jack. Unsatisfied, or at least unsure of his reaction, she asked him directly which synagogue in London his family belonged to. She nearly choked on her babka when Jack explained that he was only half-Jewish. Evie thought Bette might go into cardiac arrest then and there until he clarified it was on his mother's side, the so-called right side.

"Very nice, bubbela," Bette now responded. "Just enjoy yourself."

Excuse me? Who gave her grandmother an unauthorized lobotomy?

"Tell me, Evie, how vas ze meeting vith Dr. Gold? I'm in good hands?"

"Definitely. And I checked with my friend's husband who trained with him and he said he's a great surgeon."

"You spent some time vith him? You veren't rushing out ze door to get to one of your fakakta exercise classes?"

"You're the one who lives at Zumba Gold. I did speak to him for a long time, and as good as he seems, I still think waiting for him to operate is ridiculous. Don't you want to know the pathology already?" Evie was proud of herself for slipping in the medical terminology.

"No. I've made up my mind," she said firmly, and Evie knew the case was closed.

After hanging up with Bette, she hit Book-A-Saurus, a mom-and-pop retailer on West Seventy-Eighth Street. Everything but the megastores were going extinct on the Upper West Side, and Evie wondered if the owners had acknowledged how apt the name of their store was. She waved to Stella, the owner's college-age daughter whom she'd gotten to know over the past few weeks, and settled on an orange beanbag chair with the latest issues of *New York Spaces, Elle Décor,* and *Veranda.* Evie had grown accustomed to reading there, watching Stella open the delivery boxes, or hearing the locals complain about the erection of a new condominium that would obstruct their views. These little bits of commerce and conversation made her feel connected to her neighborhood—the one she claimed to love but perhaps didn't quite know that well when she was always at the office.

Studying the shelter magazines, Evie was surprised how easily her mind arranged a comprehensive bulletin board of the images she liked, even without the help of Pinterest. The pictures of one deco-style co-op on Park Avenue were so intoxicating Evie decided on the spot to give her studio a moderate facelift. It would be the consolation prize for not being able to afford the one-bedroom apartment she'd been keeping tabs on when the partner dream was still alive. She would repaint her kitchen (maybe in cerulean?) and buy one good piece of furniture. Fran would certainly not object to an advance on her Chanukah present.

After picking up a slice of pizza, Evie returned home with her bag of magazines and settled into her coziest sweats for the night. It occurred to her as she channel-surfed that she didn't know Harry the Greek's vintage. Caroline had been ambiguous about his work relationship with Jerome. She wondered if he was a fresh-from-business-school associate or someone Jerome reconnected with at his hundredth college reunion. Suddenly John Stamos was looking a lot more like Aristotle Onasis. She called Tracy, hoping she would do the reconnaissance for her.

Tracy's husband, Jake, picked up on what felt like the ninth ring, although she had lost count after five.

"Hello?" He sounded dazed.

"It's Evie. You all right?"

"Yeah, I'm just working. I feel like I'm really having a creative breakthrough."

"Oh yeah. With what?" She wondered what it was this time. Slam poetry? African drumming?

"I feel like my latest script's got a lot of potential, you know. I was just revising a key scene where my protagonist's vulnerability really comes through. It's when we first learn that his piano teacher molested him in his grandmother's pantry. I need to find a great director for this project."

Screenwriting. She hadn't thought of that one.

"Well good luck." She didn't dare ask about the children's music he was supposedly producing a few months ago. "Is Tracy there?"

"Evie, just the person I wanted to talk to," Tracy boomed into the phone. It was the second time she'd heard that today. Without being able to e-mail her, it seemed like her friends had lots of important information saved up to share.

"Oh yeah? And why is that? And what's with Jake? I didn't know he was a screenwriter now."

"Well, he is. He's got a lot of different projects going," Tracy responded defensively.

"Got it. I just didn't realize. So what did you want to talk to me about?"

"Well, the reason I wanted to talk to you is because I have a job for you. Seeing as you're unemployed and refusing to use the computer, I wasn't sure what your plans were to find another, um, revenue source. But it just so happens you're in luck."

Evie looked out her window across the street. It was dark, but in the apartment building opposite hers she could make out the silhouette of a man hunched over his computer with mounds of paperwork piled on either side. He looked so damn productive, as did most of the people she took inventory of as her eyes scanned the floors of the high-rise from top to bottom. Her most com-mercial activity of the last few months was a trip to the bank to deposit a fifty-dollar rebate check. She did need to go back to work. Without a job, she'd fixate too much on Bette, simultane-ously worrying about her dying of cancer and wanting to kill her for nagging about her love life.

"Okay, which firm? How did you hear about it?"

"Well, it's not a firm so much as working around a lot of people who are going to be lawyers." Tracy paused and asked Jake to bring her three scoops of Neapolitan. Evie begrudged Tracy's ability to eat anything she wanted now, even if it was only for nine months and she'd look like a house after she gave birth. The forty-calorie no-sugar-added fruit pops in Evie's freezer were an insult to the notion of dessert.

"So it's a teaching job? I would take an assistant professorship if some law school would have me. I don't have any experience, though."

"Nope. Much better. Working with me. At Brighton." Tracy literally squealed.

"What in the world are you talking about? I can't teach high school."

"Not teaching. Lawyering, or whatever you call it. Brighton's in-house counsel was just indicted for income-tax fraud, so they need someone to temporarily fill his shoes while they do a proper vetting for a permanent replacement. And I recommended you." Tracy let the indictment roll off her tongue as if it were sick leave.

"I don't think I'm qualified, Trace. I don't know anything about representing a school."

"Apparently most of the legal work is done pro bono by big firms where the school has connections. You would be more of a liaison. Besides, the headmaster seemed delighted when I suggested an eighth-year associate from Baker Smith. He wants to meet with you right away."

Evie wasn't totally surprised. Her firm's name carried quite a bit of cachet. Bragging rights were among the main things she missed.

"I really appreciate this. I do. And believe me, I could use the money. But I'm not even sure I want to keep on lawyering. Maybe this is a chance for me to start something else. You know, change course."

"And do what?"

Evie had no answer.

"So it's settled. You'll call the headmaster and set up an interview. It'll be so fun to see each other all the time. Though I'm not sure how much longer I'll be able to go in."

"Why's that?"

Tracy cleared her throat. "Something like my cervix is shortening. Or maybe it's softening, and my vagina is shortening. I don't know. Jake is freaking out. My doctor said bed rest is a possibility."

"Sweetie, that sucks. You sure you're okay?" If Evie's doctor ever told her something like that, she would spend the remainder of her pregnancy standing on her head. Hypochondria and pregnancy no doubt made for poor bedfellows.

"I'll be fine. Lots of women get put on bed rest. I just hope we can still have sex."

Tracy was insatiably horny at this point in her pregnancy, a welcome change from the nonstop puking of the first trimester. Last spring, she told the girls in her class that they should never have sex because it could lead to morning sickness. It was an unconventional abstinence lecture, but Tracy threw up so many times during class Evie wouldn't have been surprised if a few of her students had thought twice before rounding home plate, which was a good thing, because based on what Evie heard from Tracy, these city kids were running four years ahead of schedule in just about every way.

"I'll keep my fingers crossed for you. Oh, before we hang up, I need you to look up some guy named Harry Persophonis, or Persophole, or something. You have a job for me and apparently Caroline has a man for me. He works at Jerome's office. Try to figure out how old he is. I'm worried he's ancient."

"Evie, I love you, and I support your decision to quit the Internet. Frankly, it's a human experiment I don't think I'd have the strength to endure. But if you're going to do this, you've got to do it right. I'm not going to be your standby Googler."

Evie grunted into the phone. "Fine, don't. But if this guy shows up with a spare set of teeth in his pocket, you're dead to me."

"You know, I mark my students down if they use excessive hyperbole. I would have to flunk you," Tracy said. "By the way, just how long do you plan to not use the Internet for? It's quite subversive."

"It's not so crazy. Have you read *The Shallows: What the Internet Is Doing to Our Brains?*"

"Um, no. Have you?"

Evie could sense Tracy's sideways glance through the phone.

"Well, not yet. But I'm sure I'll be riveted when I do." Stella at Book-A-Saurus had recommended it to her.

"You'll have to let me know. Seriously though, are you waiting for the *New York Times* to do a feature on you?"

"Certainly not. I'm staying off-line until I turn thirty-five," Evie announced, astonished by how naturally the answer came to her. She wasn't sure she'd make it to May 29, her birthday, but it seemed a logical goal to choose. After all, she was devastated on her last birthday when she'd received only thirty-three "HBD" posts on her Facebook timeline. And she had quit the Internet in June. That would make her hiatus nearly a year long, which had a comforting circularity to it.

When she hung up the phone she snuggled under her duvet, her heels running along the edge of the faux-snakeskin bench at the base of her bed. If she got the Brighton job, even temporarily, she could buy the high-gloss gray lacquer night tables she adored. The modest makeover of her living quarters would certainly get an extra boost. She tucked the covers tightly around her body. Her skin felt electrified as it rubbed against the baby-soft sheets. She had lost her job, lost Jack, and might be losing her beloved grandmother. She had shut off the virtual world—her Black-Berry (if someone had retrieved it from the wastebasket) now in the hands of an eager new associate at the firm and her computer at the bottom of the Reservoir's murky waters. But still a faint optimism crept through her, from her tingly toes to her flushed cheeks as she drifted off to sleep.

Chapter 9

Brrrinnnggg. Brrrinnnggg. Brrrinnnggg. The ringing was incessant. Evie panicked as she watched the bronze bell rattle against the peeling yellow paint on the wall. She gripped her pencil tighter, but her fingers cramped. She wiggled them in an attempt to stop the spasms.

The question at the top of the paper on her desk read:

Discuss the symbolism of ivory in Heart of Darkness. Do you think Conrad intended that symbolism? What are some other possible interpretations of the role of ivory and how would that fit in with the overall themes of the book?

Shit! She hadn't even read that book. In fact, she didn't even remember it being assigned. All her classmates had weathered copies with dog-eared pages on their desks. How was it possible? She was an A student.

She was being asked to write about the symbolism in a book she'd never touched. And the goddamn bell was ringing. How could the class be over already? She looked down at the page in front of her. It was blank. Normally she could fill three to four pages in the sixty-minute exam period. She was going to get an F.

The ringing got louder and louder. Why wasn't it stopping? The teacher was coming down each aisle to collect the papers. How would she explain to Mr. Londino, her favorite teacher, about her abysmal performance on the final? Maybe she could lie and say a family member was sick. Wait, that was actually true.

The bell continued to sound its infernal blast. Instead of Mr. Londino coming toward her to collect the exam, she saw Jack. It didn't make sense that he'd be there collecting the papers, but all of her classmates were comfortably handing over their papers to him, making easy chitchat with him as he passed their desks. He had a Band-Aid around his pointer finger. Must have cut himself slicing again. There was a succulent turkey on his desk with a first-place ribbon pinned to the wing.

"Evie, are you done? Time is up." Jack was standing in front of her desk, wearing faded jeans and a flannel shirt. He had a crumpled half apron sticking out of his back pocket, brown spots visible on the loose strings. "You need to put down your pencil."

Evie didn't want to look up. She had no makeup on. Her clothes were mismatched. She remembered staying up until 1:00 A.M. the night before with Jack, making love and laughing intermittently. So why was he acting like she was a stranger, asking for her test paper like she was just any other student?

"I'm sorry, Jack, I need more time. Please come back to me."

She still wouldn't meet his gaze. She was whispering, and it seemed Jack couldn't hear her over the blazing bell.

"I think you mean 'Mr. Londino.' Evie, your time is up." Evie looked up to see his face. It wasn't Jack after all. It was her high school English teacher, speaking with a Cockney accent, a bizarre perversion of Jack's intonation. Mr. Londino reached forward with his arm, and she noticed the tattooed inscription of a poem on his bicep, visible through his shirtsleeve, but she couldn't make out any word other than ANGUISH. He started to pull the exam from Evie's hand, and though she tried desperately to clutch the test booklet, her fingers and wrists were limp.

And still the bell rang out so loudly she couldn't audibly beg Mr. Londino for five more minutes.

Suddenly she heard the sound of a throaty-voiced woman saying the Dow Jones futures were way up, unusual considering the start of fall was known to be a brutal time for the equity markets. But that didn't make any sense. Final exams were always in the spring. So why was this woman talking about September in her news report?

Evie's panic gave way to confusion, and then after a treacherously long two minutes of delirium, to clarity. She located her hand, buried under the pillow below her head. It was tingling from lack of blood flow. The ringing she had heard was her alarm clock, which after five minutes of growing increasingly loud automatically switched to the local news.

It was all a dream. What a relief not to fail senior English. In reality she got an A in that class and earned a five on her AP exam, all thanks to her profound exposition on *Heart of Darkness*. But seeing Jack, even in her subconscious, still left her feeling squeamish. She hadn't seen his face so vividly since the night they broke up, which was now almost a year ago. The Facebook images of him—the ones where she saw him as a grinning groom—were grainy at best. But his real face, with its shadowy cheekbones and ski-accident scar that divided one of his eyebrows in half, appeared to her in her slumber. And he looked good, with his beautiful bride reimagined as a juicy bird. *The turkey from Turkey.*

There was no need to disinter Freud, Evie thought as she hoisted herself out of bed. She was headed back to high school that day for her interview with the Brighton headmaster, Thomas Thane, an alumnus of the school and a celebrated Shakespeare scholar. The part with Jack appearing as her teacher—grading her, testing her, making her feel small, that was just another REM-sleep twist on reality.

She dressed quickly in a conservative wrap dress with a subtle checked pattern, downed a fistful of oatmeal squares cereal, and hailed a taxi outside her building. Her cell phone rang as she was giving the cabdriver Brighton's address.

"Hi, Trace. I'm on my way to the interview."

"I know. Just wanted to wish you luck."

"Thanks, I'm feeling okay. Can't imagine what he's going to ask me. I hardly think my hostile takeover experience will be relevant."

Evie felt surprisingly nostalgic referencing her Baker Smith work. She wondered if Marianne liked the new associate she was working for more than Evie and if the Calico merger had been derailed by the commodities crisis in Venezuela. When Annie last called, Evie had prodded her for office gossip but didn't get much in response. ("Haven't passed by Marianne's station lately. . . . No idea if any associates in the California office made partner. . . . The frozen yogurt machine has been broken for two whole weeks and nobody gives a damn.") A similar call to Pierce, her fellow *Gossip Girl*–aficionado from the office, yielded nothing of note. ("Sorry, Evie, the boss-man is five feet away. . . . Can't dish now.")

"Oh, it'll be fine," Tracy reassured her. "The headmaster's nickname is Headmaster Tame because he's a softie."

"Well that's good for me, I guess. I'll call you after," Evie said.

"Wait, there's one thing. I'm sure it won't come up, but if it does, I wouldn't really mention the whole off-the-web thing at the interview."

"Yeah, I can see where that might be a problem if I have to do legal research." Evie had already fretted about how she would maintain her web celibacy with a job. She vowed to only use the Internet for work if it proved absolutely necessary. If so much as a tempting pop-up ad appeared, she would log off and figure out how to be a lawyer the old-school way.

"There's that, and Brighton's whole shtick is technological preparedness. They host these lectures like 'Teach Your Kids to Google a Bright Future' and 'Is Your Child the Next Mark Zuckerberg?' I think maybe it's so the parents don't feel bad that they themselves are always checking their phones."

"Yikes."

"Yep. The administration even suggests that faculty members familiarize themselves with the class list, which I'm pretty sure means look up the parents. Sounds awful, I know. But if it weren't for a few really generous families the school wouldn't be able to give out any financial aid. I wish I could siphon some of the money for my New Orleans kids."

Evie recalled Jerome and Caroline making a sizable donation to some prestigious nursery school so that Grace could join the other three-foot titans sucking on silver spoons. And that was just for Finger Painting 101. Evie couldn't imagine the stakes for high school.

"Got it. I'm sure it won't come up anyway. I'll call you after I'm out or maybe swing by your classroom. Thanks again for setting this up."

Evie tossed her phone into her purse and focused her eyes on the TV in the back of the taxi, a marvelous enhancement to traveling around the often gridlocked Manhattan. On the screen she saw a half-naked perky news anchor with a covetous silky bob being manhandled by a grandfatherly figure in a white coat. She leaned over to the screen to turn up the volume, grateful for the distraction.

"And so, you take your hands just like this," the man in the white coat said, extending two fingers like he was directing traffic at an airport, "and work your way around the breast in a clockwise fashion, feeling for any new swelling or lumps. If you prefer, you can do a wedge or up-and-down motion. This should only take you one full minute in the shower."

The anchor kept her plastic smile firm while the old man, who Evie determined with relief was a doctor, squeezed her covered-only-by-a-lace-bra breasts on national television.

"Thank you, Dr. Liman. That was very informative." She paused to button up her red blouse. Her coanchor, a dapper man about ten years her senior with a thick coat of silver hair, leaned into the camera with a coy smile.

"Of course, JoAnne, all the better if you have someone at home who can do the exam for you." The anchors chuckled in unison while the doctor, clearly not used to being on camera, stood awkwardly, watching the banter. Evie turned off the television, thinking she really should call the physician that Dr. Gold recommended for a proper checkup.

Brighton-Montgomery was located on the northern tip of the Upper East Side, where Tracy had told her most of the students hailed from. It was housed in a handsome redbrick building with an American flag and another flag, gold and navy blue bearing a lion's face, hanging from the fourth floor. The marble-stepped entrance to the school was framed by intricate wrought-iron rail-

ings, which she admired as she climbed the steps. The building
looked more like an embassy than a high school.

Class must have been in session because she only saw one or
two students ambling in the hallway. At the front office the headmaster's assistant, a barely legal woman named Keli ("with an
i!" she proudly declared), greeted Evie. She explained that Headmaster Thane was called away unexpectedly to a lunch with an
"esteemed" alumnus who was in town from Paris, so she would be
conducting the interview. The collage of kitten photos on Keli's
computer screen and her rampant use of "like" relaxed Evie's
nerves considerably. After studying her résumé for a minute, Keli
asked a few softball questions about her work style and what excited her about the Brighton job.

After the interview concluded, Evie lingered outside the
building, debating whether to wait for Tracy's lunch break. She
leisurely traced her fingertips on the cool metal of the railing,
acclimating to the feel of the wrought iron. Everything at Baker
Smith was new and modern, with the best in Italian furniture
and sleek office equipment, but it felt more satisfying to be surrounded by something historical. When a few teachers burst
through the front door and eyed her with a suspicious curiosity,
Evie moved on. She alighted the steps and took a left around the
corner, heading north on Lexington.

The neighborhood deteriorated quickly and soon Evie was
surrounded by run-down bodegas and housing projects. The
streets were littered with soda cans and torn candy wrappers that
whirled around the scrawny ankles of the kids dancing to somebody's beat-up stereo. New York City was crazy like that—a few
blocks in any given direction could transport you from the lap of
luxury to someplace downright Dickensian.

Evie wondered if Brighton students did any community out-
reach. If not, maybe she could start a buddy program—matching

upperclassmen with elementary school children who lived just a stone's throw from Brighton's hallowed halls. At Baker Smith, Evie had done pro bono work for nonprofit organizations, helping them obtain tax-exempt status and reviewing their leases and contracts. It was definitely one of the more gratifying aspects of her job, and something she genuinely missed. When she left, she was in the midst of helping a homeless women's shelter in Battery Park City file a request for more government aid. She asked Julia to take over the project for her, and hoped she had been more successful than Evie at battling the bureaucratic red tape. The shelter was probably better off with Julia. Not only would they get her attentive legal work, but she'd probably also drop off cherry scones for the residents on the weekends.

The organizational charter for the Brighton mentoring program was already taking shape in her mind when her phone rang. She hoped it was Tracy so she could share the idea with her, but it was Paul. Her impulse for altruism would have to wait.

"Hello there Miss MIA," Paul chirped. "So nice to actually have some contact with you."

"And with you, my friend," she responded, laughing. She had been lazy about making plans recently, paradoxically finding herself less motivated to do so now that she had more time on her hands. When she was working, each dollop of free time was like a gift that had to be enjoyed to the fullest. Now that she could be social whenever she wanted, there was less pressure to reach out to friends.

"How's life among the Amish treating you? I sent out some racy photos from our jaunt to Ibiza and when I didn't get a snide comment back from you, I figured you were still unplugged."

She sighed into the phone. "Yep, still off the web. It's been okay. Boring, therapeutic, isolating, cathartic. I've got mixed feelings."

"Well, I admire your discipline. What's new with you?"

"Well, if you can believe it, I'm possibly going to be working at Brighton. I'm worried about Tracy though because—"

"I know, her cervix. She texted me from the doctor's office." Evie couldn't deny the jealousy she felt hearing that Paul was being kept up to date in real time.

"She seems to be taking it in stride, though. Anyway, my other news is that my grandmother's sick. My father's mom, Bette. You know the one I'm really close to that I visit in Florida and who comes up to see me every year. She has breast cancer." The words felt heavy on her tongue, like molasses.

"Oh sweetheart. I'm so sorry. Can Marco and I do anything for you?"

She paused before responding. Did she need anything? Maybe some company. The time when reality TV marathons could keep her warm at night had come and gone.

"Well, maybe we can all go out to dinner. I'd love to take my mind off of things."

"Done and done. I was actually calling to schedule some plans with you. Marco and I miss you. Next week's out because I need to go to L.A. for work. Some tart on the Disney Channel was caught doing cocaine in the bathroom of her little sister's elementary school in Beverly Hills. My boss thinks we should have her become a spokesperson for abstinence or something until the dust settles. No pun intended."

"Sounds scandalous. I can't wait for dinner to hear more." Evie reveled in the gossip. Without Perez Hilton and The Superficial, her only dose of Hollywood drama came from the magazines lying around her sketchy nail salon, which she was patronizing less and less since Caroline had exposed her to the real deal at the Plaza.

"But remember, I am computer-less these days. You'll need to pick up the phone again to make plans. Don't forget."

"Understood. You're living under a rock. I got it. Oh, and Evie, we have big news to tell you when I get back. Huge."

"Let me guess. You saw Hugh Jackman in a gay club, confirming what you claim to always have known."

"Wrong! This news, if you can imagine, is even bigger. But I want to tell you in person."

"Okay—well I'm looking forward to dinner now more than ever. Make sure to call me. No e-mail!"

"Yes, weirdo. I will call you. And Evie, your grandma is going to be just fine. Don't worry."

She decided to walk all the way home from Brighton, letting Paul's platitude soothe her for the time being. The sun shone brightly and the air was dry and cool. Evie cherished the clarity in the atmosphere. Central Park, as usual, was overflowing on a nice day—filled with New Yorkers eager to see sunlight reflecting on grass instead of bouncing off concrete. She passed a noisy playground on the east side of the park and paused to watch the schoolchildren and toddlers run amok gleefully. She loved the cadence of their laughter. The shrieks, the chortles and the squeals. They were all so pure.

Evie focused her eyes on a set of identical towheaded girls climbing up a slide. The girls' mother, who looked to be about her age, stood about ten feet away from them. She, chicly clad in an all-ivory ensemble and leaning cautiously against a metal fence, was gripping her PDA tightly, like it was a bomb that might explode if she stopped transmitting bodily warmth to it. She only looked up once to see her kids, presumably to check that they hadn't been kidnapped while she was busy uploading photos of them to Instagram. Ahh, the irony.

"Mom, look at London," one of the twins yelped. "She's sitting backward!"

The mom looked up for a millisecond and gave her daughter a

smile that utilized the minimum number of cheek muscles necessary to lift the corners of her mouth upward.

"Good job, honey," she said. If she'd actually been listening, she would have told her daughter to face forward and quit horsing around. Instead, she returned to her electronic cocoon, oblivious to Evie's disdainful stares.

Evie was grateful she was raised before the era of 24/7 connectedness. Fran's biggest indulgence was to bring along a *House and Garden* to flip through while Evie played at her feet in the sandbox. Sometimes Evie would grab the magazine from her, using the pictures to inspire her imaginative sandcastles. Fran was a working mother, but when she was with Evie she was truly off-duty. If she ever had children, Evie vowed to devote herself to them, and not waste the precious early years pounding away on her phone. Caroline would surely scold her for such sanctimonious thinking. "Wait until you sit on the floor for two hours playing princess," she would say. But Evie liked to think she'd be able to put down her computer if her children needed her, especially if they were precipitously dangling from monkey bars by their kneecaps like the twins she was watching were doing now.

# # #

Back home in her apartment, Evie had flopped onto her couch and flipped on the TV, expecting a quiet night, when her phone rang. The number was marked private.

"Hello?"

"Evie, hi, this is Edward Gold calling. I hope I'm not catching you at a bad time."

"No, no, I'm just watching TV," Evie said. "Is Bette okay?"

"Oh, yes, she's fine. Status quo. I'm out of the office this week and wanted to check in on you and your family. Make sure you don't have any questions for me," Gold said.

"We're good, I mean I'm good," Evie said. "The break before the surgery gives us time to rest I guess. Then the hard part starts, huh?"

"Maybe. Try to stay optimistic. Anyway, you have my number if you need me. I'll let you get back to your show," he said.

"Oh, it's fine. It's just *Antiques Roadshow*. I'm kind of addicted," Evie said.

"I love that show. Have you seen *Pawn Stars*?"

"Every episode."

"So what's the item? On *Antiques*?"

"Right now it's a hideous vase that some guy is claiming was passed down to him by his great-great-grandmother who was one of Peter the Great's mistresses."

"And what do you think?"

"Well, I know it's a reproduction. But that's because I've seen this one. I'm not that clever," Evie said, laughing into the phone.

"Hang on, let me flip it on too. Let's see if I'm any good."

Evie heard some rustling and then the echo of the TV show she was watching. What in the world was going on?

"Now that is ugly," Gold said, referring to a piano being wheeled out that might have come from Liberace's collection.

"You don't like rhinestones on musical instruments?"

"Only on my medical instruments."

"Very funny. So what do you think? About the piano?"

"I'm going to say it's authentic. No one would ever reproduce something so awful. Am I right?"

"Yes!" Evie exclaimed. "Very good. You have experience with this." She settled herself more deeply into her couch, hoping they'd continue to watch the show together.

"I'm just very smart," Gold replied deadpan. "But actually I have to hang up. My daughter just woke up crying. Enjoy *An-*

tiques Roadshow, Evie. Fill me in on the rest when I see you in a few weeks."

"Okay, bye," Evie said, and hung up disappointed. Where was he calling from? She had assumed he was calling her poolside, but with a crying kid in the next room and *Antiques Roadshow* at his fingertips, Evie surmised his vacation was far less exotic.

Chapter 10

"Here goes nothing," Evie said aloud as she ambled to her coffeemaker. At least she legitimately needed the caffeine boost this morning. It was her first day at Brighton. True to his assistant's word, Headmaster Thane had indeed called her just hours after her interview with a few questions and an on-the-spot offer for the position, which he said would remain hers until they hired permanent counsel, a process that could take up to six months.

The school was in the midst of purchasing the adjacent two-story building to create a new computer lab and student lounge, and she would be involved in the contract negotiations. Real estate wasn't her area of expertise, but after eight years of handling multibillion-dollar transactions, the project didn't seem particularly daunting, especially since she'd have outside counsel to call upon.

Grasping her warm mug, she studied her closet's offerings, hoping to find a suitable ensemble for the new position. Tracy wore jeans to teach, but Evie dismissed her denim options in favor of something more professional. She glanced over at her old work clothes. The pantsuits by this point had made their way over to the far edges of her closet, pinned so tightly up against the wall that Evie nearly threw out her back trying to pry a tailored black-and-white-pinstriped one free. Evie slipped it on over an innocuous white blouse.

To her surprise, the waist was loose. The last time she had worn the suit was on a flight to Florence. Foreign travel was one of the carrots Baker Smith dangled in their recruiting manuals. Evie realized fast it was more of a stick; business trips to Europe meant trading in one office tower for another and submitting to painful jet lag. She distinctly remembered the snug waist from this particular suit preventing her from catching even a nap on the eight-hour flight to Italy. Evie didn't really need to lose weight, but she struggled with the last five pounds like almost every other woman she knew. After a satisfactory glance in the mirror she parted her window sheers, tucking them behind the metal rings, which were already securing last year's Christmas bonus splurge: purple silk curtains with crystal detail. The sky was cloudless and Evie noted the few passersby were all dressed for a sunny fall day.

From her closet, she chose a pair of open-toe black patent leather slingbacks. They were date shoes—wearing anything resembling a sandal was tacitly forbidden at Baker Smith. Slipping her feet into the marginally sexy shoes, Evie felt brazen. She was free from the shackles of the closed-toe pumps she was forced to wear on even the hottest of summer days at the law firm. Pools of sweat would collect under her arches. Baker Smith management apparently preferred foot odor to toe cleavage.

She glanced at her microwave clock and dashed outside, shivering from an unexpected chill. The sun promised by the weatherman on last night's eleven o'clock news was missing in action. Evie realized it was practically the beginning of October. Soon jack-o'-lanterns would be on display in her building's lobby and Starbucks would begin promoting its Pumpkin Spice latte. Facebook was a month away from the deluge of children in superhero and princess costumes, not to mention the grown-ups hell-bent on dressing up as slutty versions of every decent profession.

After a torturous wait, her doorman finally succeeded in getting her a taxi, whose interior bore the heavy scent of lamb vindaloo. Now she would arrive at school smelling like she popped out of a tandoor. The traffic was abysmal. Evie observed in horror that they still had fifteen blocks to travel up delivery truck-packed Madison Avenue. Thane told her to be at work at 8:00 A.M., and the taxi TV clock read 7:53. Fuck it, she thought, and reached into her wallet to dig out a twenty.

"Keep the change," she said breathlessly and started hoofing it down the street. In a cruel twist of nature, it started to rain—first a few drops, then in sheets. The once blue sky was now a menacing gray, like a children's book illustration, and she soon was drenched. Her once-sexy, now cursed heels were wedging themselves into every sidewalk crack. Were she not acutely aware of the debris and other better-left-unsaid substances that came into contact with the New York City streets, she would have run barefoot.

After what felt like an interminable power walk, she reached the grand entrance of the school and flew up the marble steps, arriving along with the throng of students dropped off just before the first bell.

She studied the crowd quickly before reporting for duty. They were a rowdy bunch, sounding not that different from the kids she'd happened upon two blocks north of school, this bunch distinguishable only by peaches-and-cream complexions and trust funds. Aesthetically, the Brighton masses were a distant cry from the dowdy lawyers to whom she'd grown accustomed. Highlights ranging from creamy butter to roasted chestnut glistened. Chanel bags rested carelessly on delicate shoulders. Noses worthy of architectural awards pointed toward the ceiling. And that was just the girls.

The boys. They wore snug, but not too-tight, Lacoste shirts in a rainbow of colors. Their hair was equally if not better coiffed than their female counterparts, mussed to gently wind-blown perfection. It was like they had managed to get to school in a different weather pattern than Evie. They stared down at their smartphones as intensely as Evie once had but miraculously sailed through the hallway without collision, as though each of them had a personal trolley track just for them to glide on.

All faces showed the fading signs of restful summers spent soaking up the rays in luxurious surroundings. Brighton certainly wasn't the orange- and brown-tiled tribute to the 1950s high school that Evie attended in suburbia, where Gap flannel shirts reigned. She was scared. Particularly so when she looked down at her wet pantsuit. Earlier this morning she thought it gave her an air of gravitas, but now it seemed impossibly dorky, like something a middle-aged science teacher would pluck from the bargain bin.

She found her way to the administrative quarters and was shown to her office by Keli, the twenty-something feline lover who conducted her interview. It was a cubicle much like the one

Marianne occupied at Baker Smith, with a desktop computer, a phone, and a few file cabinets. How far she'd fallen from the cushy private office with the killer view. She plopped her tote bag onto a simple metal chair, comprehending how much she had taken her last professional resting place—a lumbar-support recliner with adjustable cushions—for granted. Her new space was like a fishbowl, no more than ten feet from the headmaster's leathery den. Discreetly combing the Restoration Hardware two-inch-wide sourcebook would be impossible.

"I'm going to prepare some of your tax documents now to get you set up with payroll," Keli said. "Why don't you walk around the school a bit in the meantime? The faculty lounge is on the second floor and the cafeteria is on the lower level."

"Thanks. I think I'll visit Tracy Loo's classroom."

Evie huffed and puffed up the three flights of stairs to her friend's room, wondering how Tracy could continue to do this five days a week, given her cervical or placental or whatever-they-were problems.

She entered in the midst of a classroom discussion. Seeing the kids up close, Evie noticed the gawkiness beneath the veneer of sophistication. They were still teenagers, pimples and all.

"Emma? Did I see your hand up before?" Tracy called from behind a worn metal desk, with plastic-framed glasses on the tip of her nose and a fuzzy cardigan thrown over her shoulders. She looks so grown-up, Evie thought. My friends and I aren't the students anymore.

"Yes, Mrs. Loo," a chipper brunette in the front row responded. "I thought, like, that maybe *Survivor* was based on *Lord of the Flies*? Did you ever think that?"

Tracy pushed her glasses up the bridge of her nose. "Well, yes, I suppose they both deal with groups that are stranded. But I was hoping you might have something to say about civilization versus savagery. Which impulse do you think Golding is trying to say comes more naturally?"

"Oh," Emma said. "I'm not sure."

"Anyone else?" Tracy asked, hopeful, probably pining for her third-graders in New Orleans. She looked over at Evie apologetically.

"Jamie? What do you think?"

There was no response.

After Tracy called out "Jamie?" twice more, Evie heard a smug "yep" from a student seated in the back row.

"Please try to stay with the class conversation, next time," Tracy admonished, letting him off a bit too easily in Evie's estimation.

"Will do," Jamie responded, and locked eyes with Evie. She felt vulnerable in his gaze, like her fly was unzipped, even though he was the one being reprimanded. Then he looked down, shoulders clenched and brow furrowed, clearly distressed by some diversion on the ground. She began to notice his arms twitching back and forth. The bastard was texting under his desk!

"Class, I'd like to take a moment to introduce my best friend from college. She's going to be working at Brighton temporarily," Tracy said, gesturing at Evie. "If you all work hard and stop texting during class, some of you could have a chance of going to Yale and making great friends like I did."

So Tracy was aware of the classroom shenanigans. Evie gave a friendly wave to the class.

"Stay for a bit. We're working on the first book from the summer reading list." Evie nodded her acceptance.

The students, despite Tracy's ample preparation and fluid Socratic style, just looked glazed over. Maybe it was the atmosphere. The only adornment on the faded yellow walls was a Heimlich maneuver poster and a caged school bell. It wasn't a preschool, but Evie thought much could be done to liven up the place. She'd love to spruce up the room as a surprise for Tracy while she was on maternity leave. Blowing up the covers of the books on the syllabus to decorate the walls would go a long way. She could assemble a crown molding out of famous quotes from the English canon. Soon her creative juices were bubbling over like a shaken soda can and she could barely wait to get started. Tracy would flip. After Teach for America, she'd often remark how grateful she was just to have four walls and a ceiling in her classroom.

With a head cock, Evie indicated to Tracy that she was going back downstairs. At her desk, she saw Keli had placed numerous forms that needed filling out and documents that the headmaster wanted her to read, including the school's charter, operating agreement, and financial statements from the last three years. She immersed herself in reading and making notes, back in lawyer mode as though she'd never left, and before she knew it, it was time for lunch, and the administrative office cleared out like there was a fire drill. She didn't know where to go but filed out alongside her coworkers.

Outside, her cell phone buzzed, indicating a new voicemail from a number she didn't recognize. She was surprised to hear a message from Rick. "Hey Evie, Stasia and I are just checking in to see how you're doing. Give a call if you need anything."

How silly Evie had been to worry about entering his phone number into her contacts. Instead she kept it scrawled on a loose receipt for milk she'd found at the bottom of her pocketbook. She liked to think that if she were the married one, she'd have no problem with a friend calling her husband for advice or a favor. Just as long as that friend was two dress sizes bigger than she was and had a husband of her own. But Stasia was more secure. How could you not be when your hair resembled gold silk and your legs were shaped like number two pencils, even down to the skinny ankles that looked like freshly sharpened points?

Evie picked up a sandwich at the deli across from Brighton, her mind fixated on Rick, Stasia, and their baby once again. It must be that Stasia was feeling so ill that she'd delegated her friendship duties to Rick while she remained out of commission. As she was gobbling her Havarti and hummus wrap on the sidewalk, Evie noticed a figure emerging from a chauffeured black Escalade with tinted windows about twenty yards down the street. The man who stepped out, dressed in a dark suit and tie, looked remarkably like Dr. Gold. It couldn't possibly be him, since she knew he was on vacation and would have no reason to be driven around in a rap mobile uptown, but still she squinted while his doppelgänger walked down the block trailed by a string bean of a woman in a sheath dress and red-soled heels, the kind that added another zero to the price of otherwise ordinary shoes.

Even if it was for Bette's surgery, Evie realized how much she was looking forward to seeing the real Dr. Gold again soon. She must have had a smile on her face thinking about him because as Tracy's student Jamie passed her entering the building he said with a smirk, "Someone's having a good day."

# # #

After work, Evie decided to make the thirty-block trek to see Bette, even though her first day at Brighton had been draining. The acclimation to her new surroundings was not unlike her first day of sleepaway camp. Were the coffee mugs shared or had each person already laid claim to one? Was taking a cell phone call in the office a no-no? Every office had its unwritten rules, and she had no one to turn to for the oral handbook. Actually she'd never been employed anywhere but Baker Smith, other than a million years ago at Rising Star, hawking bat mitzvah dresses to Baltimore's Jewish tweens. Remembering the code to the locked file cabinets, the directions to the faculty lounge, and even the names of her new coworkers at Brighton was exhausting.

Still Evie needed to see Bette.

Evie shuddered when she saw the apartment her grandmother was staying in. Bette absolutely refused to be a burden to Fran and Winston in Greenwich and wouldn't entertain staying with Evie in her "tiny little place." Instead, she'd taken up residence in an apartment fortuitously located less than a block away from Sloan Kettering. It belonged to her friend Esther from Boca, who had inherited the place when her mother passed away fifteen years ago at age one hundred. It was a studio with peeling wallpaper, patchy wooden floors aching to give out splinters, and the ugliest mustard-colored drapery Evie had ever seen. Bette, who stretched a tea bag until her last cup of the day was nothing but faintly tinted water, would never do anything to fix up the place during her stay.

Evie found her grandmother seated on the tattered sofa with the phone to her ear, mid-yenta.

"He's a little on ze short side, but from vhat I remember yours isn't so tall either. Listen, she's thirty-nine, she can't be so picky. I'll give him her number later on today. I gotta go, my granddaughter just valked in." Bette motioned Evie toward a chair next to the sofa.

"Vhat's that?" Bette lowered her voice. "Oh, Evie. No, nobody right now." She moved the phone to her other ear—the one farther from where Evie was hovering. "Almost thirty-five . . . I know . . . I know." Then she hung up and looked up innocently at Evie.

"Who was that?" Evie demanded. "And I'm not almost thirty-five. I just turned thirty-four." Hadn't she? It was only September. Her birthday was at the end of May.

"Carol Goldenberg, from Sunny Isles. I'm trying to find someone for her granddaughter."

The child in Evie wanted to cry out, "What about me?"

"Her daughter is an aspiring puppeteer living in San Diego," Bette continued. "As if anyone can aspire to zat. She vorks as a vaitress to support herself. Who knows vith zese kids? Anyvay, I may know someone living out zere for her."

Evie's pulse slowed. Carol Goldenberg's granddaughter was in California. *And* she was pursuing the art of marionetting. She and Evie were not in the market for the same sort of guy.

"I can't believe you're even fixing people up at a time like this. You should be focusing on yourself."

"Vy not? Doesn't hurt me to try to make other people happy," Bette said with a shrug of her shoulders. "Have you spoken to Dr. Gold?"

"He has a family, Grandma. I saw a picture of his freaking daughter when I met him."

"Vhat are you getting so angry for? I'm not trying to make a *shidduch*. I vas just asking if you spoke to him. Maybe you have questions about my care, zat's all."

Evie softened, regretting being so mercurial. "I'm sorry. I'm just so used to you trying to marry me off. Anyway, I really don't understand why you're waiting for Dr. Gold to operate anyway. I'm sure Sloan has many capable doctors."

"I'll be fine." Bette sighed. "I'm used to vaiting for things." She looked down at her lap and began twisting her sixty-year-old engagement ring around her finger.

Evie was speechless. Who compares having cancer to having a single granddaughter?

# # #

"Bette drives me completely crazy, Mom," Evie whined to her mother over coffee at a café near the hospital. "Totally, utterly crazy." She noticed Fran was wearing a messenger-style purse across her chest, in the style of the tourists who believed Manhattan was a den of pickpockets. Evie did the same thing when she first started law school. Now she walked around with her bag unzipped, usually dangling precariously open from the crook of her elbow. But she had achieved the gait of a confident New Yorker, which in her mind was all the deterrent she needed to ward off thieves.

"I know how much it bothers her that I'm single. But honestly, I have enough problems with my career and with my floundering love life—the last thing I need to worry about is how my being unmarried affects those around me. I swear I could win a Nobel Prize and all Grandma would say is that I have no one to accompany me to Sweden."

Fran quietly stirred her coffee, her expression undecipherable.

"Mom, are you listening? Don't tell me you agree with Grandma? You also hate that I'm single?" Evie slumped into her chair. "I would expect more from you. Bette is trapped in a time warp."

Fran looked at Evie. Her eyes, tender and surrounded by the beginnings of sagging eyelids, were repositories of compassion and wisdom. Evie peered into them and saw her own reflection. It made sense. Fran thought of Evie above everything else.

"Evie, it's not me that it bothers. It's you. If I believed you were okay with being single, I wouldn't care one bit. And neither would your grandmother." Her gaze fluttered down to her pocketbook, where she started digging around for something. "No, she would still care. But I really wouldn't," she added softly.

Evie didn't know whether to believe her mother, truly a woman of the glass-half-full varietal. The meltdown she'd been holding in since visiting Bette threatened to erupt. She lifted her chin, unsuccessfully willing the tears back.

"Honey, I'm not trying to upset you. I just want to have a candid conversation with you. I feel like you being single is this taboo subject between us. And it shouldn't be. I know Bette is more outspoken about these things. But I'm afraid to broach the topic most of the time."

Evie didn't know what to say. At Brighton a few hours ago, she had felt like she had a shot at regaining so much of what she'd lost when she left her old job—responsibility, self-reliance, and respect. Now at coffee with Fran, she felt adolescent.

"I want you to be happy. And yes, I'll admit, I want you to get married. Because I believe that will make you more secure. You have so much going for you, Evie. You're beautiful, smart, successful, outgoing. The list goes on and on. But the fact that you're single makes you forget all of your fabulous attributes. When I look at you, I see insecurity. It kills me. I want to shake you and remind you of all you have accomplished."

Evie continued to listen, even though she felt like she couldn't bear another moment of this honesty session. At least the coffee shop was empty.

"But to tell the truth, I don't really blame you. The world is designed for couples. Practically every movie and song on the radio opines on love. Valentine's Day. Anniversaries. Even restaurants. Not many tables for one or three, are there?"

Evie thought of Jack's restaurants. No small tables for singles. He used to complain about people making reservations for odd-numbered parties.

"It totally wastes a seat that could go to a paying customer," he'd say to her when they were up late gossiping about the evening's patrons and he was tallying the receipts. "And it just looks bad. The asymmetry is very off-putting."

Evie would respond callously, "Singles should just order in."
Maybe that's why he ended up getting married, Evie thought now
bitterly. He wanted to lead his customers by example. And she'd
egged him on.

Evie nodded at her mother to show she was at least open to
hearing more.

"And this is not some antifeminist rant you'd expect to hear
from Bette. Men too feel lonely. Winston was burned by his divorce. He couldn't wait to remarry. When you were young, you
were so precocious. You used to say to me, 'I don't need to get
married. I'm going to get straight As, go to Harvard, and become
a millionaire.' You were seven years old. Do you remember saying
those things?"

Evie essentially did—not from the time she actually said
them, but they'd been repeated to her so often that she could
picture herself at seven years old, pigtailed and chubby, walking arrogantly around their yellow-and-blue Provence-by-way-of-
Baltimore tiled kitchen telling her parents about her future. She
gave Fran another shallow nod.

"Your father and I would just look at each other and think
how much you had to learn about the world. I've never admitted
this out loud—never. But when your father died, one of my first
thoughts was that I would have to go to the Lichts' anniversary
party alone. Can you imagine? That I worried about that after
losing the love of my life? It's shameful, but it's human nature."

Evie jumped out of her seat and came within an inch of her
mother's face. The hostess looked up from her *People* magazine to
see what the commotion was about.

"Are you trying to make me feel worse? I agree with you. I
don't want to be alone, but it's not like I can walk the streets
from nine to five with a 'husband wanted' sign on my back. And

pressure from you and Grandma doesn't help." Evie settled back into her chair and folded her arms across her chest, ready for Fran's rebuttal.

Instead Fran swiveled in her seat to face the counter, turning her back on Evie.

"Excuse me, could we get our check please?"

Evie simmered. Like her father and Bette, Evie had to see any argument or discussion through to a peaceful conclusion. Her mother could just stop a fight midsentence, leaving the other person unnerved and the matter unresolved. Closure was not Fran's biggest priority, while Evie desperately sought it in all things.

"Mom, please talk to me about this. I'm sure you agree that looking for a spouse can't be my full-time occupation. I'm a bit overeducated."

Acting as though it was a big sacrifice, Fran waved the waitress away when she started coming toward their table. But then her face unexpectedly softened and she reached for Evie's hand. The warm touch made Evie shiver.

"Of course I agree. I just think, and don't bite my head off, that you chose to dive into your career to avoid rejection. Even though you complained about the work, you volunteered whenever there was an opportunity to take on additional assignments. Think about Jack, even. Your longest relationship was with a man who didn't believe in marriage. There had to be something there—subconsciously, to make you fall for someone who refused to commit. Thank God you finally broke that off. I swear, I worried you would date him into your forties before you finally grasped that he'd never propose."

Obviously Evie still hadn't told Fran that Jack was married. She didn't want her mother to pity her, or worse, to question what she had been doing wrong all that time to scare Jack off. The Baker Smith debacle had been embarrassing enough. But this was her opportunity to show her mother that she wasn't at fault for her single status. At best, she was the victim of bad luck. At worst, simply undesirable.

"Actually, Mom, Jack got—"

"Hi, everyone, I come bearing chocolates," Winston announced cheerily, his figure appearing unexpectedly in the doorframe of the café. Winston handed Evie a box of Godiva truffles with one hand and loosened his tie with the other. He gave Fran a quick peck on the cheek. Evie smiled back, relieved to put off a conversation about Jack and Mrs. Jack.

"I told Winston we'd be here," Evie's mother said, and then turned to her husband. "How was work?"

"Busy," he said, flagging over the waitress. "You have anything stronger than coffee here?"

The waitress shook her head.

"Okay, then just black coffee please. And a BLT."

"I'm going to head home. The first day wiped me out," Evie said. "Just going to take a chocolate for the road." She unwrapped the gold foil, feeling she deserved at least one truffle after the tongue-lashing from Fran. Plus her pants had been loose that morning.

When she turned to leave with a raspberry cordial in hand, she heard her mother gasp.

"Evie, your behind is sticking out of your pants. I can see your underwear! How can you walk around like that? And at a school!" Fran's shrill voice rang through the restaurant, which of course had gone from empty to semifull in the last three minutes.

"What are you talking about?" Evie asked, reaching her hand back. She palmed the smooth silk blend until the tip of her pointer finger found its way to a hole. Right in the crack.

"Oh my God! How bad is it?" Evie sank back into her chair to hide her exposed derriere. The morning's events ran through her mind in streaming video. Feeling surprised that her pants were loose when she got dressed . . . Walking around the main office to fill her coffee cup . . . Visiting Tracy's classroom and bending over to give her a hug. What if one of the students had recorded her peep show and posted it on YouTube?

She couldn't bear to face Fran and Winston, so she used the jacket she was carrying in her right arm to bury her face.

Her jacket! She had definitely been wearing it at work and had only taken it off when she got to the restaurant to have coffee with her mom.

"I was wearing my jacket!" Evie exclaimed, and she awkwardly slipped into it from a seated position. Rising, she rotated slowly like a lamb on a spit.

"It covers your behind," Fran said, less than impressed.

"Thank God," she gushed. "Now I'm officially leaving." Evie waved sheepishly at Winston and Fran. The truffle stayed behind.

As she pivoted her front foot toward the exit, she heard Fran whisper to Winston: "She complains about being single but a first step would be some decent clothes."

Chapter 11

" 'Commercially reasonable condition' and 'reasonable condition' do not mean the same thing. We've got to go with 'commercially reasonable' or I'm hanging up this phone right now."

The threat to hang up on the conference call came from Louis Madwell, senior partner and head of the white-collar crime division at Crohn and Hitchens, one of Baker Smith's rivals. Their office was located on Third Avenue in what was commonly known as the Lipstick Building due to its shape, but which Evie thought looked more phallic. Based on how Madwell was acting, her vision of his workplace was more fitting. He was a member of the Brighton board of trustees, and, as he told everyone at the start of the call, would be "running the show" for the school. His services were being offered to the school gratis, another fact he brought up at the outset when he urged everyone to be mindful of his time.

" 'Reasonable' means 'reasonable,' " Joe Cayne, a member of the opposing counsel, whose name Evie immediately noted rhymed with cocaine, chimed in. "And that's all we're willing to agree to. Besides, you're not selling anything. This is a school. Why do you need to put in the word 'commercially'?"

Madwell snorted for the benefit of all fifteen people on the call. "At forty thousand dollars a pop, we damn well are selling something. We're selling an education. Which is why when your client turns over the keys to their building so we can put in a goddamn award-winning computer lab, I want the contract to say it will be in 'commercially reasonable condition.' I don't want to come in and find holes in the walls and a rat infestation. You hear me?"

"With all due respect, Louis, my client was running a high-end art gallery in her space. There are no rats in the building. And I can assure you there are no holes in the walls," Caine retorted.

"No holes in the walls? So how did she hang the damn paintings?"

Good point, Madwell. It was time for Evie to interject.

"Gentlemen, we're getting off track here. Can I make a suggestion that I think might please everyone?"

Silence on the line.

"Why don't we change the clause to read that the building will be delivered in 'reasonably habitable' condition? That way we take out the word 'commercially,' which I think we can all agree is making the other side uncomfortable. And our side can feel good that the building will be deemed habitable for students, which I'm sure is what we're all concerned with. How does that sound?"

"I can live with that," Madwell said. "I have a three-billion-dollar lawsuit on my hands right now and I'm trying to keep a client from rotting in an upstate prison for the rest of his life. That's more important than this shit. Joe, can you agree to what the girl said?"

Evie did not enjoy being called "the girl," but she'd heard female lawyers called worse before. There was whispering on the call, which she assumed was Cocaine conferring with his client.

"That's fine with us," he said. "I'll shoot your team over a new draft of the contract and let's try to get this sale wrapped up by the end of the week."

"Thanks everyone for a productive call," Evie said. "Have a good day and please call me if any further issues arise." She rested the phone in its cradle and took a deep breath. Her first assignment as interim in-house counsel at Brighton was going fairly smoothly. She was an old pro at rehashing the meaning of everyday phrases. Similar minutiae in the M&A world might have included a week-long debate on what was better for her client: "Management will report promptly to the investors whenever a significant issue arises" or "Management will report to investors without delay whenever a significant issue arises." It all felt like a futile exercise in dictionary wars. If any problem arose, the matter would be settled out of court. Nobody would consult the contract to parse the meaning of an adverb. This was Evie's first legal assignment outside of a firm, but it wasn't proving to be that much different. Maybe some lawyers got a high from sparring on conference calls and throwing around words like "goddamn" for emphasis, but she wasn't one of them.

"Hey, I know you. Mrs. Loo's friend."

Evie looked up to find Jamie Matthews, the texter from Tracy's class, hovering near her with his book bag slung over one shoulder and a tiny paper cup in his hand.

"If I'd known I'd have an office buddy today, I would have gotten two espressos." He plopped down in the abandoned cubicle next to hers and pulled out a pain au chocolat from a crinkled brown bag.

"Yes, hi, I'm Evie. Evie Rosen. I mean Miss Rosen," she stammered. What the hell should she call herself? She wasn't a teacher. But some level of decorum felt necessary. "I'm filling in as in-house counsel for a while."

"Hi, Evie, I'm Jamie." Apparently he decided what she would be called. Whether he knew what an in-house counsel was didn't seem to matter. "We're going to be office mates. Hope you don't mind."

"Aren't you a student?" she asked, sitting up straighter, forming what Caroline's daughters called "happy back" from ballet class.

"Yep. But I got into a little bit of trouble last year and I kind of made a deal with the headmaster that I would help out in the office during my free periods so that—"

"So that what?"

"So that my suspension wouldn't show up on my student record. I'm applying to college this year. I do filing, make copies, etcetera. Whatever anyone needs, which I guess now includes you." He gave her a devilish smile.

"I'm okay. I don't need any help."

He shrugged. "Suit yourself. I'm here if you need me."

"Thanks." She turned around to face her computer, agitated by the invasion of her already cramped workspace. Who was this kid anyway, with his espresso and French pastries? In high school, she ate Pop-Tarts. At least he was cute, in a boyish sort of way.

She turned her attention back to the contract revisions, but found herself thoroughly driven to distraction by Jamie's presence. His cell phone buzzed every ten seconds, whistling something high pitched and clawing each time a text arrived. She threw a disparaging look his way, but he took no notice. The words from the document on her desk lifted off the page, the phrases "fee simple," "easement," and "right of first refusal" doing a legal circle dance. It was time for more caffeine. She rose to fill her mug from the communal pot with the plastic handle (how she missed Baker Smith's Nespresso machines on every floor) and noticed a striking young girl enter the office and head straight for Jamie's chair. He moved over to accommodate her tiny bum, and the two of them sat nibbling on his pastry and giggling.

"Evie, this is Eleanor, my girlfriend," Jamie said when he caught Evie staring.

"Eleanor Klieger," she said with poise, adding her last name, as though it was supposed to mean something to Evie. Maybe it was. "It's nice to meet you." She had one of those enviable raspy voices. Like she was on day four of a cold and all that was left to show for it was a sexy hoarseness and a throaty laugh.

"It's nice to meet you too," Evie said, feeling suddenly ancient in front of these two.

While she doctored her coffee with milk and sugar, Evie watched Eleanor's lithe body movements as she tucked Jamie's long hair behind his ear and popped a piece of puffed pastry into his mouth. She admired Eleanor's ensemble—cropped jeans, a red-and-white-checked shirt and navy ballet flats with discreet double Cs on the side. The clothing hugged her body enough to show off her excellent figure but was loose enough to make it seem like she didn't want anyone to notice. Evie knew this sort of girl. She woke up with perfectly tousled hair, had an infectious laugh, and was a good student without being too intimidating.

She was ditzy when it was cute to be ditzy; clever when it was cool to be clever.

"I have to get to study hall," Eleanor said, popping up from the chair and planting a kiss on Jamie's cheek. "Let's meet at the vending machines before practice, okay?" Of course Eleanor played a sport. Field hockey or lacrosse most likely.

"I'll see you there, babe."

Evie looked back at her contract. The words had quit their pesky dancing and she was able to concentrate. Jamie moved about the office doing random tasks, many of which involved him reaching into upper cabinets, taking his polo shirt northward to reveal a chiseled core. When he was done with his work, he tapped her on the shoulder and said, "Great to see you. I'll be back tomorrow."

Later that day, in the faculty bathroom, Evie ran into Tracy, who was struggling to snap an elastic belt she was wearing to support the weight of her tummy. Evie fastened it for her.

"One of your students works in the office right next to me. Jamie, I think," Evie said. "His desk is about a millimeter from mine. I've already met the girlfriend."

"Oh yeah. That's Jamie Matthews. I think his parents helped make that arrangement. He was apparently about to get tossed out of Brighton. Half the kids here worship him. I'm not quite sure why."

"He seems nice enough," Evie said.

"Not very good at English, though."

# # #

After a week of sartorial failures, the nadir of which was the pants-splitting episode, Evie decided it was time to invest in a wardrobe that was more suitable for Brighton. With the smug

Jamie punching in for duty almost daily and Malibu Barbie Eleanor dropping in for visits, Evie felt compelled to take her look up
a notch. She asked Stasia to accompany her on a shopping outing.

She was still peeved that Stasia had never returned her call,
especially knowing that Rick must have shared that her grandma
was sick, but she let her curiosity about wanting to sniff out a
baby bump override her grudge. They met at the J.Crew in the
Time Warner Center, which was the closest thing Manhattan
had to a mall. Evie loved walking into the front entrance of the
shopping center because of the two giant nude Botero sculptures,
known as *Adam* and *Eve,* who stood in permanent greeting. At
twelve feet tall each, they made Evie feel delicate and childlike,
and when she walked right up to them they reminded her that her
issues were quite inconsequential in a city of eight million people
with struggles of their own. Oddly enough, Evie found the feeling
of not mattering all that much comforting.

Evie waited for Stasia at the base of these two sculptures, and
when her friend showed up ten minutes late looking haggard and
ill, Evie felt sorry for making her travel all the way from SoHo
for a J.Crew run. But then again Stasia still hadn't officially announced the baby, so it wasn't really fair for her to expect special
treatment. She didn't even giggle when Evie pretended to reach
for Adam's massive genitalia.

After an hour fussing in the cramped dressing room together,
Evie was satisfied their mission had been a success. She found
periwinkle and hunter green corduroys, two A-line skirts, an as-
sortment of cashmere crewnecks, and a hot pink peacoat with
chunky buttons. Stasia provided decent commentary but seemed
preoccupied the entire time. When she didn't even try anything
on, Evie grew more convinced of a pregnancy.

"How's the new job going?" Stasia asked while Evie compiled
all of her garments to take to the register.

"Proving to be surprisingly similar to my old one."

"Well, that's good, right?"

"I'm not sure. At least I know what I'm doing."

It was Evie's turn to pay and she approached a clerk with retro glasses and a shrunken flannel shirt. Evie deduced from the U SUCK sticker he had affixed to his cell phone that he was the sort prone to eye rolling.

"Thank you for shopping at J.Crew," he said lifelessly while removing the antitheft sensors from Evie's new clothes. "If you provide your e-mail address, you can enter a contest for a thousand-dollar shopping spree."

Evie gave him a knowing smile. "And exactly how many spam e-mails will I have to endure to enter this supposed raffle?" she asked, putting air quotes around the word "raffle."

"Um, I'm not really sure," he responded with a careless shrug, his attention diverted to a ping from his phone.

"Oh, I'm sure J.Crew and whoever else they sell their mailing list to will be really considerate and only e-mail me when it's very important," Evie said sarcastically. As she spoke, Stasia gradually inched away from Evie.

"Well, guess what?" Evie went on. "I don't use e-mail. I don't even have a computer. Or a BlackBerry. Or an iPhone. Speaking of which, I don't think you're supposed to be using yours while ringing me up."

That got his attention.

"Listen," he said. "You can just opt out of the daily e-mails and still enter the raffle. Want to give me your e-mail address or not?"

"I wasn't lying. I really don't use e-mail." Despite the growing line behind her, Evie persisted. "People are so addicted to technology these days. It's really changing the way people relate to each other—and not for the better. How many times a day do you check your e-mail? Be honest. Thirty? Forty? And do you actually learn anything important from Twitter or Facebook? Think about how much time you waste with that nonsense. You get what I'm saying, right?"

"Hey, Pretentious," a voice boomed behind Evie. "Can you maybe finish up this little speech later?" A middle-aged woman carrying a pile of gray and brown slacks tapped her on the shoulder. "Some of us have lives to attend to."

"Sorry," Evie mumbled and sheepishly handed over her credit card. But she was still happy she spoke up, soccer mom with the stack of earth-tone pants be damned.

"Evie," Stasia said, pulling her by the elbow toward the exit. "I think you've got to tone it down. Like, now."

# # #

The next morning, Evie stood in her bra and underwear eyeing the spread of new clothes on her sofa, coffee mug in hand. Her stomach still looked pouchy, despite her subsistence on grapefruit since the shame of the pants-splitting. Facing the high school girls every day was rough. They were skeleton thin, despite scarfing down Dylan's candy by the bagful and drinking Red Bulls, their metabolisms still a decade away from decelerating to a grinding halt. Eleanor, the leader of the pack, had a particular lightness about her; she bubbled like a human soft drink and her peers couldn't seem to wait to drink her in.

Watching her glide like a ballerina into the office resurrected Evie's feelings of insecurity from her days at Pikesville High. Eleanor, who even managed to pull off her granny name with aplomb, was the Upper East Side version of Cameron Canon, the most desirable girl at Evie's high school. Once when Cameron wore a white jeans skirt to school in the dead of winter, half the girls showed up wearing the same outfit the very next day. Only the day Cameron wore it, a light snow was falling and she looked like a fairy princess who commanded the weather gods to produce snowflakes to complement her outfit. When the rest of the girls mimicked her the following day, a heavy rain turned the day-old powder to slush and mucked up everyone's outfits, including Evie's.

To say Cameron was Evie's rival would be to elevate Evie's social status to beyond what it was. Evie's competitiveness with Cameron was strictly internal. They were actually pretty friendly, though Evie never felt like she knew her all that well. They were in the same group, the "cool" crowd, though Evie felt at most times that she was hanging on to this group with a far more tenuous grip than its other members. She was more concerned with her grades than the rest of them. In retrospect, she couldn't pinpoint why she was so hung up on making the honor roll instead of having fun. But there was a certain security she found in her books that she could never find at a party. Study hard—get a good grade. It was a predictable path for the most part. Be nice to everyone—well, there was no guarantee that would lead to being popular.

Who would have thought Cameron would be back to haunt Evie on a daily basis in the guise of the gorgeous Eleanor? And Evie was back to her old habits, this time copying Eleanor's style while dressing for work. Mixing some of her old standbys with her new J.Crew garb, Evie chose a checked shirt similar to the one Eleanor wore the first day they met and paired it with narrow-cut beige trousers. She didn't own the Chanel flats, but there were a pair of black knockoffs in her closet that got her 90 percent of the way there. Instead of skipping makeup altogether, she worked carefully on her eyes, shadowing them with a light taupe color and finishing her face with a dusting of bronzer on her cheeks and a light gloss on her lips. Finally she wound a round brush through her hair, running a hair dryer over her locks to smooth

and contour the layers. When she was done, Evie noted with pleasure that she didn't look all that different from the senior girls.
Sure there were more laugh lines around her lips, but who could
complain about imperfections caused by smiling too much? She
topped off her ensemble with a swingy fall cape, which put a bit
of a superhero spring into her step.

With perfect punctuality, she sauntered into the office with
ratcheted-up confidence, but no one was there to appreciate her
makeover other than the school accountant, a portly gentleman
in a bolo tie who had done nothing so far to disprove her suspi-
cion that he was a mute. Jamie filed in midmorning during a
study period, and she embarrassingly took pleasure in his visible
approval of her appearance. She took up his offer to help, putting
him to work creating binders with the latest version of the sale
contract for the members of Brighton's board to review.

"I've been waiting for you to trust me enough to help you," he
teased.

To avoid having to use the Internet, she had her counterpart
at the seller's law firm e-mail the contract to Jamie's personal
account, NycLaxDude@gmail.com, which she explained away
with some absurd story about her e-mail account being hacked.
It was improper for a student to see the details of the school's
multimillion-dollar purchase, but Evie knew from sharing an
office with Jamie that there was basically zero danger of him
reading any of the sensitive material. They sat side by side, a
mismatched pair of assembly-line workers, Jamie handing her
each collated copy of the contract for her to insert into three-ring
binders. How far she had fallen from the days of merging S&P
500 companies.

"That's my mom," Jamie said, pointing to a page in one of the
contract's appendices.

"Excuse me?" Evie said, not sure she had heard him correctly.

"In the list of trustees. My mom is a board member." He ran his finger over a hyphenated last name—a double-barreled, Jack would say.

"Your mother is Julianne Holmes-Matthews? *The* Julianne Holmes-Matthews?" Julianne, and her firm Holmes (how lucky was that last name for an interior designer), was the darling of *Architectural Digest,* her projects featured every month without fail. A château in Paris, a dacha outside Moscow, a penthouse in Tokyo—her clients flew her around the world to design their residences. Her style was renowned—described usually as modern but with old Parisian flair. She'd juxtapose steel doors and apothecary tables, white Thassos countertops and vintage bar carts. It was perfection. She, the Anna Wintour of home decor, was perfection. Her offspring? Evie studied her juvenile coworker once again. Perhaps a bit less so.

"Yeah. She's a decorator," Jamie said, without the necessary alacrity. "She just did Bono's place."

Holy crap.

"Actually, she's coming in to school. She's supposed to see the new building and, I don't know, give her opinion or something."

Julianne Holmes-Matthews was coming to Brighton. She had to meet her.

"When is that?" Evie asked casually, but not really casually at all. "I like her work," she added a bit more coolly.

"Not sure. She's in Beirut now but I'll text her and find out. Do you want to meet her or something?"

"Sure, yeah. Whatever."

"Okay, I'll hook it up."

"Thanks," Evie said. "There are some provisions in the contract pertaining to the build-out that I'd love to go over with her."

That was completely false. But Jamie, as in most matters, was none the wiser.

# # #

It was the end of the workweek at last, and Evie had plans to visit
Bette again after school. She was bringing along a few accessories
to embellish her grandmother's dreary surroundings. There was a
good chance that her mom would be visiting too, since on Fridays
her theater troupe always "rested their voices," and she and Evie
would finish off their conversation from the coffee shop. Bette's illness was forcing the Rosen family into closer contact than usual.
And there was just something about cancer and hospital settings
that made everyone feel entitled to catharsis at will, especially
Bette. Her grandma had gone from tapping to pounding her sapphire engagement stone, and was prone to dropping matrimonial
references apropos of nothing. It was easier to be at work making
binders with Jamie, whose stock had basically quadrupled since
she'd discovered his esteemed lineage.

Eleanor appeared at lunchtime, undeniably pretty in her lacrosse uniform (*knew it!*), and motioned him outside with a fu-
rious wave of her hand. Evie watched their quarrel unfold just
outside the office door. Eleanor's arms were folded across her
chest and her head solemnly down. Jamie was thrashing about
clumsily, trying to put his face in Eleanor's line of view, difficult
considering she was a foot shorter. When he rested his hand on
Eleanor's shoulder, Evie noticed it droop a bit, subtly resisting
his touch. Even with their shiny hair and clear skin, Eleanor and
Jamie still couldn't escape dating's hellish grasp. They looked
like characters on one of those high school soaps Evie guiltily
watched. Only this time she was catching the live show.

Eleanor unexpectedly reached into her book bag, if an oversize
Louis Vuitton tote could ever be called such a thing. She whipped
out her iPhone, thrusting it into Jamie's face. She was so petite,
she had to stand on tiptoes to reach him. When Jamie looked at

the screen, his face changed abruptly. His eyes closed for longer
than a normal blink. He exhaled deeply and reached to take the
phone from Eleanor's grasp, but she pulled it back forcefully.
Evie gasped at Eleanor's unexpected strength and the bickering
lovebirds turned to face her.

Eleanor gave Evie a pained look and scurried away. Evie was
left alone in Jamie's gaze. She felt exposed as he walked slowly
toward her.

"She's ridiculous. Let's just get back to work." He hunched
over his desk, and she noticed that his hair was thicker than that
of any guy she'd been on a date with in the last five years.

"Want to talk about it?"

"Too long of a story, and it would all sound very immature to
you," Jamie said. "But thanks."

"Well, I'm here if you change your mind."

"It's all right. I'm gonna get something to eat actually," he
said. "Mind if we finish on Monday?"

"No, go ahead."

Famished herself, she headed to a wicker bench she'd discovered in front of a sundries shop around the corner from
Brighton. Sometimes Tracy joined her for lunch, her cervix fortunately holding strong enough to allow her to continue working, but today she had an English department meeting.

As Evie nibbled on her homemade PB&J sandwich (pear, brie,
and jambon—a Jack special) and a bag of grapes, she thought
about Jamie and Eleanor. Maybe their fighting was juvenile, but
some of the arguments she and Jack had would also have sounded
childish to an observer. They used to bicker about him flirting
with the waitresses in the restaurant, which he copped to but
said he was doing it for "morale." They tussled about him canceling multiple plans to visit Evie's family, which he defended by
saying he had calls with distributors or needed to review payroll.

Evie would always back down—Jack had a way of making her complaints seem petty, even when at the outset of the argument she was sure she was right. She had bullied men twice her age at board meetings, outmaneuvering investment bankers and corporate titans with quick-thinking and silver-tongued arguments, but Jack made her feel as much like a child as her third-grader's paper lunch bag.

"Evie?"

She heard a man's voice just as she was coughing up a bite of whole wheat bread she swallowed too quickly. She looked up, surprised to be discovered in her obscure lunch spot.

"Dr. Gold?" Evie asked, trying her best to stifle her choking. "What are you doing up here?" He was smartly dressed in a navy suit with a subtle windowpane pattern, and loafers that would have been too stylish if they weren't so worn in and faded. His horn-rimmed glasses were peeking out of his breast pocket. His yellow tie appeared conservative, but when Evie looked closer she saw it had tiny zebras all over it.

"He's here because of me," a tiny voice said in a botched British accent. A little girl appeared from behind his leg, licking a lollipop the size of her head. She had precious pigtails, tied up with satin navy blue ribbons, and wore a plaid jumper with Mary Janes that reminded Evie of the shoes she wore as a little girl. She was the spitting image of her father.

"You must be Olivia," Evie said, giving the little girl a big smile. The child was ravishing, with twinkly eyes and sun-kissed hair, appearing even more cherubic than in the photo she had seen. It was hard not to experience joy just looking at her.

"Livi, this is Evie," Dr. Gold said. "I met her through work."

"Oh, are you sick?" the girl asked, losing her accent slightly.

"No, no. My grandmother is sick and your daddy is taking care of her," Evie explained.

Olivia stuck out her tongue and gave her lollipop a once-over.

"My daddy makes everyone better," she said, looking up at him with sheer adoration.

Evie fixed her eyes on Dr. Gold.

"I thought you were away," Evie said.

"It's more of a stay-cation," he replied. "I had a lot of things to get done—one of them being getting my scrumptious little girl into kindergarten. We have our interview at Brighton today."

Brighton had a lower school located one block away from the high school. It must have been Dr. Gold who she saw the other day, but why in the world would he be emerging from a chauffeured SUV? Medicine didn't pay that well. And the wife? Evie didn't get a closeup, but she hadn't pictured Edward with a willowy style maven in Louboutins.

"My mummy is late, as usual," Olivia said. The continental affect was back.

"What's with the British—?" Evie started to ask.

"It's a long story," he said, shaking his head in a hopeless gesture. "We're working on it. Right, Livi? Speaking in your normal voice?" He gave her a kiss on the head.

"Righty-O, Daddy," Olivia exclaimed, jumping into her father's arms, her dress flying up in the air to reveal hot pink princess underwear. Evie had a strong urge to plant a zerbert on the small of her back.

"How's Bette feeling?" Dr. Gold asked Evie.

"She's good. Keeping busy meddling in everyone's lives," Evie said with a laugh, hoping he knew she didn't mean that maliciously.

"Ahh, yes," he responded with a mysterious look. "I just spoke to her briefly regarding the preop testing and she told me you were working here, which is why I'm not altogether shocked to run into you."

"Good ol' Bette," she said, wondering when her grandma and he had spoken. She'd just played Rummikub with Bette yesterday and she hadn't said a word, but then again why would she have?

"You're lucky to get such a huge treat," Evie said, addressing Olivia again. "You have a very nice daddy."

Dr. Gold leaned in close to Evie, so much so that she noticed a tiny speck of white foam on his jawline. She reached over and wiped it off of him, tempted almost to suggestively lick the cream off of her finger.

"Shaving cream," she said, surprised by her boldness.

"Thanks," he said, still leaning in close to her ear. "Livi's mom isn't really late. It's just she's not a big believer in candy, so I brought Olivia up early for something special."

"Ahh, I see," Evie said, and they shared a knowing smile. She was disappointed, though, not to get a better look at his wife, just to satisfy her curiosity. Would Mrs. Gold be gorgeous and sweet, the third piece of their flawless puzzle? Or would she be bucktoothed and ill-mannered, leaving Evie to wonder why some women had inexplicable luck to land an ideal man and spawn the loveliest child?

"What are you saying about me?" Olivia asked, tugging at her father's hand.

"Just that Mommy doesn't love sweets. And that you're my best girl."

"You're my best daddy," Olivia said. The pure love and free exchange of affection between father and daughter was enough to make Evie crumble.

"Well, I better get her face cleaned up before we get caught," he said, gesturing toward the sticky layer of pink sugar stretched across Olivia's cheeks. Evie was sad to see them go. She happily would have chatted with them longer, let anyone passing by think the three of them were actually the perfect little family.

"I'm not done with my lolli yet, Daddy!" Olivia exclaimed. She looked at Evie. "Are you a teacher here? I love my teachers. Yesterday I got three stars in school because I was the best at cleanup."

"Mommy forgot to tell me that last night," Dr. Gold said, looking at his daughter, who had settled herself on the bench where Evie had been sitting previously. She was blowing air into her cheeks like a blowfish.

"Nope, I'm not a teacher. I'm a lawyer. I'll let your daddy explain what that is. It's not nearly as cool as being a doctor. Or a teacher." Turning to Dr. Gold she said, "I know you've got to get to your interview. It was nice to run into you. I'll see you next week for the surgery Dr. Gold."

"Please, it's Edward. It was good to see you too," he said. She thought she saw him look her over approvingly, and she was grateful that she had on one of her Eleanor-inspired outfits today. He didn't know she was mimicking a sixteen-year-old.

"Bye, Olivia," Evie said, wishing she had a little toy or something to give her.

"Cheerio," she responded, full-on British schoolchild. She hopped off the bench and started to gallop down the street, pulling her father along with her, leaving Evie to wonder what the story behind that accent was.

Dr. Gold turned back to wave to her as he was dragged away. Evie gave him a sultry smile that was not an altogether appropriate way to communicate with a married man being led away by his child. She stood quietly watching their figures get smaller as they walked hand in hand down the street.

"Excuse me. I think I may have left your bag on that

bench—or someone did." A middle-aged woman with a wild streak of white hair running through a jet-black bob tapped Evie on her arm, breaking her steady concentration on the retreating figures of Dr. Gold and his daughter.

"What?" Evie asked.

"Your bag," the woman said, pointing to Evie's tote, which in fact she had left unattended on the bench.

"Oh, yes, thank you. I was distracted."

"You're welcome," the woman said. She looked vaguely familiar to Evie. Maybe she was a Brighton parent and they'd seen each other in the hallway?

"I'm just glad you didn't leave it behind. I carry my entire life around in my bag." She lifted her weighty red leather satchel for Evie to see the overflowing papers inside.

That's how she knew her! In the bag, Evie spied dozens of brochures from Allman-White, one of the city's top real estate brokerage firms. This woman, with the unmistakable skunklike hair, was the broker for the apartment Evie had been drooling over online.

"You're the broker for that one-bedroom on West Sixty-Sixth Street, aren't you?" Evie asked. "I remember your picture from the listing."

"That's me. Emmeline Fields, at your service. Were you interested in seeing the apartment? The owners have just reduced the price by five percent." She produced a business card from her wallet and placed it in Evie's hand. "This is definitely a buyer's market."

"Oh, um, not really anymore. I had been considering it a while ago."

"Well, I'm doing another open house on Sunday, so please come by. For the free bagels, if nothing else. Take a show sheet. It has all the information you need." Emmeline placed the pamphlet directly into Evie's tote bag so she couldn't even protest.

"Thanks, but I don't think I'm going to be able to come," Evie said, feeling uncomfortable. She tried her best not to look at the brochure in her hand, but the photo of the streaming sunlight pouring in through the southern exposure windows in the living room was irresistible.

"You know what's better than sex?" Emmeline asked.

"Uh, no. What?"

"Manhattan real estate. See you Sunday."

Chapter 12

It was only a matter of days before the details of the teenage drama Evie witnessed outside the school office unraveled. Evie ventured into the Klieger Teachers' Lounge, no doubt named for Eleanor's family, after she discovered with disappointment that the outdoor bench she favored had been sold earlier that morning. She overheard a few middle-aged teachers discussing the rift between Eleanor and Jamie. They were so engrossed in the gossip nobody even looked up when Evie entered and settled herself at an empty table with her lunch bag.

"Apparently, someone put a photo on Facebook of a Labor Day Hamptons barbecue at the Matthews place in Montauk, right on the ocean, and you can see Jamie in the background kissing another girl. I heard she goes to boarding school in Switzerland and her family was staying with the Matthewses. This was while Eleanor was away with her family in St. Tropez." The teacher who was speaking, a haughty-looking woman Evie recognized from the day of her interview, appeared tickled to have the scoop. Peddling teenage dirt, she didn't seem quite as intimidating as she had a few weeks ago.

"So are they breaking up?" another teacher, dressed in a dowdy navy skirt and ill-fitting floral blouse, asked breathlessly, as though the outcome of Jamie and Eleanor's relationship might have even the slightest impact on her life. The other teachers huddled in closer.

The teacher with the inside track spoke again.

"Well, apparently Jamie is trying to claim that this all happened the summer before, and now Eleanor's friends have been Skyping with some kids they know in Europe who go to school with this mystery Swiss girl to determine if he's telling the truth."

Evie was simultaneously intrigued and shocked. Eleanor and Jamie were good-looking enough to warrant attention for sheer attractiveness, let alone their social standing. But to see these teachers discussing their students' personal lives with lust was still uncomfortable. Was it possible that her teachers at Pikesville High, like Mr. Londino or Ms. Robidoux the French teacher with the permanent runs in her stockings, chatted about Evie and her friends during their free periods? Probably not. The Manhattan teens provided far more interesting fodder.

A man who had been sitting one table over rose to join the group. Evie knew from studying the yearbook she had found in the office that he was Mr. Molinetto, the physics teacher. He was a nerd from central casting, with Coke bottle glasses and a faded short-sleeved button-down adorned with a polyester brown tie.

"It's from this summer," he said authoritatively and waited for all the teachers to give him their full attention. "One of the students left their Facebook account open in the library, so I took a look. You can see a guesthouse if you look closely at the photograph. I distinctly remember that just last December Jamie's family was involved in a lawsuit with their neighbor over the construction of a guesthouse. Apparently the neighbor claimed the additional structure on the Matthews property would interfere with the sound of the waves crashing. It was covered in all the Hamptons blogs."

Which you follow? Evie questioned, stifling a sharp wince.

The other teachers looked at Molinetto in awe. They were obviously impressed with his detective skills and didn't seem remotely troubled that he had looked at a student's Facebook photos.

"Then it's settled. He did cheat on her," one of the teachers said emphatically. "The only question is how long it will take Eleanor to prove it. It's probably best they break up anyway. If they ever got married, it'd be sure to violate antitrust laws."

"Oh, she'll figure it out soon enough," another teacher said. "There are no secrets on the Internet."

With that sentiment, Evie could strongly agree.

# # #

A few days later, Paul's number flashed on her cell phone as she was walking toward Bette's apartment after work. Bette's surgery was scheduled for the next morning, and Evie was feeling thoroughly nauseated. So much was riding on whether the cancer had spread, not to mention that the surgery itself had many attendant risks. It was difficult to sleep, difficult to eat, and certainly difficult to concentrate at work. As much as Evie was dreading the next day, she also couldn't wait for it to pass already.

"Where were you last night?" Paul demanded when she answered.

"I was in pajamas watching TV. Where were you?"

"I was at Caroline's place, with everyone else, celebrating Annabel's engagement. I was hoping to set up the dinner plans we talked about. Why didn't you come?"

Annabel was Jerome's daughter from his first marriage. Evie had only met her a few times. She knew Caroline liked her well enough. Things were awkward between them in the beginning because they were only five years apart, but after some missteps they decided to embrace the weirdness and become friends.

"Oh shit. I don't even remember getting an invitation. I wish Caroline had reminded me."

"There was no invitation. This isn't her real engagement party. It was just a little impromptu thing to celebrate, since her fiancé just proposed this week. Caroline e-mailed everyone about it with details. She wanted us all to be there because Annabel's mom was coming and she needed protection."

So that's what things had come down to. How many other things had she missed because she hadn't been checking e-mail or responding to Facebook invites? Her own closest friends couldn't even remember to call her for a party. No wonder she'd been sitting home alone so much the past few months.

"Anyway," Paul went on, "you missed my big announcement."

"What's that?" she asked, not actually that curious.

"Marco and I are having a baby!" he shrieked into the phone.

"What?" Despite the noise of the traffic whizzing by, she could swear she heard her eggs, nestled inside her aging ovaries, crack open. And she barely had enough good ones left to spare.

"You're going to be an honorary aunt. How excited are you?"

Not as much as I should be.

"You there?" he asked.

"Yeah, I'm here. That's great news. But how?" It was the best response she could muster. Her voice had a thinness she couldn't mask.

"Well, obviously we were dying to become parents. So we started researching. And we found this group of women in Alabama, of all places, that are willing to be surrogates for couples trying to conceive. They're called the Belly Bringers. Isn't that name brilliant?"

"Brilliant," Evie responded, enthusiasm wanting. Paul didn't seem to notice.

"So, basically, we flew down to see Ann, our Belly Bringer, last spring to deliver our sperm to her. It took, and she's due in late January. We didn't want to say anything until after the wedding and when we were sure the baby was healthy. Anyway, she got injected with both of our sperm, so we will never know which one of us is the biological father."

Evie pictured Paul, skinny, tall, and pale, and Marco, shorter, muscular, and dark. She didn't think the baby's real daddy would be quite the mystery that Paul imagined.

"So what do you think? Amazing, right?"

Evie knew exactly what she should say. She should tell her friend, who had never been anything other than kind to her, that she was thrilled for him. That he'd make an excellent father. That the baby was lucky to have him and Marco as dads. That she couldn't wait to play with the little cutie and buy him or her tiny socks. That she might even take up knitting to celebrate the arrival of this glorious child. But she couldn't find a way to bring those words from her brain to her mouth. So instead, she said something quite different.

"Don't you think you're kind of rushing into this? You just got married. Don't you want to enjoy the child-free life a little?" She didn't offer Paul a chance to defend himself. "Listen, forget I said that. I'm so happy for you guys. Honestly, congrats. But I'm on my way to visit my grandma so I can't really talk. I'll call you back."

She walked the rest of the way down to see Bette in a huff, aggrieved by the pedestrians too busy texting to walk a straight line. Paul and Marco didn't even have biological clocks to worry about, so why were they in such a damn hurry?

She dialed Caroline from the base of Bette's building on the pretense of asking about Annabel's party. Mostly she wanted to know if Caroline thought Paul's baby news was as absurd as she did. He and Marco had been married for approximately ten minutes. After a dash of small talk about Pippa's ballet recital, Evie asked about the engagement party oversight.

"I feel terrible about that, I really do. But honestly, it was such a last-minute thing—I didn't even remember that you don't have a computer anymore. It was just a small gathering anyway. You didn't miss anything. There was no one there worth meeting."

"I do leave the house for reasons other than to meet a guy, you know," Evie said hotly.

"Of course you do. That came out wrong. I just mean it was the same old crowd. You would have been bored."

"Well, was Harry there? The guy you were going to set me up with?" She tried to sound casual and breezy. "I never heard from him."

Caroline's mind churned audibly into the phone, click click click.

"Oh, sorry 'bout that. I think he's back with his ex-lady now. That's what I'm hearin' from Jerome." There was the Texas twang. Enough said.

"Care, tell me the truth. Why didn't he call me?"

"I told you, back with an ex. Some long-distance somethin' or other," Caroline said, sticking to her story like an alibi.

"Care, it's me. I can take it. You'll be helping me by telling me the truth." Evie hoped Caroline wouldn't parse that argument, since it wasn't clear how it would help her at all.

"Fine," Caroline capitulated. "But it's ridiculous."

Evie heard high-pitched crying in the background. The cause, from what she could hear through the phone, was a lost princess costume. In the time it took Caroline to soothe her crying toddler by promising to replace the Cinderella outfit first thing tomorrow, Evie thought she would burst from a mixture of dread and curiosity.

"Okay, I'm back. Pippa is a hysteric. She could be your daughter," Caroline said, chuckling. "Anyway, I'll tell you, but you can't take this seriously. He found some picture of you online and then asked how old you were. I guess he thought you were younger."

Evie was equal parts incredulous and indignant.

"You and I are the same age!"

"I know that. I guess he didn't realize how old I was either. I swear I was too mad on your behalf to even be flattered. It's stupid. He's stupid."

Evie pictured Caroline's line-free smile and taut body, her platinum hair and wrinkle-free lids. The skin probably came from some high-priced dermatologist pumping rat poison into her and the body was the result of seven days a week of SoulCycle, but nevertheless, the results were age-defying good.

"So he thought you were like twenty-something and then saw my ugly mug and decided he better check my birth certificate?"

"Evie, stop. These finance types like dumb young models. Forget him."

"Forget the guy who thinks I need a walker? Gladly."

They went back and forth until Caroline offered to put Jerome on the phone to assure her of her youthful looks, which Evie declined before hanging up. She was no longer in the mood to dissect Paul and Marco's news.

Which picture of her was it that sent Harry running for cover? She was desperate to find it and call Google headquarters to demand its immediate removal. But she was powerless. Not that she'd even know which photo of hers he had found so unappealing. Even though she had quit the web, the goddamn Information Age was still killing her love life.

Her phone rang a minute after she hung up. It was Caroline calling back.

"I know you're annoyed right now, but I wanted to mention that Annabel met her fiancé on OkCupid. He's a statistics professor at NYU. And pretty cute," Caroline said. "There's really nothing taboo about online dating. Maybe you ought to give that a try again."

"Well you can tell him, and Annabel, that based on my experience, I believe it is 'statistically' impossible that I will find someone online," Evie said. "I'm too preoccupied with my grandma to date right now anyway."

"All right, I was just suggesting. Did Paul tell you his great news yet? About the baby? Gracie and Pippa are going to be so excited to have a little baby to play with."

"Yes, yes. It's thrilling all right. Listen, I'm gonna hang up," Evie said, ending the call abruptly. Obviously Caroline did not share her reservations about the new baby. She leaned her head back against the exterior of the building and closed her eyes, letting the harshness of the bricks massage her skull. She did not share Annabel's luck in the cyber-dating complex. A month after her breakup with Jack, when she found herself still dreaming of his creamy sauces and succulent desserts, she made a date with someone whose profile listed his occupation as "culinary industry." He was, in fact, a busboy at Katz's Delicatessen on Houston Street. To say he was a poor-man's Jack was the understatement of the century.

"Waiting for someone?"

Evie opened her eyes and saw Edward Gold, dressed in his white coat and khakis, peering down at her.

"No, no," Evie said quickly. "I was just making some phone calls before going up to see Bette."

To her surprise, Edward settled himself down on the curb next to her.

"Well, then I hope it's okay if I join you. I've got my dinner in here," he said, lifting a white plastic bag. "I just finished meeting with one of my research assistants at the office and I'm starving."

He pulled out a Styrofoam container of piping hot Chinese food. It smelled heavenly. Evie was sure it was from one of the sketchy-looking places around the hospital where she would never eat.

"Of course not," Evie said, secretly thrilled. Since their encounter near Brighton, Edward had been on her mind more than she liked to admit. She found herself bringing him up in conversation, telling Bette how precious his daughter was, and mentioning to Tracy that he was applying to Brighton.

"Want some?" Edward asked, holding lo mein noodles under her nose with his chopsticks.

"No thanks," she said, worried she'd make a mess of herself if she attempted to eat Chinese food in front of him.

"Well, if you change your mind, I have plenty here," Edward said. "So why am I finding you sitting outside Bette's building cradling your head? Are you worried about tomorrow?"

"Yes, among other things," Evie said.

"As for Bette, I promise the surgery is actually a very routine procedure, and even if the cancer has spread, there are treatment options," Edward said. "Regarding the other things, you'll need to elaborate for me to be helpful."

Evie inhaled sharply, and the grease from the Chinese food wafted so deeply into her nostrils she could feel the MSG clogging her brain, making it harder to decide whether she should share her litany of problems with Edward. On the one hand, she didn't want to bother him with her petty problems, like being jealous of her gay friend for becoming a parent before her or envying Stasia for her ideal marriage. On the other hand, Edward was outside of her circle, and it would be a relief to unload on someone who could be more objective than any of her friends. He was proving incredibly easy to talk to and seemed to have a genuine interest in getting to know her. In many ways he was a superb confidant.

"I guess," Evie started, "I'm starting to worry about meeting someone."

"Really?" He looked surprised. "I would think someone like you would have many offers."

"It's not really the offers that are the problem," Evie said. "Not that they're pouring in. I mean, I get some. It's that I need to find someone that I connect with. Everyone I really fall for has some complication. Like they won't commit or they're—I don't know—married or something."

"Married doesn't sound good," Edward said, and Evie wondered if he thought she was referring to him.

Was she talking about him?

Hard as it was to admit, especially to herself, she supposed she was. She had a crush. A crush on a married man. A man who was going to slice open her grandmother tomorrow. A man with a child. A child she'd met. This could go absolutely nowhere good.

It had been building for a while. She'd done her best to bury it, but her attraction to Edward was nearly gravitational. Even though they'd only seen and spoken to each other a handful of times, just studying the proportions of his face turned her on. Their conversations went far beyond the contrived biographical synopses proffered on first dates. No matter what he shared about himself, she always wanted more. What TV shows did he watch besides *Antiques Roadshow*? Did he read fiction or nonfiction? What was his best childhood memory? She was used to wanting guys to ask her these questions. To get them ready for the All-About-Evie quiz they'd take before her bridal shower. Now it was the reverse. And she found that thirsting for information was a hell of a lot more exciting than dishing it out.

"Right, of course. I'm not a home-wrecker or anything." She looked at Edward to judge his reaction, but his expression gave nothing away. "I don't even know why I said that."

"Of course not," Edward said. He fished around the plastic bag from which his dinner emerged. "Want one?" He handed her a fortune cookie and cracked open one for himself.

Evie ripped open the plastic cover of her cookie.

"So you think the answers to my problems may be inside?" She nudged his knee with her own, the brief contact enough to summon goose bumps to her flesh.

"Definitely," Edward said. "I make all major decisions based on fortune cookies."

They laughed together, and Evie felt certain they were sharing at least some kind of moment, albeit one clouded with ambiguity.

He unfolded his tiny slip of paper and said, " 'You are a life-saving doctor who men want to emulate and women fall in love with.' " He held the white scroll in front of her face. She leaned close to read the red lettering.

"It says 'You will learn Mandarin this year,' " Evie said, giving his arm a gentle shove. "But very funny."

"So let's see yours now," Edward said.

Evie opened her cookie, trying to think of something witty to say to match Edward. Nothing came to her so she just read aloud from the paper: "You are gifted in the art of seduction."

"See?" Edward said. "These things are foolproof."

"What are you talking about? Now I know they're crap. I wish I was gifted in the art of seduction," Evie said, batting her eyelashes in mock flirtation.

"Maybe you are and you don't know it."

Evie grunted. "Trust me, I'm not," she said, and she felt the pangs of stress and sadness return. "I'm thinking of freezing my eggs. I know that's not really your area of medicine, but maybe you can recommend someone for me to see. I'm getting older, I'm single, and I feel like it might be a good idea for me to do this. That way, if it takes me another ten years to meet someone, at least I'll have young, healthy chicks on layaway." She thought of Harry the Greek as she said the last part.

To her relief, he didn't look at her like she was possessed, nor did he inch his body away from hers.

"Evie, I think you need to slow down. Obviously we just met recently, but I do understand why you'd want to think about freezing your eggs. If you need a referral, I can get one for you. Just take a deep breath first. You're a smart and beautiful woman, Evie. You have time to sort everything out."

"Thank you," Evie said, keeping her gaze fixed on one of her shoelaces. Talk was cheap, and she didn't know how much of what he was saying was genuine or just meant to make her feel better on the cusp of Bette's critical day. "It's been a difficult few months. I appreciate everything you're doing for my grandmother." She decided to leave it at that and let him extricate himself from the awkward conversation. To her surprise, he chose not to escape.

"Evie, where's all this coming from? You seem so full of life.

You always make me smile, and I'm dealing with people who have cancer all day."

"Really?"

"Yes, really," Edward said. He began to wrap up his dinner in the plastic. She thought he'd rise to leave but instead he stayed put.

"So how in the world did you end up with the Brighton job?" he asked. "Bette said something about a 'godforsaken law firm' and a friend of yours who's a teacher. I couldn't really follow."

She offered him the long version: the years at Baker Smith, the grueling meetings, the endless hours, and the canceled dates and vacations. The only part she left out was the reason for her dismissal, making Edward think she was one of many victims in a harsh round of layoffs. She shared stories she'd never told anyone before—about the time she forgot to fax signature pages for a $200 million merger to the opposing counsel so she backdated all the documents. She told him about stealing a steady stream of office supplies for no apparent reason and about losing the epic power struggle with Marianne. She even told him about how she stashed a few shots' worth of vodka in a water bottle in her bottom desk drawer for whenever the pressure got to be more than she could handle.

"I do that too. Before a tough surgery that I'm really nervous about."

Evie eyes widened. But a moment later she registered that he was joking, and she let out a big bellowing laugh. She couldn't remember the last time she had really laughed out loud, emanating something more than a halfhearted chuckle.

"I'm fairly certain that my friend Stasia is pregnant," Evie said, diverting the conversation back inexplicably. "The one who is married to Rick Howell."

"Is that what's making you want to freeze your eggs?"

"Kind of. Well, it's contributing. I guess I just started worrying that time was getting away from me. Now that I'm not going to be a partner at the firm, I feel like I lost my Plan B, maybe even my Plan B-plus. Partnership was going to be my baby, if I never had a real one. Ideally I'd have had both, of course. Well, maybe not a partnership, but something equally satisfying."

Evie glanced at her watch. A half hour had passed already. Evie started to feel sorry for keeping Edward from getting home on time. Mrs. Edward Gold could be waiting for a kiss (still in those painful Louboutins perhaps) or a nanny might be staring at the clock, hoping to be relieved for the day. Olivia too would be missing him. She hoped Edward's wife appreciated the gem she had at home. Maybe she was a career woman herself, an investment banker still at the office where a thick pile of papers on her desk obscured a group of framed family photos. Or maybe she was a doctor too—a pediatrician perhaps. That could explain why she'd restrict Olivia's sweets. She could also be a stay-at-home mom, whipping up well-balanced multicourse dinners, paying bills, and planning fabulous family getaways without breaking a sweat.

"Go on," Edward said, and Evie surmised she had him for at least a few more minutes.

"The way I see it, there's no one I'm interested in right now. Or who is interested in me. I'm thirty-four. So let's say I meet someone a year from now. We date for two years before getting engaged. He'll probably be some commitment-phobe so it'll take forever for him to pop the question. Then we'll get married a year later. Then we'll try to have a baby, but I'll be ancient by then so it'll take forever. I'm fairly certain my fallopian tubes are tangled or clogged or something."

"You think you have hydrosalpinges?" Edward looked at her in earnest.

"What in the world is that?" She had no idea what he was talking about, but the medical jargon was kind of sexy.

"What you just said—blocked tubes. I assume you have no evidence for this?"

"It's more of a feeling. But now do you see why I want to freeze my eggs? It's insurance."

"Your logic is nuts. But I still like you." He knocked his knee gently back against hers. "Based on your fallopian tube comment, I'm going to assume biology was not your best subject in school."

"My only C. Ever."

"Ouch. Too bad I didn't know you back then. I was a biology tutor in college."

Feeling the pull of Edward's magnetic charm, she began to regret sharing the warts-and-all version of her life story. Not that it really mattered. This was no date. Still she liked the idea of him believing she had her shit together, even if it was far from true.

"I really think you've gotten ahead of yourself," he said. "But all this talk of your eggs has got me jonesing for an egg cream. Can't be any worse for me than my takeout from Shanghai Pavilion. There's a diner one block from the hospital that makes the best chocolate ones. Want to grab one before you head up to see Bette?"

She knew she couldn't say yes. It would be too painful to sit across the table from Edward and keep wishing their relationship were more than platonic. If she learned anything from her breakup with Jack, it was that self-preservation was not something to be neglected.

"Thanks, but I'd better get up to see Bette and then I've got an airport run," she responded. "Though I'm happy to see my problems were able to whet your appetite."

It was a shame to waste such a good line on a married guy, but wasn't that just her luck?

Chapter 13

Fran tasked Evie with picking up Aunt Susan from the airport the night before Bette's surgery. Susan had finally decided to grace everyone with her presence after Fran finally lost her cool on the phone. Her aunt feigned regret and said she would be there soon, apologizing for having been so busy with "stuff."

Evie didn't dare complain about the airport run because at least her aunt was taking shelter in Greenwich. So after her unexpected talk about egg freezing with Edward and a five-minute visit with her grandmother, Evie picked up Tracy and Jake's clunker of a car and headed out to LaGuardia to await her crazy aunt.

Susan's flight was delayed three hours, which Evie didn't know, since she couldn't track the flight. After arriving early and cringing when she saw the FLIGHT DELAYED sign, she found an airport lounge where she alternated a glass of white wine with sips of club soda and eavesdropped on the snippets of conversation among the motley crew of travelers. When her aunt's flight arrival was finally announced, Evie was a touch light-headed.

At the baggage carousel, the interchangeable black suitcases spinning on the conveyor belt put Evie into a trance. She zeroed in on one bag in particular, which had a bright yellow-and-pink polka-dotted ribbon tied to its handle. Who was that unabashedly joyful that they would choose a bow suited to an Easter bonnet and think *That's me . . . That's how I'll know which suitcase is mine*? Not a weathered New Yorker, a washed-up professional, or a beat-up romantic like herself, that was for sure.

She didn't notice Aunt Susan coming toward her.

"Evie, come here!" Aunt Susan enveloped Evie in a bear hug. She smelled like body odor and citrus. It didn't help that Evie's head was pressed into Susan's hairy armpit, no doubt bathed in homeopathic deodorant made from plants in her backyard.

"Hi, Aunt Susan," Evie said. Her aunt was dressed in a brown linen muumuu. Concentric circles of turquoise necklaces and a Southwestern-style poncho folded into the crook of her arm completed the look. Her hair hung long and loose, a sloppy mess of gray and chestnut waves. Susan was Henry's younger sister by seven years, but now she looked eerily older than the way Evie remembered her father, with deeper wrinkles than her dad's skin ever had the chance to develop.

"Evie, I'd like you to meet someone." Aunt Susan was beaming. *F—.*

Susan must have brought a boyfriend with her. Another crunchy hippie to smell up Tracy's car. She looked past her aunt, trying to catch sight of the dreadlocked Phish-T-shirt-wearing middle-aged man who was sure to deliver death by heart attack to Bette. There was no one like that in sight, just men in suits and mothers anxiously gripping their little ones.

"Evie, this is Wyatt." Susan wheeled over a stroller that was positioned a few inches away from her. She turned it so the baby faced Evie.

"Wyatt is my son," Susan said, and she lifted the baby from his snug car seat.

Evie was stunned. She had to be hallucinating.

"Aunt Susan," Evie said, speaking cautiously as she focused her eyes on the baby nuzzling her aunt's neck. "Wyatt is black."

"Well of course he's black, Evie. I adopted him. From Ethiopia. I know. It's very Angelina Jolie of me. But I swear I had the idea first."

"I don't think adopting a kid from Africa can be patented," Evie said, still unable to take her eyes off the tiny child curled up against Susan's body as though it was the most natural thing in the world. "Wow, Susan. Just wow."

"I know," Susan gushed. "And don't you just love the name? It had to be Wyatt."

"As in Wyatt Earp?" Evie asked, naming the only famous Wyatt she knew.

"As in Sheryl Crow. She named her adopted son Wyatt. I've always felt that she and I are kindred spirits. His full name is Wyatt Ocean Rosen. It's perfect, isn't it?"

Why not? The kid was already destined for therapy.

"Perfect."

"And what a gift for my mom. I'm making her a grandma! That's got to improve her spirits," Susan said.

Evie was aghast. "She's already a grandma. I'm her grand-daughter, remember?"

"Oh right, I'm so silly. It's just you're already so old, I forgot you're someone's granddaughter. Well, now Bette has a boy and a girl." Susan laughed giddily. "Evie, I can't wait to catch up. Your mom agreed to put me up in Connecticut, but the truth is that I wish I were staying with you. I miss life in the big city." Before heading west, Susan had lived in the East Village and sold pottery on the corner of Avenue B and Twelfth Street. She'd probably be horrified to discover how gentrified the once-beatnik enclave had become, with doormen-attended high-rises and, gasp, a 7-Eleven.

"Yeah, that's too bad. But you wouldn't want to disappoint my mom by changing plans, right?" Evie said, adding in a silent prayer.

"No, no. Of course not. Plus Wyatt will have his own room at Fran's. She said your place is tiny." So Fran knew about Wyatt. *Interesting.*

"It is. Minuscule, really." For what may have been the first time, Evie delighted in her apartment's limited square footage. If not being able to afford the larger apartment meant not putting up Susan and her imported child, then perhaps not making partner had a bright side after all.

After they got the rest of Susan's things and piled into the parked car with Wyatt strapped up tight in his infant carrier in the backseat, Evie turned to her aunt.

"So Grandma has no idea about Wyatt?"

Susan fiddled with her handbag, a crocheted monstrosity overflowing with baby paraphernalia.

"You know my mom and I aren't close. I could never give her what she wanted. She wanted me to marry a nice Jewish doctor, have kids, a white picket fence, the whole nine yards. Your dad, on the other hand, gave her exactly what she wanted. Which was easy for him, mind you, because it was exactly what he wanted too. Anyway, the point is, I felt like I was always disappointing her. The whole East Coast pace just wasn't for me. I needed someplace where I could be freer, so I moved out west. You know all this."

"And?" Evie asked, because she felt there were things that Susan wasn't saying.

"And I think that was the right thing to do," Susan said, still playing with the seams of her bag where the strings had started to fray. "But, in some ways she was right. About having a family. Which is why I adopted Wyatt. I did really start to feel like something was missing. I suppose telling Bette about Wyatt would sort of be like telling her she was right all along, and I wasn't ready to make that phone call yet. Make sense?"

Evie nodded but kept her eyes on the traffic. Susan was actually making sense.

"So, I guess she'll be in for a big surprise tomorrow when I show up at the hospital with Wyatt."

"Aunt Susan, don't take this the wrong way, but tomorrow is a nerve-racking day for Grandma. I think maybe Wyatt should stay home and just you come to the hospital. We don't want to shock her or anything."

"But I have no one to watch him."

Evie pictured Caroline's fleet of nannies and housekeepers.

"Don't worry, I've got just the place you can leave him for a few hours. He'll be perfectly safe and well looked after."

"Okay, you're probably right," Susan said.

Evie put on the radio and they listened for a while to the oldies station in silence. In the rear-view mirror, Evie could see the baby had fallen asleep sometime after "Crocodile Rock."

"So how old is Wyatt?"

"Seven months. He's an Aquarius. You know I'm a Virgo, which normally would clash, but in our case I think it's why we have such a good yin-yang dynamic going."

Evie looked at the road signs. Only eight more exits and she could deposit Susan in Greenwich.

Susan started twiddling with the tuner just as Evie's cell phone rang from inside her purse.

"Would you mind getting that, Aunt Susan?"

Susan picked up the phone.

"Hey Fran, I think we're almost there." Then she was quiet for a whole minute. "Okay, then, I'll see you first thing tomorrow instead."

Evie's intestines formed a pretzel.

"Evie, honey, your mom said Winston thinks he hit a gas valve while he was doing some renovations. They're all staying over at a friend's house tonight. Looks like Wyatt and I need to camp out with you instead," Susan said, smiling broadly.

If that gas leak turned out to be a false alarm, Evie vowed to never speak to her mother again.

# # #

"I like your place, Evie," Susan said, when they finally arrived after circling back to New York and dropping the car in Tracy's garage in Hell's Kitchen. "Good taste runs in the family. My place in Santa Fe looks kind of similar."

"Thanks," Evie said, relieved she'd already decided to redecorate.

"So, where do you want us to bunk?" Susan asked, lifting Wyatt into the air.

Greenwich.

"You can take my bed. I'll sleep on the couch."

"Thanks, I was hoping you'd say that. Wyatt is a real screamer if he's not comfortable. If it's all right, I'll start unpacking and give Wyatt a bath."

Once Evie heard the bathwater running, she called Caroline to ask if Wyatt could stay at her apartment tomorrow while Bette was in surgery.

"Fine," Caroline said. "But you owe me for this. I have no help tomorrow, so I'll have to watch Grace, Pippa, and your aunt's baby by myself."

"You have no help?"

Caroline grunted. "Hey, don't forget who's asking who for a favor."

"I know, I know. I'm sorry." Evie's call-waiting buzzed. Bette. "Listen, thanks a million. My grandma's on the other line. I gotta take this."

Evie clicked through.

"Hi, Grandma," she said. "You feeling okay?"

"I'm fine, bubbela. I just vanted to make sure zat everything vas okay vith Susan. I hear she's staying vith you now."

"Yup, everything is fine."

"How does she look? I can only imagine," Bette said.

No, actually you can't. Evie thought of Wyatt. That sweet little infant, who did nothing but coo and smile and rock his precious baby clothes, had no idea where he'd landed.

"She looked happy."

"Vell, zat's good to hear. It's so embarrassing in front of ze doctor zat my only daughter is first coming to see me now."

"Who cares what Dr. Gold thinks about us? He's not going to botch the surgery because Susan is a little kooky," Evie whispered. "Is there anything else, Grandma? You need your rest tonight."

"Yes, Evie-le. I know zis is going to sound odd to you, but it's so unusual I have you and Susan together in one room. I vas hoping to take a nice family photograph tomorrow. So I vanted to ask you to dress up, vear something beautiful, put on makeup. Do everything to look special so I can get a nice picture of ze three of us."

"But you're going to be in a hospital gown," Evie protested.

"Ve'll do it before I change. Please. It's important to me."

"Okay, Grandma. Whatever you want."

"Vonderful. You're going to look beautiful, I'm sure. Just vear a dress. Don't be afraid to put on a little extra blush."

Evie assured Bette she'd apply her bronzer and blush tomorrow with a heavy hand and wished her a good night's sleep.

After what seemed like hours of crying, rattling, and Susan bopping around Evie's apartment with Wyatt balled up in a tie-dye sling, he fell asleep.

When the apartment was finally quiet, Susan approached Evie.

"Can I ask you something, Evie?"

"Sure," Evie said. "What's up?"

"You certainly seemed taken aback by Wyatt today. I know it's shocking, but I did e-mail you about a dozen photos of him a few weeks ago. I was surprised you never even wrote back. Maybe I had the wrong e-mail address."

"Actually, I never got your e-mail. I stopped using the Internet about four months ago. Haven't checked my e-mail since the end of June. Just kind of couldn't take it anymore—the social media rat race, if that makes any sense."

"Evie, that's wonderful," Susan said. "I totally get that whole off-the-grid thing. In my community, lots of people don't even have cell phones, let alone computers. We're all about personal interaction. Not letting the Information Age overtake us. You should come visit me. I think you'd really connect with the people out there. Especially now that I know you're part of the antitechnology movement. We're more alike than you think, Evie."

I'm not part of any movement, Evie thought. But she didn't dare let her conversation with Susan devolve into anything bordering on philosophical.

"Yes, you should definitely come," Susan said, getting more excited about the idea. "You'd get to bond with your nephew more."

"Again, he's my cousin," Evie said to her aunt, who just couldn't seem to grasp family tree fundamentals.

# # #

Walking the halls of Sloan Kettering at 6:00 A.M. in three-inch heels, a shimmery dress, and bronzer applied like war paint, Evie felt like a prostitute targeting sickly men. Caroline nearly passed out when Evie and Susan dropped off Wyatt at the crack of dawn. "You going clubbing after the surgery, Evie?" she asked. Evie couldn't even wear the trench coat she grabbed on her way out the door because it just intensified the hooker look.

The operating wing of the hospital was freezing, and Evie's bare legs were goose bumped, the hair on her arms standing at attention. Thank goodness Susan's appearance took some of the attention away from her. Evie's aunt was robed in her own version of dressed-up—an extra turquoise necklace topping what must have been her nicest housedress, and yes, Birkenstocks with socks.

"Okay, my mom said we're supposed to meet in the preop room. Bette should already be there." Evie was annoyed she had to shepherd her aunt, who was visiting the hospital for the first time. "I guess that's where we'll take the family photo."

"Okay." Susan shrugged, and continued to trot alongside Evie. "Feels strange not to have Wyatt in the photo, don't you think?"

She treated Susan's question as rhetorical.

"I just want to get this picture over with and put my normal clothes back on before someone sees me," Evie said, trying to rush Susan along, who insisted on pausing in front of each hospital room to sneak a glance at the inhabitants.

"All these infirm people. Wedded to traditional medicines. I wonder how many of them have tried naturopathic remedies. You should meet my holistic healer, Evie. He grows a root hydroponically that I swear cured my arthritis."

"Let's not get into any of that today, Aunt Susan," Evie said. "Grandma's a traditionalist, and today is her surgery, so probably best not to mention your herbalist to her." They were about twenty feet away from the room where they were supposed to find Bette, and Evie wasn't sure she'd make it that far without strangling her aunt.

"I agree with you, Evie." Evie spun around when she heard Edward Gold's voice.

"Dr. Gold!" Evie turned beet red. He was garbed in teal medical scrubs and his sandy hair was pushed back by a surgical mask. Instead of the Crocs she'd seen him in before, he had on white Converse sneakers. The getup was almost too perfect, like he was playing doctor on a primetime show. It was all too easy to picture him saying, "Nurse, this patient is flatlining. Paddles, stat!"

"Edward," he reminded her. "You look great." She watched the doctor's eyes travel from the roots of her blow-dried hair to the tips of her pedicured toes. It occurred to her on some level she'd been hoping to run into him.

"I'm Susan," her aunt said, extending her hand to Edward before Evie could explain why she was dressed for a party on the day of her grandmother's surgery. "Bette's daughter. You must be one of my mother's doctors."

"Edward is Bette's surgeon," Evie explained.

"Evie didn't mention how handsome you are," Susan said, batting her eyes at him.

"Susan!" Evie yelped, grabbing her aunt by the elbow with a bit of force. To think her aunt was actually flirting with Edward.

"Evie, how could you leave that out?" Edward asked with an endearing smile. Evie wanted to crawl into his dimple and hide.

She did her best to regain composure and attempted sarcasm. "It's hard to imagine."

Edward laughed. "I forgive you. So, should we go see Bette?" he said, taking another long look at Evie before he started down the hallway.

"Yes," Evie said. "By the way, I just want to explain my, um, appearance. Bette insisted that I dress up. She wants to take a family photo, since my aunt is in town. I feel ridiculous."

"Nah, you look beautiful," he said. "Makes getting up at this early hour for surgery worth it."

Huh? Edward seemed to be overtly hitting on her. What was that about? She didn't want to lose respect for him. Even if he wasn't hers, she liked the idea of knowing men like Edward existed. Fate wouldn't necessarily collide her with another one like him, but it was reassuring to at least know these unicorns were out there. Thinking of him stepping out of the bounds of his marriage, even with just casual lip service, was disheartening. She moved to ground the conversation back in practicalities.

"So how come you're here already? I thought the actual surgery doesn't start for a few hours," Evie asked.

"I wanted to be there when Bette gets her sentinel node injection. She needs to get five hefty shots, and I wasn't sure how you and the rest of your family would feel about being in the room with her then. It's intense. She could use someone to hold her hand."

That was the Edward she knew and admired.

"That's really kind of you," Evie said, wishing she could say more. But she felt restrained in Susan's presence.

Bette was sitting up in her hospital bed when they entered.

"Susan," she gushed, and tears began streaking her powdered face.

"Hi, Mom."

Mother and daughter embraced while Evie stood to the side.

Next to Bette's bed was a huge bouquet of pink azaleas. Evie squinted to read the card: "For my favorite gal in CV Towers. Looking forward to your healthy return. Yours, Sam." It was nice to see they'd reconciled—that the rumors of him playing shuffleboard with the condo hussy were overblown. Why shouldn't old people date? If her grandmother wanted to subject herself to the misery and heartache of relationships, who was Evie to stop her?

"Back with Sam, I see?" Evie said, gesturing toward the flowers. "You haven't mentioned him in a while."

Bette shrugged her feeble shoulders. "At my age, you learn to be forgiving. I've always believed it's better to compromise zan to be alone."

"I know that, Grandma." Did Bette actually think she was telling her something new?

"I'm sure you don't agree. And you shouldn't. Don't settle, Evie-le. You don't have to."

Just when Bette did surprise her, Edward entered.

"Good morning, Bette. You look beautiful," he said. "I'm afraid though that you're going to have to take off your jewelry before we get started." Evie didn't like the way Edward was throwing around his compliments, using the same word to describe her and her eighty-one-year-old grandmother. Maybe he hadn't been flirting with her after all.

Evie stepped outside to let Susan and Bette reunite more. Her mother and Winston were in the hallway, arranging trays of coffee, yogurt, and muffins. Edward tapped Evie on the arm and motioned for her to follow him outside the room. They gathered into a huddle with Fran and Winston.

"I just want to go over the details again. The surgery itself will take about an hour and a half and then she'll be in the recovery room until all of her vital signs are strong—could be up to four or five hours. Bette will be awake but pretty out of it. There's really no reason for you to stay here if you want to get some fresh air. I'll call right away if there's any issue. And then the most important thing is to make sure Bette takes it easy for the next few weeks because we don't want her to get an infection during the recovery. This is especially important for the older patients. She will definitely be in pain for a while. I've left a Percocet prescription at the hospital pharmacy. Evie—I know Bette's insurance covers a home-care attendant for the first few weeks after the surgery, but I know you'll be helping out as well. Make sure she drinks plenty of water with the pain medication and changes her bandages. I think that's it for now. We'll talk more after."

Evie loved watching his brow furrow while he spoke, the way his face conveyed concern even unintentionally.

"All right, I'm going to get Bette started in a few minutes, so now's the time to wish her luck." Looking at Evie, he said, "And I know you've got a picture to take."

"Thank you for everything, Dr. Gold," Evie said. She felt strange saying "Edward" in front of her family. She went in to see Bette, who looked remarkably peaceful.

"Evie-le, you really look gorgeous," Bette said when Evie bent down to give her a kiss. "I'm so lucky to have such a devoted granddaughter. Your father vould be so proud of you. If something happens to me during surgery, I just vant you to know how much I love you. I have alvays been so proud. Even vith losing Henry, I still feel lucky because I have you."

Evie choked up. She reached for Bette's hand, squeezed it gently, and didn't release it until the lump in her throat subsided.

"Grandma, stop. You're going to be fine. Dr. Gold is a great surgeon. He's going to take good care of you."

"Yes, I know you're right." She sighed. "Okay, send in ze rest of zem to vish me luck."

Evie gave Bette another kiss and motioned for her mother to come in.

"You know, Evie," Bette said as Evie shifted to allow her mother to approach. "Everything happens for a reason."

Evie didn't know exactly what her grandmother meant, but she nodded anyway.

When she was back in the hallway, Edward said to her, "Evie, I'll call you as soon as the surgery is over." He put his hand gently on her back, which was exposed thanks to her dress. His touch sent unexpected chills down her spine.

"Okay," Evie said. "Thanks again." She wanted to reach up and hug him but resisted.

A nurse approached them as Evie was preparing to leave.

"Dr. Gold, Mrs. Gold is on the phone for you."

"I better take that. We're better on the phone than Twitter," Edward said, giving Evie a sheepish look, but she didn't catch his meaning.

"It's all good, Doc," the nurse said, jabbing him in the waist with her elbow.

"Thanks, Milly," Edward said. "I'm glad you've got my back." Addressing Evie, he said, "We'll speak later then." She nodded her acquiescence.

He waved at her as he turned toward the nurses' station, looking wistful as he walked away.

Or maybe it was just Evie, projecting her own disappointment onto him.

# # #

Evie didn't expect to have any free time the day of Bette's surgery. While she slipped into the jeans and sweater she had brought along, she realized they never took the family photo Bette requested. Evie hadn't seen anyone even carrying a camera. She had already arranged a personal day from Brighton, so after changing into her regular clothes, she set out for a stroll on the Upper East Side.

Fran and Winston opted to stay put while Susan set out in search of organic toothpaste and "conflict-free" baby wash, whatever that was. Evie grabbed a latte from a coffee shop on Third Avenue and sipped it slowly while she window-shopped. She stumbled upon a vintage poster shop with a *Great Gatsby* movie poster in the storefront and had a brainstorm. This would be perfect for Tracy's classroom. Inside the store, she picked out three more posters for movies based on great works of literature—*To Kill a Mockingbird, Great Expectations,* and *The Crucible*—and headed to the register.

"That will be three hundred and fifty dollars," the elderly clerk said to her. He was dressed in a woolly gray cardigan and was sipping hot tea from a New York Film Academy mug. Despite his appearance, he managed to be completely ungrandfatherly in demeanor.

"For posters?"

"Yes, these are vintage posters. We have the most impressive collection of classic movie posters in New York."

He let out a hacking cough, the signature of a lifetime of cigarettes. Evie tried to imagine this curmudgeonly poster salesman in his younger years. Maybe he was a screenwriter; someone who chain-smoked in coffee shops while aspiring actresses flirted with him so they could get parts in his movies that were never made.

This sales job was supposed to be temporary. For every star residing in New York City, there were a thousand has-beens or wanna-bes. She softened on him. Perhaps he registered this, because he leaned close to her and lowered his voice.

"I'm not supposed to be saying this, but all of these posters are available on eBay for half the cost. Trust me, I know. That's where we get our posters most of the time." He gave her a smile that was a tad sleazy.

"Only online?" she pressed. "No other stores in the area sell these posters for less?"

"Sweetheart, I just told you where you can get the posters for half price. Now you want me to direct you to other stores? You want these posters or not?"

"Yeah, fine, I'll take them," she relented and pulled out her credit card.

Quitting the Internet had definitely been cash-flow positive, even if she couldn't find these posters on eBay. She no longer made frivolous clothing buys that she'd be too lazy to send back; there was never the right size box to return them in, and going to UPS was a total drag. It had been months since the Amazon .com money pit had gotten the best of her late at night. The job at Brighton, while it was no Baker Smith, afforded her some monetary wiggle room. She had Tracy to thank for that one, so it only seemed right she should do something to express her appreciation.

Rolled-up posters in hand, she wandered the streets aimlessly for another hour, trying not to think about Bette, Edward, Jack, Susan, Stasia's baby, Paul's baby, Baker Smith, and everything else that was unhinging her. By the time she got the call that the surgery was complete, her psyche was in tatters.

Back at the hospital, she found her family gathered in Edward's office. There was no empty seat so she stood awkwardly against the wall. The degrees and anatomical posters covered practically every inch of free space, so she braced herself against an important-looking certificate from Harvard.

"Evie, welcome," Edward said. "I was just saying that all went as planned. Bette is awake and resting. You can go see her when we're finished in here, assuming she's up. We successfully removed the first-draining lymph nodes and sent them off to pathology. The lumpectomy went smoothly as well. I would imagine Bette will experience significant soreness for a few days, but other than that she should be comfortable. Remember she needs to rest. If I know Bette, she's likely to ignore the instructions from the nurse. But you guys might get through to her. We'll meet in a week to discuss the results. I know the wait is the hardest part. Stay positive. It really helps."

Evie's mother stood up and went to give Edward a hug, making Evie wonder why she had felt awkward doing the same earlier.

"Dr. Gold, I can't thank you enough. We're just all so grateful to you," Fran gushed.

Winston rose too and slapped Edward on the back, echoing Fran's sentiments.

"Please, don't thank me," Edward said modestly.

They all walked out of the office to head toward the recovery room. Fran, Winston, and Susan took the lead, and Evie and Edward fell back and walked together. She wondered if any of her family noticed a special connection between her and the doctor. If so, nobody said anything.

"She's sleeping," Winston said, looking back when he reached the recovery room. "Let's get something to eat downstairs and try again in a little while."

"You guys go ahead," Evie said, waving them off. Fran linked her arm in Winston's and they set off for the elevator.

"Feeling better, Evie?" Edward asked when her family was out of view. She assumed he was referring to their talk from the day before.

"Much," she responded truthfully. In his presence, she really was happier, especially when she succeeded in moving Mrs. Gold to the deep recesses of her brain.

"Glad to hear it," he said. "How about we get something to eat as well? I never did get that egg cream I wanted yesterday."

This time, with her energy drained from the stress of the surgery and her faculties cloudier than usual, she couldn't resist.

"I'd love to."

Evie and Edward exited the hospital and walked two blocks together in silence. Their lack of conversation wasn't totally awkward, but it didn't relax Evie either. They settled into a red-vinyl booth and Edward ordered two egg creams and a coffee for himself from a waitress on roller skates. A few other white-coated doctors from Sloan Kettering and nearby New York-Presbyterian were scattered around the restaurant. Edward nodded his acknowledgment to several of them but didn't stop to chat.

"The food is great here. You've just got to ignore the ambience a little," he said.

"It's cute," Evie said, even though it was obviously cheesy. "Thank you so much for everything you've done for Bette."

"Of course."

"You're so lucky you love what you do. I think maybe I'm just not cut out to work."

"Well, you've only tried one thing. There are a million options out there," Edward said.

"I guess so," Evie said. "But you didn't do anything before being a doctor."

"That's not true."

"Really? What did you do?"

"Well, it was just for one year, but before I went to medical school I was a journalist. I was a science reporter for the *San Francisco Chronicle*. I wanted to try out the West Coast, since Manhattan was all I'd ever known. Some of my articles are still online if you're ever having trouble sleeping."

Evie laughed. She never would have guessed Edward had been anything besides a doctor. If she'd Googled him, as she'd been tempted to do many times, she'd have known that. It was refreshing to learn something new about him directly—a fact he chose to share, not something she discovered through covert research. It was so much more satisfying watching his story unfurl like a blooming onion than to crack him open like a piñata.

"Wow, that's really cool. What else don't I know about you?" She tried to give him an opening to share what she'd been wondering, really hoping for, all along—that his marriage was stumbling, or he couldn't get her out of his mind.

"Nope. I'm quite the open book."

Evie was disappointed.

"So, former reporter, what should I do for my next job? What information have you gathered about me that will help me choose a new profession?"

"If you want to hear what I really think . . ." His voice trailed off as he stirred his coffee with skim and two sugars. It was the same drink he always seemed to choose, if she was deciphering the Magic Marker–coded Starbucks cups in his office correctly. Evie, on the other hand, liked to mix it up. One day she'd order a creamy latte with an extra shot, the next day an icy decaf espresso. It was like their coffee orders were reflections of their personalities—Edward consistent and Evie erratic.

"I do want to know what you think," she exclaimed. She was dazzled by the feeling of Edward taking a genuine interest in her life. Shamefully, she wondered if he ever thought about her outside of work, when he was picking up his daughter from gymnastics, or maybe even when he was lying in bed next to Mrs. Gold.

"I think you should be an interior decorator."

"What?" Evie gasped. "Why in the world would you think that?" She was an attorney, for crying out loud. Designing homes—which, in fairness, she did in her head all the time—was a hobby, if that.

"Bette told me what you did with her apartment. Every time I see you there's a stack of interior design magazines in your bag. I bet that tube you're carrying around has something to do with design." He pointed at the rolled-up posters she had placed next to her in the booth.

"Oh, that's different. Those are posters for my friend's classroom at Brighton."

"See! You probably don't even remember this, but the first time we met in my office, you rearranged the pillows on my couch, fanned the medical journals I keep on my table, straightened my diplomas, and angled the chairs in front of my desk differently. It actually made a big difference."

"I did?" Evie gasped. "I'm sorry!"

"You did. It was when I got a phone call. You seemed to be doing it on autopilot."

"I'm so embarrassed. I usually just want to redesign people's spaces. I had no idea I actually did it without permission. The thing is, I'm a lawyer. I went to school for that. I've invested over a decade in the legal profession. Anyone can buy throw pillows. All you need is a credit card." She doubted any of her Columbia Law School peers were choosing paint colors for a living. She shuddered to think how the Class Notes would read.

Evie Rosen, after being passed over for partner at
Baker Smith, got her start as an interior decorator
by designing her ailing grandmother's crappy pied-
à-terre. Other projects include her own apartment
and a random classroom at the Brighton-Montgomery
Preparatory School. She encourages all fellow class-
mates to contact her if they are considering buying
a new couch.

"Besides, even if I wanted to, I wouldn't know how to pursue it. I'm not very good at things that don't have clearly marked paths. College, law school, internship, law firm associate, then partner or in-house counsel. That makes sense. Breaking into something entrepreneurial or less defined—that's just not me."

Even as she resisted Edward's suggestion, she had to admit she was impressed with the way the chenille throw in powder blue, the ready-made velour window valance, and the grass cloth pillows adorning the plastic-covered love seat really did make Bette's temporary home more livable. She knew her grandmother appreciated the effort and was proud to tell visitors that her granddaughter had done all of this for her. Evie herself had really enjoyed the process—from combing Home Goods and Target to making the on-site improvements. Turning a pleasurable activity into an actual paying job was a whole other story. Switching professional gears entirely was terrifying.

"All I'm saying is that I think you'd be great at it. You could figure out a way to make it work if you wanted to," Edward said. "And trust me, not everyone can do what you do. You should see my apartment."

Evie knew nothing about where he lived, though she had always imagined the suburbs. She pictured the Golds living in a white picket fence home in Westchester, probably Rye or Mamaroneck. Their master bedroom—a place she was ashamed to admit her mind had visited—was a symphony of neutral tones and rich textures. Their kitchen was large and sunny, with top-of-the-line appliances custom built into bleached-wood cabinetry with hunter-green marble countertops. The window treatments were floral, not what she would have chosen, but perfectly appropriate and tasteful.

Now she was hearing that Edward lived in an apartment where the decor left something to be desired. Was that a little dig to the Mrs.'s taste? Her mind started to convert the tidy suburban home with its full pantry and straw welcome mat into a messy New York City apartment with IKEA furniture meant to be replaced years ago but that was still clinging to the floorboards. She wondered again what that earlier Twitter comment at the hospital was all about. Edward was proving to be full of surprises.

"Well, I appreciate the compliment, but I'm not sure how viable a career option that is for me."

"I'd buy stock in any Evie Rosen venture." Edward sucked down the remains of his egg cream and put a twenty-dollar bill on the table.

"You think I'm a safe investment?"

"My track record isn't perfect. But I've got a good feeling about you, Evie."

Too bad I can't join your portfolio, she thought.

Chapter 14

After two weeks at the framer's, the movie posters were ready for hanging in Tracy's classroom.
Tracy's doctor had ordered her to stop working
the week before. Evie hoped it would be a nice
treat when she returned from maternity leave,
and hopefully sooner if she visited the school
with the baby. After happily lugging them to
school, Evie propped them up against one wall
of her cubicle and stood back to admire her own
creativity. Edward was correct in identifying a
passion of hers. His ability to parse the layers
of her psyche and piece together clues about her
interests was bittersweet. She needed this inter-

est in her life to come from a man who wasn't off-limits. From someone whose wife Evie didn't imagine casting into a magician's box and disappearing.

"Those are lovely," a voice, faintly accented, startled her.

"Thank you," Evie said before she even turned around.

"What lovely frames. And the matting is an unusual choice. I'd love to see those hung up."

Evie looked back and came face-to-face with Julianne Holmes-Matthews. She was even more spectacular in person than she appeared in magazines and on the dust jackets of her books, each of which Evie owned: *Paris at Home, Living with Style, Signature Holmes.*

Julianne was a waif of a woman, delicate in her cream cashmere turtleneck and gray suede pants ingeniously belted with an Hermès scarf. Oversize sunglasses covered much of her face, but her enviable bone structure was apparent. She carried a Céline bag in one hand and a tote bag bearing her company name in the other. Evie wondered if it would be too solicitous if she offered to carry them for her.

"Julianne," Headmaster Thane exclaimed, emerging from his office. "You're looking marvelous on this cold day. Thank you so much for coming up here. I'm really excited to show you the new building. Your team sent over some great ideas already."

"Always a pleasure to be of service, Thomas. I just want to see my darling son before we head off. He's coming to meet me here."

"Hi, Mom," Jamie called out. He bent down and gave her not one kiss on the cheek, but two. She really did bring Paris home!

"Jamie, sweetheart, are you keeping out of trouble?" Turning to Thane she said, "I've been all over the globe recently and haven't been able to keep as close an eye on this one as I'd like."

"He's been fine, Julianne. Our new employee, Evie Rosen, has been keeping him busy." He gestured to Evie and she blushed.

"Please continue to do so," Julianne said to Evie.

"I will," Evie responded, pleased they exchanged an actual bit of dialogue.

"Shall we?" Julianne said, looking at the thin gold watch on her tiny wrist.

"Let's," Thane said, holding the office door for Julianne. They were halfway out the door when Evie, without any forethought, grabbed Jamie's hand. He looked at her in surprise. She cocked her head toward the doorway.

"Um, Mom. Can we come along too?"

"Well I don't see why not."

Evie giddily grabbed her coat, and the four of them set out together.

The future computer lab and student lounge was still set up as an art gallery. It was a three-story brownstone with large windows and a winding central staircase. They stood in the center of the top floor, a column-free expanse with an airy glass roof. The gallery used this space as its office because the direct sunlight was too harmful for the paintings. Brighton was going to use this floor for the computers. The second floor would house the student lounge; the first floor was slated to have private study cubicles, like a college library.

Julianne closed her eyes and put her hands in prayer, as though she were summoning the design gods for inspiration. Everyone else was quiet, for fear of interfering with the divine spirit.

"Thomas," she said slowly, tucking her hands under her chin. "I am having a vision. This room. We can't let this light go to waste. Would Brighton consider a hydroponic greenhouse? How fabulous would that be for the students? These city children don't know a thing about gardening."

"I love it," Evie exclaimed, even though the question was directed to the headmaster. "We can showcase some of the plant-ings on the outdoor steps leading up to the front door. Also, take a look. The railing of the central staircase has a vine pattern. So it all ties thematically. The second floor could be a combination lounge and computer room because, honestly, socializing and going online are pretty much synonymous these days. And the glare from the glass roof would make it hard to work on computers up here anyway."

"Very good," Julianne said approvingly. "I hadn't even noticed the vine detail yet. And you factored in the light correctly. You've got a great eye. Who are you again?"

"I'm Evie Rosen. Acting general counsel for the school."

"It's a pleasure to meet you, Evie. Thomas, you should bring her along when we have our first proper design meeting."

"Thank you," Evie said, looking over at Jamie excitedly to share the moment.

He flashed her a thumbs-up.

An hour later, after returning to the main office, she still should have been jumping for joy—having her talents recognized in front of the headmaster and making such a great impression on Jamie's mom. But instead, she found herself with a pounding headache and an uneasy feeling. Tracy kept a drugstore's supply of meds in her desk, and Evie headed to her room to filch some Advil.

She sat down in her friend's chair in the empty classroom, swiveling around until she got dizzy. How had she gotten to this place? This postapocalyptic world in which Jack was married, she worked in a school, her grandmother had cancer, her aunt had a baby, Julianne Holmes-Matthews told her she had a great eye, and she hadn't used the Internet in five months. She never looked up Edward's old science articles, though she would have liked to see his byline in print. She missed his face terribly, from the three lines across his forehead to the connect-the-dot freckle map she had memorized on his nose, and especially his dimple. The old Evie would have found a picture of him on the hospital's website and masochistically stared at it late into the night.

With Bette's surgery over, she knew she would be seeing Edward less and less. Exactly seven tension-filled days after the lump was removed, she, Fran, and Bette had regathered in Edward's office to discuss the results. Evie almost felt guilty about the amount of effort she put into her appearance before heading to Sloan, wondering how she could possibly have the presence of mind to try on six outfits and choose between four lipsticks all while her grandmother's fate hung in the balance. Evie sat clenching her grandmother's hand, the rapid pulses in both of their wrists drumming against each other.

To Evie's surprise, Edward had greeted them in jeans and a hooded zip-up sweatshirt. He explained that after their meeting he was headed to chaperone Olivia's nursery school class trip to the Bronx Zoo. Are you trying to destroy me? Evie wanted to ask him. Do you need to be so damn perfect every time I see you?

Edward said Bette's nodes tested negative, which meant the cancer hadn't spread beyond the tumor. Evie, Fran, and Bette hugged each other tightly and Evie felt her shoulders melt back to their proper alignment for the first time in a month. It had been agonizing trying to remain calm around her grandmother following the surgery, and Evie found herself picking fights with Bette's deer-in-the-headlights home attendant over how much liquid her grandmother had had to drink or when her bandage was last changed. Edward reported that Bette would still need radiation for six weeks, and then hormone therapy for the next five years, but chemotherapy would not be necessary. The immediate threat was over, but even when Evie heard the news and squeezed Bette's liver-spotted hand in joy, she recognized their time together was still limited by life's natural cycle.

Evie vowed to make the most of having Bette in the city for the next few months and promised herself she would get to Boca at least twice a year for extended stays. Maybe she and Bette could hit Art Basel Miami together and return to their old tricks—this time pretending to scout Hirsts and Murakamis for billionaire clients. Edward concluded their meeting by saying he needed to help keep some four-year-olds' fingers away from the lion cage, and they all embraced in an awkward group hug. She missed his arms around her, even if Bette and Fran were squeezed in there too. All of this she thought about while she rotated herself around in Tracy's desk chair like she was meat on a spit, waiting for the pain reliever to kick in.

"Hello?" a female voice sounded.

Evie looked up and found Eleanor standing in the doorway to the classroom.

"Sorry, I didn't mean to disturb you. I was just wondering if you knew where Jamie was. We were supposed to meet in the cafeteria and he didn't show."

"I saw him a few minutes ago with his mother. Maybe they left together," Evie suggested. She actually knew that to be true, having seen the two of them step into a chauffeured town car parked outside the school.

"Oh," Eleanor said. "I didn't realize Jules was back. Thanks."

Jules? Eleanor's familiarity with the Holmes-Matthews clan made Evie feel spiteful for absolutely no good reason at all.

# # #

Life fell into a comfortable rhythm after Bette's surgery. The work at Brighton continued at a manageable clip, and Evie made acquaintances with some of the younger teachers. She continued to enjoy long walks to work and found her way over to Bette's at least once a week after school for a quality visit. Bette seemed

eager to return to Florida, griping about the cold, but Evie wondered if her desire to go home had something to do with Sam.
Fortunately Evie and Fran convinced her to stay local while she
convalesced, though no exact time frame was agreed upon.

Edward kindly dropped in on Bette several times during her
recovery, but it seemed like the timing was always off for them
to catch up—he'd be leaving to do rounds just when Evie arrived. When *Antiques Roadshow* came on in the evenings, she daydreamed about calling him to watch it together. Sometimes she
thought of fictitious questions to ask about Bette's treatment but
worried that Edward would see through them. What would she
do if Mrs. Gold picked up his cell phone? Of course she would
never act on anything with Edward. She just missed hearing his
voice. And listening to him rattle off medical jargon on a phone
call. And seeing him in scrubs. She missed the way she felt in his
presence—noticed, special, worth analyzing. In his presence, her
memories of Jack vaporized; only Edward could morph Jack from
lifelike zombie to translucent ghost.

Jack.

Sans the web, she never did find a photo of his wife, whose
name, Zeynup Kayatani, Stasia had triumphantly discovered
through means Evie wasn't quite clear about (the Turkish Records Bureau came to mind). She also didn't look at the photos
of Wyatt that Aunt Susan said she had sent her, even as Evie
found herself missing the sweet little baby and wondering what
new milestone he'd reached in New Mexico. He'd only stayed with
her for two days before Susan whisked him back to Santa Fe (days
before Bette's results were even known), but it was enough time
for the adorable infant to settle himself into Evie's heart. She even
missed the way his baby accoutrements filled every inch of her
apartment. Looking at the pictures of Wyatt Susan had e-mailed
was truly tempting, but that would mean logging into her e-mail,

where she'd inevitably comb her inbox for word from Luke Glass-cock, or the orthodontist she'd botched the date with, or even a message from Jack confessing his marriage to Zeynup was a huge mistake. If she had to guess which of those messages was likely to be there, she'd have to choose (D): None of the above.

Which is why she was fortified in her decision to keep her distance from e-mail until she reached the looming finish line of her birthday in May. And it wasn't just Gmail that she was better off for cleansing. She no longer patrolled eHarmony, JDate, or Match for hours. She didn't self-flagellate by comb-ing Facebook for enviable photos and posts. Nor did she creep around the Internet looking for news of divorces or scandals, the sort of searches she used to do in secret when she was feel-ing particularly bad about herself. She hadn't been on *BigLaw-Sux* since her own humiliation, though she would have relished the comment threads about the grueling hours and abuse from power-trippy partners. Abandoning the web had undoubtedly started with painful withdrawal, and while she sometimes got the urge for a fix, it was proving to be a positive adjustment in her life. She was definitely less obsessed with what everyone else was doing when she didn't have the virtual yardstick to measure herself against.

But still, she wasn't happy. Something was missing. It wasn't the web. But it was something.

# # #

After autumn took its leave, winter showed its face quickly with a snowfall that dusted the city canopies like confectioners' sugar. The old radiator in the Brighton main office started pumping heat into the air, and Evie started to suspect that Jamie had a crush on her. He volunteered to help out in the office twice a day and would often pass by to give her an ironic salute en route to

class. She used it to her full advantage, often prodding him for
details of his mother's projects while she had him look up phone
numbers, e-mail signature pages, and Google contract terms.
How did his mother get her start in interior design? Where did
she source her antiques? What was Bono like? These were just
a few of her nagging questions, but Jamie didn't seem to mind.

This week her task had been to mark up the contract from the
construction team that would be renovating Brighton's new building and circulate a draft to the board members. The legal work
wasn't particularly challenging, and Evie found she did most of
it on autopilot. Up the penalties on the contractor. Stretch out
Brighton's payment schedule. It wasn't rocket science. She was
grateful for the paycheck and to have her days occupied, but lawyering in this capacity wasn't any more exciting or suited to her
interests than M&A had been.

"Evie," Headmaster Thane said, surprising her from behind
one morning. "I need to speak to you about an important matter."
He motioned for her to get up.

Her stomach flip-flopped. Had he noticed that she never used
the computer? That she delegated all Internet work to a high
school senior on probation? That she interrogated the poor kid
about his mother, a Brighton trustee, every chance she got? She
followed him into his office, anxiously reliving the moment the
partnership committee announced she was caput.

"Have a seat," he said, and she settled into a leather armchair
opposite his desk.

"Evie, what can I say? Your work has been exceptional. We are
all very impressed with the way you have handled the contract
negotiations and dealt with the sometimes difficult members of
our board. I know Julianne was very impressed with you. We're
hoping you will consider accepting our offer of full-time employment. Initially, we were looking for someone with experience in

the education sector, but I just don't think it's necessary. You've been fantastic."

Evie exhaled deeply. She wasn't being reprimanded. Thane had no idea she was lawyering like a Luddite or that she was using her "intern" (as she'd taken to thinking of Jamie) inappropriately. On the contrary, she was being commended. It felt so nice to have her hard work and skills appreciated that it took a moment to sink in that she had a decision to make.

"So what do you say? I know we can't pay you like your firm did, but your hours would be a heck of a lot better and you'd have a great deal of autonomy."

And I'd get to work for someone who wears bow ties and elbow patches every day, Evie thought, looking at the professorial-looking Thane. Brighton, and especially Thane, had her pining for her college days—a happier time, and definitely a calmer period in her life, when she didn't feel like the clock was running out on her to GET THINGS DONE. A period of her life when dating was for fun, not for marriage, and friends were drinking partners—not life coaches. The offer was certainly worth consideration.

"I'm very flattered. But I need time to think it over."

"Of course. Take a week or two. We'd love to have you on board."

Back at her desk, Evie found Jamie in his cube listening to his iPod. He pulled out his earbuds when he saw her.

"In trouble with Headmaster Tame?" he teased.

"No, quite the opposite. He offered me a full-time job."

"Congrats. You gonna take it?"

"I'm not sure. Lots to think about."

"This place is pretty cool. I mean, they let me work here instead of—"

"Jamie," she interrupted. "I need help hanging these posters in Mrs. Loo's classroom. I can't leave them lying around the office anymore."

"Sure, let me get those for you," he said, lifting up two of the frames and trotting alongside her up the stairwell.

#

"I guess a hammer and nails would have been useful," Evie said, a touch out of breath. "Not sure why I didn't think of that."

After an unsuccessful stop in Tracy's classroom, she and Jamie were cramped into the supply closet, located in the school's sub-cellar. He was on a stepladder fishing through a toolbox.

"It's cool," Jamie said. "I was planning to skip Spanish anyway."

"Sorry about the trek up and down the three flights. I know these posters are heavy."

"I don't mind at all. But you look like you're freezing down here."

She was. There was no heat in the basement, and Evie was wearing a thin blouse.

"Take my sweatshirt," he said, offering her a generously sized zip-up.

She slipped it on gratefully.

"Hey! I found something," he said, producing hooks and a bag of nails. "Now we just need a hammer."

He climbed off the ladder and started opening random boxes. Evie did the same, and together they combed the four-by-six stor-age shed, bumping into each other apologetically.

"I think I see one," he said, reaching for the box behind Evie's back.

"Great, because I'd love to get this done today. Tracy, I mean Mrs. Loo, is going to have the baby any day and I'd really love it if—hey, what are you doing?" she shrieked.

Jamie had snaked his hand up the back of her shirt. He was fumbling with her bra clasp. Before she could say another word, his mouth was on hers.

His lips felt plump, the skin around them baby smooth. She almost did it. She almost kissed back. Jamie, after all, was not your average hormonal, acne-laden teen. How easy it would have been to meet his tongue with hers. To have a victory over Eleanor, and a symbolic win over Cameron Canon. But no. It wasn't okay, no matter how fabulous his mother was. She was not going to make out with a student. That was sick.

"Jamie, stop it. This can't happen." She pushed him off of her.

"Don't worry, I'm eighteen," he said, lunging back at her.

"That is not the issue," she said.

"Then why not?" he whined, like a little boy used to getting whatever he wanted. "You've been leading me on for months."

"I've what? No I haven't!"

"You ask me to send e-mails for you. Seriously? That's clearly just a way to have us work together. And the other day you asked me to describe my bedroom to you."

"That's because of your mom! I worship Julianne Holmes-Matthews. I was curious how your room was decorated."

He looked so hurt and confused, Evie actually felt sorry for him. What had she done?

"What about all the touching in the office?"

That part was true. Their flimsy excuses to touch each other ("You dropped something . . . There's a thread on your pants . . . Here let me help you with that") were as transparent as they come.

She had just wanted to feel another human. Was that a crime? Jamie represented something she felt she'd no longer be able to attain at her age—a partner without baggage. If Edward was an open book, then Jamie was a blank book. The way she was at that age. Before her father died, before she gave nearly a decade to a thankless job, before Jack shredded her heart to smithereens, and before technology fast-tracked the pace of everything around her. Back when her world was still whole and complication-free.

"I don't know what you're talking about. I mean, we do work six inches apart, so of course we knock into each other."

"Well, what about the computer stuff? Why are you always asking me to Google things?"

"Because I don't use the Internet. I haven't for six months already."

She might as well have been a one-eyed Martian the way Jamie looked at her in that moment.

"That's weird. It just really seemed like you were into me. You gave Eleanor the stink eye every time she came to visit. C'mon, Evie. I think you're just holding back because I'm a student. I won't tell a soul, I promise."

"Jamie, I'm sorry, but it's just not going to happen. I am flattered though. Seriously."

"Whatever," he said, pushing open the door to the supply closet. He looked back and whispered, "It's not cool to be a tease. Guys don't like that."

Dating advice from a high school student. And there she had it—she'd sunk to a new low.

# # #

"It's a boy!"

"What?" Evie asked groggily. She tried to focus her eyes on the alarm clock next to her bed but the red numbers just did a blurry dance. After painful squinting, she registered that the clock read 3:30 A.M. She clenched her fingers over the receiver in her hand and ascertained she was not dreaming the phone call.

"It's a boy," she heard again. "A perfect, angelic boy." She recognized Tracy's voice upon hearing it the second time.

"No he's not," Evie said defensively.

How the hell did Tracy know what went down?

"Evie, trust me, he's a boy. He was circumcised one hour ago."

The baby. Tracy had a baby boy.

"Oh, the baby's a boy. That's amazing. Sorry, it's the middle of the night. I'm just so out of it."

"Well, get up and come meet him. I feel shockingly okay. Percocet's pretty awesome."

"Now?"

"Yes, now. You need to meet Henry."

"You named him Henry?" Evie asked, suddenly paralyzed.

"Yes. Cutest name, right? He's named after Jake's uncle."

Evie was speechless. She never expected to hear her father's name. Not in this context.

"You there?"

"Um, yeah. I think it's a great name," Evie said. "It was my father's name."

"Oh, Jesus, Evie. I'm sorry. I hope you don't mind. Honestly, we didn't even think about that. You don't mind, do you? We can both have Henrys. Someday."

Evie knew Henry was a common name. She couldn't very well lay claim to it, especially when it was unclear if she'd ever have a chance to use it for a son of her own.

"It's okay, really. Let me get dressed and I'll come see you guys. You're at New York Hospital, right?"

"Yes. And thanks, Evie—I hope my Henry is the kind of man your father was. You've always spoken so highly of him."

"I'll be there soon."

By the time Evie reached the labor and delivery floor, Tracy had transitioned from exuberant to unconscious. The new father was also asleep, his body scrunched into a sideways child's pose to fit onto the tiny hospital couch. The baby lay quietly in the hospital-issued bassinet against one wall of the room. Caroline and Stasia were already there, seated on mismatched plastic chairs they must have dragged from the waiting room.

"She just fell asleep," Caroline said with a big yawn. Nocturnal secretions crusted the corners of her eyes and lips. "You all are so lucky I had the girls in the daytime."

Evie approached the crib cautiously, worried that her footsteps would wake the baby.

"Don't worry, you won't wake him," Caroline said, intuiting Evie's concern. "They sleep like, well, like babies at this age."

Henry was swaddled in a fuzzy white hospital blanket and was wearing a tiny blue-, pink-, and white-striped beanie. She had to admit he was a cute newborn, with flushed cheeks and a thick swath of black hair visible from where his cap ended.

"Evie, you missed Tracy's very detailed account of the birth," Stasia said. "Before she passed out she asked me to check if her vagina was still intact. I sincerely hope Jake isn't serious about making a documentary. If I were Tracy, I would have smashed his video camera in two."

Jerome stumbled in at that moment, clearing his throat.

"Coffee, anyone?" He was carrying a full tray. Evie was surprised to see he had come along with Caroline to the hospital. She had presumed that rich people, particularly rich old people, didn't do things that weren't convenient for them, which would certainly include a middle-of-the-night trip to meet a new baby. But there he was, rubbing Caroline's shoulders after passing out the coffee.

"Is Rick here?" Evie asked, noticing that Stasia was also eyeing Jerome's warm gesture to Caroline.

At that moment, Tracy's eyes flitted open and Evie jumped out of her chair to approach.

"Hi, Trace! Congratulations!" Evie said. "I hope I didn't wake you. How are you?"

"I'm fine, I think. I just felt a contraction. But he's out of me, right?"

Caroline laughed. "Yes, he's in the bassinet. You're having after-birth contractions. They really suck and will last for a few days."

"Just when I thought I was done," Tracy said, rubbing her eyes. "Okay, I need to go back to sleep if I have a prayer of taking care of this kid. Wake me when Paul arrives, okay. I think he said he'd come. He and Marco want to get a handle on the newborn thing before Maya arrives."

So Paul and Marco already knew they were having a girl? Evie calculated that over a month had passed since she'd spoken to Paul.

Tracy's eyes closed again, and everyone kept their voices down, even though they could see from her jerky wincing every few minutes that she was not asleep.

"Does this freak you out?" Evie turned to Stasia. "Seeing how much pain Tracy's in?"

"Why would it freak me out?" Stasia asked with a blank stare.

Let's see how you handle pushing out a watermelon from a hole the size of a peach pit.

"Well, I'd be nervous if I was going to have a baby someday soon, seeing how tough it is," Evie hedged. Stasia still hadn't told her about the pregnancy so she treaded lightly.

"Well, I'm not pregnant. So nothing to worry about." Stasia offered up a close-lipped smile.

Maybe she'd had a miscarriage? Evie had been so sure Stasia was keeping something from her.

"Well, you and Rick are doctors. When the time comes, you'll probably both handle this in a much more clinical way. Rick was so nice, by the way, about my grandma. Is he coming?" Evie repeated her previous question. In the other corner of the room,

Jerome and Caroline were silently looking through pictures on Jerome's iPad. She knew they were looking at the girls, because every time Jerome's finger scrolled to a new picture, goofy parental smiles would spread across their faces.

"He's not coming, Evie. Why do you keep asking?" Stasia's voice boomed, shattering the calm in the room.

"Okay, I'm sorry, I was just making conversation. Sorry if I was being annoying." Evie couldn't understand why Stasia was so rattled.

"Whatever," Stasia went on, choosing not to lower her voice from her initial outburst. "We're getting divorced, okay? Now you know." Suddenly the room was sucked of all its air, Evie suffering the most of all from foot-in-mouth suffocation.

"Does everyone else know?" It was a petty question, and Evie knew it. But it was the first thing she thought to say and her filter didn't operate well in the middle of the night.

Stasia started crying. She cradled her head in her hands and nodded her head. It was so subtle that Evie couldn't tell if she was trying to say yes or her head was just being moved in that direction by her hands.

"So that's a yes?" Evie asked.

This time Stasia nodded more deliberately.

"Why didn't you tell me? I could have been there for you."

By this time, Caroline and Jerome had stopped studying pictures and were listening intently to Evie and Stasia.

"It's not an easy thing to share. And honestly, you wouldn't understand." If Stasia was intending to be hurtful, she succeeded with her undue emphasis on the "you."

"I did have a terrible breakup with Jack after dating for two years. I'm not an asexual amoeba, for God's sake. I know a thing or two about relationships," Evie snapped.

"Hi everyone, what did we miss? Something about sexuality?"

Marco asked as he and Paul swooped into the room, carrying armfuls of shopping bags tied up with curly ribbons.

Nobody answered.

"Awkward," Marco said and settled the presents down gently. Even so, the sound of crinkling tissue paper was jarring.

"I told her," Stasia said, looking directly at Paul.

"Oh."

"Told me?" Now Evie was steaming.

"Yeah, told you. About the divorce," Paul said, his voice the temperature of ice water. Marco motioned for Evie to follow him outside of the hospital room.

"What the hell was that ambush?" Evie demanded of Marco when they were stationed in the hallway. Stasia flew past them in the direction of the elevator with her coat tucked under her arm.

"I'm just going to say it," Marco said. "Paul is pretty angry at you."

"What, why?" She tried to appear flabbergasted but had more than an inkling of what was coming.

"When was the last time you talked to him?"

"I don't know, a couple of weeks ago," Evie lied.

"Much longer than that. Not since he told you we were having a baby. We invited you to this baby shower cocktail thing at our place and you didn't show. And he said you were less than enthusiastic about our family plans."

Evie's toes curled. She hated being wrong. And worse, she hated being called out on it. She assumed a defensive stance.

"Well, things have been crazy for me. I was basically unemployed, my grandmother had major surgery, and I've been taking care of her. You know Jack got married out of the blue. It's just been a really shitty time. So I think it's pretty understandable that I didn't have time to hear about crib shopping." The coffee Jerome gave her was seeping into her veins. Mixed with her lack of sleep, the caffeine high was making her the lethal combination of anxious and hyper. She continued her rant, transitioning from assumed defensiveness to legitimate anger.

"And what the hell? I never got invited to any baby shower."

"We sent an Evite. Actually, it was Paperless Post. Paul said Evites are passé."

"Well, news flash, I don't use the Internet anymore and you both knew that."

"Which is why he also called you and left a message. Paul said you never returned the call. He also said you practically hung up on him when he told you about the baby. I mean, you said congratulations and all, but apparently it was very half-assed."

Evie didn't answer. The voicemail from Paul was still on her phone, unlistened to, as it had been for a while already.

"But tell the truth. Would you have wanted to be there anyway?" Marco asked, his eyes penetrating whatever facade she was foisting on him. It felt like having her insides skewered.

"Of course," she bellowed on impulse.

"Well, we weren't so sure. You were jealous, Evie. And that's okay. But Paul doesn't quite get it. You know my older sister Paola is still single so I'm more understanding of these things."

"These things?" She was outraged. Was Marco saying that single people are given a pass on egregious behavior because of their pitiable state? What year was it? 1950? "Well, I'm not jealous, so I guess you don't have me quite as figured out as you think."

He ignored her protest.

"And this thing with Stasia. I know she was planning on telling you about the divorce. But it was like you had this exalted view of her marriage. I think she knew you saw her and Rick as perfect, and it killed her to have to admit to the person who idealized them so much that the envy was misplaced."

Evie looked at her watch. It was close to 5:00 A.M., but she could see out the window that it was still pitch-black. Had Stasia ventured out or was she huddled in the hospital cafeteria, waiting for daybreak? Evie wished it was lighter outside, so she could flee down the hallway and run the whole way home to seek refuge in her bed. Marco read her inner monologue.

"It's the middle of the night. Go back into Tracy's room. Talk to Paul. You set us up. He can't stay mad at you forever."

Evie inhaled deeply, letting her body communicate her assent to Marco. They walked back down the hallway together. Tracy's parents had arrived in the meantime, and the new grandparents were busy cooing at the baby in the bassinet. Paul was next to Tracy, deep in conversation. Whether they were trading secrets on baby bottles or he was venting about the fight, she didn't know. He didn't glance up when she entered. Jerome rose to offer her his seat next to Caroline, which she gratefully accepted. It was as if her legs had turned to jelly. She was finding it hard to support the weight of her body, let alone her stress.

"This night is insane," she whispered to Caroline. With Tracy basically out of commission for the next forty-eight hours, or more likely the next month, Caroline felt like Evie's only friend.

"It'll be fine. Stasia's just going through some really rough times. He was cheating on her, you know?"

"Wow, I didn't know. She never so much as uttered a single complaint about him to me in all the years they were dating or married."

"You know she thought he was in love with you, don't you?"

"Me?" Evie was honestly in shock.

"I guess he used to suggest including you a lot. It made Stasia paranoid."

Evie remembered Stasia's call to her a few months ago while she was in line waiting to have her computer fixed: Rick wants you to come see a movie with us. There had been many more invitations like that in the past. She recalled Rick's eagerness to talk to her on the phone and his message checking in on her. And the time she heard him saying in the background that she shouldn't go on the blind date with the orthodontist if she wasn't feeling up to it.

"But Stasia's gorgeous. If he was cheating on her, it was probably with a supermodel. He wouldn't have wanted someone like me," Evie countered with genuine modesty.

"Evie," Caroline said wearily, shaking her head from side to side. "We can all agree that Stasia is smart and beautiful. But so are you. You just don't know what you have, do you?"

"I have nothing."

"I'm not dignifying that with a response."

"Marco accused me of being a jealous person. Do you agree?" Evie hoped her eyes were conveying how much she was counting on Caroline to give her an honest answer.

"I think you're . . ." She paused, and Evie could tell she was running through her mental dictionary to find the proper word. "I think you're contemptuous of married people."

"What? I am not!"

"Sometimes you say things about Jerome, you know about him being older and having been married before. I know you've made fun of Jake for not having a traditional career. What's motivating all of that?"

"I never said those things!" Evie rebutted indignantly. "I love Jake and Jerome."

"Listen, I'm not upset with you. If I weren't sleep-deprived I probably wouldn't even be having this conversation. But since we are, let me ask you something."

Evie looked up at Caroline with trepidation. She wanted to beg, *I'm fragile. Go easy on me.*

"Yes?"

"What are you so worried about? That you'll end up alone, tending to a parrot and joining the local community board so you have something on your calendar?"

If only her life were as simple as a cliché.

"No," Evie said truthfully, linking her arm through Caroline's. She rested her head on her friend's shoulder and felt just how tired she was. "In fact I'm worried I won't do that. I'm much more scared of settling."

The truth reverberated through the room, but the only audible reaction to Evie's admission was a knowing sigh from the nurse changing Tracy's bedpan.

Chapter 15

The moment the sun came up, Evie took her leave from the hospital, kissing Tracy on the forehead and blowing a kiss to baby Henry. When Jake woke up from his new-father-induced slumber, she was extra ebullient with her good wishes.

Outside, the streets were only sparsely filled—a homeless person here, an eager-beaver investment banker there, and a few uniformed workers closing out their night shifts. She recognized pangs of hunger in her belly.

The hospital where Tracy delivered was not too far from where Bette was being treated. She decided to eat breakfast at the same 1950s diner that Edward had brought her to. She left a message on the Brighton main office voicemail saying she would be out sick that day. Jamie would probably wonder where she was, maybe even think she was traumatized by his advances. What difference did it make?

She slumped into a booth by herself and studied the pictures of the food on the menu.

The waitress approached, wearing a poodle skirt and black-and-white saddle shoes. The restaurant's shtick had seemed cute when she was there with Edward, but today the sound of "Hound Dog" blaring from the jukebox was excruciating.

"What can I getcha this mornin'?"

Evie's eyes gravitated to the picture with the most food.

"I'll have the Truck Stop Special," she said. "And an egg cream."

"You sure, hon? That's two of everything. Two stacks of pancakes, two eggs, two pieces of french toast, two pieces of bacon, two pieces of—"

"You heard the woman. She wants the Truck Stop Special. Actually, make it two, please."

Evie turned around in surprise. Edward Gold was behind her booth, smiling broadly. "So you liked this place, huh?"

"Oh, um, my friend just had a baby last night at New York Hospital. I'm so hungry because I think when you're up all night you're hungrier than normal. I don't normally eat like a pig." Why was she babbling?

"I hear you. When I had the midnight-to-six shift in the ER, I'd be starving by the time I was done." He gestured toward the empty seat opposite her. "Can I join you?"

"Of course!" She was ashamed she hadn't thought to offer him a seat sooner.

Edward sat down and removed his winter coat, a handsome navy Barbour parka. Underneath, he wore reddish-purple scrubs.

They were short-sleeve and showed off sizable muscles. She hadn't seen him in his doctor's getup since Bette's surgery. He had Ray-Bans tucked into the V-neck of his shirt.

"So your friend had a baby. Mazel tov."

"Yep, in the middle of the night. A baby boy. Henry." Evie rubbed her eyes for effect, hoping to excuse her unfortunate appearance.

"Your father's name." Edward paused deliberately after saying that and looked at Evie pensively. "Is that tough for you?"

She was touched he remembered.

"It was, especially when I first heard it. But it's nice, I guess."

"All right," he said simply, and Evie sensed he didn't want to push the issue. "So what's with the Brighton lacrosse sweatshirt? Does that mean you are coming around to your job?"

Evie flushed when she looked down. She was wearing Jamie's gigantic hoodie, which said VARSITY and had two crossed sticks on the sleeve. She took it home after the supply closet fiasco and must have grabbed it when she was getting dressed in the dark.

"Oh, this? Yeah, they give these out to the teachers. I was just wearing it as a pajama top," she answered, instantly regretting her cover story. She wanted Edward to visualize her in a lace teddy, not an oversize gym shirt. Especially not one belonging to the half-wit jailbait who had just pounced on her, claiming she'd led him on.

The waitress arrived with their oversize plates, sausages steaming and bacon sizzling. On a separate plate, pancakes jiggled delectably against a voluminous pile of eggs. Evie inhaled deeply as her stomach rumbled. It was the first time in a while she could remember being truly hungry.

"The Truck Stop Special was definitely the right call," Edward said, lifting a forkful of syrupy pancakes to his lips. "If I hadn't run into you, I would have ordered a low-fat muffin.

You've definitely tempted me. Again." He smiled in a way that was more seductive than friendly. Evie shifted self-consciously in her seat, like a hot potato had fallen into her lap. She was uncomfortable, but happily so, if such a thing was possible. She tried to convince herself the meek flirtations of a married man were harmless enough. That is if he was even flirting with her. It was hard to tell on so little sleep.

She returned the volley to him with a sweet smile and a deliberate eyebrow raise.

"Glad I could be so tempting." Their coy banter, albeit surprising, temporarily relieved her of the drama she had left behind in Tracy's hospital room.

Unexpectedly, Edward began shoveling forkfuls of eggs into his mouth. Evie thought maybe she had been misreading signals until he said, "Sorry, I just caught the time. I have to be in preop in ten minutes. Which doesn't leave me much time to ask you—"

The waitress interrupted.

"More coffee for you, sir?"

"No thanks," Edward said hurriedly.

She turned toward Evie with the pot. "Miss?"

"Yes, please." Damn it. Why did she ask for coffee? It seemed to take the waitress forever to fill Evie's cup and drag over more sugar and milk from a nearby table. When she finally sauntered off, it looked like Edward had lost his train of thought. He was staring into the distance, as though he was trying to identify someone at another table.

"You were saying," Evie started cautiously, her voice lilting upward. "You wanted to ask me something?"

"Yes, I did. Bette has bragged to me many times that you went to Yale. My niece is thinking of applying there. I was hoping maybe you could tell her about it."

"Huh?" She questioned, a look of surprise no doubt spreading across her face. What had she been expecting? This married man to ask her to meet up in the hospital basement for illicit sex amid the syringes and catheters? Whatever she thought he'd say, she was undeniably let down that his question was so platonic.

"Would you mind? Talking to my niece?"

"Um, sure. You can give her my e-mail address. Actually, wait, not e-mail. Have her call me." Evie reached for the syrup and methodically filled every indented square of her waffle—anything to avoid looking at Edward.

To her surprise, he reached out and put his hand on top of hers, the one that was grasping the handle of the syrup dispenser. Evie's hand shook a little upon contact, and syrup spilled out abundantly, drowning her plate. She emitted a reflexive laugh.

Edward spoke. "Wait. That's not at all what I wanted to ask you. I don't even have a niece. I'm an only child."

"So am I!" Evie exclaimed. She thought back to her own imaginary niece, the one she told the clerk at the computer store threw up all over her computer. But why in the world was Edward finding it necessary to invent family members for her benefit?

"I know." Edward took a deep breath. "What I wanted to ask you was, will you have dinner with me? I'd really love to take you out on a date. I've wanted to ask you out for a really long time." He exhaled. "God, it feels good to get that out. What do you say?"

Evie's jaw dropped.

"But you're married! You have a daughter. You wife doesn't let her have sweets!"

"I'm divorced, Evie. Recently divorced. But we've been separated for over two years. I figured you knew that."

"How would I know you're divorced?"

Edward chuckled. "Because everyone knows I'm divorced. It's all over the Internet. Though it's actually quite refreshing to find someone who doesn't know the intimate details of my personal life."

"Why is your divorce on the Internet? Are you famous or something?" Evie's mind raced to keep up with the information it was receiving.

"No, I'm not. Well, maybe in some medical circles. What am I saying? I'm not famous. But my ex-wife is. Georgina Cookman."

"Cookman's Cookies? I loved those things when I was a kid. Still do." She noticed a shadow darken Edward's face. "Oh sorry, I mean, they were terrible. Tasted like burnt rubber."

"No, it's okay. I had a hard time giving them up. They're in every vending machine at the hospital. Anyway, until four months ago, I was married to the cookie heiress herself. Trust me, there was nothing sweet about her. And I never saw her bake one thing the entire time we were together. Family recipe, my ass." Evie had never seen this side of Edward before. Raw, unadulterated emotion was guiding his tongue. She liked it.

"Georgina Cookman." Evie let her name swish around in her mouth like she was savoring one of their oatmeal raisin cookies. "That woman is everywhere. I once went to a fund-raiser to restore the gardens of Versailles that she cochaired. Don't ask what I was doing there."

Edward rolled his eyes. "Please don't bring back those memories. I can't even tell you how many hours that woman devoted to saving Venice."

"But wait, I'm still confused. What was all over the Internet?" He looked at his watch again.

"I really do have to get to surgery. Can I tell you later?"

"At least give me the short version now. How did you get together?"

"Fair enough. I met Georgina at a fund-raiser. It was when I started my fellowship and the chief of medicine dragged me to this lunch. Anyway, Georgie was speaking about some grant from her family's company and we made eye contact during her talk. As I was leaving to get my coat she approached me. She was beautiful. And very sophisticated."

Evie eyed her tattered lacrosse top once again. She placed her hands on her lap to hide her gnarled nails. Edward must have noticed.

"Stop it, Evie. You're stunning. I have no doubt you've noticed me staring at you many times."

She had, in fact, noticed. But she'd always told herself she was misconstruing the signals: there had to be a poppy seed in her teeth; or Edward was just the kind of guy that liked to make intense eye contact. How oblivious she must have been to the signs the last few months. And the ones she did pick up on, she couldn't give herself enough credit to accept, attributing them to a misunderstanding or the harmless overtures of a possibly bored married man. She gave him a slight nod.

"Anyway, I had been living in the library for five years during my residency, subsisting on Rice Krispies and coffee. Social plans for me meant playing cards in the doctors' lounge during my on-call hours. I had no time for dating. Then came Georgina. She hit me like a tornado.

"Things were good at first. G took care of everything—our schedule, our apartment, our finances. I had time to focus on my patients and my research. We got pregnant right away—with Olivia. After she was born, I really felt like divorce was off the table, though we both knew things were deteriorating. And I know this sounds like a terrible idea, but a part of me wanted to stay with Georgina to give Olivia a sibling. I still want that for her. Not with Georgina though, obviously. But I hope to have more kids someday. Anyway, Georgina and I had nothing in common. All she wanted was to be photographed for the society pages. She resented my hours because I couldn't accompany her to benefits. I thought she left Olivia with the nanny too often for silly things, like Botox or hair appointments. And I'm sure I was distant too—burying myself in work to avoid confronting our problems. We finally called it quits about a year ago. Because we have a child and the amount of money involved, the divorce was a disaster. We kept it private for as long as we could. But it got out a few months ago, and the media had a field day with it."

"How so?"

"Let's see. Let's start with the headlines. 'Cookie Heiress Crumbles Her Man,' 'Cookman's Marriage Goes from Sweet to Sour,' 'Spouses Battle to Split the Cookie Jar,' 'Cookie Heiress Finds New Man to Satisfy Her Sweet Tooth.' I could go on and on. I feel the worst for Olivia. Thank God she's not old enough to go online." Evie hoped that was true. Caroline recently found five-year-old Grace on the American Girl website, browsing out-fits for her Julie doll.

"When I moved out, Olivia started acting up a little. And that's when the British accent appeared mysteriously."

"Wow, that's terrible. I had no idea." Evie shocked herself when she reached across the table for his hand, which felt warm and ready to receive hers.

"And then there was the Twitter incident."

"Twitter incident?" She flashbacked to Edward's comment in the hospital that he was better on the phone than on Twitter.

"Honestly, I'm ashamed to tell you. Let's just say I found ways of being cruel to Georgina in a hundred forty characters or less. I just felt like I had to fight back. But I swear, Evie, that's not the real me. I was going through a really shitty time."

"Edward, it's okay. I was waiting to discover you weren't per-fect." She thought back to when he said he was going to chaperone Olivia's class trip, when his level of perfection felt almost stifling.

"Far from it." He chuckled. "But you still haven't answered my question that got this all started. Will you have dinner with me?"

"I would love to." She felt the corners of her mouth reach her ears, the widest smile she'd cracked in ages.

"That's great," he said. "I had my doubts about whether you could possibly be interested in me."

Evie furrowed her brow. She had been mesmerized by his TV-star looks, quiet confidence, and natural humor from their first conversation, and try as she did not to let it show, some of her more-than-friend affinity for him had to have surfaced. Why would he doubt she'd like him?

"I mean, I thought you might, but then you started telling me about wanting to freeze your eggs. I couldn't imagine you considered that flirting."

"Yeah, I typically wait until at least a third date to tell guys about my fertility concerns," Evie said, managing to make a joke despite her embarrassment. "To be fair, I did think you were married."

"I wanted to ask you out right then and there just to shut you up, but I felt like I should do the surgery first and avoid any ethical gray areas. I was worried you'd accept a date with me just so I wasn't in a bad mood when I operated on your grandmother. In fact, I've been waiting to formally discharge Bette as my patient before asking you out. Which I am pleased to say I officially did three days ago."

He placed enough money on the table to cover both of their breakfasts, then reached for his coat and stood up to leave.

"So I'll call you later to arrange a date and time, okay?"

"I'm looking forward."

He headed toward the door but turned around suddenly.

"So before I go, can I ask you, how is it you managed to escape reading tales of my bitter divorce?" He gave her a quizzical glance.

"Oh. That." Evie giggled. "I haven't been on the Internet for, um, let me think. Five months and counting."

"Ah," he said. "Evie Rosen, I knew I liked you from the minute we met."

"Well, thank you," Evie said gingerly. "Now, let me ask you something,"

"What's that?" he asked, eyebrows raised.

"The heiress of a cookie company doesn't let her child have sweets?"

"That's correct," Edward responded, deadpan.

"Now I've heard everything," Evie responded, with a playful smile.

When he was gone, Evie spontaneously pulled out her cell phone and dialed Headmaster Thane. She thanked him for his generous offer of full-time employment but politely declined, promising to stay on until the school's building purchase was complete. Even though she dreaded facing Jamie, her conscience dictated that she wrap up the project. She owed that much to Tracy.

Although her friendships with Paul and Stasia were teetering, sitting alone with the remains of her Truck Stop Special before her, Evie couldn't deny that the world felt wide open. She was going out with Edward, someone she'd secretly fantasized about since probably day one of meeting. She would find employment someplace totally out of the box to which she'd historically confined her future. Maybe she could actually make a go of decorating—though an apprenticeship with Julianne Holmes-Matthews was firmly off the table. Her Mrs. Robinson days were definitely over. And so, possibly, were her lawyering days.

# # #

Jamie was gnawing on his fingernails when Evie entered the office the next day. She hoped he'd lay low for a few days—and that after a weekend had passed, what had transpired between them wouldn't seem as big of a deal. No such luck. She sat down at her desk and immediately began to work, or at least to pretend to. Thank God the gallery purchase was set to wrap by the end of the week and she'd be done with her Brighton commitment.

"Evie," he whispered. "Can I talk to you outside?"

She didn't look up from her papers.

"There is nothing to talk about," she murmured. "Let's just forget about it."

"At least listen to me. I'm really sorry for what I did. It was not cool of me. I get it. I just thought we sort of had something. It sounds nuts, I know. But I can usually read chicks."

"Jamie, please, Thane is in his office. I don't want to discuss this now. Or ever."

"Do you still want to see my room? I could show you pictures of our apartment like you asked." He reached into his back pocket for his phone.

"No, no, no." My god, had she really asked for that? No wonder he made a move on her. "I think you misunderstood what I was saying. I need to work, Jamie. I'm not taking the full-time job here, but I still have to finish up this contract."

"My mom thought you were awesome, by the way."

"Really?" she said, perking up her head.

No, Evie, focus.

"That's nice," she added, less enthusiastically.

The bell rang signaling the first period was starting in three minutes. Jamie gathered his book bag.

"I'm really sorry again, Evie. Are we cool?"

"We're cool," she said, giving him a reassuring smile. He actually was a decent guy. If he was five years older and she was five years younger . . . maybe. What a home his mother could design for them. She pinched herself.

"We're cool," she repeated, and gave him back one of his signature salutes. "Eleanor's lucky to have you. I hope you guys work things out."

# # #

Edward and Evie's first date was at the movies. She had a queasy feeling in her stomach all day before he came to pick her up. Had she built him up too much because she thought he was unavailable? Would she suddenly notice a bulging vein in his forehead or a mole with a hair sprouting out of it on his neck? Maybe he had permanent garlic breath or dropped French expressions into casual conversation. Paul was always her go-to friend for a pep talk before an anxiety-provoking date. He'd say something like "You're hot, he's hot, what's the problem?" She didn't have the nerve to call him though, especially to ask for help. If he rebuffed her, as she expected he might, she'd never be able to enjoy the date.

When she went down to the lobby to meet Edward, she recognized what a runaway train her mind had been on. Seeing him standing comfortably in his date attire, looking absolutely perfect, she actually did a double-take. His faded jeans hit his suede driving loafers at just the right spot. Under his three-quarter-length overcoat Evie could see a checked button-down shirt layered beneath a gray V-neck sweater. She was pleased to see he was wearing his horn-rimmed glasses. They kissed on the cheek.

"Hi there," she said, feeling genuinely, butterflies-in-her-stomach, excited.

"Hi there," he repeated. "You look great."

"Thanks," Evie said casually, as though her black jeans, riding boots, and turquoise cowl-neck sweater weren't the tenth outfit she tried on that day.

"Ready to go? I want to make sure we have time to get popcorn," Edward said, touching her back.

"If we can't have popcorn we might as well not even go," Evie joked, feeling the tension melt from her shoulders. What a pleasure to be on a first date that wasn't essentially an after-dark job interview.

The movie was a romantic comedy, as fluffy as cotton candy. Their fingers kept touching when they reached for popcorn at the same time until Edward finally grabbed her hand and teased, "Hey, stop taking my popcorn." He didn't let go for the rest of the movie, resting their clasped hands on his left thigh.

"Want to get some dinner?" he asked, when they were walking out of the theater.

"Definitely," Evie said, stuffed from the popcorn. They wandered off hand in hand down Broadway until they found a sushi restaurant.

"So, are we telling Bette about this? The fact that we're out on a date?" Evie asked as she lifted a piece of spicy tuna to her mouth. "I saw her twice this week but didn't mention it. I guess I wanted to make sure we had some traction first." She had, in fact, been dying to share the news of her date with Edward and it was taking tremendous restraint to keep it in.

"Traction, huh? I like the way you phrased that. It's really up to you about telling Bette. But I'm pretty sure your grandmother will be quite pleased with herself," Edward said, leaving Evie to question his meaning. Was he saying that her grandmother would be glad that her illness brought them together? That was almost definitely true.

"I'm going to tell her when I see her for lunch tomorrow. It's basically criminal to hide dating a doctor from a Jewish grand-mother, really."

"I think I learned that in Hebrew school."

"Temple Israel? That's where I learned to French kiss." She popped an edamame into her mouth, loving the way she made Edward smile. She could get used to seeing that dimple every day. "After class, anyway."

"Hebrew school must have a universal curriculum."

"So, now that we've bonded over Hebrew school, you can tell me the truth. Have you ever left anything inside someone while doing surgery?"

"Not that I know of," Edward said. "I did lose my cell phone once during a surgery. But I figure my patient would have com-plained if she woke up in the recovery room and her chest was ringing."

Evie burst out laughing, an edamame bean nearly lodging in her throat.

"Ever commit malpractice?" he asked.

"Only once," she said, after a few sips of water. "But the client really deserved it."

"I'm sure you were totally justified." Edward expertly lifted a biteful of seaweed salad with his chopsticks. Evie liked watching his surgical hands at work. "I have to say, I feel a little guilty having such a great time right now with all the craziness in the news today. I don't think the cease-fire lasted more than two hours. Terrible, isn't it? Over one hundred civilian casualties."

Israel? Russia? Iraq? Evie didn't even know which continent had a war going on. Without her morning perusal of *theSkimm*, she was utterly lost. She really needed to subscribe to an actual newspaper.

"Terrible," she said, nodding vigorously. "I can't even begin to talk about it."

That bullet dodged, the rest of the date was sublime. They both agreed that desserts at Japanese restaurants were terrible, so after dinner they set out in search of ice cream in the crisp November weather. Thanksgiving was just a week away. She wondered what his plans were. Fran and Winston announced they were going on a one-week Galapagos cruise while the TWASPs celebrated with their mom. They invited Evie to join them, but she didn't feel comfortable tagging along. Even Bette, a visitor in New York, had plans. An old friend of hers from the Baltimore Hadassah, now living in Brooklyn, had invited Bette to Thanksgiving dinner with her bridge group. Evie would probably join Caroline's family for their Thanksgiving feast, where the food— all imported (even, inexplicably, the turkey)—had a shot of being as delicious as her last Turkey Day meal, which Jack cooked for the two of them. She was already dreading dinner at the Michaels', knowing she would feel like an interloper, but it still beat sitting home alone.

"Do you want to see my apartment?" Edward asked, when they were walking with their ice cream cones. "I live just a few blocks from here." He gestured beyond the triangular Apple Bank building, one of Evie's favorite New York landmarks.

Evie busied herself licking the ice cream drips off the cone so it wouldn't look like she was hesitating. The truth was that she wanted very badly to see where he lived and to do much more than that. But she didn't know what was appropriate anymore on dates. She was out of the game. Besides her time with Jack, the last few years had been a string of get-to-know-you dates with total strangers, very few of which she had been inclined to take to the next level. Edward and she were already close, even though it was only now officially turning romantic.

"Sure, let's go," Evie said, trying to make it sound like she wasn't vacillating.

Edward lived in a charming two-bedroom which occupied the full floor of a brownstone, located just five blocks north of Evie's building. She liked that they shared a neighborhood. They could have passed each other countless times at the dry cleaners or pharmacy. But he probably lived someplace much fancier when he was with Georgina, and she preferred not to think about that time in his life.

His block was lined with town houses, and a few impatient owners had already put up holiday lights. New York City, with its bustling streets and infinite options for distraction, could still feel like the loneliest place in the world during the holidays. Manhattan was about to get lit up like a giant Christmas tree, and even the city's most sensible, feet-on-the-ground inhabitants could lose themselves in the blinding lights. Evie wanted to lose herself in Edward. She hoped very much they would share the holiday season together.

"So this is it," Edward said, taking her coat. "Let me give you a tour. Suggestions on how to improve the appearance are certainly welcome."

He walked her through the living and dining room combo, the kitchen, his bedroom and finally Olivia's room. With the exception of the little girl's room, everything was neutral and lacked verve, like Edward had just ordered the pieces straight from a Pottery Barn catalogue. Olivia's room, on the other hand, was magnificent. The carpet was wall-to-wall magenta, and the furniture was creamy lacquered wood. All the accents were done in rose-colored toile.

"This is stunning," Evie said. "A dream room for a little girl."

Edward blushed.

"Thanks, I tried to make it special for her. Even hired a designer to do this room. Too bad I didn't know you then."

"You did great, whoever you hired and whatever you did," Evie said, reaching for his waist. She was surprised at herself for initiating physical contact in the apartment. But watching this gorgeous man exhibiting such obvious love for his daughter—it was very hot.

They started kissing. They shared soft, light pecks at first but both grew hungrier and more impatient. Edward tugged at her hand and she thought he was taking her to his bedroom. Instead he settled them on the living room couch, away from the prying eyes of Minnie Mouse and Dora the Explorer, who were perched on Olivia's shelves.

He rubbed his hands up and down her back and she found herself hoping he would be more aggressive and reach inside her shirt. Her wish came true. He worked his hands to her chest and starting running the lace of her bra between his fingers. Evie gasped when he reached inside and began caressing her breasts.

His touch started off soft and sensual, but the pressure gradually increased until Evie felt like her breasts were melons being squeezed for ripeness.

She scooted away from him abruptly.

"Are you feeling for lumps?"

"What? No. Of course not." He feigned shock.

Evie threw him an accusatory glance.

"Okay, okay. Maybe I was a little. It's an occupational hazard. But I promise I'll stop." He raised his arms in the air like he was facing a police officer with a pistol drawn.

"Okay," she said, and cracked a smile. It was pretty humorous, actually. A first date she'd certainly never forget. She relaxed and pulled him toward her. Edward planted a trail of gentle kisses from her collarbone to the top of her neck.

"I promise I know what I'm doing in this department," Edward whispered when he reached her ear. "And in checking for lumps, but I'm referring to, you know, this." He continued to kiss her but she found herself stiffening again.

"Everything okay?" he asked.

"So, did you feel anything? Lumps, I mean."

"Nothing, I promise. But you really should go for a baseline mammogram now that you're thirty-five."

"I'm not thirty-five," she exclaimed. "I'm thirty-four and a half," she faintly added.

"Wow, I thought only Olivia used halves to describe her age."

By now they had pulled apart from each other, both of them looking up at the track lighting like they were stargazing.

"So no lumps?" Evie asked again.

"No detectable lumps." He paused. "But why didn't you see the doctor whose name I gave you?"

"How do you know I didn't make an appointment?"

"I checked up on you."

"Isn't there, like, doctor-patient confidentiality or something?"

"Oh, you really believe in that?" Edward asked, laughing. "Kidding, of course."

"I hope so!" Evie exclaimed, opening her eyes in wide surprise.

"Of course," Edward said. "You know, I have never cared so much about any girl I've been on a first date with that I felt compelled to give her a breast exam. Just saying, this is highly unusual."

"Well maybe I'm an unusual girl," she said coquettishly.

"That's what I like about you," Edward said and cupped her chin with his hand, pulling her closer.

"In that case," she whispered as their faces were less than an inch apart, "there's also this mole on my thigh that I'd love for you to check out. I think it's spreading."

"No problem," he said. "But would you mind terribly if we kissed first?"

"Oh," Evie giggled. "That would be nice." She let him take the lead and felt her body unfold into a sequence of electric kisses, ravenous touches, and passionate embraces which stopped just short of them making the ultimate connection.

Around midnight, Evie stood up to leave and Edward walked her downstairs to put her in a taxi. He thanked her for an amazing evening. With her confidence soaring, she debated asking him again to examine her suspicious mole before they separated, but in a rare moment of restraint, she reined in her neuroses and let their evening together end with her acceptance of another date.

Chapter 16

It was the first New Year's Eve in recent memory that Evie could recall actually feeling happy. She didn't need to create a list of ambitious and untenable resolutions. The year before she was single, newly separated from Jack and beyond lost. She had found a project at the office in which to bury herself, and rang in the New Year at her desk while a lonely janitor vacuumed around her bare feet.

It wasn't much better when she was with Jack. The first time they celebrated New Year's he let her down by refusing to accompany her to a party at Caroline's place, saying he couldn't break away from JAK for even one hour. The second time they celebrated together, Jack was in a foul mood all night because the truffle delivery from Italy never arrived, killing his prix fixe menu. Her hopes of a fun night had already been dashed the day before the mushroom debacle when Jack's mother announced she was getting remarried and Jack said she must be suffering from dementia to make the same mistake twice.

At last, this year was different. She was spending the night with Edward, who to her delight wanted to enjoy New Year's Eve with a lovely dinner and be home by eleven thirty to watch the ball drop.

This would be their fifth date. In Evie's head, this was the date, the one when they would sleep together.

Their past dates had been heavenly, and, as expected, Bette was beyond thrilled when Evie told her she was seeing Edward. "*Nachas*, Evie. You give me so much *nachas*," she said. Following their movie date, they did a bowling and beer night. A week later they watched the Macy's parade from an apartment on Central Park West belonging to one of Edward's friends and later ate Thanksgiving dinner together in the hospital cafeteria because Edward was on call (Caroline didn't mind at all when Evie bailed). Edward confessed his love of all traditional Thanksgiving foods, gobbling up his own tray and portions of Evie's turkey, stuffing, relish, and sweet potato pie and bemoaning that people only ate that way once a year. The highlight of the date was when he told Evie he knew he wouldn't be on call the following Thanksgiving and was looking forward to celebrating with her properly. It was like he'd looked into a crystal ball and seen her face clearly in the reflection. On their latest date—the one she thought would have been the date—they took a horse and carriage ride through Central Park. They were with Olivia, who Edward was unexpectedly asked to watch so her mother could attend a holiday party.

He was going to cancel their date, but Evie wouldn't hear of it. The three of them set out on a cold evening to enjoy the holiday season in New York like tourists.

When Olivia fell asleep with her head in Evie's lap, Evie felt a level of contentment she'd never experienced before. As the little girl's chest rose up and down, Evie stroked her blond curlicues and let her fingers graze Olivia's impossibly soft cheek. None of this was for Edward's benefit. She was positively captivated by Olivia, loving everything about her small figure, raspy voice, and undeniably cute grammatical errors. The feeling seemed to be mutual. Olivia reached for Evie's hand during their carriage ride and snuck a sip of Evie's coffee when Edward wasn't looking, pleading in a whisper to try some "caffeine." It was almost too easy to Photoshop herself into the Gold family albums, that is until Edward's phone buzzed and Evie sneaked a peek at the text message: "E—remember to unpack O's hippo from her overnight bag and make sure you tell her Mommy misses her. G." Edward reached over and squeezed Evie's hand after he read the message. She didn't know if that was meant as reassurance or was just a simple gesture.

If there was anything else about their dates that left Evie feeling uneasy, it was how smoothly everything was going. Edward didn't play games. He didn't confess to being a commitment-phobe. He didn't say he'd never marry again. He called when he said he would. He told Evie how much he liked her. They didn't struggle to make conversation. They made each other laugh—a lot. She liked who she was around him. But instead of taking pleasure in the ease with which their relationship was progressing, Evie constantly needed to remind herself that there was nothing wrong with everything going right. That she deserved this level of joy after enduring nearly thirteen years in the New York City dating scene. It was just that dating Edward was the opposite of dating Jack. With Jack, she was masochistic, growing more attached to him the more aloof and unattainable he was. With Edward, she liked him more the closer they got and the more he gave himself over to her.

Her excitement about ringing in the New Year with Edward was mitigated only by her distance from Paul and Stasia. Stasia wasn't practiced in loneliness, and being a jilted wife on New Year's Eve had to really sting. Evie called her first thing in the morning to check in but wasn't shocked when voicemail picked up after only one ring. The same thing had happened when Evie called her a few weeks after Tracy's son was born, and she was ashamed to admit she hadn't tried again until this morning. She knew from Tracy, who barely had a minute to talk because Henry was permanently attached to her breast, that Rick had moved out and had taken up residence with his twenty-two-year-old girl-friend, his indoor cycling instructor. "What a fucking cliché," Tracy had said. It made Evie sick to think how shitty Stasia must be feeling, and even sicker knowing there was nothing she could do to make her feel better.

Paul was known to sulk whenever his feelings were bruised, so instead Evie called Marco, hoping to mend fences via an overture toward his partner. But Marco didn't pick up either. Caroline called her last week to say their baby arrived early (a phrasing that led Evie to envision a crying infant popping out of a FedEx box), and the new dads were obviously overwhelmed. Evie's neglect of both situations meant that repairing those friendships would have to wait for the new year—she just hoped forgiveness was among Stasia's and Paul's resolutions. Not that she particularly deserved it. For someone who had depended so much on the kindness of her friends throughout the years—resuscitating her after both her father's passing and breakup with Jack and attending faithfully to her just-below-the-surface loneliness—she'd been pretty rotten in return, at least of late. No matter where things headed with Edward, fixing these friendships had to be a priority.

Edward didn't tell her where he'd made a reservation for that evening, but she imagined it would be fairly nice given the occasion. She looked forward to dressing up for him. The only time he'd seen her fully decked out was when she wore a cocktail dress to Bette's surgery for the photo that was never taken. While studying her closet the morning of their date, her home phone rang. All she could hear through the receiver was crying.

"Who is this?"

"Evie, you've got to help me," the voice sputtered. Caroline.

"Care, what happened?" Evie asked, cradling the phone to her ear.

"Jerome is going to kill me. What am I going to do? He comes back from his business trip tonight," Caroline choked out and started wailing again.

"Calm down. What is going on? Why is your husband going to kill you?" Evie braced herself for hearing another tale of infidelity.

"Because I lost four hundred thousand dollars," she cried into the phone. "Four hundred thousand dollars. Gone."

"How is that possible?"

Caroline's sobs subsided to noisy sniffles.

"Let me come over, I'll tell you the whole story."

"Sure, of course, I'm home. I'm just getting ready for New Year's Eve."

"Oh, that's right, that's tonight. It's just that Jerome is going to kill me." The waterworks started up again.

"It's going to be okay. I'll see you in a bit."

Two minutes later, Evie heard a knock at her door. A mascara-streaked, red-faced Caroline stood quaking in her doorway. Her normally blow-dried locks were assembled in a bun that seemed to challenge basic architectural principles. It was the least put together Evie had seen her friend look since their hungover Sunday brunches in college.

"How the hell did you get here so fast?"

"I was in my car, downstairs. I figured I'd just stalk your apartment until you came back if you weren't home. I really need your help." She collapsed on Evie's couch but popped up again a moment later.

"This place is so beautiful. You have the best taste," Caroline said. "I love these pillows. Where did you get them?"

"Um, thanks. But can we talk about my apartment later? Tell me what's going on with you and Jerome."

Caroline, seemingly oblivious, began inspecting the wine-glasses that Evie had displayed on floating shelves above her TV.

"Care? You called me hysterical. Now you're appraising my apartment. What is going on with you?"

Caroline flopped into the armchair adjacent to Evie's sofa.

"Ooh, this is comfortable too. Is this calfskin?"

Evie glared at her, refusing to answer.

"Okay, okay. Let me explain. Jerome's birthday is next week, so I wanted to do something special for him. He had talked about redoing his home office for a while but was always too busy at work to focus on it. So I told him for his—" Caroline hesitated, and then went on. "Oh whatever, what's the difference?" She seemed to be talking to herself. "I told him for his sixty-fifth birthday I would redecorate his office for him and surprise him with it when he returned from the hedge fund conference in Gstaad."

So that's how old Jerome was! Caroline had been very cagey about his age since they first met. There was no trace of it on JCM Capital's website or even in the articles written about him. Now that she knew, Evie wasn't as appalled as she thought she'd be by their thirty-year age difference. Her friend was happily married. That much was clear. The rest—the biographical details, the résumé minutiae, the stuff of the *New York Times* wedding announcements and the search engine returns—that was just background noise, particulars that so often obfuscated what really mattered.

"Anyway, I found this decorator. Pierre Von Warburg," Caroline said his name disdainfully. "We were introduced through Kiki Krauss, you know my friend who always carries that little Maltese around with her. Remember, Jack used to say she looked like a young Cruella de Vil?"

Jack *always* did that. This one looked like an Indian Mickey Rooney; that one looked like a skinny Oprah. Evie would always gallantly agree. But was he even remotely on the mark? His wife Zeynup, at least in pictures, looked like an anorexic Padma Lakshmi. Did he see that resemblance?

Evie nodded.

"Anyway, Pierre was apparently so desirable that you had to be introduced to him through a current client in order for him to consider taking on your job. I was really excited when he agreed to redo Jerome's office."

Evie rolled her eyes. "Care, you sound like you resurrected Michelangelo to paint the ceiling in your den."

"Stop it, Evie. This is serious. I know you think I'm wasteful, and whatever, maybe I am. But I really need your help right now. And by the way, I wouldn't be so mean to me. I'm basically your only friend at this point in time."

Evie trembled. Caroline was right—it was proven just moments earlier when both Stasia and Marco wouldn't take her call.

"You've got me there. I'm sorry. Go on."

"Anyway, we met a few times, he showed me pictures of the things we were ordering. I thanked Kiki for the introduction and even took her out to Degustation for lunch."

"You what?" Evie jumped. "I thought we agreed all of Jack's restaurants were banned."

"I'm so sorry, I know. But that's where Kiki wanted to go. Trust me, I regret the whole thing now. You forgive me?"

"Yeah, yeah. It's fine." The truth was, since she started dating Edward, Jack crossed her mind less and less. But now her curiosity was piqued. "How was the food? Is it nice inside?"

"Honey, the worst. The meat was overcooked, the salad was wilted. I bet that joint closes in a year. Kiki even found a damn hair in her foie gras." Evie hadn't heard Caroline's Texas-speak since she said that Jerome's colleague Harry was back together with his ex and that's why he didn't call her.

"Is one word of what you just said true?"

"No." Caroline shook her head from left to right sorrowfully. "The food was delicious. It's stunning inside. I'm sorry."

"Was he there?"

"No, sweetie." Caroline gently touched Evie's knee. "I didn't see Jack."

"It's fine, really. Honestly. I'm so excited about Edward that it almost makes hearing about Jack's success tolerable. Just tell me more about Pierre the Terrible."

"So I paid for all the furniture up front, which I think is actually standard. It came to just over four hundred thousand dollars."

"Jesus, Care, what did you order, a credenza made of solid gold?"

"No! Not even. Just a few things. But he said they were being custom-made in Vienna by the world's foremost furniture maker."

"Let me guess, the stuff never arrived."

"Exactly. Everything was supposed to come yesterday. I stayed home the whole day waiting for the deliveries. Nothing came. I tried Pierre's cell and office phones. Both were disconnected. I called Kiki. Her housekeeper said she's on vacation and can't be reached. I think they ran off together with my money. And

Jerome comes back tomorrow. He's expecting to see the new office when he gets home. And he knows how much I spent because we discussed the budget. So it's not like I can replace it without him knowing. He's going to think I'm an idiot."

"Care, Jerome will understand. This isn't your fault. Pierre's a con artist, plain and simple."

"But it is my fault. Jerome wanted to use the same decorator that designed his company's offices, Julianne something-or-other."

"Holmes-Matthews?" Evie asked through a clenched jaw.

"Yes, that's her. But I fought him on this. I told him Kiki said Pierre is the absolute best and does all the top residences in Europe. Jerome said he didn't feel comfortable using someone he'd never heard of but finally gave in after I badgered him for a week."

"Still, Care, he'll understand. You guys surely have enough money that losing four hundred thousand dollars doesn't mean you won't be able to feed Grace and Pippa."

"Yes, of course. But you don't get it. It can be hard being with someone so much older. Someone I feel—I don't know—subordinate or something, like I have to prove myself." Caroline's hysterics had subsided, but a few tears slid down her cheeks. It was very dramatic for nine in the morning when Evie was still precoffee.

Evie fetched her a box of tissues. She crouched down next to her friend and started to wipe the black coal from Caroline's face.

"Don't forget, you may be younger than Jerome, but you are more than capable. You have an amazing education and before you got married, you were an investment banker at Goldman Sachs for crying out loud."

"Thank you. It feels good to hear that."

"I want to help you fix this, but what can I do?" Evie asked.

"Well, nobody in the world has better taste than you. Remember the *Yale Daily News* photographed your dorm room sophomore year? Look at what you've done with this apartment. It looks like a showroom. You turned your grandmother's place around overnight. And Tracy's classroom—which I still want to come see. You never did tell me why you turned down the offer from Brighton."

"It's complicated. Suffice it to say I'm ready to do the soul searching necessary to find employment that does more than just pay the bills. The kind that doesn't make me dread Sunday evenings."

"Well, in that case, good riddance. You'll find something better. You need a more creative field. I've always thought so."

"That's what Edward thinks too. But enough about me. Back to the issue at hand—you want me to decorate Jerome's office in one day on what, like, a thousand dollars?"

"No, don't be silly," Caroline said, waving her hand. "Ten thousand. I have a little money set aside that Jerome doesn't know about. Kind of a rainy day fund." She looked uneasy but went on. "It was something my mom suggested when I first got married. She said, 'Caroline Ashley Murphy, you may be marryin' someone with all the tea in China, but it ain't gonna help ya if you get tossed out of China.'"

"Sounds like something my grandmother would say." Evie laughed.

"I think it's something that every woman with experience in life would say," Caroline said ruefully. "So, can you help me?"

"No problem. I can replicate a room that was supposed to cost four hundred thousand for ten thousand dollars in one day. When I'm done, I'll just cure cancer and discover a new planet. I heard they knocked Pluto off the list."

"Please, I'm desperate. You've got to help me."

"I want to. But I'm not a decorator. Good taste doesn't qualify me as one. I wouldn't know where to start." Which actually wasn't true at all. She was already placing the burgundy lounge chair with the nickel trim that she spotted in a recent Crate & Barrel catalogue in the corner of Jerome's office. Together with the striped velvet drapes with the wooden grommets from Restoration Hardware and a sisal rug from ABC Carpet, the look would be masculine and warm. Jerome's office had a coveted southern exposure, and the natural light would balance the darker tones of the furniture perfectly. The project was actually exhilarating to Evie. On any other day. But she had to prepare for the date.

"It'll be fine. Jerome won't be examining the rug fibers. Please," Caroline whined. She looked up at the wall clock in Evie's living room, a treasured art deco find Evie had scouted at a flea market in the West Village a few years ago. "Listen, if we can finish before five P.M., I can make you the belle of the freakin' ball for tonight. We'll go to Bergdorf Goodman. Any dress you want. Then we'll head to the salon upstairs to get your hair, makeup, and nails done. Everything on me."

"You'll throw in new shoes too?" Evie was half-kidding.

"Heels to match your dress plus flats to wear the next day when you come over to see how much Jerome loves his new office." Caroline made a puppy-dog face.

Evie looked out the window. The weatherman said it was eighteen degrees, and you could actually see the bitter cold in the air. Snow was predicted for later that afternoon. It wasn't the climate for trekking around the city on a shopping binge. But then she thought back to the day when Caroline showed up at her apartment after her downfall at Baker Smith to force the much-needed spa day on her. She realized she had mentally agreed to help from the minute Caroline walked in crying. Why else would she have changed out of her pajamas while Caroline was filling her in? She vowed to be a better friend, and there was no time like the present to start.

"What the hell? Let's go shopping."

Caroline threw her arms around Evie and they both grabbed their coats and hats.

"One more thing, though," Caroline said, linking arms with Evie, as though to preempt her from changing her mind.

"What's that?"

"The whole office needs to be done in feng shui. Something about the balanced chi being good for Jerome's hedge fund."

# # #

Evie and Caroline were at the last store, the furniture department of Bloomingdale's, after having scoured every reasonably priced furniture store in all of Manhattan for upward of six hours. On the ground floor, they were assaulted by perfume spritzers wishing them "happy new year" from behind scented clouds of gardenia, vanilla, and hibiscus. The assorted bouquet was giving Evie a headache and she was losing steam fast. They were in search of a "bureau plat," which Pierre had promised would be the pièce de résistance and for which he had convinced Caroline to fork over $50,000 alone. Caroline had been so excited about it, she couldn't resist telling Jerome. Now it was up to Evie to find one for her. They had $212.39 left to spend.

"Should I ask someone for help?" Caroline called out, sounding overwhelmed and exhausted. She was lying prostrate on a mattress in the bedding department, attempting a nap on a Frette display. Evie was off studying some bronzed bookends a few yards away.

"I guess so. Honestly, I'm not sure we're going to have much luck finding one. But it's worth asking, I guess." She headed toward an elderly saleswoman standing near the glassware. "Our best bet is that Jerome doesn't know what a bureau plat is, so we can just buy a nice lamp and tell him that's it."

As Evie approached, a singsongy voice rang out from the fine china section. "Can I get some help for my registry please?" The salesperson took a detour to attend to the high-pitched chirping.

"My fiancé and I need help deciding which pattern to choose," she heard the girl say. Evie gagged. There was nothing worse than an engaged couple walking around a department store with one of those stupid price guns, selecting gifts like they were at target practice.

A familiar male voice emerged to join the conversation.

"Yeah, we're looking for something that would work for dinner parties but that we could also use casually, for when we start a family."

"Aww. He's the best," she said, and Evie could actually hear the smooch.

The girl stepped out first from behind a tall display of dishes. She was a petite redhead wearing a bright purple turtleneck with slim olive pants; she could have been wrapping Christmas presents in a Banana Republic catalogue. Maybe it was the smattering of freckles across her nose, but she just looked too young to be getting married. Every gesture of hers seemed intended to accentuate the engagement ring on her finger. She kept checking on it, as though it might vanish into thin air.

The fiancé stepped into view a moment later. He seemed to take notice of Evie before she saw his face, because by the time her eyes met his, he was ashen.

"Um, hi there. It's been a while since we last—talked," Evie said. It was Luke Glasscock, Paul's cousin. He looked exactly the same. Hazelnut eyes. Nice head of wavy hair. Only this time Evie felt repulsed.

She turned to the redhead.

"I'm Evie. You must be the future Mrs. Glasscock?" Evie extended her hand, which the girl reluctantly accepted.

Luke just stood there dumb-faced. He offered nothing toward facilitating the introduction.

"Yes, I'm Emily. How do you two know each other?" She turned to Luke for explanation.

"Oh, we met a long time ago at a party." To Evie, he said dismissively, "Anyway, so good to see you. Take care."

"It wasn't that long ago," Evie corrected him.

"Yeah, I guess I don't remember that well," he said. "Well, again, great to bump into you. I hope everything's good."

"So how long have you two been engaged?" she asked Emily, pretending to be oblivious to Luke's curtness.

"Thirteen months. Long engagement, I know. But wedding planning is really hard work," Emily said, as earnestly as humanly possible.

"I can imagine," Evie responded, dripping with empathy.

She recognized the power she was holding. She could persist in the conversation with Luke and Emily, explain to this wide-eyed young girl with the sparkly ring that she met Luke just over seven months ago at his cousin's wedding. Emily would go to sleep questioning how bizarre the interaction in Bloomingdale's was, and wonder why her fiancé was so awkward and rushed. She'd wonder why Luke didn't take *her* to the wedding.

"Anyway, we've got a few other stores to get to today, so we've got to go now," Luke said, this time more firmly.

"Wait a second," Evie said. She even reached for his arm to hold him in place. "There's something I need to say."

Luke looked like he might expire. She took great pleasure in watching him squirm. Emily sensed the tension in the air. She looked like she was bracing for what Evie would say.

"Yes?" Luke asked, timid as a tadpole.

Evie leaned in and signaled to Luke and Emily to come in closer. When they were huddled together in an unlikely trio, she could hear Luke's labored breathing.

"The china pattern you guys are considering," Evie said. "It's gaudy. I would definitely consider something more elegant."

Emily looked like she might burst into tears. If having her taste criticized was enough to make her cry, Evie wondered how she'd react to hearing her future husband was a cheat.

Luke smiled for the first time since running into Evie.

"She's right, Emily. We really should reconsider." Luke shot Evie a grateful look.

The couple stepped away to analyze different dishes as Caroline glided over to Evie.

"Who were those people?" she asked.

"Nobody important." Evie thought to herself for a moment and added, "You know what is so weird, Care?"

"What's that?" she asked, yawning.

"How you can obsess over something so much and concoct a million different scenarios in your head, and then when you discover the truth you realize you had no idea what was really going on, so fixating on it was just a big fat waste of time."

Caroline yawned again. "I have no idea what you're talking about, and I'm beat. Forget the bureau plat. Let's just go and make you beautiful."

Chapter 17

Caroline delivered on her promise to transform Evie for her date with Edward. After they finished furniture shopping, they headed straight to the European designer floor at Bergdorf. Evie winced at the prices of the clothes she was trying on, but Caroline waved her off.

"I'm going to rescind on my offer if I see you look at another tag."

Evie settled on an elegant Christian Dior black cocktail dress. Despite her promise, she sneaked a glance and saw it was almost $3,000. For that same money, Evie had purchased velvet drapes, a leather love seat, a desk stained to look like it was walnut, faux-silk lamp shades, a substantial desk blotter with matching pen set, and a wool throw blanket.

But once she tried it on, the dress almost seemed worth the exorbitant price. The fabric, a wool crepe, was the softest and most luxurious material to ever touch her skin. The fit was impeccable. Small silk bows were stitched atop the shoulders and at the bottom of the zipper, just at the base of her spine. The dress had a subtle sheen, the result of the meticulous weaving of iridescent silver threads. The Bergdorf dressing room was bathed in lavender and illuminated with soft, indirect lighting, and Evie suspected just about anyone would have a shot in there. The saleswoman had three stacks of shoe boxes brought over (Caroline appeared to be something of a Bergdorf VIP), from which Evie selected a pair of four-inch-high nude stilettos. After the salon worked her over, coiffing her hair into a falling tower of loose waves and penciling in eyebrow arches worthy of a design patent, Evie's confidence was sky-high.

"You look unreal," Caroline said, when they were back at Evie's apartment. She pulled out her phone and snapped a photo of Evie. "Can I post this? I know you're above computers these days, but surely you'll allow me to broadcast this image."

Evie shrugged. "Sure, if you want to," she said. Not too long ago she would have been delighted to float this image into the digital universe. Hell, she would have taken a selfie. Now she was indifferent at best. She just wanted Edward to appreciate her.

"Okay, I'm going to split before he comes to get you." Caroline grabbed her fur coat and buzzed Jorge. "You look gorgeous. Edward is going to pass out when you open the door."

Evie hid her pleasure. "With my luck, he's probably taking me skating. I'll end up looking like an Ice Capade."

"Stop the negativity, lady! You look too pretty to be pessimistic. It's New Year's. You're going to have a great night."

"Let's hope so. I'm going to tell Edward about Jack tonight. I feel like it's important, you know? I wanted to marry the guy, for crying out loud. I wish I'd just told Edward weeks ago, when he told me about Georgina. But he was in a rush, and I was still in shock over him asking me out. Now that I didn't, it's like this big thing that's snowballing every day. It'll at least explain the motivation for going off-line. Partially, anyway."

"You should tell him about Jack," Caroline said, pulling on a pair of sumptuous leather gloves. "And the Internet. You obviously want a future with Edward, so you have to be up front with him."

"I know. I think I've been scared to say anything because it makes me look crazy—giving up a major means of communication because my ex got married. But it was more than that really. I felt like the whole world had voluntarily signed up to be on *Big Brother*. I couldn't keep up. And I didn't want to. Do you get it?"

"I do get it, though obviously I have not followed in your footsteps." Caroline extended her palm with her iPhone balanced on it like a tray. "As for telling him about Jack, of course you should. It's always a good idea to be up front about significant exes—or wives, in Jerome's case." She smiled sheepishly.

"I guess I'm also a little embarrassed. Like Edward will wonder why Jack didn't want to marry me, especially because he married someone else so soon after. He's going to think I'm so foolish—believing all of Jack's no-marriage crap, wasting my time like I did."

"Evie, Edward's a big boy. He can make his own decisions. He's not going to be influenced because someone out there, some guy that he doesn't even know, didn't want a happily ever after with you. I would hate to think you would break up with someone if you found out they had been dumped before."

"Thanks. I know you're right," Evie said. The old Evie might have done just that very thing, ditched a perfectly good prospect because someone else had deemed him unsuitable. "It'll probably be like a five-minute conversation and then we'll move on. I don't even know what I'm so worried about."

Caroline blew her a kiss and headed out the door. "Anyway, Evie love, thank you, thank you, thank you for your help. I hope you'll come by tomorrow. Feel free to bring Edward."

Feel free to bring Edward. That sounded nice.

Ten minutes later, her doorman called up to announce that Dr. Gold was downstairs. She told him she'd be right down, but the doorman said her guest would like to come up. Edward had never been to her apartment before. They always met in her lobby and ended their evenings at his place.

She propped her door slightly ajar and watched with glee as a beautiful bouquet of flowers was the first thing to poke into her apartment. At least three dozen white roses obscured Edward's face. The blossoms were artfully assembled, long stemmed and thorn trimmed, tied with a heavy grosgrain ribbon.

"These are for you," he said as he handed them off to Evie, adding with an adorable head bobble, "obviously."

Evie motioned him inside, noticing a tiny bit of stubble on his jawline when they kissed. It made Evie think how much better off they'd be when they got ready together—she'd point out a patch of hair he'd missed and he'd zip up her dress. She'd remind him to take his phone, he'd help her with tricky jewelry clasps. Maybe her mother was right: it was a couples' world.

Tonight Edward had replaced his usual horn-rimmed glasses with contacts. He was still a few inches taller than she was in her skyscraper heels. She was glad she had let Caroline make her over because Edward was looking his absolute best that night, in a black velvet blazer, suede loafers, and the darkest shade of indigo jeans. She thought she even detected the slightest hint of hair gel, which gave away that he too had gone through extra effort for the night.

"The flowers are gorgeous," she said, and leaned in to give him another kiss. His spicy aftershave wafted pleasurably into her nose.

She headed toward the makeshift bar area she had created in her kitchen and grabbed a vase for the roses.

"You look incredible," he said. "That dress is really pretty."

"Nice of you to notice," Evie said. "My friend bought it for me, actually."

"Nice friend," he said. Evie kicked herself for telling him her friend bought her the dress. Why couldn't she just accept the compliment without diminishing herself in the process?

"Yeah, well, I did her a big favor so I kind of earned it."

"Being married to Georgina I learned a lot about fashion. Plus Olivia is already into shopping, even though she mostly wants sparkly princess costumes." He rolled his eyes with a smile and Evie enjoyed seeing his parental pride surface even while he was technically complaining about his daughter. She brushed off the Georgina reference. If she was going to have a real future with Edward, it would mean hearing about Georgina from time to time. She'd just have to get used to it.

"Your apartment is amazing," he said. "Not that I'm surprised. Just affirms my opinion you should start an interior design business. I know you thought I was crazy when I first said it, but you have real talent."

"Thanks. I've actually had the chance to play decorator quite a bit recently. I guess I'm test-driving your career advice. It's a far cry from being a lawyer, but a hell of a lot more enjoyable."

"I told you so," Edward said and gave Evie a warm shoulder squeeze. "I love the coffee table. It could be in a magazine."

Evie beamed. Edward had singled out her favorite piece of furniture. Unable to find a coffee table that she liked in her price range, she had assembled one out of coffee-table books. Four stacks of neatly piled books about everything from religious iconography to modern architecture made up the base of her table. She topped the books with a heavy glass top from a table that had rested in her father's home office in Baltimore.

Edward walked around her place, examining the furniture and the artwork closely. He approached her bedroom and turned back to Evie to ask, "May I peek?"

"I'll show it to you later," Evie said with a wink. She loved how flirting with Edward came so naturally to her. He made her feel sexy and desirable, giving her the confidence to say things that would ordinarily get stuck on her tongue.

"Sounds good to me," Edward said and looked at his watch. "We should go. The place we're going to is really popular. I don't want them to give away our table."

Evie was famished. She and Caroline only had time to scarf down some frozen yogurt during their shopping expedition.

"So we're not going ice-skating?"

Edward looked at her curiously. "No, we're not going ice-skating. What a strange question."

"Never mind," she said, reaching for his hand. "Let's go."

"We can walk. It's only a few blocks away." Edward put on his coat and helped Evie into hers.

She wondered where they were going, hoping it was the new Italian place on Amsterdam that was recently featured in *New York* magazine, which emitted the most heavenly garlic smell through its front door. She'd been dying to try it, but the tiny candlelit tables and soft music made her feel unwelcome as a single.

They walked several blocks south from her apartment, giggling each time they passed a group of New Year's Eve revelers in tiaras and oversize numerical sunglasses. Evie started telling Edward all about her adventures decorating Jerome's office on a shoestring budget. She forgot all about the Italian place she hoped they were going to, which was in the other direction, and let herself be led by Edward, who was clasping her gloved hand.

"We're here," Edward said, putting his hand on Evie's arm to halt her from walking. She was looking down at the street when they stopped and noticed that the rattan doormat at her feet seemed familiar.

"I hope you like French food. This place is supposedly the best on the Upper West Side. Have you been here? It's called JAK."

"It's very good," she whispered, her appetite, her confidence, and her enthusiasm vanishing simultaneously. Before she knew it, she was on the other side of the door, and cursing herself for not making an excuse for why they should go elsewhere. Not that they could have gotten in anywhere. Jack had once told her New Year's Eve was the busiest night of the year for restaurants. In fact, she knew that to secure an 8:00 P.M. reservation, Edward had to have arranged the dinner a month in advance. She wished she could have appreciated his foresight, but in the moment she was too wrapped up in the stress of her surroundings.

Once the restaurant door closed behind her, she might as well have stepped into a time capsule. The smell of brown butter and rosemary, which Evie knew came from Jack's famous filet of sole preparation, thrust her olfactory sense into déjà vu. She was transported back to when she'd drink red wine at an empty table after midnight while Jack reviewed the evening with his staff. Jack would admonish her for putting her bare feet on the tablecloth; Evie would tease him that the crème brûlée was overly torched. Looking at Edward, all she could think was that they were both entering this relationship with a trolley full of baggage.

Their table wasn't ready, so they stood at the crowded bar. She fixed her eyes on the glossy purple of the Montepulciano in her hand—anything to avoid looking around. Edward ordered himself a Scotch, neat, and if she weren't so distracted, she would have taken the time to appreciate his taste in manly drinks. They strained to talk over the din, Evie doing her best to appear as normal and composed as possible. When they were finally seated, Evie was stressed their conversation was waning—a first for them, but she just couldn't focus on anything Edward was saying. Fortunately the server came over right away to hand them menus. Evie used hers like a burka, hiding most of her face except for her eyes, which were darting around the room, looking for Jack. He was nowhere in sight. Maybe he was at Degustation or Paris Spice for the night.

The waitress ran through the list of specials, not even glancing down at the pad in her hand once. Jack always insisted his waitstaff memorize the plats du jour.

"And finally," the server said, "our master chef, Jack Kipling, is in residence, so if you have any special requests or questions about the menu, he is available to speak with you."

So much for him being elsewhere. Please, please, please let nobody in this restaurant ask him any questions. Let him stay in the kitchen all night long, and maybe even burn his hand on a Crock-Pot.

"Should we meet the chef?" Edward asked. "Could be interesting. Maybe ask him to whip up some fantastic dessert for us."

"Um, let's not. I'm sure he's busy." Busy ruining my life, she added to herself.

"Okay then," Edward said, looking a little disappointed. "Are you ready to order?"

"Let me give you two a moment," the server said, perhaps registering Evie's look of abject distress.

Evie was frustrated. It was a small matter, but she didn't want to seem like a party pooper shooting down the suggestion of meeting the chef. She had planned to tell Edward about her relationship with Jack that night. Then she could ring in the New Year Jack-free—and with no significant parcels of her life story left untold to Edward. Was that so much to ask? Now, flustered and flailing at her ex's restaurant, there was no way she could imagine getting through it.

Evie reviewed the menu. Many of the dishes were new, but her favorite appetizer and main course remained. They were among Jack's specialties, and he'd often prepare them for her at his apartment, especially if she was feeling under the weather. That was one of the things she loved most about him. The way he could ignite her senses with his craft, waking her with the smell of freshly prepared waffles or drawing her to the kitchen with the sound of turkey bacon crackling in the pan. Jack said he liked to see the pleasure on her face while she ate his food. Maybe it was self-referential. More about feeding his ego than feeding her soul. But maybe it wasn't. Maybe he just liked seeing her happy. And maybe that's why he kept those items on the menu. Even Jack was subject to sentimentality.

When a different server returned to take their order, Evie said, "I'm going to have the macaroni and cheese with asparagus to start, and then the branzino with—"

"Broccoli instead of haricot vert?" the waitress asked, smiling at her. "I switched tables when I spotted you over here."

"Tasha?" Evie squinted her eyes to focus on her face, still in disbelief of her surroundings.

"Yep, it's me. Still working here, still pursuing acting. Got a speaking part on *Law & Order* but it's only two words. Did get my SAG card though. What's going on with you, girl?" Tasha's eyes shifted her gaze to Edward.

"I'm good," she said. Then realizing everything she said would get directly reported to Jack, she added, "Actually, I'm great. Never been better."

Edward beamed, oblivious to her reason for amplification.

"Well that's good to hear. Happy New Year to you both. Enjoy your meal, hon," Tasha said, and bounded straight into the kitchen.

"Wow, you're famous," Edward said. "I thought I was well known after my picture appeared in the paper for six days straight, but nobody knows my order by heart."

"I used to come here a lot." At least that was true.

"Well then I'm glad I chose it." He leaned in closer. "I made a reservation after our first date. I was hoping we'd be together on New Year's."

"So thoughtful," she said, knowing it wasn't enough but somehow unable to say anything more.

"I made it on OpenTable about five minutes after you left that first night. Call me optimistic."

"Uh-huh," she said, again not delivering nearly what she should.

"Obviously I could live without online reservations, but seriously how do you function without the Internet? And, I guess more to the point, why?"

She took a deep breath and swept the room one more time for a sighting of Jack. "It's a long story."

"That's okay. We've got until midnight," Edward said, glancing at his watch jokingly. "I assume you'll be done before the ball drops?"

"I think I'll just finish up in time," Evie said, with mock gravity. She reached for her water glass and took a deliberate sip. "I did quit because of something specific, but there have been all these other reasons for me to keep—abstaining, I guess is the way to put it best. Functioning is trickier, though I think my fingers have slimmed down." She flexed her wrists, knowing how she would balk if Edward tried to dodge a serious discussion with a silly joke.

"I could never do it. I use the Internet all the time for research and to communicate with my patients. Don't get me wrong—I also waste a ton of time online. ESPN.com is my nemesis."

Actually, your nemesis is in the kitchen, dicing vegetables for your soup right now, she thought.

"Oh really? Yankees or Mets?" she asked, seizing her opportunity for a detour. "I'm Orioles all the way. They have the best chili fries at Camden Yards." Her father, his face splattered with Worcestershire sauce and shouting from the bleachers, appeared before her. What would he say to his daughter if he knew how panicked she was feeling right now? Probably, "Talk to your mother."

"Yankees, of course. I think Olivia is ready for her first game next season." He went on about the Pixar movie he had taken her to the day before, tabling the Internet discussion, much to Evie's relief.

Why had she clammed up? She could have said Facebook had been too much of a time drain. That she finally saw the absurdity in Foursquaring her location. Or in Instagramming like her life was a perpetual photo booth. Even the truth about her dismissal from Baker Smith. She had multiple Jack-free versions of why she was off-line at her disposal, all of which had sizable grains of truth. But Jack was the undeniable catalyst, and lying—or sharing a partial truth with Edward—didn't feel right, especially when her ex was fewer than twenty feet away and she could barely gather her thoughts just knowing he was nearby. Because she knew that in fact it was the moment she saw something she wasn't meant to see—Jack's body, hand in hand with Zeynup's, his face just moments after saying I do—*that* was the moment she wasn't equipped to handle, the one that led her down this rabbit hole.

When Evie's and Edward's first courses arrived, she paused to admire the familiar preparation before sinking her teeth into the perfectly crisped macaroni and cheese. The familiar taste of the creamy mozzarella and sweet asparagus tips topped with seasoned bread crumbs exploded in her mouth. The aromatic steam made her eyes water. She had missed this dish more than she remembered and found herself savoring every morsel. Her plate was nearly licked clean when Tasha cleared it.

"Everything here to your satisfaction?"

Evie flinched when she saw a stained apron out of the corner of her eye. She looked up, and there he was. Looking down at her table, wearing his toque, Jack looked the same as the last time she saw him just over a year ago. Still handsome, still with his confident stance, still with his watery blue eyes that looked like they were on the verge of springing soulful tears. He did seem to have a bit less hair than she remembered. And maybe the beginnings of a gut. Never trust a skinny chef, her mother had said when she showed her Jack's picture two years ago.

"Yes, the food is wonderful. The butternut squash soup was sublime," Edward said. "This is my first time here but I'd heard wonderful things."

Evie wanted to shout "Stop kissing his ass! You're the one who saves lives." Instead she just sat in her chair, uncomfortably twisting her fork with her fingers.

"And you?" Jack asked, turning to Evie.

"And me what?"

"Are you enjoying your dinner?" Jack asked, staring at her intently. Edward seemed unaware that the conversation before him was not taking place between strangers.

"It's good. And I'm good. Never been better, like I told Tasha," Evie said. Now Edward looked confused.

"Excuse me," Jack said, turning to Edward. "Would you mind if I borrow your date for one minute?"

Edward mumbled "of course" as his perplexed look morphed into displeasure.

"Sorry," Evie mouthed to Edward and rose to follow Jack to the back of the restaurant, toward his office.

When the door was closed behind them and they were in private, Jack spoke first.

"Evie, I have to say this: you look brilliant. I have never seen you so magnificent. You're incandescent."

"Caroline bought me this outfit." God damn it. What hope was there for her if she could repeat the same mistake twice within an hour?

"So she and moneybags are still going strong then?" Jack asked, and Evie felt wistful hearing Jack's familiarity with her friends. It took so long to build history with someone—to get to the point where you could exchange a glance and know exactly what the other was thinking. Or even just to know the foibles of the people in each other's network of friends and family. There was so much effort involved in bringing a new person up to speed, Evie felt lethargic at just the thought of it. Maybe that was part of why she hadn't told Edward about Jack yet—pure exhaustion.

Evie faintly nodded at Jack.

"Well, she may have bought the dress for you, but you're the one wearing it so well."

"Thanks," Evie said, looking down at her peep-toe pumps. For some reason, Jack's compliments were making her feel smaller, each kind word from him taking a quarter inch off of her heels. If he kept going, she'd shrink into a pile of nothingness. Just a designer dress lying bodiless on the ground.

"So Tasha's still here," Evie said to fill the silence.

"Yeah, I feel bad. I think she's got a thing for me."

Evie didn't respond. She was accustomed to his cockiness. Shamefully, she found it was still a bit appealing.

"So why are you here, Evie? You weren't missing my mac 'n' cheese that much, were you?" Jack asked with an eyebrow raise.

Asshole. He probably thinks I got all dolled up to show him what he's missing. Evie tried to turn the humiliation around on him.

"No, definitely not. My date chose the restaurant, not me." She pictured Edward sitting at the table, abandoned and confused. He was her future—her ticket to a happy new year—so why was she in Jack's office, trapped in her past? "How do you even know what I ordered anyway? Checking up on me with Tasha, I see." She returned his barb with a haughty eyebrow raise of her own.

"No, I didn't check with Tasha," he said, then lifted his pointer finger toward her face. "You have asparagus in between your two front teeth."

Evie ran her tongue over her teeth, feeling the stringy bit with the tip. It wouldn't dislodge.

"Don't worry, I have toothpicks in my drawer," Jack said, and then surprised her by pulling her arm toward his desk. It was their first physical contact in a year. She felt the texture of the burn on his index finger. She wondered if he felt her goose bumps. In a movie, this was the moment that he would throw her down on top of the scattered papers and extract the asparagus with his own tongue. She thought he might actually do it. But instead he guided her by the wrist over to the desk where in fact he did have a stash of toothpicks. She reached for one, her hand unmistakably shaky.

She sneaked a glance at the framed photographs arranged on his desk. Next to a picture of Jack standing with his father in front of his first restaurant, a now-shuttered American nouveau café in Chelsea, was a picture of him with his wife in Turkey at what could have been their rehearsal dinner. It was a more professional version of a shot Evie had seen on Facebook.

"That's Zeynup," he said, taking note of Evie's prolonged stare.

Evie avoided looking back at Jack. He didn't know she knew he was married and she didn't want her face to give away her lack of surprise.

"It's kind of funny you're here, actually," Jack said. Unless it was "opposite day," the game she used to play as a grade-schooler, there was nothing remotely comical about this situation. It was proving to be the third New Year's Eve in a row that Jack had ruined for her—and this one when she had been poised to be so happy. "I've been thinking about you a lot in the last year. Well, since I got married." When she still didn't spin around or collapse on the floor, he added, "I'm married now. Can you believe it?"

"Good for you," was the most she could utter. She didn't expect it to hurt so much—hearing what she already knew. Her better instincts told her to walk straight out of his office and get back to Edward, preserving as much dignity as a girl with food in her teeth could possess. But curiosity was a stronger impulse for her than hubris had ever been.

"You certainly changed your tune on that one," she said, finally looking at him. "How's it going so far?"

Jack focused his eyes on something in the distance, avoiding Evie's face. Whether it was out of guilt or shame or pity, she wasn't sure.

"It's interesting, I suppose. Good, bad, fun, tiring, all that stuff." If he was gunning for a prize in cryptic answers, Evie was ready to hand him a trophy.

"You know what I mean, right?" he asked.

No, I don't, she thought. Thanks to you. "Totally," she said. "Any kids on the way?" she asked, a nervous laugh escaping.

"No, no, no," he said quickly, which relieved Evie until he followed it up with, "not yet, anyway."

"Well, congratulations." She would have loved to share news that would rival Jack's announcement. An engagement. A pregnancy. A promotion. Nothing came to mind. "I'm not at Baker Smith anymore," she said, pursuing at least a topic change.

Jack seemed surprised, genuinely so. All the times she daydreamed Jack was thinking about her, looking for photos of her with a new boyfriend or checking on her law firm's site to see if she'd make partner yet, those had all been illusions.

"I quit a while ago," she said. "I'm pursuing a totally different career now."

"Good for you, Evie," he said, in a way that made her feel like he was a politician trained to use people's first names. "What are you doing now?"

She could, with some modicum of honesty, tell Jack she was the new CEO of Couch Potatoes, a very, very small company based out of her apartment. But surprising even herself, she responded, "I'm a decorator. My business is called Manhattan Maison." Where the hell was this coming from? She gave herself an invisible pat on the back for inventing such a good name with no forethought.

"That's wonderful. I definitely recall you rearranging my pitiful flat over and over. I could never find anything. You should redesign JAK, actually. It could use a facelift."

"It certainly could."

"Oh, really?" Jack said, like he didn't actually think his restaurant needed any help. "What refurbishments do you have in mind?"

"Well, the carpet is dated, the light fixtures are casting a fluorescent glow, and the dining chair fabric feels synthetic," Evie said, her voice gaining bravado with each criticism.

"Then it's settled. You'll help me. I'll e-mail you tomorrow to set up a meeting."

Evie scrambled for a response. "Well, I don't really do, food, I mean, commercial spaces yet. I will do them soon. Of course."

"Well, if you're interested, you know where to find me." He winked, or at least Evie thought he did. She had been looking at her toes.

"You should be getting back to your date now, shouldn't you? We've been in here for at least ten minutes," he asked, with a glance at his watch. It was shiny and looked to be solid gold, maybe part of Zeynup's dowry.

"Yes, yes. Of course. Edward hates to be kept waiting." She wanted to make sure Jack didn't think she was on a first date, that in fact she knew Edward very well. But all she had done was make her date sound like a prick, when she should have said that she was missing him and wanting to get back to the table.

"Well, then you better go. Happy New Year."

Jack held the door open for her. She paused when she caught sight of a book on his shelf.

"You still have this?" she said, running her finger along the spine: *"Secrets of a Jewish Mother: Recipes for the Soul and the Digestive Tract."* A gift from Bette to Evie. Three-quarters of the recipes included prunes. Jack insisted he had to have it when he found it stashed in her closet. Said it was the funniest thing he'd ever laid eyes on.

"It makes me think of you. We had some great times together." Jack squeezed her elbow gently and said, "I'll e-mail you tomorrow," as though it was obvious to both of them that they needed to finish an important conversation. She was about to say "No, call me instead," but Jack had already disappeared back into his office before she could formulate the response.

"Everything okay?" Edward asked when she returned. "I was getting worried about you."

"Yes. I'm so sorry about that," she said, draining her glass of Merlot and then winding her neck around to signal Tasha, who ambled over much too slowly.

"Tash, I need a refill," she said, pointing to her drained glass. "Fast."

"You got it, girl," she said, and dashed off to the bar.

"So what in the world was that about?" Edward asked.

Here goes.

Chapter 18

"Jack Kipling, the chef and owner of this restaurant," Evie said, eyes fixed steadily on Edward's face, "is my ex-boyfriend. We broke up last December. He's married now." She leaned in closer to him, so none of the busboys or the slippery sommelier could report to Jack what she was saying. "He's the reason I disconnected myself from the Internet. I found his wedding photos on Facebook. He always told me he didn't believe in marriage. It's why we broke up. And then six months after our relationship ended, he was somebody else's husband. I took it really hard. As you can see."

"Wow," Edward said, shifting in his chair. "I didn't see that coming." He absentmindedly returned the sourdough roll that he'd already buttered to the breadbasket.

"There's more, actually," Evie said. "That is, if you want to know."

"Go on," Edward said, reaching for his drink. The ice cubes clanked sharply against the glass as he lifted it, and Evie felt the sound was symbolic of her life cracking open before him—finally.

"I lost my job because of how much time I was spending online. My BlackBerry was basically stapled to my hand because of work—and then I got fired for sending too many e-mails. It was very hypocritical." Even as she said it, she was barely convincing herself. Baker Smith wasn't to blame for her addiction. The compulsion to stay connected, the fear of missing out, that was all her own. "Anyway, that was yet another sign I should go off-line."

Edward nodded but didn't say a word. She took that as a sign she should keep going and not hold back. The Baker Smith portion she believed Edward would be able to understand. The Jack part of the story—that worried her, so she treaded lightly.

"Anyway, I thought I knew Jack. We had two pretty wonderful years together. Frankly, I still don't understand what made him come around on marriage, but it doesn't matter. Maybe Zeynup's some kind of sexual goddess or something." Evie attempted a mood-lightening grin. "She looked quite limber in the photograph."

"Zeynup?"

"Jack's wife. She's Turkish."

"Listen, Evie, we've all got exes. You know I do. The only question is whether you still have feelings for him."

At that moment, Tasha returned to refill their waters. Evie took advantage of the extra few seconds to collect her thoughts.

"I don't," Evie said with as much conviction as she could muster. She reached across the table for Edward's hand. "Since our first date, I've been walking on cloud nine. You can't even imagine how much I've been looking forward to tonight."

"That's all I need to hear," Edward said, squeezing her hand. He started playfully twisting her cocktail ring around her finger, and Evie noticed that the contours of his frame had relaxed back into their natural posture.

"Of all restaurants for me to choose," he went on, with a defeated chuckle. "There has to be—I don't know—ten thousand to pick from in the city and we end up here."

"Eighteen thousand actually," sounded a voice from above their huddled faces.

"I hope you don't mind but I've taken the liberty of serving you myself," Jack said, setting a piping hot plate of roasted chicken with braised leeks in front of Edward. "Your branzino will be right out, Evie. I've prepared a special sauce for it that is still reducing. My sous-chef will bring it out in a moment."

"Thank you," Evie muttered, refusing eye contact. She couldn't believe he was intruding like this. It seemed beneath the Jack she knew.

"I'm sorry about before, stealing your date like I did. Let me properly introduce myself," Jack said, extending his hand to Edward. "Jack Kipling. And I understand you are Evie's lucky companion for the evening."

Companion? Evie bristled. Jack's phrasing made Edward sound like a paid escort.

"Edward Gold," he said, returning the handshake. "Evie was just telling me about you."

"Don't believe a word," Jack said, with a wicked smile. It was more a movie line than genuine dialogue, and it made Evie uncomfortable—the slickness of it all.

"So, Edward Gold, how do you pay the bills?" Jack asked, in a tone that suggested whatever he responded could not measure up to restaurateur.

"He's a surgeon," Evie intervened. "He cured Grandma Bette of cancer this year."

"Well, I'm not sure I 'cured' her, but yes—I did remove her tumor," Edward interjected, with infuriating modesty.

"Well done, chap," Jack said, gingerly patting Edward on the back. A sinewy chef with a long, blond ponytail appeared and placed Evie's plate in front of her. "Thanks, Arianna," Jack said, addressing her in the tone he used with all his female staff: one-part condescending and two-parts flirtatious.

"Evie here has just agreed to redesign JAK. We're going to discuss it further soon, I hope," Jack said, gaze securely set on Evie as though Edward was not even at the table.

"Has she?" Edward asked, and Evie saw his shoulders creep up in tension again. She shook her head no but wasn't sure either man noticed. Her voice box had quit on her.

Jack smiled innocently. "Well, I suppose we still have some details to iron out. But with her new business, I don't see why this wouldn't be a great opportunity."

Evie leaned over her plate, hoping to disappear in the cloud of steam that was heading to the ceiling. No such luck.

"Well, let me allow you two to enjoy your meal in peace," Jack said. "I have to drop by a lot of the tables tonight." He gestured toward the restaurant, where every seat was occupied.

"Yes, and we've got a party to get to," Evie said, desperate to keep pace with Jack.

"We do?" Edward asked, his look of annoyance surpassing his surprise.

"Yes, didn't I mention it?" Evie said innocently. "Anyway, good-bye, Jack."

"Happy new year, Evie," he said, and brushed a light peck on her cheek. Extending his hand to Edward once again, he said, "Don't let her get away."

Like you did? Evie was more than baffled.

"What was that about a party, Evie?" Edward asked when Jack was out of earshot.

"Oh, I was just trying to hurry him along," Evie said, hoping to be convincing. She noticed Edward didn't even ask her about redesigning JAK, or her so-called new business.

After Jack left their table, Evie and Edward's dinner conversation wasn't entirely mangled, but it lacked the natural quality it typically possessed. She answered too many of his statements with "uh-huh" and he barely showed his dimple. She tried not to worry too much about it. Outside of JAK, on neutral territory, she and Edward would return to their old ways.

For the next hour, while Evie and Edward worked their way through their main course and decadent servings of tiramisu and mille-feuille, Jack milled about the restaurant, shaking hands, lighting flambés, and toasting with patrons. Evie heard the people at the next table comment that it was already 11:00 P.M. She wondered if and when Zeynup was going to appear. Where was she right now? Downing champagne with a gaggle of glamorous foreigners downtown? Would she be here to kiss Jack at midnight while the onlookers cheered? Evie would have liked to see this woman in the flesh. Sensing Jack was keeping an eye on her, Evie tousled her hair, sensuously brought her wineglass to her lips repeatedly, and throatily laughed until her neck hurt. She even uncharacteristically spooned her dessert into Edward's mouth when she noticed Jack at the adjacent table. Edward didn't seem to know what to make of Evie's affections, and appeared to alternate between confusion, flattery, and concern.

"I think we should get going," Edward said when their dessert plates were cleared. She hadn't noticed that he'd already paid the check. He gathered their coats and ushered Evie onto the street before she had a chance to protest their departure or spot Jack one last time.

Outside, the blast of cold air hit her face like a speeding truck. The streetlights looked like dripping paint, and she clutched Edward's arm for support. The wine had gotten the best of her. By the time they made it into a taxi, she was slurring something about Dick Clark and his balls dropping.

With her forehead propped against her apartment door, Evie struggled to fit her key into the lock. Edward pried it from her determined fingers and easily opened the door. Evie truly didn't know what would happen when they were inside. Would they consummate the relationship, the way she had expected to welcome the new year, or was the seismic shift that she was perceiving since they arrived at JAK a reality? She collapsed onto the couch and planted her head into a velvet throw pillow, unable to think straight. What a night.

"Where are the lights, Evie?" She could hear Edward tapping on her walls. There was, unless she was mistaken, a never-before-heard chill in his voice.

"To the right of the front door," she mumbled. Maybe there was still a chance to turn the evening around. She could put on some music, slip into her favorite silver nightie, and take Edward to her bed.

"That's where I am," Edward said. She heard him swatting at the switch.

Evie slowly got to her feet. The journey from intoxicated to hungover had already begun. Boulder-size lumps had taken up residence in the back of her skull. Each of her muscles felt sluggish, as if on strike until the alcohol was purged from their surroundings.

She flicked the switch. Nothing happened. She tried it several times more, but the room remained a black canvas, save the sliver of light shed by her battery-operated clock.

"Sorry, I don't know what's going on. There's another switch by the screen," she said. "Next to the big photograph. Try that one."

Right outside her bedroom hung a vintage photograph of the French singer Edith Piaf. Evie found it on a trip to Paris with Jack over a year ago, while they were browsing antique shops on the outskirts of the city. The vacation had proved a watershed moment in their relationship. At the outset, Evie had felt like her life could not get any better. Suspending what she knew in reality, she harbored a belief that Jack would propose in Paris. She visualized him dropping down on one knee at Versailles or the Eiffel Tower. She fantasized that Jack had been lying all along about his views on marriage just to take her even more by surprise when he produced a ring.

But by the day they entered the antique shop where she found the lovely black-and-white photograph of Edith Piaf, the trip was nearly over and Jack had not proposed. In fact, she'd even broached the topic a few times, carefully choosing her moments. She brought it up on a sunny day when they were strolling in the Tuileries eating ice-cream cones. And then again after an extraordinary performance on her part in the bedroom that had involved a striptease and a skillful blow job. But each time she spoke about their future, Jack rebuffed her coarsely, saying some variation of "Let's just enjoy the trip." Crushed, Evie was in a foul mood for the last leg, and when Jack went to pay for the Piaf photograph Evie pushed his hand away and insisted on paying for it herself.

"What's the point?" she had said gruffly. "It's not like we're married." Jack had simply slipped his wallet back into his pants pocket and said nothing while Evie whipped out her credit card.

She liked the picture too much to take it down, even though it resurrected painful memories.

"Nice photograph," Edward called out.

Heart-wrenching is more like it, she thought.

"Evie, this isn't working either. Maybe the building had a power outage," he suggested.

"That must be it," she said. She pressed the intercom button. "Are we having a blackout?"

"No, Miss Rosen. If we had lost electricity, then we wouldn't be answering the intercom now."

"Well my apartment is pitch-black so can you please send the super up? We want to watch the ball drop."

"It's New Year's Eve. He's off," the doorman said unsympathetically.

Edward came over and put his hand on her shoulder. "Evie, it's okay. We'll handle this tomorrow."

We'll handle this tomorrow. The words reverberated in her brain.

"What a nightmare," she whined. It was 11:43 P.M. She lit a candle by her bedside table, the words from Fiona Apple's "Shadowboxer" echoing in her mind as she struck the match: *Once my flame and twice my burn.* God damn Jack. She reached for her flannel pajamas.

"Tomorrow, you'll call up your electric company, find out what happened," he said. "I'm sure it was an accident. It's not like you don't pay your bills."

She thought about that for a moment, not able to remember the last time she had paid an electric bill.

"You're right," Evie said. "I think I need to go to sleep. Will you stay over with me?"

# # #

Morning hit her unapologetically. The sunlight streamed through her window with a mighty force, making it impossible to stay asleep and pretend the night before had never occurred. She took a good look at the man lying next to her in bed. Their first sleepover had definitely not gone according to plan.

Edward, in an undershirt and boxers, looked remarkably comfortable in her bed. Overnight the coarse hairs on his chin and above his upper lip had sprouted and the shadow made him look more brusque. Her mind immediately did a side-by-side comparison of him and Jack. Edward was more classically handsome, that was for sure, but Jack still had that certain something that she could never fully articulate, even to herself. She still couldn't believe she saw him last night.

"Good morning," Edward said, after she started stirring.

"Morning to you," Evie said. There was something reassuring about his stillness in bed. If he was plotting his escape, she couldn't tell.

"So, just to make sure this wasn't a dream, I don't have electricity, do I?" Evie asked.

Edward turned toward her and propped up his head in his hand, so they were mirror images of each other.

"I'm afraid not. I got up an hour ago and tried to make coffee and realized that an electric coffeemaker plus unrefrigerated milk poses a significant problem. So I went back to sleep."

Evie moaned. Last night she hadn't even thought about all the food in her refrigerator and freezer going bad. Fortunately only milk, frozen waffles, and a container of egg salad from Han's Happy Deli were lost.

"I can't believe we saw your ex-boyfriend last night. At the restaurant I chose. What are the chances?" Edward swung his legs over the side of the bed and reached for his clothes. She didn't take that as a great sign.

"It was crazy," Evie said, touching his back lightly before he put on his shirt. "But we just won't go back there. Like you said, we have eighteen thousand restaurants to choose from."

"Actually, Jack said that," Edward said, twisting around to face her. "Listen, Evie, I'm sorry if I'm speaking out of turn, but I think you may have some unfinished business with him." He put his arms through the sleeves of his button-down and rose to get his pants.

She wanted to protest. To tell Edward that she was over Jack and totally ready to move forward with their relationship. But she found it hard to do so convincingly when she was replaying every line exchanged between her and Jack over and over, searching for signs of his longing for her, and asking herself why he called her back to his office. She made up a new business to impress him; invented a story about having another party to go to. Edward witnessed this behavior. How could he not accuse her of having unresolved feelings? The question was where she and Edward would go from this fucked-up place.

"I'm really sorry about all that." It was the best she could do in the moment.

"It was an interesting night." Edward leaned over and gave her a kiss on the cheek. "Good luck with your electricity situation." Evie wondered what happened to "We'll deal with this in the morning."

"Thanks. So we'll talk soon?" Evie said, hating that her voice climbed about eight octaves.

"Of course," Edward said, waving from the door to her bedroom.

When she heard the front door close, she let out a guttural "Arghhh." It was a hell of a way to start the new year.

After tearing apart every cabinet and drawer looking for correspondence from Con Ed, she finally found a letter confirming activation of a new account buried deep in her night table. After a torturous ten minutes on hold listening to Donna Summer's "Bad Girls" on repeat, the customer service representative explained that their system had been hacked and everyone's stored credit card information lost. Her power was shut off because she hadn't paid a bill in three months.

"Why didn't you call me to get my payment information? I deserved a warning," Evie demanded.

"Ma'am, it says in your file you specifically refused to give us your phone number. You asked to be contacted only via e-mail."

"I see," Evie said, shrinking on her end of the phone.

"And, ma'am, did you not receive the letters we sent you in the mail?"

Letters? She must have dumped them along with her junk mail. She'd never needed to open anything before to have light in her apartment. Maybe she didn't have Internet service either. She had no idea. Just six months earlier, an Internet outage would have sent her scaling rooftops in search of a signal. Now she was truly unaffected.

"My neighbor steals my mail. Can you turn my power back on?"

The lights flickered moments after she gave the representative her credit card number. Relieved, Evie went to the kitchen in search of carbs to soak up the alcohol residue. Luckily she found a box of English muffins on the counter. As she chewed her way through the nooks and crannies, she thought back to the day she moved into her apartment.

Paul was there. He was helping move her stuff out of her Columbia Law School dorm and into a new rental apartment, the place she still called home today. After three long years hitting the books in Morningside Heights, Evie was moving to the Upper West Side, arriving in the "real" Manhattan a single girl with a J.D. on the wall, a sophisticated job, great friends, and membership in the twenty-something club. The threshold of her new abode lay rife with possibilities, and Paul was there to help move her into the next chapter. It was a quid pro quo for Evie setting him up with Marco, who at that point Paul was still calling "the guy with the hottest body I've ever met." Nowadays Paul referred to his husband as "Mr. Love Handles," even though Marco was at most three pounds overweight. In some ways that day seemed light-years away from her current station, but in other ways it was very much the same—she was, again, finding herself at a crossroads.

Move-in day had been exhausting. She remembered sprawling out on her new couch with a dish towel spread over her eyes. Paul was still bustling around, shelving her plates and hanging her clothes (the latter with ample commentary). It was a boiling hot summer day and both of them were drenched in sweat. The strong AC promised by the building's in-house real estate broker was not showing its best self.

"Now we need to set up your cable, Internet, and electric, okay?" Paul said.

Evie had just groaned and passed Paul some paper that had come inside her lease package.

"You want me to do this?" Paul asked, incredulous.

"Marco," was all Evie said, to remind him of what brought him to her apartment in the first place.

"Fine," he grumbled and got to work. "But not because of Marco. Because you are a great friend and I love you."

The memory hurt.

She suddenly needed to see Paul at once, to wrap her arms around him and offer a heartfelt apology for her lukewarm reaction to his baby news. She still hadn't met Maya. The Edward situation may have gone haywire, but that didn't mean she couldn't right another wrong today. She reached for her phone.

"Paul, it's Evie. I know you're pissed at me, but I really miss you and want to meet the baby. I'm coming over," she said to his voicemail. Sending a contrite e-mail would have been a million times easier, but a one-way conversation would have been a cop-out. Whether Paul would have accepted it was beside the point. He deserved an apology face-to-face.

She grabbed her coat and headed downtown in a cab. The streets of New York City on January first were the perfect tableau of heartbreak. Singles walked with heads hung low, dressed in their party attire from the night before, cursing themselves for already breaking their top New Year's resolutions: (1) cut back on drinking; (2) no more one-night stands; (3) get eight hours of sleep a night; and (4) exercise every morning. Couples too looked out of sorts—fighting about where to have brunch or gossiping about the other guests at the New Year's Eve party they attended out of obligation. Almost everything was closed on New Year's Day except for restaurants, and the city dwellers didn't know what to do with their free time except gorge themselves and over-think their lives.

When she arrived, Marco answered the door of their third-floor walk-up carrying a swaddled infant in his arms. She was more blanket than baby at this point.

"Hi, Evie," he said. "Happy new year. Meet Maya."

She melted at the vision of the newborn baby girl wrapped in her pink cashmere cocoon, eyes closed and rosy cheeks puffed out, crimson lips in the shape of a rosebud.

"She's gorgeous," Evie gasped, and threw her arms around Marco.

"Thank you," he said through a big smile and motioned her inside.

"My God, I haven't been here in a while," she said. Their apartment had been transformed from a sleek and modern oasis into a shrine to Buy Buy Baby. Everywhere she looked, she saw baby swings, bouncy seats, playmats, blankets, toys, and books all in the brightest shades of pink, purple, and yellow.

"We went a little overboard," Marco said, registering Evie's look of horror.

"No, no, it's great. It's just a big change."

"Let me show you the baby's room," Marco said. "Paul went to the hardware store to bribe someone to help put the crib together. He won't be back for another hour at least. Transitioning Maya from her Moses basket to a proper crib was our New Year's resolution."

Maya's room was bright and cheerful, the walls painted in Pepto-Bismol pink. But bags of unopened toys and adornments lay everywhere, including a lamp shaped like a lamb and a tall stack of animal decals still in their shrink-wrap. Evie never understood why jungle animals were a part of every baby's early education. How often in real life were most kids going to encounter a giraffe? The large pieces of furniture, a changing table, a sweet love seat in crushed ivory velvet, and a rocking chair in chocolate brown suede, were situated oddly in the center of the room.

"You said he'll be gone for an hour?" Evie asked, looking at Marco as he adjusted the blanket to cover Maya's exposed toes.

"At least. He didn't even know where to find a hardware store. Come to think of it, I doubt they're open on New Year's Day anyway."

"Take Maya for a walk, okay? I've got some stuff to do here," Evie said, gently pushing Marco out of the room and toward the stroller.

"You sure?" Marco asked.

Evie nodded.

"One hundred percent. I owe this to Paul," she said. "Let me do this for him. And for you."

Marco just whispered thank you and set off with a well-bundled Maya.

Closing her eyes in the style of Julianne Holmes-Matthews, she took a moment to visualize the room taking shape. Behind closed lids, she saw the glider gravitate to the window and the crib migrate to the west wall. The stuffed animals took their positions, the oversize giraffe standing sentry by the door. The toy chest found its way into the closet. Opening her eyes with a plan in mind, she got to work. Evie resituated the furniture and hung the decals around the room in a thoughtful, but not overly stylized, fashion. She assembled the lamp and rolled out the area rug and put the tiny toys and board books out on the shelves. It was like doing exactly what Paul had done for her move years earlier, but with miniatures.

The work proved to be an effective distraction from her New Year's date with Edward (and her hangover) until she recognized an oversize plush Minnie Mouse similar to one in Olivia's room. It had been over a week since their horse and carriage ride. She longed to cool Olivia's hot chocolate with her breath and ride next to her at the carousel in Central Park. She found a precious princess clock in one of the shopping bags from Toys "R" Us that she was sure Olivia would adore and vowed to pick one up for her later that day. When, and if, she'd be able to deliver it to her was another story.

When she heard the key in the door, Evie felt sufficiently pleased with her progress.

"Oh my God," Paul gasped when he saw the transformation. "Evie, this is unreal." He went over and swept her into a big hug. "Marco texted me that you were here and that I shouldn't come home for another hour. I knew you'd work magic in here."

"You're welcome," she said. "I've been an ass. I'm really, really sorry for being so selfish. But with my grandma sick and my job situation sucking and my love life having been nonexistent until recently and Jack getting married . . . You know what? I shouldn't make any ex—"

Paul stopped her by putting his finger to her mouth.

"Evie, it's okay. Maya's room looks incredible. Let's just call it even, okay?" Only in the context of a really old friendship could schadenfreude be forgiven in exchange for a freshly decorated baby room. Eight years ago she and Paul had bartered a New York City apartment move-in for a setup.

"I appreciate that," Evie said, but Paul didn't seem to hear. He was inspecting his daughter's new room with an ear-to-ear grin.

"All right, but for the record, I am sorry," Evie continued, unwilling to let her expert placement of a rocking chair wholly absolve her wrongdoing.

"I get it, Evie. Here, let me show you some Maya pictures. We've gone a little camera-crazy." He pulled his iPad out from his messenger bag and starting scrolling through pictures.

Watching Paul at work, she craved feeling the smooth metal of her own Mac notebook. She missed being a touch away from her pictures. She longed to hear the rhythm of her fingertips tapping the keyboard. But more than anything, she wanted to check her e-mail. Jack said he was going to contact her about designing his restaurant. She wondered if he actually would, and if he did, would it even matter to her? What really mattered was that she had messed things up with her actual boyfriend. So why was she thinking more about Jack? It didn't make much sense.

But really, few things did anymore.

Chapter 19

In the first weeks of January, during a freeze that weathermen were describing as the "Big Apple Chill," Evie could palpably feel the distance Edward was putting between them. He called to follow up on her electricity situation, but when he didn't suggest getting together, she was crestfallen.

It was hard not to wonder if Edward had diverted their relationship from the path to something serious to a fun interlude on the dating superhighway. The only stumbling block so far (at least in her mind) had been the macabre New Year's Eve dinner at JAK. Though she tried to suppress it, and even rewrite the course of the evening in her mind (especially the parts that were fuzzy from the alcohol), she knew all too well the way she had come across. Like a girl who wasn't over her ex. Who still got flustered in his presence. Who cared a little too much what he thought of her. Who had something to prove. Now she felt compelled to show Edward that she was wholly ready to commit to him, even if inside she was coming to wonder if Jack might always occupy at least a slice of her heart.

She surprised him at the hospital a few days later and took him to lunch at Spice on Second Avenue. Over coconut-curry soup and veggie dumplings, they talked about anything but Jack and New Year's Eve, and by the end of lunch, they seemed to have gotten back into their familiar rhythm. Back in his office, she produced a gift from her pocketbook.

"I have something for you." Evie paused before handing over the silver-wrapped package.

Edward looked at the small box curiously.

He peeled apart the silver paper, at first trying not to tear it but then getting impatient. His face glowed when he saw the present, a newspaper article framed in antique silver. To the corner of the frame Evie had affixed a sticky note that said, "Mine certainly did when we first held hands. xx, Evie."

"I really wanted to read some of your old science articles, but since I don't use the Internet, I couldn't find them. So I decided to go to the library and I tracked them down in the stacks. It was harder than it sounds. Anyway, I photocopied the one you wrote about whether hearts actually skip beats when people get excited." She tried to stifle her smile.

"Arrhythmic palpitations," Edward said, with a scholarly head bob.

"Exactly." Evie smiled. "The medical jargon is really hot." He could spout the most esoteric medical knowledge without being pedantic, unlike Jack, who spoke about reducing a sauce like it was designing a rocket ship.

"So I've been told. Seriously, though. This is amazing, Evie. I love it." He embraced her.

"I really hope you like it," Evie said, watching as he set up the frame next to Olivia's picture. She still felt anxious, though, and didn't want to wait for him to ask her out again.

"Are you free to see a movie this weekend?" she asked while his back was still turned.

"Definitely," he responded, and Evie could feel her fingers tingle.

"Oh, and guess what? If you had any doubt how much I respect your opinion, I have news for you."

"Really? What kind of news?"

"I'm going back to school. One day after visiting Bette, I dropped by the New York School of Interior Design to ask about their classes. It's right on Seventieth Street on the East Side. It turns out they have a one-year certification program and Bette offered to pay part of my tuition. Apparently her washing out Ziploc bags all those years led to some amount of savings. Edward—walking into the building, seeing the designers walking around with portfolio books, discussing their projects, I felt like I was finally in the right place. It was electrifying."

"That's wonderful! I'm so happy for you." He hugged her again.

"It was weird, just enrolling like that. The registrar was a little surprised when I asked if she needed to see my SAT score."

"Not everything has to be difficult," Edward said.

She was coming to learn that.

"And to be clear, this has absolutely nothing to do with redesigning JAK. I have no intention of doing that. I need you to know that."

"I trust you," Edward said, with a gentle squeeze of both of her shoulders and a peck on her forehead. "The design school is right near the hospital. We can meet for lunch."

She exhaled a deep breath of relief hearing his forward thinking. "Thanks. I start in September. Caroline ended up telling Jerome that I designed his office and he insisted on paying me for the work. He even hired me to remodel their guesthouse in the Hamptons. So with that and Bette's contribution I won't have trouble covering the tuition."

"And you balked the first time I suggested this to you," he said playfully. "Listen, I have to deliver grand rounds in twenty minutes. But I'm excited to hear more about this."

It was after seeing another romantic comedy, this one about a doctor falling in love with a hypochondriac so she keeps inventing things that might be wrong with him, that they did finally sleep together. Before the date, Evie had taken painstaking care to look great, splurging on a new minidress and ankle boots and having her hair professionally blown out. She waxed, plucked, shaved, combed, trimmed, and polished everything that needed attention. It felt a bit like going through a human car wash, but when Edward picked her up looking especially adorable in faded gray corduroys and a gray zip-up sweater, she was glad she had gone to the trouble.

Within minutes of returning home from their quick bite of pasta after the movie, her new dress and boots lay in a careless pile in her living room, her lace bra and panties resting on top like the cherry on a sundae. The sex was even better than she expected it would be, the wait they had to endure to get to that moment only heightening the intensity. The first round was fast and ferocious, both of them desperate to explore the other's body, maybe even make sure they were as compatible sexually as they were otherwise. Once that box was checked, they slowed down a bit, taking time to kiss and speak softly to each other in between passionate embraces and rounds of love-making. She found their bodies fit like lock and key. Her head rested perfectly in the dip between his shoulder and chest. His feet reached just the right length under hers so he could tickle her toes with his. Each climax felt like putting in the last piece of a jigsaw puzzle.

Life was good.

# # #

The registrar at the New York School of Interior Design had said Evie was welcome any time to visit and collect materials for the upcoming semester. She could barely wait. With the syllabus and recommended reading list in hand, Evie walked home from the school in a happy fog. When she got to West Sixty-Sixth Street, she detoured left unexpectedly. Before she knew it, she was on the other side of the revolving door of The Hamilton, the building that housed the one-bedroom the broker Emmeline Fields had tried to entice her to see.

"Can I help you?" the doorman asked. He was dressed in a maroon and black uniform with gold tassels, as elegantly clad as a Buckingham Palace guard.

"Yes, in fact you can," Evie said. "There's a one-bedroom apartment for sale here. Or there was. Represented by Allman-White. I was wondering if I could see it. I don't remember the open house schedule."

"Sorry, ma'am. That apartment sold at the end of January. A couple with a new baby purchased it."

"Okay, thank you," she said, more disappointed than she thought she'd be.

"There is another apartment on the market," the doorman said, putting his hand on the door to keep her inside. "It's a two-bedroom. A great family apartment with river views. It's another Emmeline Field exclusive. I can ask the super to call up and see if anyone is home to show it to you."

Evie pictured Olivia's toile cocoon in Edward's town house. How she'd love to create something even more beautiful for her here, in this family apartment.

"Well, I don't have a family. Or a husband. Yet," Evie added, inexplicably confessing her personal life to the doorman. "I hope I will soon. And when I do, I'm coming here to look first."

"Good luck with that, miss."

"Thank you, sir. You can let Emmeline know I stopped by. Tell her I'm the one whose bag she found near the Brighton school. And that I'll be back."

"Will do. The building has a gym, a playroom, and a—"

"I'm so sorry," Evie said, ringing cell in hand. "I've got to take this."

She rushed out of the building, staring at the screen of her phone. Those ten digits. It had been a long time since she had seen them. But she'd never forget them.

"Jack," she said. "How are you?"

"I've been better, truthfully. I'm perplexed as to why you haven't returned any of my e-mails. I must have sent you half a dozen since I saw you on New Year's Eve. I've been checking my account constantly."

"Well, I'm sorry about that. I've been very busy with work," Evie said, proud that she didn't blame it on quitting the Internet. It was far more delicious to let Jack think she saw his e-mails and chose not to respond.

"No matter. Have you given thought to whether you'd like to help me with a remodel? It'd also be just nice to catch up. Our conversation was cut short at the restaurant—I didn't want to keep you away for too long from what's-his-name."

"Edward. His name is Edward."

"He seemed like a decent guy. You deserve it. Too bad you didn't meet Zeynup. She arrived just before midnight."

Was it too bad? Did he really want her to meet his wife? It didn't seem likely, if he was calling her now. Unless he sadistically wanted to rub it in her face, which didn't seem like Jack.

"Too bad. Listen Jack, what's going on?"

"Evie, we have a history together. I wanted to hear your voice. I won't bother you again if you don't want me to."

There was a long, pin-dropping pause.

"The food was delicious. On New Year's Eve," she said finally. "I have to admit that I missed it. You're really talented, Jack."

"Evie, it feels really nice to hear you say that. I always respected your opinion. You looked so beautiful that night. You missed my food, but I missed your face."

"Jack, I need to hang up now, okay? I think it's better that you find someone else to work on your restaurant."

"I understand, Evie. I hope you're happy. You're happy, aren't you?"

"I'm hanging up, Jack. Good-bye."

She was trembling when she put the phone back in her purse.

In her heart of hearts, she knew Jack was only calling her because she was unattainable. The question was whether she could fault him for it when she had been guilty of the same. Hadn't she been fixated on him in part because he refused to get married? These issues danced in her head like an unrelenting tap routine, supplanting any of the joy she'd been feeling about design school moments earlier.

"Miss?" the doorman at the Hamilton poked his head outside. "Emmeline Fields just came through the back entrance of the building. Do you want me to ask her to show you the two-bedroom?"

"Not now," she said, and took off down the street without looking back.

# # #

Evie wasn't totally shocked when Edward asked if they could get together to talk a few weeks after Jack called. They had been out twice more but she was preoccupied on the dates, fidgeting when she should have been still, silent when she should have been conversing. Even during sex she felt like she was floating up above it, looking down at their coupling through a haze. The worst was when Olivia bounded into Edward's living room dressed as Peppa Pig. "It's my favorite show," Olivia said, diving for Evie's lap. Finally Evie understood the provenance of her British accent. "That's nice," she replied, with about a quarter of her typical effusiveness. When she looked up from her magazine moments later, she found Edward whispering something into a forlorn Olivia's ear.

She met Edward in Central Park on a Sunday morning. She arrived early, admired the glistening snow on the treetops from a park bench, and tried to let the cold wind flush her mind. The park was the place where Evie found peace after she went offline, where long walks eased her Internet addiction and helped her digest the reality of Jack's marriage. But it wasn't a panacea, and when Edward arrived right on time, she wasn't at all calm about what he would say or prepared for what she herself would tell him.

"Evie, you know I'm crazy about you," Edward started off. "I don't play games or pretend otherwise."

"But . . ." Evie heard him continue in her head, waiting for the thud of the proverbial other shoe.

"And I'm going to keep being truthful with you. I want a future with you. But I feel like something is holding you back,"

he said. The wind was blowing his sandy hair, and the flap of
his overcoat was beating up and down. Evie noticed that he left
almost a foot between them on the bench, like he was pulling
away physically as well as emotionally from her. "I love you. I
haven't said it formally yet, though I hope you already knew it.
But I need to hear how you feel. And where you see this going. I
need to know Jack is out of the equation."

In the dark days following her breakup with Jack, she might
have toyed with exploiting her sense of power over a man with coy
and ambivalent answers. But a full year had passed and she had
changed. Edward had changed her. Being with Edward, or Jack
for that matter, wasn't about shifting her Facebook status from
"single" to "in a relationship" or never having to go on another
blind date. It was about finding happiness and discovering what
real love is—building a merger unlike any she had been a part of
at Baker Smith, where she always felt at arm's length from the
outcome. If she and Edward were going to move forward, it would
need to be with a full investment and the results would really
matter—to them. And now he was asking her what she wanted
for the long term, maybe even forever.

Edward Gold was the most thoughtful, sincere, earnest, and
caring man she'd ever dated. And he had the other stuff too—the
looks and the job and the pedigree she used to fixate on, and probably always would to some extent. But something about getting
what she had always wanted was making her question if it would
be enough for her. Maybe that was the pull of Jack all along. He
never made her settle on a long-term plan. By always making
her think marriage was out of the question, she'd automatically
decided it was something she desired because she never had to
see the consequences through. Or perhaps it was something else,
something darker keeping her from forging a life with Edward.
Maybe she wasn't sure she deserved the best. Clearly Edward was

picking up on her issues, which scared her. She didn't want to lose him because of her own craziness.

"I'm very happy with how things are going," Evie said truthfully, and put her hand on his knee, trying to bridge the space between them. "I feel so blessed that you've come into my life."

Edward looked relieved. She could tell because his dimple made an appearance for the first time in the conversation.

"Evie, I want you to be as happy as I am," he said, and scooched over so he could put his arm around her.

"I am," Evie said, "I promise. And I love you too." She rested her head on his shoulder. To anyone passing by in the park, they were the portrait of bliss.

"And Jack?" Edward asked.

Evie tugged at her scarf, tightening the strings around her index finger until it puffed up.

"He has been in touch," Evie said, not wanting to elaborate further, even though she had no right to keep it to herself.

"I figured as much. And?" Edward pressed her.

"And I think he might want me back. But I'm with you now, and that's what I told him." Evie exhaled deeply after uttering those words. They felt very final, which frightened her though she knew it shouldn't.

"Good," was all he said in response. Maybe that was enough for him, Evie marveled. It wouldn't be enough for her. But Edward was her complement, not her mirror image.

"I want to explain a little bit more about why I quit the Internet. I gave it kind of short shrift at JAK and you deserve more than a half-assed version of the truth," she said. She swiveled to face Edward squarely. "Like I started to tell you, I found out that Jack got married by looking at pictures of someone I barely know on Facebook. I ended up throwing up on my computer in the midst of trying to Google his wife. I was nervous about tell-

ing you that he married someone else after he and I broke up.
Like that would diminish me in your eyes. Let's see what else.
I lost my job because I was always sending personal e-mails instead of working. I researched the wrong guy before a blind date
and got called out on it. An industry blog ridiculed me. I stalked
ex-boyfriends. I measured myself against other women's photographs and résumés. I relied on dating websites to meet people
when it was really just an excuse for me to avoid putting the real
me out there. I could go on."

"I thought it might be something like that. Listen, Evie, I get
it. My ex-wife and I battled over Twitter, inviting the world to
take sides in our divorce. The Internet is a crazy place."

"It certainly is."

"There's good stuff too, though. Olivia and I use FaceTime
when she's at Georgina's place. Do you know how grateful I am
for that? Plus I can review X-ray imagery from patients around
the world. And when you're ready for e-mail again, I have some
pretty awesome forwards that have gotten passed around the hospital."

"I'll let you know when I'm ready," Evie said and placed her
hand on top of Edward's. She pulled him to standing.

"Let's walk a little," she said. "I heard on the news the ground-
hog didn't see his shadow."

"Oh good," Edward said. "I love spring."

"Spring's my birthday," Evie said, unable to believe she was
going to be thirty-five in a few months.

"I know," Edward said. "We'll do something special to make
you feel better about getting so old." He tickled the inside of her
wrist playfully.

They started to walk hand in hand down the famous elm
tree path, the personification of perfection. But the demons just
wouldn't quit.

"Edward, I do love you." She stopped walking. "But I need some time."

She broke her hand free and headed off in a different direction, leaving Edward and possibly her entire future behind her, surrounded by elms that were due to get their leaves back soon.

# # #

Sam Blumberg was everything you would want to find in an eighty-seven-year-old retiree living in a senior center and more.

Though Bette was due to return to Florida in a few weeks, Sam had flown up to visit her. Evie met him on the screened-in porch of Fran and Winston's home. Bette was temporarily lodging there ever since her neighbor in the apartment building started a noisy renovation that was taking her "kishkes" out. Bette looked vibrant and strong, not at all like a woman whose life was upended by cancer months earlier. Her hair was newly frosted and her nails lacquered in a rich burgundy color. She tapped her ring when Evie arrived. Old habits die hard, Evie reminded herself.

While Evie reclined on the outdoor love seat, Bette and Sam sat on identical rocking chairs, swaying back and forth in the opposite direction so that they crossed at the midpoint.

"I'm so glad to meet you, Sam," Evie said, after she released his wrinkly hands from hers. He was really a cute old man, his skin crinkled like an overripe peach and sprouting with patches of fuzzy white hair. Even in his seated position, Evie could see his stature was stooped. His body, like Bette's, was a collage of soft-edged parts held together by a big heart.

"Evie, you're every bit as gorgeous as your bubbe said you were. The Rosen women make me weak in the knees. Of course, that could also be my osteoporosis."

"Sam, you must be killing it in Century Village," Evie said.

"It's either me or old age because they're dropping like flies down there."

Evie giggled.

Bette beamed. In the sunset of her life, with all the wisdom she'd amassed over decades, she was still proud to have landed "a catch."

"Listen, Evie, I hear from Bette you're spoken for, but if things don't work out I've got a grandson for you in the city that would put all those other cards to shame. My Barry is tall, makes a nice living, and let me tell you, he knows how to treat a lady. You could do a lot worse. Such a shame he hasn't found anyone yet."

It was all Evie needed to hear to know Bette and Sam were perfectly matched.

"Thanks, Sam. I will definitely keep Barry in mind."

"Maybe you have a friend for him?"

"You said he's tall?" Evie asked. There was no harm in introducing him to Stasia, though the idea of Evie finding a boyfriend for her most desirable friend was still an unsettling reversal.

"Listen, he's no basketball player, but he's tall enough. You need a lightbulb changed, call the handyman. What's with these girls today, Bette?"

"Don't get me started, Sam."

"Things were better in the old days. All right, beautiful ladies, I'm going inside to call my stockbroker. My new glaucoma medication has been working miracles and I want to pick up some Glaxo." Evie watched Sam rise slowly, bracing his hands on the arms of the chair to lift all 120 pounds of his sagging flesh.

"So, Evie-le, what can I do for you?" Bette asked innocently once Sam was out of earshot, even though she knew damn well Evie was there for advice.

"I'm confused," Evie said, prepared to elaborate. "I mean, since we last talked—"

"Let me guess. Jack's a putz arriving just in time to screw you up and things vith Edward are too good. I'm right, no?"

Evie was done with dishonesty. She hadn't taken the train out to Greenwich to share partial truths. She looked at her grandmother squarely and said, "I think that basically sums things up. Jack called me. And e-mailed. It's such an about-face from where he and I left things."

"Zat Jack did some number on you." Bette sighed. "Of course zis is also your fault. You alvays vant ze unattainable. You don't vant to be a part of any club zat vill have you as a member. But you're not Groucho Marx."

"I know that, Grandma."

"So listen to me. You vanted Jack for so long. You can't imagine letting him go after you pined and pined for him. But now you have Edward. A real mensch. Much better for you. Of course, it has come too easy. He doesn't make you sveat vaiting by the phone. So naturally you aren't sure he is good enough for you. You only vant someone you need to convince."

"That's really not true, Grandma. Of course I want someone who really loves me. Not someone I have to tranquilize to make sure he shows up to our wedding."

"You know vhat you are doing, don't you?" Bette took a deliberate sip of tea and then folded her hands together, like an aging Jewish Buddha.

"And what am I doing?" Evie asked, though she could hear the predictable answer in her head. "You're being meshuga," "You're shmucking up your life," or some variation on the same theme.

"Vhat you are doing," Bette said, "is looking for lumps."

"Looking for lumps? What in the world are you talking about? This has nothing to do with cancer. Nor my hypochondria. Which is getting better, thank you very much."

"I'm not talking about ze cancer. Listen to me, bubbela. I

have spent my life vorrying. Looking for lumps. But you know vhat? I didn't ever imagine I vould lose my son. Ve never know vhat really comes next, no matter how hard ve try to prepare or to predict. You are not really in control of how life vill unfold. So just live and stop being afraid to be happy."

"Okay, maybe you're right. Maybe I do look for lumps, as you put it. But even if I can put my craziness aside, I'm not sure if Edward will still have me. His daughter just had her fifth birthday party and I wasn't invited. He said he didn't want to get her hopes up too much unless we definitively were going to have a future."

Evie had called Edward the day after she left him in the park to apologize for her rash and confusing behavior. He took her call at work but was more curt than usual. She found herself stumbling over her words and not saying much of anything at all. She wanted to beg for his patience, to explain how hard it was to let Jack go a second time—even if she wasn't sure he was even hers for the taking. But that would have sent Edward running for the hills, so instead she simply suggested they meet up that night for a drink to talk more. He listened to her patiently but said that he didn't want to see her until she had sorted out her feelings for good. Bette winced as she listened to Evie recounting these details.

"Evie, please," Bette said. "Don't make me regret fixing you up vith him."

Evie shot up. "What do you mean, fixing me up?" she asked, totally in shock. Evie told Bette months ago that she and Edward were dating and Bette never mentioned that she played a role in getting them together, beyond being the obvious source of their meeting.

"Evie-le, give me some credit, please?" Bette said. "Who do you think told Edward all the vonderful things about you? I showed him pictures of you from your high school graduation party. I vanted him to see vhat you looked like vith a little blush. That's vy I had you come to ze hospital all dressed up on ze day of my surgery. I vanted Edward to see how beautiful you are. Vhen you try, of course."

"But I yelled at you when I thought you were trying to set me up with a married man. You knew he was divorced and didn't tell me? I confided in you that we were seeing each other right after the first date. You could have told me then."

Bette shot Evie a look that sent prickles down her spine.

"Vhat can I say? I felt it vas better you didn't try to date him right away. He's so handsome. And successful. I believed it vas best you vere yourself around him. Not too nervous, not all ze time trying so hard. And if you knew I vas ze one behind zis, you never vould have given it a chance. I'm only telling you now because you two have already gotten to know each other." Bette took the blanket she had on her lap and tightened it around her chest. It was eerie to see any bodily frailty in a woman who was such a force of nature.

Evie wanted to be angry with Bette for deceiving her. She could have avoided the horror of asking Edward about egg freezing, among the other embarrassing things she shared with him. But what Bette was ultimately saying, albeit in a backhanded way, was that she knew if her granddaughter acted like herself around Edward, he would like her. The rest would fall into place, just like it did. That is until Jack came back into the picture, sending an otherwise smooth courtship into a tinderbox.

"And Edward?" Evie asked. "He was in on your little plan?"

"Not at all," Bette said. "You vere both my pawns. I told him I didn't even know if you had a boyfriend, who you vere seeing, etcetera. Spark his interest, you know? Things aren't so different today zan zey vere in my day. But, Evie, I can't tell you vhat to do."

"You can't?" Evie asked, wondering if the radiation treatments had somehow eradicated the part of her grandmother's personality that entitled her to tell other people how to live their lives. She should tell Aunt Susan it was safe to move back to the East Coast.

She kissed her grandmother on the head and helped her out of the chair. Together, with linked arms, they walked back into the house, where Fran was waiting with a plate of cookies and fruit and Sam was, true to his word, on the phone with his broker. Evie had only a touch more clarity, but she was feeling very grateful for her loving family nonetheless.

On the train ride back to the city, Evie couldn't stop thinking about Bette's ruse. What her grandmother didn't realize, being an octogenarian, was that her plan only worked because it coincided with Evie's Internet hiatus. If she was still Googling every person she met, particularly every man, then she'd have known Edward was not married. She would have seen him as a potential mate and acted entirely differently around him, just like Bette said. Or she would have been turned off by his high-profile divorce and had the totally wrong impression of him. Their initial conversations were so comfortable because she wasn't trying to ensnare him in her fishing net. Instead she was just herself, the good, the bad, and the ugly all in plain sight. And still Edward liked her.

But being off-line had also brought Jack back into her orbit. He copped to as much when he said that her ignoring his correspondence was driving him insane. Who would have thought chucking her computer in the reservoir might have helped him propose to her a year ago?

Most surprising of all was that disconnecting had helped her professionally—remarkable in a city where smartphones were more common than underwear. If she were still on the grid, she'd have posted her résumé soon after leaving Baker Smith and would probably be grinding her way through another thankless big-firm legal job by now. Then when Caroline asked her to re-design Jerome's office, she would have barked that she was knee-deep in some billion-dollar merger and didn't have an ounce of spare time. There was no chance she'd ever have enrolled in the New York School of Interior Design.

Going dark had changed the course of her life. Evie just hoped it was for the better.

# # #

Stasia called her unexpectedly a few days after her visit with Bette.

"I miss you, Evie," she said, in a voice that sounded tired but genuine. "Can we meet for coffee?"

"Anytime, anyplace. Thank you for giving me another chance."

They arranged to meet at Starbucks later that afternoon. Too many months had passed where Evie had let her preoccupation with Edward, and now Edward and Jack, divert her from the task of repairing that friendship. She finally understood that the only barrier between them all these years had been her own envy. And it was misplaced envy at that. All that time, Evie had avoided sharing romantic troubles with her, feeling like her friend—who'd never seemed to know loneliness or heartbreak—could not relate. Now things were different, and Evie suspected there would be more reciprocity in their discussions, even though she was dis-tressed that it took a marital crisis to get to that point.

Stasia looked thinner than Evie had ever seen her, and her normally shiny hair was lackluster and unkempt. She was still a beauty, though, like the true ones always are.

"How are you?" Evie said, though she felt foolish asking the question.

"I'm healing. Rick moved all his stuff out last month. Not seeing his disgusting boxers every day has been helping. I came really close to burning his things, but I restrained myself. What about you? Things with Edward still going strong? I've been keeping tabs on you through Tracy and Caroline."

"Actually, things are rocky now. I'd love to get your advice."

"You sure? It's nice to know someone thinks I'm capable of giving romantic advice given my husband's disappearing act."

"Hey," Evie said in a stern voice. "Nobody was better than you at getting every cute guy in school to fall in love with them."

"That's true," she said, shrugging in earnest. "But believe me, this has been very humbling."

"I'm so sorry, Stasia. I wish there was something I could do to make you feel better. I know it doesn't compare, but I've been humbled before too. Giving Jack the marriage ultimatum and seeing him willing to let me get away—that was a doozy. And now, well, I just don't know where I stand with anything."

Evie filled her in on her string of dates with Edward and running into Jack on New Year's Eve.

"I acted pretty nutty after I saw Jack. We had this talk in his office. I don't know—it just felt like something was still there. Then I went back to the table and Jack came over to introduce himself to Edward. They shook hands, and I'm telling you, it was like watching my past and future implode simultaneously. Jack said to Edward, 'Don't let her get away.' What does that mean? Why would he say that if he didn't have regrets? Anyway, the rest of the dinner was a disaster. Half the time I was trying to make Jack jealous by throwing myself at Edward, the rest of the time I was trying to prove to Edward that Jack was history. Then get this—Jack called me. Told me he's been e-mailing me too. Said he missed talking to me. And my face. Now Edward wants to hear me say that I definitely have no more feelings for Jack. And I can't seem to get myself to utter that simple sentence."

"Well, do you?" Stasia asked. "Still have feelings for Jack?"

"I don't think so. I mean, I love Edward. That's for certain. But there is a part of me that needs Jack to know I'm winning or at least make him regret he didn't marry me. If I still care about that, does that mean I'm not really there with Edward?"

Stasia took a sip of her chai latte and didn't respond for a long minute. "I really don't think so. Take me, for example. I genuinely despise Rick now, but I'd love for him to think that I'm dating some superstar right now. Does that mean I want to get back together with him? Not one bit. But I still want him to think I'm doing great."

"I get that," Evie said. "I really get that, actually. That's kind of what Facebook is all about."

"Totally. Oh, did you happen to see my lab equipment when you were at JAK, by the way?"

"What in the world are you talking about?" Evie asked, wide-eyed.

"I lent Jack a whole bunch of test tubes, droppers, and beakers when he was experimenting with molecular cooking. He never returned them. It was like five hundred dollars' worth of stuff, but it was right before you guys broke up so I couldn't say anything."

"Sorry, hon, I don't recall any science instruments lying around," Evie said.

"Asshole," Stasia clipped. "Edward is so much better than that."

"So what do you think? How can I show Edward that I'm committed to our relationship? I don't want him to think I'm still into Jack, or worse, that he's my rebound guy."

"Well, I hate to borrow a page from Jack's book, but you can never go wrong with food. Why don't you cook a really fabulous dinner for Edward at your place? Make his favorite foods. Light candles. And then sit him down and do what you were planning to do on New Year's Eve. Tell him how much you care about him. How you haven't been this elated in ages—or ever. Reassure him about Jack. Tell Edward how hurt you were when Jack let you go and got married so soon after you guys broke up. Keep in mind that Edward has been married before. You worry that there's no room for Jack in your psyche if you move forward with Edward. That's not how things work. Rick will always be a part of me. These people who take up space in our lives, they don't just vanish entirely. They leave scars. Do you see what I mean?"

"I think you're spot-on," Evie said. "All this time I was feeling guilty whenever Jack crossed my mind. But it's not like I can feign amnesia about an entire two years of my life. I think Edward would understand if only I could explain myself coherently for once. He said himself that Georgina will always be a part of him."

"Exactly. So, is there anything else? I'm on a roll."

"That's all for me. What about you, Stas? I'm really worried."

"I'll be okay. I have great friends." She put her hand on Evie's.

"Not me so much. I should have been banging down your door after that night at the hospital or at least putting out a hit on Rick. I got caught up in my new relationship like some teenager."

"Stop it. I'm happy for you that you've found someone," Stasia said.

"Speaking of finding someone, how do you feel about accountants?"

"I feel positively. Rick did our taxes. It's almost April and I'm screwed."

"I mean romantically. My grandmother's boyfriend's grandson is apparently looking for love."

"Oh dear. Let me think on that. I've recently joined something frightening called Hinge. Anyway, you have a phone call to make and cooking to do. And I'm heading to the lab."

"The lab? It's Saturday."

"I prefer the rats to men these days. Though they have a lot in common."

"Things will work out for you," Evie said.

Stasia raised an eyebrow and said, "You never believed us when we said that to you."

Evie laughed. "I guess I'm an optimist now."

"Jeez, maybe I should quit the Internet," Stasia said. "I could use an attitude adjustment. And the focus at work. I check Rick's Facebook status about every five minutes. Not good for all those people counting on a better Alzheimer's drug."

"Ahh, the Facebook stalk. I know it well," Evie said wistfully. "Or should I say I knew it well?"

Evie took a last sip of her drink and asked, "So you really are just going to let Rick get away with this? No revenge? You are a better woman than me."

"Well," Stasia said, her voice but a whisper. "Remember I told you my father was appointed to the Committee on Homeland Security?"

"Yeah," Evie said, unsure where this was heading.

"He added Rick to the no-fly list. I cannot wait for him to take his little spinning mistress on a trip to nowhere."

# # #

Evie called Edward the moment she parted with Stasia to invite him to a home-cooked meal at her place that night. She said she needed to see him. That she missed him terribly. And that she wanted to feed him. Luckily, he agreed.

She dashed to the oversize gourmet grocer in her neighborhood. When she passed the yams, her menu was inspired. She would cook Edward a Thanksgiving meal, in January. He told her he regretted that he only feasted like that once a year, so she filled her cart with turkey, green beans, gravy, a prepared pecan pie, and the ingredients for sweet potato fluff. Confused by the different checkout lanes—did "13 items or less" mean she had to count each individual yam or did the bag count as one?—Evie felt like a tourist in the grocery store. She was used to ordering online through FreshDirect, lazily selecting "refill existing order," even though it meant receiving multiples of cumin and cilantro and other aspirational items that had no business in her kitchen. When she couldn't do that anymore, she bought cereal and other essentials from Duane Reade and the corner store.

Afterward she visited the liquor store and picked up two bottles of award-winning wine recommended by the manager—a white from the Rhone Valley and a red Bordeaux. Then she rushed back to her building. The grocery bags were piled high in her hands so that she couldn't see two feet in front of her. She fumbled around for the proper elevator button and hoped she was getting off on the correct floor.

"Need some help?" a familiar voice said, startling her. The brown paper bags blocking her vision came crashing down to the floor.

"Jack? What are you doing here?" Evie asked, without even looking down at the mess of food at her feet.

He was seated outside of her door, dressed in a button-down and the bottom half of his chef uniform, with a newspaper open on his lap.

"Finally, you're here. I've been rereading articles."

"Sorry to keep you waiting," Evie said caustically. "Why are you outside my apartment?"

"First let me help you. I never knew you to cook. I don't suppose this is for Edward, is it?" Jack bent down in front of her, and the familiar scent of butter and garlic mixed with his ginger shampoo wafted up to her. Evie inhaled deeply in spite of herself.

"It is. Let's get this stuff inside." Evie fumbled with her keys, annoyed that her hands were trembling. She looked at her watch. There wasn't much time for her to prepare the meal and get dressed. She really should ask Jack to leave.

"How's Manhattan Maison going?" he asked, arranging the groceries in the fridge. Evie's face froze as she tried to remember what he was talking about. It clicked by the time he turned around to face her.

"Oh, terrific. I just did a huge project on the Upper East Side." Caroline and Jerome lived there, so at least part of what she was saying was true.

"I'm happy to hear it. You know, Evie, I said I'd leave you alone if you wanted, but I'm finding it harder than I expected. I also wanted to run something by you. I'm opening another restaurant and I'd love you to collaborate. JAK was just going to be a renovation, but here's a chance for you to execute a vision all your own."

Another restaurant? She couldn't help begrudging him. Edward had recently been awarded a prestigious teaching prize, and she wanted to share that with Jack. But it seemed too obvious, too out-of-left-field to bring up casually. So she said nothing.

"Anyway, I tried to contact you through your website but I guess you haven't gotten around to setting it up yet. I was thinking of pretending to be a stranger. Maybe then you'd take the job," Jack said. "Anyway, I'm doing a high-end French-Argentinean concept in Midtown. For theatergoers, but definitely not for tourists. Just locals."

How could Jack be such a New York snob when he was from an entirely different country? Edward would never act so uppity, and he was Manhattan born-and-raised.

"Sounds great," she said, not protesting when he started chopping the vegetables she had bought.

"I'm calling it Evita," he said, looking up from his knife work. "Do you like the name?"

"It's nice," Evie said neutrally. Was he implying that the restaurant was named after her? Was that even possible? She honestly didn't know how to react.

"I hope you think it's more than nice. It's inspired by you," he said.

By now he'd moved on to prepping her sprouts. His hands worked effortlessly. She remembered him telling her that knife skills were all about the wrist. If your bicep bulges, you're doing something wrong.

"After all, you supported me before I really made it," he said. This was news to her. By the time she and Jack met, he was already a well-regarded name in New York City's competitive culinary sector. She doubted if she would have even gone out with him if he'd in fact been a struggling restaurateur. Either Jack was trying to flatter her, or he'd rewritten history in his mind.

"Whose is this?" Jack asked, picking up one of Wyatt's baby bottles that was left behind.

"Aunt Susan's, if you can believe it. She adopted a baby."

"Oh dear. That lady thinks I'm rubbish," Jack said. "Didn't she say I was poisoning my customers when she found out only half my produce was organic?"

"She definitely said something about you being toxic. But I talked her down."

"Well, I still don't think she's going to root for me."

"There's nothing to root for. I have a boyfriend. And if people aren't rooting for you, it probably has more to do with the fact that you're married than knowing your broccoli gets sprayed with pesticide."

"Touché," he said with a forlorn expression, and Evie warmed to his conciliation. "Listen, Evie. I know my reappearance in your life is sudden. But I know you. You require complication."

"I don't know," Evie responded truthfully. A marriage was more than a complication. And she was annoyed with his presumptions about her. He never had especially good insights into her needs, except when he was putting a plate of spaghetti Bolognese in front of her.

"I'm sure your wife is very proud of you," Evie said, trying to focus the conversation on the more important matter at hand—why the hell Jack was naming a restaurant after her when he was married to someone else.

"Zeynup? She likes the publicity," he said, with a one-shouldered shrug.

Evie delighted in hearing Jack insult his new wife, but she didn't let the pleasure creep onto her game face.

Opening score: fifteen-love, Evie.

"But yes, of course, she's very proud of me and has been really helpful," he added. It was just like Jack to give with one hand and take back with the other. Evie resented his ability to alter her emotional state within seconds.

Fifteen, all.

"Well that's good," Evie said. "I would hope so, seeing as you married her." She didn't mince words. As her aggravation with Jack escalated, she grew more certain that she was entitled to some sort of explanation about why he suddenly up and got married.

"About that, Evie," Jack said, putting down the knife on her counter. She thought he was signaling it was time for a serious conversation, one that involved his full attention. But instead he reached for the raw turkey and ran it under the faucet. He raised his voice to speak over the running water.

"I know you must have been surprised to hear I got married.

To tell you the truth, it was all a blur. Zeynup got pregnant and I just panicked and proposed."

Aha! She knew there had to be a baby involved.

Thirty-fifteen.

"She miscarried, but by that time the wedding plans had all been set in motion. And I do love her."

Damn it. Thirty, all.

"And now?" Evie asked, moving to stand next to him at the sink. Even though she thought Jack's reason for following through with the wedding seemed cowardly, she still reached for the turkey, letting her fingers linger on his hands.

"And now, I can't get you out of my mind. Evie, when you came into my restaurant with that other chap, I thought I would die," he said.

Forty-thirty, Evie.

"Edward."

"Well I gather from this feast you're attempting that Edward is still very much in the picture. He's very lucky," Jack said, but he put his free hand on the back of Evie's neck at the same time, sending shivers down her spine.

"When you didn't respond to my many e-mails I nearly went crazy. I swear I checked my Hotmail every three minutes hoping you'd finally decided to get in touch with me."

Now you know how it feels, Evie thought. To not have the upper hand for once.

"What about Zeynup?" she asked, moving slightly away from him but not removing his hand from her body. His fingers started creeping their way through her messy bun until he pulled out her rubber band and her hair fell around her shoulders.

"Evie, she'll understand. I think she knows the truth about how we got to where we are now. This wouldn't come as a surprise to her," he said. By now the chopped vegetables that he put into a frying pan were sizzling and sending their caramelized scent upward. Evie turned down the flame, musing over the symbolism.

"But has anything changed, Jack? I'm not ashamed anymore to say that I definitely want to get married and have a family." She knew it was Edward giving her the confidence to say these things outright. A wonderful man who saw more of her real self than anyone else, who also wanted these very things with her, or at least she thought he did. He was often making references to the future. So why shouldn't Jack?

"We'll talk through all that later," Jack said, bringing the score to deuce. He snaked a hand around her back and ran his fingers over her breast. She hated that her nipples reacted to his touch by hardening and protruding. Stupid reflexes. Jack had to notice.

"I'd like you to go." She took a full stride away from him so he was no longer at arm's length.

"Please call me," Jack said as he let Evie start to push him out the door. When he was on the other side of the threshold he said, "Are you sure you don't at least want me to stay so I can cook this dinner for you?"

"No. Just go." Game-set-match.

But when she closed the door on him and looked back at the mess in her kitchen, she'd wished she'd accepted his offer. It was the least he could do for all the hell he'd put her through. Maybe it was advantage Jack after all.

But no, Evie thought, it wasn't so. He had no more advantage over her. Jack could maybe win a game or two. But she would win the set.

He knocked a moment later. She opened the door a crack, and Jack forced his way inside.

"Evie, please. I need you." He lunged for her, putting his

mouth on hers. His saliva tasted like acid. She recoiled, disgust moving across her face like a shadow.

"Jack, no more warnings. You need to leave now and not come back."

# # #

"Bradley Winter!"

"Brad Winter?" Evie was back at Book-A-Saurus, relieved that it had yet to be shuttered. Her mother called just as she was read-ing an article about innovations in Venetian plaster painting. She wanted to impress on the first day of school. "Why are you bring-ing him up?" Evie asked Fran. She was off to meet Caroline for a movie in a few minutes and had no time to discuss one of her high school boyfriends.

"Do you know where Bradley Winter is now?" Fran asked, obviously eager to share.

"No idea. Haven't seen him since graduation."

"Well, I know. He's the U.S. ambassador to the Czech Repub-lic. And guess what else? He married a swimsuit model. They have three kids." Fran's voice brimmed with satisfaction.

"How in the world do you know that?" Evie asked.

"Facebook. After you quit the damn thing, I joined just to see what the hell it's all about."

"And why are you telling me this?" Evie said, surprised to hear her mother cussing.

"Because you dumped Bradley Winter when he sent you roses and chocolates for Valentine's Day. You thought if he was so into going steady with you, then you were settling by being with him."

That was actually true. At the time she told Fran she dumped Bradley because his house smelled like whitefish.

"Look, you play the part of the insecure girl with the misfortune of being single when all her friends are married. But the truth is that you don't think anyone's good enough for you. Anyone, that is, except for the one person that didn't want you. He's apparently the guy you'd be willing to marry. But trust me, if Jack did ever actually marry you, his novelty would wear off pretty quickly."

"Yikes, Mom. How long have you been saving up this speech?"

"Not long. I had an epiphany after seeing Bradley's Facebook page."

"Congratulations. The only thing Facebook did for me was make me suicidal," Evie said, a bit too contemplatively. "Exaggerating, of course!"

"Well that's your own doing, Evie," Fran said. "You've got to think about your future. Long-term happiness. What you deserve. Who is going to be the better father? Who is going to be the better husband? Who do you love? And by love I mean come home to at the end of a long day when your feet are aching and—"

"Mom, I got it. Please don't worry about me."

"I really hope so. I had to catch you before I left with Winston for New Haven to see May play in her squash match."

"Be sure to tell her I say hello," Evie said in a sarcastic tone.

"Evie, cut it out. Winston's girls are lovely. They practically worship you. What do you have against them?"

"Worship me?" Evie scoffed. "May never so much as asked me about Yale."

"Evie, please. Don't play dumb. They are intimidated by you. You're beautiful and successful and live this big life in Manhattan and you see them as sheltered babies. They know that. I wouldn't feel comfortable asking you for advice either. I gotta hang up because Winston is nudging me out the door. I love you," Fran said.

"Love you too, Mom."

Chapter 20

"I'm officially old," Evie said, flexing her feet in bed to work out the morning cramps. She couldn't believe it was her birthday and how much had changed since last spring. At least the last couple of months had been uneventful—in the absolutely best way possible.

"You look as young as the day I met you." Evie could hear the familiar sounds of the morning routine from the bathroom—the toothbrush clinking against a glass, the foam of the shaving cream emerging from the can.

"Very funny," Evie responded, cozily tugging the blankets around her neck. Though she was rather pleased if he meant what he said. A lot had transpired. If she'd resisted some extra wrinkles along the way, that alone was reason for celebration.

"I think it's time to wake up, birthday girl," he said, appearing beside her with two mugs of steaming hot coffee, hers prepared just the way she liked it. "You excited for tonight? Should be fun." Caroline was having a party at her house later to celebrate Evie's birthday. Evie made her promise to keep it small and casual, but Caroline was not capable of hosting anything to which either of those adjectives could be applied. At least she promised not to serve red wine out of respect for the new furniture Evie had ordered for the living room.

"Yeah, it's nice everyone will be there." She sat up in bed, resting her head dreamily against the headboard. "But truthfully, I'm more looking forward to the after party." She clinked her mug against his, and they both took sips through big smiles.

"So what do you want to do today? Anything you desire, I'm at your service."

Evie was disappointed. While the sentiment was kind, she had sort of expected that the minute she bounded out of bed an elaborate day would unfold, one that might even involve a proposal by night's end. But now it seemed like she was being left to plan her own birthday.

"I don't know. I haven't thought much about it," she lied.

"C'mon, surely you can think of something you'd like to do."

Evie glanced out the window. It looked like a perfect spring day, one of the perks of being a May baby.

"Well, I guess we could go for a walk, maybe get some breakfast?"

"Sounds perfect."

"Okay, I'll throw on my clothes," Evie said, reaching for the jeans and tank top on the floor next to his bed.

"You look beautiful in the mornings." He stood next to her with a towel wrapped around his waist. Evie inhaled his freshly scented skin. It was hard to be mad at him, especially after her erratic behavior just a few months before.

"Thank you, Edward. I love you." She stood on tiptoes and pressed her lips against his. "I'm so happy to spend my birthday with you. Wait, happy's not enough." Evie paused and touched her pointer finger to her chin to show deep contemplation. "I'm elated. That's a much better word."

"Me too," he said, wrapping his arms around her waist.

"I bet all the women at the hospital are jealous of me, right?" Evie teased as her fingers grazed his beeper.

"No, I don't think so," Edward said, scratching his head. "Wait, what am I saying? They hold a daily vigil praying for your untimely demise."

Edward. He was so sure of himself, he didn't need to impress Evie with stories of being sought after, like Jack used to do. She had grown accustomed to hearing about needy waitresses requesting cooking lessons and saucy bartenders asking him to test their latest concoctions after closing. At first when Edward never mentioned a nurse or a patient's family member hitting on him, Evie questioned if she was alone in finding him so irresistible. By now she recognized, and appreciated, that Edward didn't feel the need to share such occurrences, and maybe, just maybe, he was too in love with her to even notice.

They left Edward's place, where Evie had basically moved in, and set out hand in hand toward Zabar's. Evie tried her best to mask her disappointment that a proposal was unlikely looming. Bette had already left her a voice message at the crack of dawn wishing her a happy birthday, and Evie was purposely waiting to call back in case she had news to share. But now she figured she might as well just call back sooner rather than later so her grandma didn't get her hopes up too much during the day. Bette was thankfully doing well, power walking around the Boca Beach shopping center and playing canasta, and now enjoying a new tradition—watching Sam's informal stand-up act on Sundays at the complex's pool.

After about ten minutes of strolling through the midmorning pedestrian traffic, Edward said, "Let's run up to your apartment for a minute if that's okay. I need to use the bathroom before we load up on sugar and fat."

Lovely. So not only were they not getting engaged today, but Edward was also sharing his bodily functions with her. If they weren't married, she shouldn't have to hear about his plans to poop.

"Can you just go at Zabar's?" Evie asked, not feeling especially compliant.

"No, I can't. I want to use your apartment," Edward insisted. Suddenly Evie's mood reversed. This must be it! Edward was trying to lure her to her apartment where no doubt one of his friends had set up champagne and roses. An emerald-cut diamond would be sitting in a velvet box, waiting to encircle one of the most ready fingers in all of New York.

"Okay, honey, sorry. Let's go upstairs."

In the elevator she caught a glimpse of herself in the reflective railing. If her big moment was coming, she had better spruce up. She pulled out her ponytail holder, slicked on lip gloss, and used a dash of moisture from her mouth to smooth her wayward eyebrows.

"It's just Zabar's," Edward joked as she primped herself on the ride up to the nineteenth floor.

"Just want to look good on my birthday."

When they reached her door, Evie inhaled deeply. The moment

was upon her, and the anticipation was every bit as delicious as she'd suspected it would be. Her heart fluttered in her chest like a hummingbird's tiny wings. Her stomach was a wreck. If an oxygen mask had dropped down in front of her face, she'd happily have put it on.

"Well?" Edward said, "I really have to go to the bathroom. Can you open the door?"

"Yes, yes, of course," Evie said, flustered. Her fingertips were tingling.

When the door opened, the first things Evie noticed were the purple cardigan and thin checkered scarf she had worn the day before. They were lying in a crumpled ball on the arm of her sofa, where she had left them after changing her outfit. If Edward were about to propose in her apartment, he surely would have cleaned up first.

Edward disappeared into the bathroom, and Evie began a frantic search behind the curtains and inside every drawer, looking for evidence of an impending proposal, but she came up empty.

"Okay, I'm ready," Edward said.

"Fine, let's just go," Evie said, replacing the couch cushions.

"But wait, don't you want to know what this is?" Edward asked, extending his arms.

The bathroom. It was the one place she hadn't looked.

Edward was carrying a wrapped box that looked about the size of a book.

"Happy birthday, baby," he said, handing over the package. Unless it was a box containing a dozen other smaller boxes inside like a Russian nesting doll, it didn't seem likely the contents would please her.

"Thanks," Evie said, surprised by the weight of the package. "I can't imagine what it is."

"Well, before you open it, let me say a few words. I know this is something you don't have. And I believe you are ready to enjoy it. Plus I think you're really going to need it."

At this point Evie became convinced he was describing a vibrator. She didn't have one. She would enjoy it. And if Edward wasn't going to propose on her thirty-fifth birthday or sometime soon after, then she was definitely going to need it.

"So, go ahead, open it," Edward said with a huge grin.

"Okay, here I go," Evie said, ripping open the paper. It was gold foil, totally not her taste, and had a cheesy poly bow affixed to it. "Wow, a new computer."

The present may have been expensive, but it entirely missed the mark. Even a cheesy ankle bracelet would have been better than this unromantic hunk of machinery.

"You don't like it?" Edward asked.

"No, no, I love it. Really useful. Who doesn't love typing?" she hedged with humor.

"Well, it's just that I know your old computer broke. And you said when you turned thirty-five you were going to go back to using the web," Edward said.

It was true. With her first semester at the New York School of Interior Design beginning in just a few months and actual projects to display on her business website, using a computer would be essential. And given how happy she was with Edward, she felt ready to go back online. Other people's wedding and baby photos would no longer send her in search of a Zoloft. She told Edward she planned to buy a new computer, and an iPhone and iPad too. But she promised herself she'd be so much smarter about using the Internet this time around—refusing to let herself get obsessive and miss out on the chances for her life to happen organically. And her stalking days were definitely behind her.

Apparently he'd been listening. Because she was holding an

eleven-inch MacBook Air with a 1.7GHz Intel Core i5 Processor. At least he'd thrown in lots of the fancy extras, like the portable charger and an external CD-ROM.

"So, let's fire this thing up," Edward said. "I already set everything up for you. Aren't you curious to read your e-mail after all this time?"

A single tear rolled down her cheek. Edward noticed immediately and pulled her close.

"What's wrong, sweetheart?" he asked gently.

"It's just, it's just—" Evie tried to talk. Maybe she should tell Edward the truth. "I don't know, I guess, I'm always disappointed on my birthday. It usually rains."

"Well, it's a beautiful day. Check your e-mail and then we can go for breakfast. I bet you have over fifty thousand e-mails waiting for you. You going to start reading at the oldest or the most recent?" Edward seemed unusually insensitive to her fragility.

"I don't know. What's the difference?" Evie said.

Edward looked deflated.

"All right, let me get at this computer," she added with more vigor, making a show of opening the laptop and stroking the keys.

"I took the liberty of buying the domain name www.Manhattan Maison.com. You should check it out. I even made you a logo. It's pretty pathetic but at least it's a start."

"Okay, okay, let me see." She sat down cross-legged on the floor and threw her hair up into a bun. She actually felt exhilarated facing a computer screen for the first time in nearly a year. Maybe the gift wasn't all that bad.

She typed in the Manhattan Maison web address that Edward had reserved for her. The page was blank save for one line: "In order to access this web page, you will need to authenticate your identity. Please click on the link in the e-mail from edward.r.gold@hotmail.com to verify your identity."

This kind of computer crap she didn't miss.

"Edward?" He had disappeared into the kitchen. "Can you make coffee?" If she was really going to look at all of the e-mails she missed over the past year, Zabar's would have to wait. He didn't answer.

She opened her Gmail. Her inbox registered 24,612 unread messages. Jesus. Where to start?

It was clear that she was in an unquestionably better place today than she was a year ago, so she chose to scroll to the most recent e-mail in the list. It was from Edward. The subject of the e-mail was "Manhattan Maison Authentication."

She clicked it open, and suddenly the butterflies returned to her stomach. The e-mail contained just one line, but it was the best thing to ever appear on a screen, or anywhere. In Times New Roman, size 30 font, all caps, Evie read the following:

EVIE ROSEN, WILL YOU MARRY ME?

She spun around and Edward was behind her, on one knee, with an open box. The ring looked very familiar. It was a sapphire, surrounded by diamonds.

"My grandmother's ring," Evie gasped.

"She insisted when I told her I was going to propose."

Evie was stunned speechless, relying on the reserves in her vocal cords to deliver the only word she needed to say.

"Yes," she whispered. Then, summoning more strength, she repeated the same. "Yes, yes, yes, yes, and yes."

EPILOGUE

Dear Alexia,

I really appreciate everything you've done so far for me and Edward. Thank you for helping us to book the Brooklyn Botanical Gardens. We know it'll be an exquisite setting for our wedding, even if the beetle exhibit will still be on display in the reception hall and the bathrooms will be under renovation. What's a wedding without "The Royal Flush" Porta Potties?

It has come to our attention that you are related to two of the vendors you passionately encouraged us to hire. Thanks to Facebook, I have determined that DJ Rhapsody is your son and Flowers Flowers Flowers is owned by your cousin Stephan. I feel you should have disclosed these affiliations to us prior to saying that they were the only people up to the job.

As an interior designer (and the unofficial new set designer for the Greenwich Town Thespians), I am confident that I will be able to create the wedding of my dreams without your assistance, even though you told me my taste in table linens was "questionable." Further, there is nothing "cliché" about an all-white wedding. It is classic and tasteful, and it suits our style.

We have mailed you a check for the portion of your services which you have already rendered.

Very best regards,
Evie Rosen

P.S. You really need to contract with a new calligrapher. I don't know if she's your relation as well, but Charlotte Appleby ("the best of the best" you promised) addressed a number of the invitations incorrectly. We had a hard time explaining to the matron of honor why her invitation was addressed to Mr. and Mrs. Jake Poo. It's L-O-O!!! And you are lucky my grandmother B-E-T-T-E doesn't see so well, because her name was misspelled as B-E-T-T-Y. This is a woman who is planning to frame both the invitation and the envelope. (I guess she wasn't certain this day would ever come.)

"Well, Susan, what do you think?"

"It's perfect, Evie. You have a way with words. Besides, you don't need a wedding planner. I'm here to help."

"You are?" Evie asked in disbelief. "I thought you were here on business."

"There's time for everything."

Susan had e-mailed her a couple of weeks earlier asking if she and Wyatt could stay for a few days. Evie had Edward's place now to seek refuge, so she didn't object. She was dying to see Wyatt anyway.

"Whatever. I'm just glad I can fire her over e-mail. I would not have relished doing this face-to-face, or even on the phone. Thank God I'm back online."

"Back online?" Susan asked, confused.

"I told you I quit the Internet, remember? You said I could be part of the New Horizons antitechnology movement." Evie tried to jog her aunt's impaired-by-God-knows-what memory.

Susan smiled patronizingly. "Evie, honestly, going off-line? That is so passé. What matters now is Responsible Internetism."

"Glad I'm with the times."

"Indeed. Listen, Evie, you're an angel to let me stay with you again. We had such a good time when I was here last."

"Grandma was having major surgery then. We didn't know if she was going to live."

"Well, yes, I know. But you and I got to catch up. And you met Wyatt."

Upon hearing his name, the darling boy toddled into the room, holding one of Evie's shoes. He had the drunken gait of a new walker. Wyatt had grown so much in just a few months. Now he had the face of a little man and could feed himself Cheerios, one sloppy handful at a time.

"Mama!" he exclaimed, grabbing at Susan's ankle.

"Yes, sugar. You're going to spend time with Aunt Evie this week."

Aunt! Still!

"So why exactly are you in New York again? Your e-mail was a bit confusing."

"Yes! Yes! You need to meet my business partner before I fully explain. He'll be here any minute. It's my friend Anton. He also lives at New Horizons. Even though I came up with the idea, I cut him in because of his marketing expertise. You'll love him. I'll get him to make you some of his famous tempeh empanadas."

"Speaking of food, I ordered you a vegan meal for the wedding."

"Oh, that's going to be a problem. Didn't I mention to you in my e-mail that I'm only foraging now?"

"Not at the Brooklyn Botanical Gardens, you're not. You better BYO or else you're going to be very hungry."

Susan just let out a whimper, to which Evie paid no mind.

"He's here!" Susan exclaimed when Evie's intercom buzzed moments later.

Anton greeted Susan with a kiss on the lips. Some friend. He was a dead ringer for Jerry Garcia, if the singer had subsisted on a strict diet of Cherry Garcia. And why was he carrying a suitcase?

"You must be Evie," he said. "It is so nice of you to put us up while we're in New York."

Us?

"Anton, I didn't ask Evie yet if you could stay here too. Evie, you wouldn't mind would you?" Susan gave Evie puppy-dog eyes, but there was nothing irresistible about a sixty-plus lunatic who couldn't keep her family relations straight.

When Evie didn't answer right away, Anton said, "We'll happily put you and your fiancé up at New Horizons whenever you like."

That was doing less than zero to sweeten the deal. Even though she could flee to Edward's, she wasn't crazy about the trio of Susan, Anton, and Wyatt (damn cute but quite the little devil) crashing at her place unsupervised.

"Fine. One night though, okay. I'm back in school now and I have a lot of reading to do. So what is this business you two are working on?"

"We are starting an online wet nurse business. People who can't breastfeed for medical reasons or because they adopted often want their babies to get breast milk. But there's no guarantee the wet nurse is eating a strictly organic diet. My business will help mothers connect with organic wet nurses. You can be an investor if you'd like. I'm offering the opportunity to family and friends first."

"Um, thanks, but I'm feeling a little strapped."

"Well, if you change your mind, you know where to find me. Let me show you something." She yanked the rubber band off a rolled-up poster in her duffel bag. The sign said MA NATURE'S MILK and had a picture of an Asian baby suckling the breast of a robust black woman while she ate leaves directly off of a tree.

"Pretty great, don't you think?" Susan said. "Anton used to be a graphic designer for Coca-Cola."

"It is professional-looking," Evie said. "And very diverse."

"Thank you. I'm doing this all for Wyatt. Now I have another mouth to feed. With Ma Nature's Milk, of course."

"Anton's wife is in charge of PR," Evie's aunt added nonchalantly. "We're going with a strictly social media campaign."

"Wait, wait, wait. Anton—you're married? Your wife doesn't mind your, um, friendship with Susan?"

"Not a bit," he said.

"Rain's my best friend. She loves that I keep Anton off her back," Susan said with a wink, reaching into Evie's cupboards. "Do you have spelt? I need to feed Wyatt."

Evie must have looked incredulous because Susan sat down and put a hand on her knee.

"Evie, honey, there is no one set path. Life is much better with complication. Trust me," Susan said, brimming with conviction. Her words echoed what Jack had said on the phone months earlier.

What a crock.

She only wished Edward was with her at that very moment to exchange an intimate eye roll. She'd tell him later, once they were tucked cozily into their shared bed after an ordered-in dinner and an *Antiques Roadshow* marathon.

# # #

The bulbous, fleshy boob of an unfamiliar Asian woman was the first thing Evie and Edward saw when they returned hand in hand to her apartment late the following afternoon, light-headed from a day of choosing wines for the reception. Susan, Anton, and Wyatt were supposed to have relocated to the Holiday Inn on Fifty-Seventh Street by now.

"I'm Angela," the topless woman said from her perch on Evie's beloved sectional. At her feet were three babies, including Wyatt, chewing on various of Evie's treasured objects—an expensive cashmere throw, the cover of an out-of-print Chanel coffee-table book, and most catastrophic of all, her new fuzzy slippers.

The dining room table, where she had her spread out her books and sketches from design class, was now covered with enough electronic equipment to service a Kinkos.

Around the table sat several other strangers. Susan and Anton were nowhere to be seen.

"Hi," Evie said tentatively, when no one in the room offered any explanation for their presence.

"Are you here for the shoot?" a bald man sitting at the table asked her. He had a pack of cigarettes poking out of his breast pocket. Evie would kill him if she found out he had smoked in her apartment.

"The shoot?" Evie asked.

"Yeah, for Nature's Best Milk."

"It's called Ma Nature's Milk," a gaunt woman with blue hair, also seated at Evie's table, corrected and returned to crocheting.

"Okay, everyone, sorry about that. We're back," Susan announced, entering the apartment. "Oh good, Evie, Edward, you're both here. You can give us input." Anton followed behind Susan, carrying a camera with a ten-inch lens.

"Aunt Susan, what the hell is going on here?" Evie demanded, gesturing toward the naked woman on her couch.

"Don't worry about a thing, Evie. Everyone will clear out in just a few minutes. Anton left our PowerPoint presentation for the investors at home, so we had to quickly scramble to put something together here. I hope you don't mind. We just need to shoot a few pictures, and then your apartment will be back to normal."

"How did you get all these people here on such short notice?"

"Craigslist."

Of course.

"Susan," Edward spoke up. "Evie is really stressed about the wedding. She has school projects to do. I think you've got to find another place to work."

"We're almost done. I promise," Susan said. "By the way, I'd love your input on our model, since you are the breast expert. Do you think her chest will photograph well?"

"Evie," Edward said, pulling his fiancée back out the door. "I have to go. Like right now." He looked dangerously close to hyperventilating.

"I know, I know. But I need to stay until these people clear out. Our response cards are here. My dress is hanging in the closet. I can't leave with these crazies milling about."

"Five minutes tops, Evie. I promise," Susan said, completely unoffended.

"Angela," she directed. "It's go time. Let's use Wyatt in this shot. Put him to your breast and hold the apple with your other hand. And don't forget to smile."

"Okay everybody," Anton called out. He lifted the camera to his face. "SAAAAYYYY FACEBOOK!"

"That's it," Edward said, wrapping his arms around Evie. "I'm quitting the Internet too."

"I don't think you'll be alone after this."

"Forget the response cards, Evie. I just want to leave this apartment, take you to my place, kiss you, and celebrate how normal we are. Can you live with that?"

"Forever."

Acknowledgments

It takes a village to write and publish a book and I am deeply indebted to the many people who helped make *Love and Miss Communication* a reality.

The team at William Morrow couldn't have been better. Thank you to my brilliant and quick-witted editor, Lucia Macro, for responding so enthusiastically to the novel and embracing Evie wholeheartedly. Major gratitude is owed to the marketing team, specifically Jennifer Hart and Molly Birckhead, and to my publicist, Katie Steinberg, for helping this book reach so many diverse readers. Shelly Perron did an excellent and precise job of copyediting, no doubt a tireless task. Jeanie Lee was a wonderful production editor. Julia Gang, who designed the cover, totally nailed it on the first try and for that I am so grateful. Nicole Fischer, you were so on top of everything, I really appreciate it. Finally, thank you to Liate Stehlik, the publisher at William Morrow, for taking a chance on this first-time novelist. I'm so proud to be a part of the William Morrow family.

My agent, Linda Chester, who has more publishing experience in her thumb than I do in my entire body, did an amazing job bringing this book to market. Thank you for supporting my efforts, believing so strongly in the importance of good books, and encouraging my career so passionately.

Tanya Farrell of Wunderkind PR did an amazing job of spreading the word about this book and organizing so many special appearances for me.

Anika Steitfeld Luskin: Where do I start? Only you know how helpful you were to me. You not only made *Love and Miss Communication* a much better book, you also made my life so much richer through your friendship.

I had many early readers, and in particular I want to thank Jennifer Belle, Sara Houghteling, and Cristina Alger, all extremely talented authors, for their invaluable comments. A special shout-out to another Houghteling, Charlotte, who is just the most optimistic and encouraging human on earth. I am also indebted to Dr. Jaime Knopman and Dr. Lynn Friedman, who kindly took time from their busy schedules to educate me about breast cancer fertility issues.

My husband, William, is my rock and my best friend. I feel like the luckiest person on earth to have him by my side. With equal parts encouragement and coddling, he nursed this endeavor and pushed me to keep on going. And of course I want to thank my beautiful children Charlie, Lila, and Sam. You may have interrupted me at least a thousand times while I was trying to write, but it was worth it every time just to see your faces. I love you infinitely. My parents, Shelley and Jerry Folk, are pretty much a child's dream come true. They provided me with everything I needed and more to succeed, and they continue to sustain me with boundless love. In particular my mom, to whom this book is dedicated, listened to me talk about this book ad nauseam for the past few years and truly is my biggest fan. To all my extended family—my loving in-laws, Marilyn and Larry Friedland; the Folks; the Meyers; the Rabinovicis; and the Friedlands—it feels amazing to be surrounded by so much love every day. You guys are the best. To my friends, too numerous to name (lucky me!), you make me smile and laugh every day and truly enrich my life. Finally, Jason, if you were here today, I know just how proud you would be.

About the author

2 Meet Elyssa Friedland

About the book

3 A Note from the Author

9 Reading Group Guide

Insights,
Interviews
& More . . .

Meet Elyssa Friedland

© PhotoOp

ELYSSA FRIEDLAND attended Yale University, where she served as managing editor of the *Yale Daily News*. She is a graduate of Columbia Law School and subsequently worked as an associate at a major firm. Prior to law school, Elyssa wrote for several publications, including *Modern Bride*, *New York* magazine, *Columbia Journalism Review*, CBS Market Watch.com, *Yale Alumni Magazine*, and *Your Prom*. She grew up in New Jersey and currently lives in New York City with her husband and three young children. Visit her at www.elyssafriedland.com. ✑

A Note from the Author

#SOCIALMEDIAGIVESMEANXIETY

Many people have asked me why
I decided to write a book about a woman
who gives up the Internet. They want
to know if I gave up the Internet myself
and if I think people should live off-line.
The answers to those questions are *no*
and *no*. But I am fascinated, and often
overwhelmed, by the way our world is
changing due to the prevalence of the
web and social media, and writing *Love
and Miss Communication* was my way
of trying to make sense of our new
reality. I wanted to create a character
who is driven to quit the Internet and
then manages to live off the grid in
a society where that basically seems
unthinkable. Imagining how that
would change the course of her life
was so intriguing that I couldn't wait
to find out where it took her—and me.

We all see the way pins, posts, Tweets,
hashtags, and "likes" have infiltrated
society as we know it. For me there were
a couple of specific incidents regarding
the Internet that particularly hit home,
and by that I mean sent me into
something of a nervous spiral about
how quickly the world around me was
evolving.

The first occurred at my college
reunion. Instead of "catching up" in the
traditional sense, classmates who barely
knew each other in college were joking
about shared photos and congratulating
each other on major life events. People ▶

3

I couldn't remember ever laying eyes
on during college approached me to
say, "Your son had the cutest Halloween
costume" or "Congrats on the new
apartment." I congratulated them
in turn on their promotions and
asked about their recent vacations.
All of this happened because we were
Facebook friends, which meant that
despite having never been actual
friends, we knew *a lot* about each
other (including the results of the
Facebook quiz "Which Golden Girl
Are You Most Like?"—for better or
worse I was Sofia). In a strange way,
our class was more connected ten years
out than we were when we all lived
together on campus.

Shortly after the reunion, my husband
and I tried to set up a friend of ours with
a great woman we both knew very well.
We were unable to produce a photo of
her (how she managed to escape the
Internet's prying eyes we aren't sure),
but our friend simply refused to call
her without seeing a picture. We
realized that the blind dates of our
parents' generation were officially over.
So were job searches. Employers readily
admit to checking out an applicant's
online presence before making a
decision. We are all on display, and
there are few mysteries left. That's partly
why my husband and I decided not to
find out if our third child was a boy or
a girl (we found out with the first two).
I wanted to experience a real surprise
because it had been so long since any

information I sought had been more than the click of a button away.

How much *is* appropriate to share on social media? And how much snooping is appropriate? And more importantly, how does all this posting and searching make people feel?

I'm a moderate poster. By that I mean that I put up pictures of my family about two or three times a month. It's actually really nice. When my children celebrate birthdays, I get tons of "likes" and "HBDs" and it makes me feel great—cared for, cheered on, admired. Of course, my posting has also backfired. I have what I consider to be an undesirable birthday from a social media standpoint. It's July 3, and many people are away celebrating the long weekend, hence they lack the time to check in and wish me a great day. I'm left floundering on what should be a joyful day. I'm not even friends with half of my "friends"—so why do I need their electronic well-wishes?

As most of us are realizing, all this posting can definitely take away from "the moment." I find this happening most often when I'm with my children, who are by far my most valuable asset to show off online. We could be having the most glorious day: Picture apple picking when the temperature is a crisp 66 degrees and we've all just busted out our quilted vests for the first time this season. Cuteness abounds. But then I pull out my trusty iPhone and start clicking away. "Smile!" I shout. "Don't ▶

make funny faces!" "Move closer to your sister!" "Stand back, I can't see your whole outfit!" I start barking orders at my children like a drill sergeant, all in the name of that elusive thing—a perfect family photo for Instagram, or at least a sixty-plus "hearts" photo.

While I'm a moderate poster, I'm not a moderate checker. I look at Facebook and Instagram at least five or six times a day, scrolling through pictures of friends and acquaintances for long stretches of time, and often when one of my children is clamoring for my attention. It's partly voyeuristic, but mostly it's out of boredom. When exactly did this happen? When did it become unbearable to wait to cross the street without whipping out our phones? Why was the installation of Wi-Fi in the New York subways such a cause for celebration?

Now, I won't pretend that I'm not interested in other people's pictures and posts. They are more than just diversions from my children's petty fighting or the tedium of standing in a long line. I stare at my Instagram feed and think: Why is my ex-boyfriend still dating that not-so-cute girl? Whose children are grasping chess trophies (and when did they start lessons)? Who is on a glamorous vacation? Why wasn't I invited to that party?

So what does all this have to do with Evie Rosen? Evie is, in my estimation, bright and capable with a good head on her shoulders. She's competitive and driven and looking for love. The problem is that she's doing it in the age of the Internet. There's a virtual yardstick out there, and Evie is constantly checking to see how she measures up. How could she not? Men and women alike are scrutinized with a forensics lens even before a first date. New friends' pasts are unearthed after a first greeting. And everyone is posting pictures showcasing the very best in their lives. For someone like Evie, who is at a crossroads in her life, this pressure becomes unbearable. Who can blame her for checking her e-mail a hundred times a day at the office? She's at a job that can be painfully boring and is living in a world that is changing by the millisecond. She just wants to keep up—that is, until all that keeping up derails her career and Jack's wedding pictures crush her heart.

Unlike Evie, I didn't quit the Internet, though I have given myself long stretches without it. I thought going off social media sites would make me feel isolated. In fact, it had no effect on my relationships. Maybe that's because the connections made through "likes" and Tweets and hashtags cannot replace a good phone conversation or a lengthy catch-up over a meal. What my brief periods of abstinence really did was make me evaluate why I was posting pictures. Most of my close friends see me and my children regularly. So why do I feel the need to broadcast ▶

A Note from the Author *(continued)*

my daughter in her darling ballet leotard, my baby in nothing but a diaper, with his glorious rolls on display, or my older son with, yes, a chess trophy? Call it a desire to share, call it a compulsion of our generation, or call it simply showing off. All are true.

For Evie, the Internet is at times destructive, but it also enables her to connect with her friends while she is tethered to her desk. Her journey reflects the ways in which the Internet can be both the single most unifying force and also the most isolating. Going off-line also leads Evie down paths she never would have stumbled upon otherwise, and has certainly left me wondering where I would be if I fully disconnected.

But I am still posting, so please do be on the lookout for my latest crop of posts and grams. I implore you to like or heart them. ☺ ∿

Reading Group Guide

1. How do you feel about Evie's dismissal from Baker & Smith? Do you think it was justified? How much time do you spend on personal matters during the workday? What do you consider excessive?

2. Evie's previous boyfriend, Jack, says he doesn't believe in marriage, yet she pursues a relationship with him and continues to pine after him long after they break up. Why do we always want what we can't have?

3. Have you ever been tempted to quit the Internet, or at least quit social media? Evie says she knows that what she sees online is not reality, yet it still upsets her. Do you have similar negative reactions to social media?

4. Evie yearns for Bette's approval in her life. Do you think she shares Bette's traditional worldview more than she'd like to admit? Does this shape the choices she makes?

5. Before going on dates with men, Evie uses Google to her advantage. Do you think she should have regrets about her former dating habits, or is it a safe rule of thumb to know your date? Do you believe Evie and Edward would have gotten together if she had, in fact, Googled him?

6. What are the top three dating tips that you would share with Evie from your own personal experience? ▶

7. Evie struggles with being the only single one in her group of close friends. Do you think she handles it well? Do you think it's possible for friends to be close when their situations in life are so different?

8. There is a recurring theme of jealousy and self-absorption throughout the novel. Are there any times that you may have let jealousy, especially fueled by social stalking, get the better of you? Discuss the ways Evie may or may not have evolved by the end of the book.

9. Fran is the ultimate mother— supportive, loving, and not judgmental. Yet Evie seems closer to Bette. Why do you think that is?

10. In marrying Edward, Evie will become a stepmother to Olivia. Do you think she is ready for that role?

11. What do you think about the Steve Jobs quote at the beginning of the novel? Is technology really "nothing"?

12. Do you think Evie was particularly addicted to technology, or is that the way most people are "wired" these days?

13. Aunt Susan tells Evie that life is better with complication, and Evie dismisses the comment. Do you agree more with Susan or with Evie?

14. Do you believe Evie could have had a happily ever after with either Jack or Edward? Or is there only one right person for her? ❧